SHEIKHS, LIES & REAL ESTATE

THE UNTOLD STORY OF DUBAI

JR Roth

For M, the bravest person I know...

Disclaimer

This is a work of fiction. Names, characters and incidents in the story are products of the author's imagination, or are used fictitiously and are not to be construed as real. Although real people, places and incidents are referred to throughout the book, they are intermingled with the fictional people and events that make up the story. Any resemblance to actual events, locales, organisations or persons living or dead is entirely coincidental.

No part of this book may be used or reproduced in any manner whatsoever without the prior written consent of the author, except in the case of brief quotations embedded in critical articles and reviews.

CONTENTS

Preface

1 On the Cusp

2 Opportunity Knocks

3 Camels to Cadillacs

4 Arabian Nights

5 The British Invasion

6 Bullshit Talks

7 Bullshit Walks

8 A Grand Affair

9 Other People's Money

10 Something to Celebrate

11 Passing the Grenade

12 Driven to Decision

13 The Property Tour Bus

14 Boiler Room

15 A Tale of Two Cities

16 Twisted Fate

17 The Laundry Business

18 Buy Now, Pay Later

19 The Boy Who Cried Wolf

20 Paradise Lost

21 Faulty Towers

22 The Great Escape

23 Apocalypse Now

Epilogue

About the Author

The Romans have done great things but their time is past. What they have done we can do. We should rule the world.

Attila the Hun

The moment you say 'I am on top and nobody will reach me' – that is when people will catch up with you. What we are trying to do in Dubai is to extend the distance between us and everybody else. If they really want to catch up, they will have to go two or three times our speed, and in doing this they will run out of breath. So we are looking to maintain the gap by not stopping anytime soon.

HRH Sheikh Mohammed Bin Rashid Al Maktoum

Preface

Sandcastles never last.

As a child I would spend countless hours on the beach with my bucket and spade, meticulously constructing an opulent palace fit for a king, only for a cruel tide to wipe it out of existence for ever.

Standing forlorn on the shore in disbelief, the tears rolling down my rosy cheeks, it was the sense of utter helplessness that was the hardest to swallow. Perhaps this was an early warning of the fickle nature of humanity's great triumphs, a humbling reminder that our proudest achievements are irrelevant against the infinite annals of time. But little did I know then this harsh lesson would come back to haunt me again years later in a distant sheikhdom in the mysterious Middle East...

At the dawn of the twenty-first century, a desert storm in the Persian Gulf was gathering pace. The timeless dunes were shifting to make way for an exotic new land where money flowed more freely than water and sand could be turned into gold. A new metropolis soon emerged from the barren desert as a thriving centre of business, a glamorous tourist paradise and an opulent playground for the super-rich; thousands flocked to its shores to claim a share of its spoils.

An estimated $600 billion of petrodollars, 'hot money' and cheap credit transformed the remote Emirate of Dubai from a Bedouin backwater into a contemporary utopia in less than a decade. Fortunes were made in the blink of an eye on the roulette wheel of Dubai's property casino, and everybody emerged a winner. And with such instant and outrageous wealth came all of its inevitable trappings: fast cars, lavish parties, exotic women, and piles of cold hard cash.

Far away from the desert miracle in a forgotten corner of British suburbia, I was a hopeless young dreamer trapped in the mundane grind of London's corporate rat race. Desperately seeking an escape, I was infatuated from the moment I heard of this exciting city of boundless opportunity, and obsessed over the thought of eloping to find my fortune. As the stars aligned and I plucked up the courage to leave behind my humdrum life, I found myself thrust into the middle a fairytale world of wealth and excess, cowboys and crooks, hookahs and hookers.

But it was not to last. As the great desert party approached its final hours, the lights went out and the music abruptly stopped. The shockwaves of the global credit crunch had reached Eastern shores, and the tsunami that followed not only wiped out the sandcastles, it took the entire beach with it. Fairytale became tragedy and greed turned to fear, and as Dubai's envious naysayers revelled in glee from the sidelines, thousands scrambled to avoid the bleak fate of a dark foreign jail cell or being drowned in a sea of debt.

The following story is inspired by actual events during the Dubai property boom between 2002 and 2009. Much has been written and discussed about the dramatic rise and fall of Dubai, but few have heard the shocking true story, until now.

This is the remarkable tale of a rude awakening from an Arabian dream...

1

On the Cusp

A familiar figure stands a thousand feet high above the turquoise waters of the Arabian Gulf. As a dusty breeze blows gently against his spotless white polo shirt, he shields his eyes from the beaming desert sun and peers out over the edge to absorb the breathtaking view below. He sees an endless coastline of pearl-white sand gently kissing the ocean bed. In the hazy distance there are vaguely visible clusters of emerging skyscrapers, roads and villas surrounded by acres of unspoiled desert extending as far as the eye can see. Directly below lies a manmade marina with dozens of luxury yachts scattered around the clear blue water like stars in the night sky.

There is an impressive intensity in his eyes as he takes a deep breath to focus. Bending his knees and lowering his head, he pauses for a moment in preparation before taking an almighty swing! He hears a gasp from the on-looking crowd amid a chorus of camera shutters singing in unison behind him as the white speck flies high into the air and is swallowed by the cloudless sky above, never to be seen again.

The man is golf legend Tiger Woods and he is standing on the fifty-sixth-storey helipad of the opulent Burj Al Arab, the tallest hotel on the planet. Tiger is the guest of the Jumeirah Group, Sheikh Mohammed of Dubai's luxury hotel brand, who has invited him to do what he does best against the most remarkable backdrop in the region. The event is billed as the meeting of two icons: the world's greatest golfer and the world's only seven-star hotel. Woods is reported to have been paid $1 million for this single appearance, and Dubai is later to become the home of his own signature golf course.

Then, in 2004, the relatively unknown emirate of Dubai was on the threshold of greatness – thousands would soon be arriving from around the globe to join those already chasing the so-called Dubai Dream. A modern Arabian fairytale was taking shape in the desert, and it was only a matter of time before the rest of the world would sit up and pay attention.

***

'*Ahlan wa sahlan*, and welcome to sunny Dubai!' announced the chirpy air stewardess through her huge cabin-crew smile.

It was about time. I had never been a very comfortable flier, and the seven-and-a-half-hour journey from London had drained me of every last drop of patience. I tried hard to sit back and close my eyes in those final few moments, but I was too restless to relax. Like an adrenaline junkie on the cusp of a death-defying bungee jump, there was a nervous energy pumping through my veins and I was now itching to break free from the shackles of my economy-class seat.

As at last the seatbelt signs switched off, I clutched my bags and pushed my way to the front of the crowd to ensure I was first in line. And then, seconds before the aircraft doors opened, it hit me. After all the pondering, worrying, reflecting and planning, this was it. There was no turning back now.

From the moment I set foot in the airport, I was swallowed by its enormity. The terminal was a colossal emporium of glass, silver, marble and gold. Infinite arrival gates stretched as far as I could see, and giant indoor palm trees towered over the bustling marble atrium below. The vast building surrounding me was nothing short of a feat of modern architectural endeavour; a far cry from the mud huts and tents I had been expecting to see on my arrival in the Arabian Desert.

As I strolled along what seemed like an infinite gangway, I glanced at the awe-struck faces of my fellow travellers. They were businessmen and Bedouins, Western tourists and African traders, bright-eyed Filipinos and emaciated Indians. Some had come to lounge on the beaches, browse at the gold souks, and bash the dunes on the must-do desert safari. But others had bigger plans. They had been seduced by Sheikh Mohammed's great vision and had gambled everything to start anew. Many followed in the footsteps of friends, kin and countrymen who were already living prosperous lives with regular work and high salaries in the city. To these ambitious dreamers, this was not just an airport but a modern-day Ellis Island: a gateway to a bright future of unspeakable riches.

3

I followed the mob onto the escalator to the lower floor, where I was engulfed by familiar designer boutiques like Gucci, Dior and Prada, curiously juxtaposed with traditional souk-like stalls selling Arabian perfumes, garments and dates. It was part bazaar and part modern mall, and I felt as if I was at once on Fifth Avenue and in old Baghdad. The contradiction seemed to resonate well as the high-end designer outlets were brimming with brand-hungry Arabs and layover businesspeople killing time, while the old stalls satisfied every tourist adventurer's hunt for souvenir treasures to take home as mementos of a journey to exotic lands.

Right in the centre of the terminal sat a sparkling silver Lamborghini, shamelessly teasing every captivated bystander. I sniggered at the thought that this was perhaps some sheikh's VIP parking spot while he popped to Paris for a spot of weekend shopping. The super-car was in fact the grand prize in the Dubai Duty Free raffle, which offered punters a one-in-a-thousand chance to become its lucky owner. A display board stood beside it featuring dozens of photographs of ecstatic former winners, all proudly holding up their new keys as proof of their prize. It was a fitting metaphor: 'anybody could win in Dubai'. It was the very promise of this mantra that was attracting new dreamers to this exciting city every day. Indeed, I was one of them.

On my way towards the Arrivals hall, I was unexpectedly struck with a nose full of spicy Arabian incense from one of the nearby stalls which made me feel rather dizzy. As I struggled to regain my senses I clumsily stumbled into the path of something that sent me crashing to the ground. I looked back to see that I had stumbled into a five-piece designer luggage set, which was now scattered across the floor. A large Arab man dressed in a spotless white tunic, sandals and traditional headdress suddenly towered over me. Most of his chubby face was engulfed by a messy stubble, and he stared at me disdainfully through his aviator sunglasses.

As he launched into a tirade of abuse in Arabic, I tried to make amends by collecting his stray bags. My gesture didn't seem to do the trick; instead he huffed at me like a raging bull, snatched his luggage from my fingertips and charged off into the distance. I felt a little sheepish for a moment, but in spite of the scolding I was also rather pleased; I had just had my first cultural exchange with a 'real' Emirati!

It wasn't on the best of terms, but being acknowledged was surely a first step to acceptance by the locals. I skipped towards Passport Control with a smug smile on my face. I was starting to fit in already.

After collecting my luggage, I was finally ready to venture into the city. I put on my sunglasses and stepped out of the airport with the swagger of a rock star. But nothing could have prepared me for the shock that followed. My legs turned to jelly, beads of sweat formed across my burning forehead and my face turned scarlet with panic. I felt as if I had put my head into a blazing oven wearing a woolly hat, balaclava and ear mufflers. It was unbearably hot. I stopped dead in my tracks, turned around and made a desperate dash back to the air-conditioned sanctuary of the terminal.

I took a seat on the benches inside for a few moments to recover from the ordeal. I had heard temperatures in Dubai were known to creep up a bit, but I was not expecting the heat to be this ruthless. As I peered nervously outside to plot the cleanest route possible to the taxi stand, I was distracted by an animated figure out of the corner of my eye. A tall, slim man with curly hair appeared to be jumping around and waving frantically in my direction. He wasn't very old, perhaps 30, Middle Eastern in appearance and dressed in an oversized suit. I assumed for a moment he was a heat-induced hallucination, but the more I tried to ignore him the more enthusiastically he vied for my attention. Who was this stranger and why was he so pleased to see me? As I cautiously made my way to the exit to investigate, he rushed towards me and snatched my bags, almost taking my arms with them.

'Hello, sir! Welcome to Dubai!' he shouted in a high-pitched Arabic accent, shaking my hand vigorously. 'I am Fadi, your driver! I hope you had a nice flight?' His hospitable manner was flattering, although I was rather relieved that he didn't try to kiss me, which for a brief moment didn't seem to be out of the question.

'Thank you, but there must be some mistake. I didn't book a driver...'

'Compliments of the hotel, sir! We are honoured that you are staying with us! Please, sir, my car is this way. Follow me!'

The short distance to the car park felt more like a trek across the Sahara in the unforgiving heat, but the chariot awaiting me at the other end was worth the effort: a black luxury Mercedes, glistening under

5

the piercing desert sun. It was certainly a far cry from the Nissan minicab that had taken me to the airport back in London. While Fadi loaded my bags into the trunk, I sank my sweaty behind into the soft leather, air-conditioned sanctuary of the back seat. Awaiting me were two ice-cold bottles of mineral water, both of which I gulped down in a matter of seconds. I never remembered water tasting so damn good! Cool and refreshed, I sat back and made myself comfortable. This was more like it. Finally, I had arrived.

'More AC, sir? Or it is okay?' asked Fadi, as we eventually pulled out of the car park.

'Thank you, it's perfect. Fadi, I must say your English is very good.'

He looked overjoyed by the compliment. 'Thank you, sir! I learn from James Bond, Prince Charles, The Beatles!'

'I see, and where are you from?' I asked, curious.

'I am from Egypt, sir,' he replied proudly. 'From Cairo.'

'Have you been in Dubai long?'

'About four years, sir.'

'And how do you find it here?'

'It is okay, sir. Sometimes good, sometimes bad! Dubai is really for people like you, not like me.'

Before I could ask what exactly he meant by 'people like me', I was distracted by the view from my rear window. We were in the middle of the desert, but there was not a single sand dune or camel herder in sight. Hundreds of luscious date-bearing palm trees lined every street amid perfectly manicured beds of colourful flowers, exotic plants and flawless lawns. The city outside was nothing like I had imagined. The paths were clean and untarnished, the roads wide and spacious. There was a familiar pattern of traffic signals and road signs, each of them in both English and Arabic, and every second car passing us was a luxury Mercedes, Lexus or Range Rover.

'Fadi, are women allowed to drive in Dubai?' I asked.

'Oh yes, of course, sir. Dubai is not like Saudi Arabia. Dubai is free!'

6

As we stopped at a red traffic signal, a spotless white BMW pulled up beside us. In the driver's seat was a beautiful Emirati woman with flawless fair skin and dark Christian Dior sunglasses. Her head was only half covered with a thin black veil, revealing a modern bronze fringe straight out of the pages of *Vogue* magazine. Seductively miming the words to the Arabic pop song blasting out of the stereo, she seemed too preoccupied to notice me gawping as she reached for a vanity mirror in her handbag to top up her perfect pink lip gloss. The lights turned green and she revved the powerful engine before speeding off into the distance, leaving Fadi behind in her slipstream. It seemed that not only did women drive in Dubai, they were full-blown petrol heads; and I have to admit that in a way it turned me on.

We approached the centre of the city and my attention quickly shifted to the looming silhouette of the hazy vista ahead. I remembered how *Vanity Fair* magazine had called it the 'skyline on crack', and it was now clear why. Each building was unique in shape and design, ranging from the astonishing to the grotesque, like the manifestation of both an architect's wildest fantasy and most surreal nightmare.

'You see this building, sir?' asked Fadi, pointing at a dirty and dated-looking white tower.

'Yes, what about it?'

'This is called the World Trade Centre building, sir. It is a very famous landmark in Dubai. Only ten years ago this was the tallest tower in the Middle East. And look at it now!'

Today it was an awkward anachronism; its dated architecture and thirty-nine storeys dwarfed by the more impressive modern structures surrounding it. I wondered why it hadn't been demolished to make way for the contemporary towers. Perhaps its very purpose now was to act as a yardstick of progress against which the emerging Dubai could be measured; a benchmark for just how far the city had come.

'We are now on the Sheikh Zayed Road, sir,' said Fadi, as we merged into a vast, twelve-lane highway. I sat up eagerly. Named in homage to the nation's much-revered founding father, the busy highway was the main artery running through the centre of Dubai, from the Emirate of Sharjah all the way to the UAE's capital city Abu Dhabi. It was something of a landmark, and most journeys in Dubai involved at least a brief stint on the 'SZR'. I had read and heard much

7

about this famous road and it was quite exciting to finally be driving along it.

Nevertheless, the single fact about the highway that I remembered most vividly was that it was considered one of the most dangerous in the world, and it was now clear why. There were six lanes in each direction, and with each the raw speed of the cars was more intense and terrifying. Sports cars, 4x4s and minivans rushed around us at dizzying speeds, aggressively jostling for position like rival title pretenders in the final lap of a grand prix. The leftmost lane looked like a sheer death trap that only the foolish dared enter at their peril. Much to my relief, Fadi cruised sensibly in the third.

I leaned forward to get a better view of the buildings now towering over us on either side, but I was distracted by a flashing light in the distance behind me. I tried to ignore it at first, but the flickering only seemed to get closer and brighter until I had no choice but to shield my eyes. I looked at Fadi, who was nervously mumbling something to himself under his breath. And then without warning our car swerved violently to the left and I was thrust back into my seat with a force that almost snapped my neck in two!

'You crazy guy!' screamed Fadi, slamming hard on the brakes. He followed with excessive honking of the horn as he battled to regain control of the wheel. From nowhere, a scarlet Ferrari cut across us in a death-defying move, inches away from taking out our car and three others in an instant. My eyes briefly caught the face of my would-be assassin: an Emirati man of no more than 20 wearing traditional headdress and dark aviators, chatting away on his mobile phone. Oblivious to the chaos he had almost caused, the insane driver pushed into the perilous leftmost lane and sped off into the distance with an ear-splitting roar of horse power.

'I am so sorry, sir! These drivers are crazy,' said Fadi apologetically.

My heart was racing hysterically. 'Don't worry, I'm fine,' I replied, urging Fadi to keep his eyes on the road.

'This is a big problem in Dubai, sir. Every day on the Sheikh Zayed Road they will come up close behind you, and if you don't move they will do some crazy move to overtake. They don't care about others here! Many people have died this way.' This tragic reality

8

seemed genuinely to sadden Fadi and he didn't say much more for the rest of the journey. Perhaps he felt he had somehow let me down, but I was just grateful to be alive and unharmed. It seemed that the unforgiving Sheikh Zayed Road had lived up to its sinister reputation and I was certain this wasn't the last time such a senseless near-fatal incident would occur. Thankfully, we were not too far from the hotel now.

My new employer, Imperial Bank, had offered to put me up at the Emirates Towers for a month while I found a permanent place to live. Overlooking the Sheikh Zayed Road, the twin skyscrapers were two of the most contemporary and iconic buildings of the Dubai skyline, and their distinctive sharp edges and reflective glass made them an unmistakable symbol of 'New Dubai'. One of the towers featured one of the world's most distinguished business hotels; the other boasted the most exclusive office space in the region, including Sheikh Mohammed's own private offices, which occupied many of the higher floors. The Towers even boasted their own shopping mall, The Boulevard, where lonely housewives wasted countless hours in high-end boutiques while their overworked husbands slaved away in the offices above to bankroll their lavish spending habits.

'Welcome to the Emirates Towers, sir,' said the impish Indian valet attendant, dressed in a grey uniform and matching hat. He opened my door and I stepped out and thanked him, walking towards the giant revolving doors of the lobby as his colleagues unloaded my bags.

'Goodbye, sir! Goodbye! I wish you best of luck and prosperity!' I turned around to see Fadi waving at me frantically, before getting into his Mercedes to leave. I had warmed to him over our short ride as he preserved me from the heat, become my makeshift tour guide and even saved my life. I smiled and waved back with genuine appreciation before he drove away to pick up the next unsuspecting visitor.

The lobby inside was brimming with sharply dressed international businessmen and executives sipping on cappuccinos, discreetly watching the passing guests over the pages of the *FT* or the *Gulf News*. There was a chic ambience that resembled a day spa rather than a hotel lounge: a subtle water feature trickled serenely near the entrance, and the gentle music from the female pianist added a touch of sophistication. At the far end, a futuristic glass elevator transported guests up and down the soaring atrium at breathtaking speeds like a scene from a science fiction movie.

As I waited patiently by the check-in desk, I was approached by a frail old Emirati man dressed in a traditional *dishdasha* and sandals, who offered me local coffee and dates in what seemed to be a customary welcome gesture. I happily obliged, but as I sipped from the tiny porcelain cup its unfamiliar bitter and spicy taste almost made me gag. It was a far cry from a Starbucks cappuccino and I handed him back the full cup, desperately hoping I had not offended. He didn't seem too amused and abruptly walked away shaking his head. Clearly, I still had some cultural adjusting to do.

While the pretty European receptionist tapped away on her keyboard to check me in, I looked up and noticed a giant portrait of Sheikh Mohammed Bin Rashid Al Maktoum, Dubai's illustrious ruler, watching over the room. His black beard was perfectly trimmed, his nose large and noble, and his *khaleeji* headdress flowed over his shoulders. There was a boldness in his deep green eyes as he seemed to stare well beyond the parameters of the picture frame, perhaps into an affluent future for his ambitious new city. And then something altogether peculiar happened. By some inexplicable miracle, he began to speak to me!

'Welcome to my city, my friend, whatever you need just shout,' said the bellowing voice. I couldn't believe my eyes. Was the picture really talking to me? I looked around to see if anybody else had observed the wonder, but they continued with their business. Before I could pluck up the courage to thank His Highness for his kind hospitality, the receptionist interrupted.

'Here is your room key, sir. You will be staying in a wonderful room on the twenty-seventh floor. We hope you enjoy your time at the Emirates Towers.' The tiny piece of plastic she handed me was hardly a key in the conventional sense; rather, it was an ingenious mini replica of the building itself, a clever gimmick, except that the sharp edges dug into my groin when I put it in my pocket.

'Thank you,' I replied keeping one eye on the painting above.

Before leaving the desk, I looked up at it again and nodded in acknowledgement. This time there was no response.

'Is everything okay, sir?' asked the receptionist, confused.

'Yes, fine thanks. Just fine.' She looked up at the portrait and back at me with bemusement as I walked towards the elevators.

The moment I entered my room on the twenty-seventh floor, I rushed towards the giant window to absorb the awesome spectacle. It was more than just a view; before me was an incredible animated snapshot of a great vision being brought to life. There were construction sites in every direction as hundreds of men in blue overalls and yellow hard hats worked industriously in the beaming desert sun. Dozens of cranes moved giant blocks of concrete and steel amid an intricate web of scaffolding. For every completed tower there were three emerging in the distance, currently only half-built shells but soon to be competing for air rights in the Dubai skyline. And there again was the dream weaver himself; a giant image of Sheikh Mohammed across the façade of an adjacent building, like an omnipotent shepherd watching over his flock.

I eventually sat on the edge of the bed and began thinking about how far I was from home. A sudden bout of homesickness overcame me as I pondered what had possessed me to embark on this insane journey into the unknown. Was it a desperate bid to escape the daily routine of the London rat race? Perhaps. Was I responding to an innate need for adventure and excitement? Possibly. Or had I fallen victim to the irresistible lure of the so-called city of the future? Whatever the reason, the fact remained that I had left behind a safe and secure career on the hunch that in 2004 there was no better time or place in the world than this tiny Emirate to achieve my greatest dreams.

This was my time to shine.

2

Opportunity Knocks

Since my earliest memory, I always wanted the good life. When asked the familiar question 'What do you want to be when you grow up?' by my unsuspecting primary school teacher Miss Penny, my answer was somewhat unorthodox for a boy of 6:

'I want to be really rich so I can buy a boat and sail around the globe, and I can have my own plane, and live in a big mansion and drive a Porsche, and I will be really happy...'

Miss Penny was speechless as the other kids began to question their own lowly aspirations to be firemen, bakers and nurses.

Growing up, I was never too interested in fame and celebrity. The thought of paparazzi camping on my front lawn, or images in the gossip magazines of me stumbling out of a nightclub with my arms around two blondes seemed like a frightful inconvenience. But money, on the other hand, meant so much more. Money could buy independence, choice and freedom to live the good life without a worry in the world. This to me was a worthy pursuit indeed.

I am sure I had my mother to thank for instilling such immense ambition into me at an impressionable age. Despite my modest upbringing, she had always taught me to aim high and expect the very best in life. My parents had emigrated to the UK from Pakistan as teenagers. They had met at college in London and married young, and I was born soon after a passionate honeymoon in Paris. My father was a builder by trade, while my mother had worked as a secretary in a small shipping company. It was my father's idea to call me Adam, a universal name that he believed would bridge the cultures of my ethnic roots and the Western world. Ironically, as I grew older I didn't seem to fit in to either.

I was never very comfortable with the peculiar customs and traditions of Pakistani culture, which were often imposed on me by

12

visiting relatives against my will. They were all so foreign to me, and I never understood the point in odd rituals like arranged marriages and blowing strange prayers over food. Yet being the only ethnic kid at a white school also meant that as much as I tried to be one of the lads, I would never be wholly accepted there either. It didn't help that I looked more Middle Eastern than Asian, and taunts like 'camel herder' and 'rag head' became part of life. And so caught between two opposing worlds, I took it on myself to make wealth my passport to freedom from the petty concerns of identity. With money, I convinced myself, people would respect me regardless of who I was or where I came from. Once rich, I could live comfortably on my own terms without the pressure to 'fit in'.

Sadly, my parents' marriage didn't last the stresses of working-class life and they separated when I was 10. After the divorce, I left with my mother to live in a tough suburb of North London. Life was quite different there. Most other kids in the neighbourhood belonged to gangs, and fights and stabbings seemed to be an everyday occurrence. Out of fear of falling into the wrong crowd, my watchful mother constantly reminded me of the need to study hard to make a future for myself. I did as I was told, stayed out of trouble and kept my head in my books. Needless to say, my mother was overwhelmed with pride when at the age of 18 my efforts were rewarded with an offer to study at Oxford University; a passport to the distinguished life I desperately craved.

Apparently getting into Oxford was a big achievement for an ethnic kid from an inner-city school, but pretty much from the day I arrived I knew that I didn't belong there. Most of my fellow students were private-school brats who had never had the misfortune of associating with state-school plebs like me. I had never played rugby, nor did I row or fence, so there was little common ground there. I tried my best to relate to their stories of picnics at Henley and weekends rambling in the Cotswolds, but the only interesting anecdotes I had to offer in return were of friends being mugged, or neighbours burgled in the middle of the night. I quickly accepted it was a lost cause. We were chalk and cheese, and Oxford was not for me.

Lonely and depressed in my dimly lit dorm room, I received an unexpected phone call one weekend that would change my life for ever. Some old school friends invited me to join them for a private party at a members-only nightclub in the West End of London called The Rooms. The club was world renowned as one of London's most exclusive night spots and a regular haunt for celebrities and movie stars, so it was an invitation I wasn't going to turn down. It would be a welcome change from yet another boring evening in the dreary college bar, so I dressed in my best shirt and took the coach from Oxford to London for an adventure.

From the very moment I passed the velvet rope into The Rooms, I was spellbound. The intoxicating music, the discerning crowd and the irresistible ambience captivated me. As we cracked open the champagne and danced on the tables until the break of dawn, for the first time in my life I felt like I belonged. There was no class divide or snobbery here; instead the revellers were united with a single, overarching purpose: to party hard and have fun. My eyes had suddenly opened up to a new world that I had never even known existed; where I could be anybody I wanted without a care in the world. And for those few exhilarating hours, I was free.

That night changed everything. Every week as another grim schedule of lectures ended, I jumped on the coach to London to get my weekend party fix. I became a regular at The Rooms and I soon became good friends with the club's owner, an eccentric Italian American called Gino del Primo. Gino was kind enough to offer me my own guest list at the club, which meant I could earn a cut of everything my invited guests spent, whether that was a single bottle of vodka or a Nebuchadnezzar of champagne. Considering the average spend on a table was over £2,000, it was an opportunity to make some good money.

And so I was soon living a double life as an insignificant Oxbridge geek by day, and a promoter at the most exclusive club in London by night. I never waited in a queue, everybody knew my name and I was rubbing shoulders with the cream of London's in-crowd. I partied with movie stars, sports personalities and royalty. In stark contrast to the monotony of Oxford student life, I was recognised and respected here; I was a 'somebody'. And it wasn't long before I had my first encounter with the so-called kings of London nightlife and every promoter's best friends: the infamous sheikhs.

The sheikhs were Arab businessmen, nonchalant royals and thrill-seeking oil barons who left behind their unsuspecting wives (many had more than one) to head to London for a summer of unspoken indulgence and excess, far from the judgemental eyes of their conservative societies. They were usually from one of the oil-rich Gulf States – Saudi, Kuwait, Qatar or the United Arab Emirates – where most of the 'evil' vices of the West were forbidden by the strict Islamic regimes.

They would ship their customised Ferrari and Aston Martin sports cars over for the weekend to race down Park Lane and valet-park pretentiously outside the entrances of the most exclusive clubs and restaurants. They stayed in the penthouses of the luxurious Park Lane hotels and they dined in the finest Michelin-starred restaurants. The sheikhs were gaudy, ostentatious, often overweight, terribly dressed (albeit drenched in designer labels) and spoke poor English. But despite their shortcomings, there was one thing about them that kept restaurant owners and club promoters salivating across London: their bulging wallets brimming with cash, waiting to be squandered.

Luckily, The Rooms was one of their favourite London hotspots and Gino did everything in his power to ensure that their every whim and desire was attended to every Friday and Saturday night. They reserved the best VIP tables, smoked the finest cigars and ordered the most expensive champagne. And with the excessive spending came a harem of gorgeous women: Russians, Italians, Lebanese and English, all competing for attention and desperate to be spoilt for the night. Seldom were they disappointed, and many found their night ending in the penthouse suite of a Mayfair or Knightsbridge hotel.

The sheikhs' decadent lifestyles fascinated me. I was soon on a first-name basis with many of them, as they entrusted me to take care of their every need while they partied into the night. The tips alone would be enough for me to live well for months, so I did whatever was required to keep them spending. I was sure it helped that I looked a little Middle Eastern as they probably saw me as one of them, although when they spoke to me in Arabic I always just nodded or pretended I couldn't hear. After a few glasses of champagne, they didn't seem to mind.

I lived my dual existence for over two years, but as my university days drew to an end, the pressure was mounting to make the all-important decision I had been dreading: a future career path. The ultimate dream for most of my peers at Oxford was to sell their souls

15

in a Faustian pact to an investment bank or magic-circle law firm in the city of London. But a grim existence of sitting in a poorly lit office in front of a flickering computer screen while it sucked out my soul for twelve hours a day simply didn't excite me. I wanted wealth, freedom and prominence like the sheikhs, and my new-found significance as a club promoter had given me confidence that I could make money without compromising my integrity. So while my classmates shamelessly whored themselves to the corporate reps who flooded the campus like vampires looking for virgins, I was notably absent. I had bigger plans.

But as the sheikhs left London for the Gulf over the winter, business at The Rooms dwindled and the tips dried up, I grudgingly accepted that club promoting was not my life's calling and I needed to find something else. I was also constantly being reminded by my mother of the need to build a future, and with mounting student debts I decided I had no choice but to bite my tongue and take a 'real' job.

In the autumn of 2004, I reluctantly joined an investment bank in the City of London as a trading desk assistant. It was apparently a position that many graduates would have killed for, but for me it was a well-paid time-filler while I pondered what I really wanted to do with the rest of my life.

The crux of my new role was to capture trades for equity-linked structured derivatives, and to monitor trading positions and risk limits. Every day, irate traders would shout at me over the phone about a trade dispute or an upcoming corporate event. It wasn't that I didn't know what they expected, but rather that I didn't give a damn, and wasn't going to let some guy who was earning ten times what I was talk me into a panic about something that had no bearing whatsoever on my life. All of my preconceptions about corporate life were ringing true: the work was boring, the hours were lengthy and the commute was a nightmare. It wasn't long before I was deeply de-motivated and began looking for a way out.

To get a fresh perspective on my dreary life, I arranged to have lunch with Cameron, a close friend I had not seen for over a year. I had first met Cameron on the London party circuit in my early promoting days. At the time he was making a fortune exporting mobile phones to Africa, and he had since invested in a fashionable wine bar in the West End that had become a regular haunt for the hedge-fund crowd. Today he had his finger in a number of other pies, from software companies to urban dance schools. He was well connected with club owners and promoters at all the trendiest London clubs and restaurants, and had introduced me to some of my biggest Arab clients.

Cameron oozed success; he was a natural-born entrepreneur who seemed to excel in everything he touched. He was a living example of the unshackled lifestyle I had always craved, and I admired him for making his fortune on his own terms, having never worked for anybody in his life.

As I arrived at the restaurant near Green Park, I instantly spotted him flirting with an attractive brunette waitress who was giggling like a school girl while he showered her with his boyish charm. This was classic Cameron: his success with women was legendary and few could resist his chiselled good looks and piercing blue eyes. He usually wore a permanent copper complexion owing to his penchant for travelling to exotic locations, but I noticed that today he was more golden than ever. As I approached the table, he handed the waitress a business card and she scuttled off with a huge grin.

'Well, well, if it's not Mr Party Time himself!'

'How are you doing, Cam?' I replied, smiling. 'You look great!'

'Why, thank you. You don't look too bad yourself after all the late nights you've had. Take a seat, buddy.'

We ordered some drinks and caught up. He told me how his wine bar had recently won numerous prestigious awards, how he was dating an up-and-coming Brazilian supermodel and that he was now thinking of launching his own lingerie line. He listened carefully as I told him about my mundane new job, how it lacked the thrill of the old promoting days, and that I was desperately seeking a new direction.

'My advice to you is you need to think outside the box, buddy,' said Cameron after some thought.

'What do you mean?'

'Well, you're doing what everybody is doing. You're a sheep and you need to be a wolf. You need to do something that nobody else has the balls to do.'

'Okay, now you've completely lost me.'

17

Cameron paused and stared deep into my eyes. 'Do you know where I've just come back from?'

'Let me guess, somewhere ridiculously hot and sunny,' I replied sarcastically.

He smiled wryly. 'Go on, take a guess.'

'Cannes, Ibiza, St Tropez...'

'You know me well!' he laughed. 'But you're wrong. I've actually been somewhere quite different this time. I spent last week in a crazy little place called Dubai.'

'Doo-buy?'

'Yes, Dubai. The world's fastest-growing city. Surely you've heard of it?'

I vaguely recalled one of the sheikhs mentioning he was from Dubai once at the end of a night as I ushered him into a taxi with a Romanian blonde, but I didn't know much else about the place. 'Isn't it somewhere in the Middle East?'

'Spot on, mate!' He sat back and lit a cigarette. 'It's a city in the United Arab Emirates in the Persian Gulf. Dude, believe me, it's going places. Think of Ibiza, Monaco and Vegas combined. That's what Dubai will be in a few years. It's the city of the future. I was completely blown away!'

'Really? As far as I know the Middle East is shepherds, camels and terrorists. That's why the Arabs are always in London, isn't it?'

Cameron's demeanour changed suddenly. 'Mate, do you know the world is changing? The days of the West's dominance are coming to an end! Countries like India and China are booming. A new world order is emerging. Mark my words, Western civilisation will soon be eclipsed by the emerging East.'

'Okay, Cam, thanks for the lesson in international politics,' I laughed. 'But what has this got to do with thinking outside the box?'

He didn't look amused. 'Think logically for a second, man! India and the Far East are the new manufacturing hubs of the world, and there's one natural resource they need more than any other to sustain their industry.'

'And what is that?' I asked.

'Take a wild guess!'

'Oil?'

'Exactly!' he said, as he pointed at me with his smouldering cigarette. 'Black gold, my friend. It's the life blood of the global economy. And where does most of it come from?'

'The Middle East...'

'Bingo!' I was finally beginning to understand where he was going with this. 'The problem is they can't keep pumping it for ever, it's running out. And so oil prices are only going one way: up. The higher they go, the more money flows into Gulf countries like Qatar, Saudi, Kuwait and the UAE.'

'Okay, Cam, I understand that, but these guys have been raking in the petrodollars for years. This is nothing new. The problem is they spend it all on Ferraris, weapons and whores. Even I've lived pretty well on squandered oil money. I really can't see that changing any time soon.'

'You're right. And that's where Dubai comes in. The ruler of Dubai, Sheikh Mohammed, is not like the others. He has seen an opportunity and has started a revolution. He knows the oil-rich countries can't keep wasting their limited resources for much longer. They need to reinvest in themselves, build a real economy and a future beyond oil. So he's constructing a new city with a bloody great big pile of petrodollars. And let me tell you, the plans this guy has got will blow you away!'

'What kind of plans?' I asked curiously.

'Where do I start? The sheikh is planning to build the world's tallest buildings, the biggest malls and the most incredible skyscrapers. Think of the finest restaurants, best golf courses and most luxurious hotels; they are all being built right now. Dubai is the home of the Burj Al Arab, the planet's only seven-star hotel. Yes, seven stars! But that is nothing compared to the most outrageous project of all; they are actually creating a giant manmade island shaped like a palm tree in the middle of the freaking ocean! When it's finished you will be able to see it from space. Can you believe it? There are just no limits in this place!'

I had never seen Cameron speak so passionately. But as fascinating as it sounded, it also seemed too good to be true. What could these backward Bedouins possibly know about building a great city? As I struggled to get my head around it all, Cameron continued.

'The sheikh has recently allowed foreigners to own freehold property for the first time in designated areas across Dubai, and the smart money is going in now. People are literally flocking to Dubai with suitcases of cash. Mark my words, it's the beginning of a modern-day gold rush. Anybody who wants to make serious money should be in Dubai property right now.'

'I hear you, but if this place is really the city of the future as you say, how come you're not over there now? I thought Cameron always followed the money?'

He sat back and smiled. 'Trust me, if I could be I would, but I have too many business commitments over here right now. Besides, I did the next best thing. I just bought a five-bedroom villa in Dubai.'

I almost choked on my drink. 'Are you serious?'

'Yep. It's in a project called the Emirates Hills, which is going to be like the Beverly Hills of Dubai. It's a beautiful property surrounded by palm trees, lakes and a world-class golf course designed by Colin Montgomerie himself.'

'Wow, congratulations! So when are you moving in?'

'Well, it's not even built yet,' he smiled. I bought the villa off-plan. I just put down a deposit of 10 per cent and I pay another 10 per cent every six months until it's complete. Simple. There's no mortgage debt or interest owed.'

'Wait, you're telling me that you bought something that's not even built yet in a new market with no track record? That sounds pretty risky to me, Cam!'

'Not at all. It's being built by a developer called Emaar, which is practically government owned, so they can only go bust if the Dubai government goes bust, and I can't really see that happening with all the bloody cash they have. There's virtually no risk! But do you want

20

to know the best bit? If I want, I can sell it tomorrow for a profit of around 20 per cent without a single brick being laid.'

'How?'

'I just flip it to the next investor. And he will probably flip it again, and maybe again after that. I don't really care, as long as I get my profit. The demand is there, believe me. A 20 per cent return on investment in less than a month. Easy money, mate! Don't think your hedge funds can get you that kind of return.' It was certainly a phenomenal return by any measure. 'Listen, we have known each other for a while and I consider you a good friend. If there is any advice I can give you it's this: opportunity waits for no man. "Someday" is a disease that will rob you of your dreams. You have to act now if you want to make some serious money! I suggest you get over there as soon as you can. Life's short, take a gamble! Besides you look like one of them, so you'll fit right in.'

And so the 'Oracle' Cameron had spoken and bestowed his pearls of wisdom, and I left lunch feeling enlightened.

From that day on, I couldn't escape Dubai. Newspapers, magazines and television shows swooned over the emerging desert paradise. Dubai was where celebrities vacationed, supermodels partied and sports stars trained. Legendary performers like Tom Jones, Elton John and Tina Turner had all played to sold-out audiences in Dubai. Celebrity icons like David Beckham, Michael Schumacher and Michael Jackson had all reportedly purchased luxury villas, and Michelin-starred chef Gordon Ramsay had chosen Dubai to open his first international restaurant. The Emirate was hosting its own golf tournament, ATP tennis championship and horse-racing event. It seemed everybody who was anybody was either talking about Dubai or was already on their way there.

And as I waited on the wet platform for my late-running train home from work in the bitterly cold British winter, I was at my wits' end. This dead end reality was a far cry from the life I had envisioned for myself. Surely, I was worth more than this. I was a thinker, an intellectual, an entrepreneur. The choice was clear: either I accepted this trivial and insignificant existence for the rest of my life, or I took a chance, here and now. At that very moment, I made a decision. This was an opportunity I was not going to miss. I had to act now.

21

As soon as I got home that evening, I dropped my bags and soaking umbrella and rushed over to my computer. I looked up every Dubai-based recruitment company's website I could find. One by one I went through them all, noting down any vacancy that was vaguely relevant and emailing my CV across by the dozen. I didn't even think about sleeping, instead I worked industriously into the night. By the time I had finished it was almost 3am. I was completely exhausted and finally surrendered to my fatigue. There was nothing more I could do now but wait.

A week passed with no replies. And then another, and another. I sent a few follow-up messages, but nobody came back and I began to lose hope. As much as I refused to believe it, in the back of my mind I knew the reason why. Employers in Dubai were looking for specific skills and work experience to fill the massive talent gap in the region, and for that they were willing to pay handsomely. A young upstart like me offered little value to a skill-deficient economy and few companies were willing to take such a gamble. And so a month after my résumé blitz, I resigned myself to the fact that nobody wanted me and abandoned my silly pipe dream. I obediently slipped back into my daily routine and never spoke of Dubai again.

***

'Hi, mate! Long time...'

'Anthony, how are you?'

'I'm great! Sorry I haven't been in touch lately, work's been a killer.'

My old friend Anthony had lived on my street as a child and we had been inseparable best friends since the age of 6. Although we had gone off to different universities, we had kept in touch until recently, when Anthony had started working at a large American law firm. These days he was regularly in the office up to sixteen hours a day and I was surprised to hear from him at all.

'Listen, dude, I can't talk for too long, but I need a big favour...'

'Sure, what do you need?' I asked.

'Well, my first cousin has recently moved to London from Canada. He's working for a bank close to where you are in the City. He doesn't know many people and I was wondering if you could maybe take him to lunch and show him where to get good coffee and sandwiches. You know what I mean?'

With the way my luck had been going I wasn't exactly in the most charitable mood, but I was willing to make an exception for old times' sake. 'Sure, dude. No problem, I would be happy to.'

'Thanks, I knew I could count on my old bud! His name is Chad. I'll drop him your number. Listen, I gotta go, things are pretty busy, but I appreciate it, man. Let's catch up soon, okay?' He hung up before I could even say goodbye.

Anthony's cousin Chad called me a day later and we agreed a time to meet for lunch. Chad was a tall and well-built man in his early thirties, with curly hair and a messy stubble. I took him to a great little burger joint in Farringdon that in my opinion did the best milkshakes in London. After devouring his cheeseburger and chocolate milkshake, we sat and chatted for almost two hours. Chad explained how he was born and raised in Toronto and had recently moved to London with Imperial Bank to trade corporate bonds. It had always been his dream to work in the City and he was clearly excited about his new job. I instantly took a liking to him. His calm and measured manner was endearing and I somehow felt like I could trust him.

Our conversation moved on to my frustration with my job and how I was possibly looking to move, although I was careful not to mention the 'D' word.

'Well, if you are willing to look at opportunities internationally, we have just opened an office in Dubai,' Chad said. I sat up eagerly at the news. 'Our bank has very big plans for the Middle East and Dubai is going to be our regional hub. I would be happy to make some calls to see if we're recruiting if you like.'

After all the recent disappointment I wasn't exactly hopeful, but I had nothing to lose. 'That would be great, Chad, if you don't mind.'

'No. Of course not. I would be happy to!'

After taking care of the bill, we exchanged numbers and I rushed back to work expecting never to see him again.

A week later, Chad called me at the office.

23

'Listen, Adam, I made some calls for you, and it turns out that Imperial Bank is looking for a guy at your level to go out to Dubai to work in the Institutional Sales team. Would you be interested?'

I was struggling to contain my excitement. 'Yes, absolutely!'

'Perfect. I'll set up a time for you to speak with the head of sales over there. His name is Asim Ali. He will be expecting your call.'

I was astounded that Chad had called me back at all. Clearly something about my dire situation had struck a chord with him, and I was overwhelmed that he had made the effort for me.

'Thank you, Chad. I really appreciate this.'

'Hey, don't mention it. Good luck!'

Within a day, he emailed me with a time for a phone interview with Asim Ali, the Regional Director of Sales for Imperial Bank in Dubai.

Asim didn't waste much time on formalities and cut straight to the point. 'So tell me, why do you want to leave a global financial centre like London to come to Dubai?' he asked in a strong Asian accent.

'Well, as I said, I want to get some international exposure on my CV, and with my current experience I think I can add a lot of value to your team in Dubai,' I replied, trying my best to sound confident despite the butterflies swirling in my belly.

'But don't you think it is a bit early in your career to be making the transition?'

'No, not at all. I think it's important to take risks early on in one's career. I also want to be part of the growth of Dubai as one of the world's leading financial centres, which I'm very confident it will become.'

I couldn't exactly tell him the truth. It wasn't my intention to come to Dubai to develop a conventional career at all. If I had wanted that, I would have stayed in London. I was looking for a way into the world's fastest-growing city and a position with Imperial Bank would be my Trojan horse. Once inside, I planned to do whatever it took to make my fortune.

Asim sighed and paused for a moment in deep thought. 'Okay, well, you sound like you want this and your résumé is outstanding. When can you start?'

I couldn't believe it! My bullshit seemed to have worked and Asim made me a formal offer within a week. As I was only a junior banker, I would not receive the full expat package of a housing and car allowance that more senior expatriates were getting, but that didn't bother me too much. All I really wanted was the break. I was convinced that within a couple of years I would be sailing around the clear waters of the Persian Gulf in my own private yacht, so petty matters of allowances were trivial in the greater scheme of things. I immediately resigned from my dreary job and urgently made the last minute preparations to leave my life in London behind.

The night before I left to begin my new life, I sat on my bed for the last time and stared at the giant poster on my wall. It was the object of my childhood fantasies and the thing I desired more than anything else in the world: a Porsche 911 Turbo. As a kid, while my friends had drooled over pictures of Pamela Anderson and Carmen Electra, it was this fine example of human engineering that had got my testosterone flowing like nothing else. For me, the Porsche 911 Turbo represented the ultimate status symbol: a feat of human engineering and an icon to show that one had truly made it. I had always dreamed about making one of them my own, and I was convinced that the pot of gold waiting for me in Dubai could turn that dream into reality in no time.

I lay back on my bed and pondered the adventure that lay ahead. I felt like Columbus on the cusp of his journey to discover a new world. Yes, I was a little afraid and I would miss my dear family and close friends. But I couldn't wait to see the back of my banal job and pushy boss. I was destined for greater things and I was determined to make the most of the rare opportunity I had been given.

Little did I know that the journey that lay ahead would be the most important of my life.

3

Camels to Cadillacs

Once upon a time, in a distant corner of the Arabian Peninsula lay a sleepy nation called the United Arab Emirates. The UAE was made up of seven autonomous cities ('Emirates') where seven kings, or sheikhs, benevolently ruled their respective territories according to strict Islamic laws and customs. Life across these Emirates was docile and conservative, governed by the old Bedouin tribal customs of centuries before. Despite the bounties of oil wealth and the temptations of the modern world, these rulers remained insular and reactionary, and their people were suspicious of change.

Yet of the seven, one was desperate to break away from the chains and shackles of tradition. In a region where *shway shway* ('slow, slow') was the overarching mantra, this Emirate's visionary sheikh was brimming with ambition to embrace the New World and cement his legacy for ever. For years his predecessors had watched with envy as the Western world surged ahead, leaving the envious East in its shadow. No longer would he settle for second best. Although many dismissed his grandiose visions as the foolish dreams of a madman, his resolve grew to the point of obsession. Money was of little importance and time was a mere inconvenience. This sheikh would not stop until the world was at his feet and the name of his city was spoken in the same breath as London, Paris and New York.

That man was Sheikh Mohammed Bin Rashid Al Maktoum, and his great project was Dubai.

***

The origins of the great Dubai experiment can be traced back to the 1800s, when the formidable Bani Yas tribe dominated the remote deserts of the Southern Arabian Peninsula. The Al Abu Falasa clan, a faction of Bani Yas, broke away from their brethren to a remote and uninhabited corner of the desert where a new settlement was established under the auspices of Sheikh Maktoum bin Buti in 1833.

With the support of the British government in exchange for protection again the Ottoman Empire, the settlement soon attracted other Bedouin settlers, and the foundations were laid for a new city of trade and commerce to emerge. They called it *Dubai.*

The city leaders' flair for shrewd business was clear as early as 1901 when the savvy Sheikh Maktoum bin Hasher Al Maktoum established a free port by abolishing tariffs and persuading wealthy Iranian merchants to relocate their trading activities to the Dubai Creek, a natural harbour where traders could dock their goods and import and export freely between Europe and the Far East. In the 1950s, before oil was discovered, Sheikh Rashid bin Saeed Al Maktoum dredged the Creek with a loan from the Emir of Kuwait to expand its capacity for trade. And in 1959, Sheikh Rashid founded Dubai airport and established the emirate's first hotel, cementing the foundations for his city's bright future.

Oil was first struck in the Emirates' capital city Abu Dhabi in 1958, transforming the fortunes of the nation. However, Abu Dhabi's incumbent Sheikh Shakhbut bin Sultan Al Nahyan failed to visualise the potential to develop his city by utilising its new-found revenue stream. He was replaced in a bloodless coup in 1966 by his more ambitious British-backed brother Sheikh Zayed bin Sultan Al Nahyan, who immediately went to work to unite a land beset with tribal rivalries, and inspire its transformation from a modest trading outpost to an economic powerhouse.

Zayed was a man of great principles and values; a Bedouin before a statesman. He won the loyalty of his people by establishing a welfare state that offered them free healthcare, comfortable housing and education. His religious tolerance of Christians and the freedoms given to Western expatriate workers were unprecedented for the region, and he was also one of the world's first environmentally friendly statesmen, remembered as 'the man who turned the desert green' after ordering the planting of thousands of trees in the barren sand. After the British withdrawal in 1971, Zayed continued to utilise the country's immense oil revenues and instilled a program of infrastructure development and national investment, which led to the building of new roads, schools, nospitals and utility plants. Despite being one of the wealthiest men on the planet, Zayed chose to live a modest and traditional life, which won him great praise from the masses as a man of the people.

Then, with the aid of big brother Abu Dhabi's oil revenues, Sheikh Rashid Al Maktoum surged ahead with Dubai's own modernisation program. Rashid was a realist and understood well that the gift of oil was finite and that urgency was required to modernise and prepare his city for an uncertain future. His famous words summed up his sentiment:

'My grandfather rode a camel, my father rode a camel, I drive a Mercedes, my son drives a Land Rover, his son will drive a Land Rover, but his son will ride a camel.'

Sheikh Rashid astounded his advisers with a decision to build a new mega-port, the $3 billion Jebel Ali Free Zone and a cornerstone for the commercial development of the city. The construction of the colossal million-ton capacity Dubai Dry Docks project was entrusted to his younger son Sheikh Mohammed bin Rashid Al Maktoum, Dubai's precocious future ruler. It was a great example of financial clairvoyance that Sheikh Rashid bequeathed to his sons when he passed away in 1990.

On 3 January 1995, Sheikh Mohammed Bin Rashid Al Maktoum became the Crown Prince of Dubai, marking a new era of decisive leadership and economic growth. An RAF-trained pilot, a keen falconer, talented poet and accomplished endurance equestrian, Mohammed outlined his ambitious plans in his 2006 book *My Vision: Challenges in the Race for Excellence*, in which he compared Dubai to Cordoba, the medieval capital of Arab Spain and a centre of intellectual enquiry, debate and interaction, revealing his vision to revive the glory of the Arabia of yesteryear.

Sheikh Mohammed shared his father's urgency and built on his legacy of modernisation. The late 1990s saw the emergence of new real estate projects the scale and size of which had never been seen in the entire region. Among these were the iconic Emirates Towers, which became the tallest and most contemporary commercial buildings in the Middle East. Mohammed also established tailor-made business parks like Media City and the DIFC, which offered 100 per cent foreign ownership and tax-free incentives to the world's top companies to make Dubai their regional hub.

However, the crowning glory of the new Dubai was to be the opulent Burj Al Arab, the tallest free-standing and only seven-star hotel. The magnificent sail-like structure instantly became the iconic symbol of Dubai's ambitions to become one of the globe's leading destinations. Sheikh Mohammed's decisiveness and the impressive speed of his execution won him great praise from his peers. He was the entrepreneur sheikh; the chief executive of a new giant city-corporation, later aptly nicknamed 'Dubai Inc.'.

Yet despite the sheikh's monumental efforts throughout the 1990s, Dubai remained utterly insignificant in the corridors of global power. The West's close alliances with the Gulf's other oil-rich regimes had served them well to keep supplies up and providing useful cash-rich customers for weapons and Treasury Bonds when coffers were low. But the reputation of the region remained that of a mysterious backwater of old-fashioned Bedouins beset by tribal bickering. Dubai's lack of any significant oil reserves ensured that it would never be given the same respect as its neighbours Saudi Arabia, Kuwait or Abu Dhabi.

In 2001, a quite unexpected event would disturb this longstanding status quo for ever. This single incident served as the unlikely catalyst to catapult Dubai onto the global stage and usher in a new era of recognition and respect. That event was 9/11. Within days, wealthy Arabs pulled billions of dollars out of US and European capital markets through fear of a political backlash from Western governments. There were reports of planes loaded with gold bars and dollar bills flying across the Atlantic in a frantic display of financial repatriation as Middle Eastern regimes scrambled to bring their money out before the tide turned against them.

With such enormous wealth flooding home, it needed to be parked somewhere safe and lucrative. Dubai's visionary sheikh saw his opportunity. In May 2002, His Highness Sheikh Mohammed announced the ground-breaking Dubai Freehold Decree, which allowed the open purchase of property in Dubai for the first time in its history. A surge of pent-up demand was unleashed and this piece of legislation proved to be the stroke of genius that would win Sheikhs Mohammed the praise his craved.

From Dubai's perspective, the 2002 decree was the latest step in the progressive history of a modernising city that had begun in the

29

early twentieth century. But to the outside world, 2002 was the beginning of history for Dubai. It represented the tiny Emirate's arrival onto the global stage like a tremendous 'big bang' that kick-started its ascendancy as a global destination for tourism, trade and investment. The timing could not have been more perfect. Destitute funds returning from the West were welcomed with open arms by Dubai's government-backed property developers Emaar and Nakheel to bankroll their grand real estate ambitions. They were soon followed by hundreds of private developers, and the subsequent gold rush would transform the city's skyline for ever.

After decades in the shadows of obscurity, Dubai had finally found its place in the sun. It was now time for Sheikh Mohammed to step up and show the world just how high he could reach.

4

Arabian Nights

'*Yalla, habibi, yalla…!*'

I was abruptly woken from my blissful slumber by the repetitive Arabic pop song blasting out of the wall-mounted television above.

'Let's go, oh baby, let's go…!'

As I scrambled for the remote control to get a few extra minutes of much-needed snooze, I caught a glimpse of the vivid images and jumped up to get a proper look. An attractive Lebanese bottle blonde was prancing provocatively around a forest dressed in a skimpy school uniform, which was conveniently too small for her buxom physique. The pop video was littered with sexual innuendo as its voluptuous star teased her audience with the guile of a stripper. Was this mild pornography really allowed to be broadcasted in the conservative Middle East? I was eventually startled out of my trance by the bellowing echo of the Muslim call to prayer from a nearby mosque. It signalled the crack of dawn and time to get ready.

As I brushed my teeth, I looked down at Imperial Bank's state-of-the-art office block from my twenty-seventh-floor window. From this vantage point I could see that it was only a short walk away from the Emirates Towers, so I took my time to shower, shave and get dressed. But it was as I was applying my complimentary rose-scented shower gel that I remembered I had failed to consider one important factor in my scheduling: the punishing desert heat outside. Considering my brief encounter with the Dubai summer at the airport yesterday, the prospect of even walking to the other side of the road caused a shudder down my spine. Throughout breakfast I formulated strategies on the back of my napkin with the tenacity of a military general in preparation for round two with the sun.

After a couple of false starts by stepping outside the lobby and running back inside to the amusement of the hotel staff, I went for it. The first five or six steps were fine. Seven and eight were okay. But it

31

was around my tenth stride that the blazing sun decided to strike again. Once again, my face turned bright red and large rings of sweat formed under my armpits and around my groin. I felt sticky and wet, and within a few moments I resigned myself to the fact that I couldn't go a single step further. I stopped, turned round and staggered back to the hotel lobby.

After some deliberation, I accepted that there was no option but to do something highly embarrassing, but necessary. It was something I would never have dreamed of doing back in London, but there was simply no other choice in the circumstances: I took a taxi to cross the street.

As the cab pulled up, I jumped in the back head first to avoid the gawping valet attendants who had now gathered in a huddle to mock me. But before I could utter a word to the driver, I was struck with the most appalling odour: a hideous fusion that could only be described as curry, sweat and rotten eggs. I held my poor nostrils together as tightly as I could, but the smell alone was not the worst of it. The sound of strangely repetitive Indian flute music was pumping out of the struggling stereo at full volume, and the seats were sticky and damp. The only redeeming feature of this taxi from hell was that the air conditioning was working reasonably well, which was enough to keep me planted in the back seat.

'Where you go?' shouted the driver at me in a strong Asian accent. He was an older man with oily hair and hairy ears, and he looked like he hadn't bathed for weeks.

'To the DIFC, please.'

'Dubai Internet City, no problem,' he said and slammed his foot on the gas.

'No!' I screamed. He braked abruptly and turned to stare at me with his beady yellow eyes. His breath was unbearably foul. 'I said *DIFC.*'

'You say DIC!'

'No, I said D-I-F-C. Dubai International Financial Centre.'

He looked utterly bemused. 'Where is this place?'

'You don't know where the DIFC is?' He shook his head. 'It's there, across the street.' I pointed desperately.

'There?'

'Yes, there.'

'If there, why no you walk?' It was a reasonable question.

I sighed and muttered sheepishly under my breath, 'It's too hot.'

'It's too hot?'

'Yes, it's too hot to walk.'

'Not too hot!'

'Yes, it is. It's just too hot to walk today. I tried, but I can't do it. Please, I'm begging you, just drive me there.'

My driver had forced a confession and he didn't look too happy. He had assumed, quite correctly, that passengers from the Emirates Towers at this time of the morning usually went to work at the city's other business districts like the Dubai Internet City or the Media City, which were both a fair distance away. Nobody ever took a taxi from here to the DIFC! By accepting my pitifully short fare he was probably sacrificing a better one elsewhere, and he didn't hide his frustration. He turned up the hypnotic Indian music and began singing at the top of his voice. I was sure it was a small act of revenge, and it wasn't long before I cracked under his torture tactic and decided to attempt some small talk just to make it stop.

'That's, erm, very interesting music. Where is it from?' I shouted over it.

'From Peshawar.'

'Ah, I see. Is that where you are from?'

'Yes, I am from Peshawar in Pakistan.' He stared at me again in his rear-view mirror. 'Where are you from?'

'I'm from London.'

The driver began to shake his head as if I had told him a massive lie. 'You are from London?' he asked. 'Your face looks like Arab. Where your mother, father from?'

'Well, their roots are in Pakistan. But they live in London.'

'So you are from Pakistan!' he shouted, now clearly overjoyed by our shared ancestry.

'No, like I said...'

'Which *pind* is your father from?' he interrupted.

'I'm sorry, *pind*?'

'*Pind*. How you say, village?'

'I have no idea...'

'Very, very bad! You should know your *pind*!' Great, that's just what I needed right now, a history lesson from a taxi driver. 'You speak Urdu?'

'No, only English I'm afraid.'

'*Yaar*, very bad,' he scolded. 'You should speak Urdu. You think you are from England?'

'I *am* from England!'

'No, you are from Pakistan!'

This conversation was clearly going nowhere, so I conceded I was an ignorant immigrant with an identity crisis. It was the first of many lessons on f Dubai's social hierarchy. The colour of one's passport meant very little. Whether you were British, Indian or Chinese, your social status in Dubai was determined ultimately by ethnicity. If you had blond hair and blue eyes, you were considered a Westerner, no matter where you called home. And if you were of Pakistani or Indian origin, you were Pakistani or Indian first, even if you were British. It was all rather confusing, but it was the way Dubai society had functioned for decades, a clearly defined social pecking order based on skin colour. I seemed to present an unwelcome spanner in the works of this well-oiled system, as I had a British passport yet was of Pakistani ethnicity and looked like an Arab!

The journey was embarrassingly short. After driving down the ramp from the hotel lobby and around a small roundabout, we were pretty much there.

'Here, DIFC!' he shouted in a patronising tone.

34

'Thank you,' I replied sheepishly and paid him a handsome tip to offset the humiliation, although I gathered he was now more upset about my lack of knowledge of the regional tribes of Pakistan than the short fare.

'Never forget your country, my friend,' he warned before driving away to the sounds of his strange music. I was just grateful to escape the dreadful smell.

I stood at the foot of the financial centre and glanced up at the colossal stone that towered over me. The iconic arch of the Gate was even more impressive from this vantage point than from my hotel room. It reminded me of Paris' Arc de Triomphe, except this structure incorporated glass in its walls, looking into the numerous offices inside. The surrounding six buildings were positioned like a giant semi-square around the Gate, all of them recently finished and many still unoccupied. Covered cloisters ran around the perimeter of the buildings, and a few empty restaurants and cafés with outdoor pavilions overlooked the grounds below.

The creation of Dubai International Financial Centre in 2004 marked the city's claim to becoming one of the world's great financial centres. It was established as a Federal Financial Free Zone, offering over a hundred acres of prime office space for investment banks and financial institutions to set up their regional offices in Dubai on an attractive tax-free basis. The elites of global finance and banking were coaxed into establishing operations in the DIFC and it soon became the world's fastest-growing financial hub, comprising almost five hundred local and international companies and employing more than eleven thousand professionals.

In theory, it was an excellent idea. The DIFC bridged the time-zone gap between London and Singapore and offered a convenient hub to access Africa, the subcontinent and the near east. But as Dubai threw millions of dollars into gleaming tower blocks and tax breaks, the only thing it couldn't buy was credibility. That would take much longer to earn and the Emirate wasn't best known for its patience. Imperial Bank had been one of the first international institutions to move its entire regional operations to the DIFC, and building number four was to be the location of my new office. I entered through the revolving glass doors and announced my arrival to the Indian security guard at the reception desk.

'Hi, my name is Adam. I'm here to meet Asim Ali at Imperial Bank.'

'Welcome, sir. Please, one moment,' he said and picked up the phone beside him.

A few moments later, my new boss Asim came downstairs to greet me. He was just as I had imagined, a slim-built Pakistani man in his mid-thirties with a dark complexion, a side parting in his hair and an ill-fitting suit. However, he seemed surprised by my appearance and stared at me curiously for a moment, as if he had pictured me completely differently. It was obvious that I wasn't exactly what he had been expecting.

'Adam?'

'Hi, Asim! It's great to meet you finally.' I enthusiastically shook his hand.

'Yes, you too.' He hesitated. 'You look quite different to what I was expecting.'

'Oh really, how so?'

'Well, with a name like Adam and an Oxford degree I was expecting you to be, well, white...' He looked a little disappointed.

'Well, this is me!'

'Indeed. Let's head upstairs, I'll show you to your desk. Nice suit, by the way.'

As I followed Asim into the elevator and out into the bank's dealing room, I was struck by how quiet it was. The trading floor felt more like a library than an investment bank. There were no salespeople shouting at clients on phones, or traders yelling at salespeople, like I was used to in London. Instead, rows of Indians, Pakistanis and Emiratis sat obediently in front of their computers, intensely involved in their work. It was a far cry from the dynamic, money-making boiler room I was familiar with, and it made me a little concerned.

'Meet Deepak, Ram and Sanjay,' said Asim, and I shook hands with three identical-looking Indian men with thick moustaches and side-parted hair. They seemed distracted by my arrival and reluctantly tore themselves away from their screens to greet me.

36

'What is your good name?' asked one of them in a robotic voice.

'Sorry, my good name?'

'Yes, your good name.'

'Do you mean my name?'

'Yes, your good name.'

'It's Adam.'

He then sat back at his desk and got back to work. It was already obvious there was not going to be a great deal of banter between us.

I made myself comfortable at my new desk and began to ponder whether I had made the right decision to take such a huge gamble with my career. I tried to take solace in the belief that I was a pioneering young banker in a fast-growing global financial centre, well placed to ride a wave of expansion in one of the world's most up-and-coming regions. My first impressions were hardly encouraging. I desperately hoped my hunch was right.

***

That evening, I wanted nothing more than a quiet drink alone. The stress of the past few weeks had taken its toll and I was craving some time by myself to relax and switch off. After a long shower, I took the elevator up to Vu's Lounge, a trendy hotel bar on the fifty-first floor of the Emirates Towers. I took a seat on the deliciously comfortable red-leather sofa and scanned the extensive drinks menu.

The bar was not too busy at this early hour and I was glad I could hear myself think over the soft jazz music trickling out of the speakers. I treated myself to a Monte Cristo cigar and a Mojito cocktail and as I puffed away gently, I looked out onto the hazy sunset falling over the city skyline and the ever-busy Sheikh Zayed Road below. The view of the city from this unique vantage point was breathtaking, and I hadn't felt so relaxed in days. I sank further into my seat to make the most of this rare moment of bliss.

Ping. The elevators doors opened and out strolled a stunning blonde who nearly made me fall off my chair. Dressed in seductive skinny jeans, a fitted white jacket and five-inch heels, she could have easily passed for a supermodel. I almost burned my leg with cigar ash as I watched her strut into the bar with an irresistible swagger. She looked European, perhaps Russian. As she walked over in my direction, she seemed to spot me staring from the corner of her eye before taking a seat at the bar. She was too beautiful to ignore, yet I didn't want to make my interest too obvious so I decided to play it cool.

'It's a beautiful sunset, don't you think?' I asked, as I casually leaned towards her. There was no reaction. Not even a look. Taking the hint, I sheepishly went back to my drink.

'Where are you from?'

It seemed she had heard me after all. I looked up to notice her scanning me from head to toe, as if to assess whether our conversation had any long-term potential.

'I'm from London.'

'You are born in London?'

'Yes, I am.'

A vague smile. 'You don't look like you are from London. You like Arab.'

'Yes, I hear that a lot.'

'What you do in Dubai?'

'I'm banker.'

Again a smile. 'Very good. And where do you stay?'

'I'm actually staying here in the Emirates Towers right now.'

She now turned around to face me. 'You look very young,' she said, lighting a cigarette that she pulled out from her gold Gucci handbag.

'Thanks, I'll take that as a compliment.' I was sure she was younger than me, but I got the impression she was comparing me with other men she knew. 'So what's your name?'

'Irina.'

'It's nice to meet you, Irina. I'm Adam.' I shook her perfectly manicured hand. And where are you from?'

'From Russia.' Bingo.

'You're a long way from home.'

'You are further from home,' she replied confidently.

'Yes, I guess I am.'

Her cross-examination of me wasn't over yet. 'So you make a lot of money?'

It was an odd question and I was a little taken aback by her directness. 'Erm, I guess my salary is okay.'

'And do you have plans tonight?'

This conversation was now moving a bit too fast for comfort. I hesitated for a moment but before I could answer, we were interrupted by the imposing presence of a large Emirati man in traditional dress towering over us. He was tall with broad shoulders, and was holding praying beads in one hand and a glass of champagne in the other.

'*Habibi*, I would like you to join me and my friends for dinner tonight,' he said to Irina in a deep, uncompromising tone. My presence seemed utterly insignificant to him, as if I wasn't even there. I caught her staring intensely at his gold Rolex watch before she whispered something back to him, and they left together for the corner of the room where what looked like a negotiation ensued. I guarded her bag like a gentleman until she returned, hoping we could resume our banter.

'I have to go,' she said nervously as she returned and hurriedly prepared to leave, while the Emirati man waited impatiently by the elevator. 'My friend is waiting.' She seemed a different woman to the confident seductress I had been speaking with moments before.

'Yes, sure. But is he really a friend of yours? It looked like you just met him.'

She ignored my question. 'Where is your phone?' she demanded.

'Pardon?'

'Give me your phone!' I did as I was told. After typing something in, she tossed it on the table, rushed over to the elevator and was gone. I sat scratching my head and nursing my bruised ego, trying to piece together what had just happened. But a glance at my phone made it all somewhat clearer:

You're cute. Call me anytime you are lonely. 050 747 8855. Irina xx

The events fell into place and I guess I couldn't blame her for choosing the better offer. I took comfort in the message, which proved who she would rather have had a drink with, and with a smile I decided to order one last cocktail before calling it a night.

'*Yaani*, is anybody taking this seat, my friend?' said a voice from behind me just as I prepared to leave. I turned around and saw a good looking young man dressed in a smart blazer and trendy jeans. He had a trimmed goatee and his hair was tied back in a sleek ponytail.

'No, feel free,' I replied politely. 'I was about to leave anyway.'

'Thanks!' He sat down beside me. 'What are you smoking there, buddy?'

'It was a Monte Cristo number five,' I said as I extinguished the stub in the glass ashtray at the bar.

'Very nice! *Yaani*, a true connoisseur's cigar. You know they say they roll these on the thighs of virgins. But they don't tell you if she's a hot virgin. *Yaani*, she could be butt ugly for all I know. Maybe that is why she is a virgin!' I gathered *Yaani* was the Arabic equivalent to 'like,' and was obviously a staple of his vocabulary.

'Very true,' I laughed.

'I'm Hani, by the way,' he said, extending his hand.

'Adam. Nice to meet you.'

'Am I, erm, disturbing you?'

'Well, I was just about to call it a night,' I replied, trying not to appear rude.

'Ah, I'm sorry, my friend. Don't let me keep you. Good evening.'

As he turned his attention towards his drink, for some reason I hesitated. There was something strangely endearing about this chap that made me want to find out more about him, so I decided to stick around a little longer. 'Actually, it's okay, I'm not in any real rush.'

He looked pleased. 'Great! Take a seat! Let's get you another drink.'

'So do you work in Dubai, Hani?' I asked.

'Yeah, I work as a journalist for a Lebanese TV channel in the Media City. I am Lebanese, if you didn't notice already. But I can't tell where you're from, though. You sound British but...'

'I *am* British.'

'Cool! *Yaani*, I thought maybe you were an Arab, but your accent gave it away. You know you look like an Arab?'

'Yes, I have heard that.'

'And what do you do here in Dubai?'

'I work for an investment bank.'

'Wow, great. Good for you! That's where the money is, my friend. *Yaani*, have you been in Dubai long?'

'Just a couple of days.'

'Wow, that's all? Welcome to Dubai!' he said, and raised his glass. I toasted his back and smiled. Hani's warm personality was endearing and I felt as if I had known him for years.

He took a long swig of his drink and slammed the empty glass on the bar. '*Yalla*, so do you want to party tonight?'

'Tonight?'

'Yeah!'

On any other night I would have jumped at the invitation, but tonight my fatigue had got the better of me. 'I really appreciate the offer, Hani, but I'm very tired. Besides, it's a week night and I have work in the morning.'

'*Yalla*, come on! Everybody is working tomorrow! One thing you have to learn is that in Dubai every night is like a weekend. You work hard and play harder. You're new to this city. Let me show you around!'

'I really would love to but...'

'Come on, man! Let me show you the real Dubai!'

'Listen Hani, I don't know if...'

41

'One night only! We won't make it a late one'. He wasn't yielding. '*Yaani*, I promise it will be the night of your life!'

I paused and sighed, 'Okay, but do you promise I will get home at a reasonable time?'

'Of course, bro! Just leave it to me.'

We left the bar and jumped into his black Ford 4x4 parked at the hotel entrance. As we pulled away, the sounds of Lebanese pop music blasted out of his expensive sound system and the heavy bass caused a shudder in the soft leather seats.

'Nice ride, Hani,' I said, genuinely impressed.

'Thanks, buddy. She's my pride and joy, this baby. You gotta have a big car here in Dubai, otherwise people won't respect you on the road. There are some pretty crazy drivers here.'

I suddenly remembered my near-death experience the day before and how lucky I was to be alive.

'So, tell me, do you like *shisha*?' asked Hani.

'Yeah, I love *shisha*!'

'Great! Let's start with some *shisha*. And I promise you never had *shisha* like you will have tonight.'

The memories came flooding back. I had smoked *shisha* regularly as a teenager with my friends in London's famous Arab district on Edgware Road, where we would sit for hours playing cards and puffing away into the night. Also known as the hookah or hubbly-bubbly, *shisha* was a traditional Arabic glass pipe of flavoured tobacco and water smoked through a hose. Its origins dated back to the royal courts of the Mogul Emperors, but it was enjoying a modern revival across the Arab world, and Dubai was the undisputed Mecca of *shisha* smoking. Socialising in Dubai often revolved around getting together with friends at one of the hundreds of restaurants or cafés to chat, eat and smoke. *Shisha* transcended boundaries of class, ethnicity and wealth as people from all walks of life regularly indulged in what had become the nation's favourite pastime.

Our first stop was the Shu Lounge on the Jumeirah Beach Road, which Hani described as the 'Rolls-Royce of *shisha* cafés'. It was one of the city's most fashionable spots for Dubai's young and affluent

42

crowd to be seen at. As we pulled up, Hani handed his car keys to the valet attendant at the entrance and we entered through an arch into a large outdoor pavilion directly overlooking the busy road. Inside, dozens of young locals were scattered around large tables and VIP enclosures. The decor was chic and minimalist, with clear plastic tables, gaudy chandeliers and Andy Warhol-inspired pop art. The waiters wore black Japanese-style kimonos and straw slippers, and on the walls hung fifty-inch flat-screen televisions showing the latest Arabic pop videos from Lebanon and Egypt. There was a constant flow of Ferraris, Lamborghinis and Aston Martins pulling up at the entrance and out of each super-car emerged yet more sexy young girls and tanned macho men, drenched in designer labels, dark sunglasses and gleaming jewels.

Hani spotted his friends waving at us from a table near the back of the courtyard and we walked over to join them.

'Hey, guys! I have a new friend with me. This is Adam. He's just arrived, so let's show him how we rock it in Dubai!'

He went around the table and introduced me to the group one by one. There was a Lebanese photographer called Marwan, a Moroccan web designer called Sami and two Palestinian sisters called Selma and Nawal, both of whom worked as real estate agents. We ordered a range of *shisha* flavours including mint, strawberry and apple and a few plates of delicious Lebanese *mezze* to share between us. The *shisha* and food arrived shortly after, and as Hani had promised it was the smoothest I had ever had.

'So how do you guys like living in Dubai?' I asked the group.

Sami replied enthusiastically. 'You know, Dubai for me has everything. It has great shopping, nice restaurants and a vibrant nightlife. It is safe and I am free here. As a young Arab, what more could I want?'

'I agree completely,' added Nawal. 'In my country, Palestine, I had no job and no future. Dubai has given me real career prospects. I can really be somebody here.'

'Yes, Dubai offers us hope,' added Marwan. 'I no longer have to go and chase the American dream like so many of my friends have. I can be successful here in my own region, where I know the culture and speak the language. I don't have to socialise in a pub or a bar, instead I can smoke a *shisha* with friends like we are doing now. This is what Dubai offers us.'

While the Western media continued to portray the Middle East as a region of instability, repression and fear, it was clear that Dubai offered something that had never existed before for these young Arabs: a sense of hope. In a region traditionally ravaged by war and frustration, Dubai represented job prospects to the unemployed, a voice to the disenfranchised and freedom to the repressed. In this city the young could reinvent and express themselves as they wanted and families could live without the fear of a repressive regime. To these Arabs the Emirate stood for more than somewhere to make a quick buck; it offered them a real future.

I got on effortlessly with Hani's friends as we sat chatting for over two hours about everything from movies and music to history and politics. I was astonished by how much we had in common and the lack of any cultural barriers between us. We shared stories of our childhoods and our aspirations for the future as we laughed, cried and laughed some more. My new friends personified young Arabia perfectly: a fun-loving, intellectual and ambitious generation who would lead the region boldly into the bright future, and I felt somewhat proud to be so close to this cultural renaissance. I was content to sit there and chat away for the rest of the evening, but I could see Hani was getting restless.

'So, guys, are we just going to sit here all night? I don't know about you, but I want to party! *Yalla*, let's go!'

We settled the bill and all squeezed into Hani's truck for our next exciting destination, which Hani simply referred to as the 360. Nestled in the luxurious wave-like Jumeirah Beach Resort, 360 was a popular nightspot for the city's trendy youth to party into the hot desert night. Located at the end of a manmade pier extending two hundred metres into the ocean, the bar offered stunning panoramic views of the marina and the endless waters of the Persian Gulf. Most nights of the week, Dubai's affluent social elite would dress in their finest beach attire and head to 360 to enjoy the majestic sunset in all its glory.

We arrived at the hotel at around eleven and jumped into a golf-buggy shuttle to make our way to the end of the pier. The flashing neon lights of the bar could be seen for miles and the music penetrated the air as far as the boats in the marina and along the adjacent beach. As we strolled up to the entrance, the hypnotic bass line of progressive house music and the rapturous screams of the revellers inside were enticing.

The atmosphere inside was electric. Sexy young models sipped exotic cocktails while they danced provocatively to the beats spun by the DJs. Hani had already reserved a prime table for us next to the balcony with bean bags and oversized loungers. We introduced ourselves to a group of tanned European girls drinking from champagne flutes at the table next to us, and we smoked more *shisha* and danced to the music, which had the entire crowd under its spell. The vibe was as thrilling as any night spot in Ibiza or Miami and everybody here felt alive.

But as midnight struck and the party at 360 was approaching its peak, Hani decided it was time to move on. Once again, we jumped into his party-mobile and headed to the next hotspot.

'Hani, it's getting kind of late,' I shouted over the pumping stereo. 'It's been a great evening, but perhaps I should head back to the hotel, I have work very early tomorrow.'

'Nonsense,' he interrupted. 'We are only just getting started, my man. You haven't seen anything yet!'

'Come on, Adam,' added Nawal. 'It's your first night out in Dubai. Relax and enjoy yourself. Work will always be waiting for you.'

I decided that any attempt to disagree would be futile, and I was secretly quite excited by what the night still had in store. I sat back, shut my mouth and went with the flow, trying not to think about the sleep-deprived day that surely lay ahead.

Hidden deep in the Dubai Marine Beach Club Hotel on the Jumeirah Beach Road was The Boudoir. In the early evening it was a chic restaurant serving the finest French food in Dubai, but as the clock struck midnight the tables were promptly cleared away and it was transformed into one of the hottest nightclubs in the world. Again, Hani had reserved a table for us directly on the dance floor, so we didn't have any difficulty getting past the large and uninviting doormen.

45

Inside, The Boudoir looked like a high-class Parisian brothel, boasting a gothic ambience of enormous crystal chandeliers, giant drapes and opulent red-suede sofas. Stunning fashionistas danced on the table tops while groups of muscular men drank from two bottles of champagne at a time. There were beautiful women everywhere: at the bar, in the DJ booth and on the tables. Hani ordered a giant bottle of vodka for our table and moments later, two muscle-bound barmen brought it to us on their shoulders like the entrance of Cleopatra into Rome. They laid it on our table while the club watched on in awe. Hani jumped onto the table and held the huge bottle above his head to the roar of the crowd. He then proceeded to pour its contents over the girls below him, before taking a large swig himself.

I don't remember much of what happened after that. The rest of the night was a bit of a blurry haze. But I was certain it was one of the best nights of my life.

The sun was already rising when the taxi dropped me back at the Emirates Towers. As I stumbled into the lobby, my ears were still ringing and my sight was blurry. Despite having to get to the office in less than three hours, I was too pumped up to sleep, so I decided to sit in the lobby for a while before going up to my room. By day the chic lobby lounge would be bustling with businessmen and executives, power lunching and shaking hands on million-dirham deals. But at this hour the deal makers were replaced by exotic women of various nationalities, all sitting mysteriously alone. In my innocent naivety I assumed they were hotel guests who were suffering from a bad case of insomnia like me. But I had a suspicion that there was something more to this peculiar scenario, and that the Emirates Towers lobby was living up to its reputation as a premier 'business hotel', although the nature of this business was somewhat more sinister.

I eventually headed back to my room, and after an hour of channel surfing through old Arabic movies and American shopping networks, I decided to call it a night. As I was scrambling through my suitcase for my pyjamas, I found a scrap of paper under some socks with a phone number on it. I suddenly remembered that a former colleague at work back in London had given me his brother Jerome's number and told me to get in touch. Jerome had moved to Dubai a few months before me, and so he could be a good contact. Oblivious to the time, I decided to call him there and then.

The phone rang continuously for over a minute without a reply, until finally a gruff voice answered.

'Yeah?'

'Erm, hi, is this Jerome?

'Yeah, who is this?'

'Hi, Jerome. I'm Adam, a friend of your brother's from London. He asked me to call you when I arrived in Dubai. He said you would be expecting my call.'

There was a long pause followed by a female voice giggling in the background.

'Oh yeah, he mentioned you. How you doing?' There was yet more commotion and I began to feel like I was disturbing something. 'Listen, I'm in bed at the moment. It's been a heavy night, man, had a couple of drinks, you know how it is.' I glanced at my clock and I suddenly felt quite embarrassed. 'Let's meet up tomorrow evening at the Shangri La hotel. A few of the guys from work are getting together for some drinks. Let's say nine in the lobby. Is that cool?'

'Erm, yeah, sounds good,' I replied sheepishly. 'And sorry for calling so late, I mean early.'

'Don't worry about it. See you tomorrow.'

I lay back in bed and thought about the night's events. Hani had opened my eyes to the real Dubai and I finally saw what Cameron had tried to tell me back in London. Every doubt I had previously about my decision to move here disappeared in an instant and I felt a sudden burst of excitement rush through my veins. There was something utterly electric about this young city. It was bustling, energetic and alive, and I was more determined than ever to make my mark.

All I needed now was a plan.

5

The British Invasion

There is certainly an expatriate type. To be willing to leave behind home comforts and family ties for a new life in a foreign country is not for everybody. It calls for admirable character traits like an ardent sense of adventure, an outgoing nature and a keen ability to make new friends. But there is often a darker, almost sinister side to the expat persona. In the insatiable pursuit of tax exemption and endless sunshine, many expats turn into obnoxious versions of their former 'indigenous' selves. They tend to drink and misbehave, fuelled by greater disposable incomes and a false air of importance. Blinded by delusions of grandeur, many transform into full-blown egomaniacs, showing little regard for their host country's customs and etiquettes without an ounce of shame.

From 2002, over 120,000 British expats came to Dubai in pursuit of sun, sea, sand and tax-free cash. Many were serial property investors looking to recycle their cash in the 'next big thing'. Others were tax evaders, VAT fraudsters and money launderers wanting to clean their money and their reputations. Most were undervalued middle-class professionals trying to revamp their flagging careers and upgrade their lifestyles in a new untapped and skill deficient market.

Lured by generous tax-free packages of inflated salaries, housing allowances and company cars, these Brits lived wonderfully indulgent lifestyles with an active social calendar of glamorous brunches, dinner parties, BBQs, nightclubs and beach clubs. They lived in newly built apartments and villas in exclusive gated communities, kept a housemaid and a chef, drove a gas-guzzling 4x4, and dined at the restaurants of the globe's finest chefs. They played golf on world-class courses and shopped in the most luxurious malls on the planet. Life was dynamic and exciting and the sun shone every day of the year. It was a far cry from the drudgery of city life in London, Birmingham or Manchester. In Dubai, the Brits found themselves at the top of the social food chain based on the colour of their skin and their passports, and they lived like royalty.

This expat influx was not new. Western workers had been relocating to the Middle East since the early 1970s on short-term contracts to meet huge skill shortages, particularly in the booming oil and gas and construction industries. Back then a position in Saudi, Kuwait or Abu Dhabi was considered a hardship post; a sacrifice made by the employee for his company in return for a generous salary and benefits package. But there was nothing 'hard' about living in new Dubai. The desert had become a playground for wealthy expats to enjoy every excess and vice they could fathom. Ten years ago a contract in the Gulf was an opportunity to save for retirement; today expats were piling up on credit cards to supplement their overblown salaries and fund an extravagant and indulgent lifestyle. With the added opportunity to own their properties and invest in the booming real estate market, the Gulf was no longer just a temporary stopgap for expats, but somewhere to place roots and build a future.

Every outrageous whim and desire of Dubai's affluent Western community was met by an army of foreign migrant workers from India, Pakistan and the Philippines, who formed an often invisible blue-collar underclass of helpers and servants. They worked inhumane hours bagging groceries, pumping petrol and running errands for measly wages to support their own poverty-stricken families back home. They were nervously attentive and unreservedly committed to please, driven by an ever-looming fear of upsetting their fickle overlords and, worse still, being replaced.

When they were not stuck in the office, on a building site or in an endless traffic jam, the preferred citadels of entertainment of the Western expat were the city's grand hotels. Each of them featured an eclectic selection of fine-dining restaurants, fully licensed bars and poolside *shisha* lounges where the social elite would flock after work and at weekends to meet, drink and be seen. The luxury beach hotels of Jumeirah featured pool bars, cocktail waiters and afternoon BBQs, while sun-starved tourists roasted for hours under the scorching desert sun. And as night fell over the desert, the hotels hosted exotic themed events offering indulgent buffets, wine tasting and live entertainment, attracting expats in their hordes to eat, drink, and hobnob late into the night.

But the undisputed weekly highlight of the discerning Dubai expat's social calendar was the infamous Friday brunch. Against the

49

echoes of the Muslim call to prayer on the holiest day of the Islamic week, the brunch became a weekly ritual of unbridled indulgence as hung-over Europeans, Americans and Australians came in their masses for a day of gluttonous excess. Copious quantities of food from every major cuisine were brazenly displayed to catch the appetite of the insatiable diner, and for a set price one could sample the best of Chinese, Indian, Italian, Mexican, Arabic, French and English cooking in a mass gastronomical orgy.

And with the food came champagne by the bottle and beer by the jug. It was no surprise that things often turned rowdy, and a few overindulgent foreigners had to be forcibly removed on the orders of the nervous hotel management. Despite their best efforts to contain the revelry, sometimes the unruly expatriates, fuelled by a deadly cocktail of booze, food and sunshine, were unleashed onto the city outside. Well-publicised incidents of abuse of the locals and public displays of excessive affection were unfortunate reminders that despite the city's best efforts to segregate opposing worlds, there was an ever-present risk of two cultures colliding with disastrous consequences

***

After work the next day, I jumped into a taxi to the Shangri La hotel and waited for Jerome in the lobby as we had agreed. I didn't have a clue what he looked like, but I assumed, perhaps naively, that he would resemble his brother, so I was confident I would be able to pick him out. I took a seat on a large beige sofa and scanned the lobby. It was the most impressive I had seen so far, with a three-tiered atrium of restaurants and bars overlooking a giant marble floor. Above the revolving doors hung an imposing giant tapestry of red, brown and beige made entirely out of glass beads. The lobby was trendier than the business-like Emirates Towers, with a younger and more fashionable clientele of Emiratis and foreigners sitting around smoking cigarillos while they browsed on their laptops or chatted away on their state-of-the-art mobile devices.

I felt a hand grip my shoulder from behind. 'What's up, matey?' I turned around to see two piercing green eyes staring directly into mine.

'Jerome?'

'Yep, that's me,' he replied, in a deep and raspy British accent. 'Good to meet you finally.'

I stood up to shake his hand. He was dressed in a tailored navy suit and crisp white shirt that fit his athletic physique perfectly. He was not very tall, but his chiselled features made up for what he lacked in height. 'It's great to meet you too. How did you know it was me?'

'Simple, my brother told me to watch out for a good-looking, well-dressed guy who looks like an Arab.'

'Ha-ha, I'm flattered, but that could be anybody in this city.'

'Yes, but you're the only one here who still looks impressed by the big shiny buildings. It's an instant giveaway!'

I smiled sheepishly. 'Is it that obvious?'

'Yep, afraid so,' said Jerome with a cheeky grin.

'By the way, Jerome, I want to apologise for calling you so late last night.'

'Hey, don't worry about it,' he interrupted. 'I think I got a pretty good idea what you were up to at that hour, you rascal!' I gathered what he was implying and I played along with a wink. 'Listen, come over and join me and my colleagues. We're having a world wine- and cheese-tasting night.'

'Sounds good, lead the way!'

I remembered Jerome's brother had told me that he worked for a small, London-based recruitment company in Dubai called Manning-Clarkson. The firm had seen the upcoming opportunity in the Emirate early and had set up a regional office two years ago, before the competitors had arrived. With first-mover advantage, Manning-Clarkson was perfectly placed to take advantage of the massive recruitment surge and business was booming. To capitalise on the demand, the firm had transferred half its London staff to the Emirate on attractive packages; as a top performer, Jerome had been one of the first to make the move.

I followed him through the lobby and past a giant arrangement of cheeses from France, Belgium, America, Argentina and Australia. They were meticulously arranged and each block was individually labelled with a little flag notifying its country of origin. In the centre of the grand display was a swan with open wings carved from a single block of cheese. It was impressive, except that the horrendous odour

51

was now spreading relentlessly throughout the lobby. As we approached Jerome's table, he let rip a piercing wolf-whistle, which startled everybody within a hundred metres.

'Everybody, your attention please! This is Adam, a friend from the UK. He is new to Dubai, so I want everyone to make him feel at home.'

His introduction was met with a reassuring roar of approval from the table, which I noticed was littered with empty wine glasses, bottles and plates still piled with cheese. I went around introducing myself to everybody one by one. They were an interesting mix of young and middle-aged Brits, all with beaming wide smiles and glowing red like overcooked lobsters. Most of them were clearly rather tipsy, as they slurred their names and 'nice to meet you's.

'Okay, buddy, I'm going to leave you in the hands of Jamie here, 'cos I'm sitting at the other end. Don't worry, he doesn't bite. Just keep an eye on your private parts. He's a bit unpredictable.'

'You rascal!' screamed the blond-haired, freckled man opposite me, who I gathered was Jamie. 'You didn't complain too much in the toilets this afternoon, Jerome.'

'No, Jamie, I think you're mistaking me for your mum.'

'Bastard!' replied Jamie in defeat. Jerome scuttled off to his seat, leaving me in the hands of his potential rapist friend. 'Your mate Jerome can be a right fucker sometimes. But he's still a legend,' said Jamie incoherently. 'So you recently moved here?'

'Yes, just this week,' I replied.

'You're gonna freaking love this city, mate! Coming here was the best decision I ever made. It's quality!' He guzzled down another glass of wine.

'Thanks, that's very reassuring. So what brought you to Dubai, Jamie?'

'Sun, booze and cash! Back home my career wasn't really going anywhere. The money was rubbish, I had no prospects and the weather was shit. Life was a bit grim, to say the least. But out here I'm making more money in a month than I would probably have made in a year in

England, and it's all tax free! I play golf every weekend and I'm out drinking almost every night. What more could I possibly want?'

'Well, then it sounds to me you're not working hard enough!' interrupted an older, overweight ginger-haired man sitting to my left in a strong Yorkshire accent. 'I'm Colin, by the way.'

'Colin's my boss, so I should probably watch what I say,' whispered Jamie.

'Damn right, Jamie. We wouldn't want you losing your job, now. How would you pay for that Jeep Cherokee you just bought?' Colin laughed heartily.

'Okay boss, understood,' replied Jamie and saluted his superior.

'I gather from your accent that you're from the north of England, Colin,' I said.

'Yep, I'm from Leeds, mate. It's a fucking world away from this place!'

'Colin just got divorced,' interrupted Jamie in an attempt to get his own back.

'Oh, I'm sorry to hear that Colin,' I said, genuinely.

'Don't be! It was the best thing that ever happened to me. I sent the old bag packing and now I can take my pick of a new girlfriend every night. God bless this city!'

'Oh, so it didn't work out?'

'Mate, I was an idiot! When you come to work in a place like Dubai you don't come with baggage. I got married when I was a hopeless nobody in a dead-end job in Leeds. Life wasn't going too far, so I thought, why not try Dubai? Since giving her the shove, I'm driving a brand new BMW and shagging every night. Life couldn't be better.' He exploded in a fit of laughter.

'Oh, Colin, you are so fun-unny...' said a large blonde woman in a flowery frock and glasses who was sitting next to him and listening attentively.

'Fun-unny? What the fuck is fun-unny, you drunken cow?' Colin pointed at a random bottle of wine and beckoned the waiter. 'Oi, we need another bottle of this stuff, pronto!'

The young Indian waiter nervously scuttled away and did as he was told. He returned in a flash, but as he showed the label to Colin before pouring, Colin didn't look pleased.

'Hang on, hang on. This is not what I fucking ordered!' The poor waiter froze with fear. 'I ordered a bottle of this one here!' Colin pointed at a similar bottle on the table, which I noticed was different to the one he had originally indicated.

'Sir, I am very sorry,' the waiter replied nervously.

'This is not good enough. I think I need to speak to your manager,' continued Colin remorselessly.

'No sir, please! I will get the correct bottle now!' There was a desperate plea in the waiter's voice that Colin callously ignored. I felt bad for the poor guy.

'Call your manager over right away!' screamed Colin. It seemed that the jolly northerner I had met moments ago had turned into a sociopathic manic.

'It won't be necessary to speak to the manager,' I interjected. 'Please, just get us the correct bottle.' Colin stared at me with surprise, while the waiter's eyes lit up with the appreciation of a slave pardoned from execution.

'What the fuck are you doing?' screamed Colin.

'Come on Colin, the poor guy is terrified for his job. Give him a break!'

'With all due respect, I think I know a little more about the customs here than you do,' said Colin, fuming at my interference. 'In this country you have to give these guys shit to keep them on the ball. It makes them work harder and not get too lazy. If you're too polite, you get walked all over. You clearly have a lot to learn about how this city works, mate. Now excuse me, nature calls.'

As he left the table abruptly, I peered over at Jerome at the far end. A pretty blonde dressed in a revealing off-the-shoulder blouse and mini skirt was sitting on his lap. She was attractive, but clearly older than him, and while she continuously rubbed his face and kissed his cheek, his nonchalant manner was frustrating her. I figured it was her voice I had heard giggling in the background when I called him last night. Jerome spotted me watching and winked before running his hand up her thigh.

As everybody got drunker, the table was becoming increasingly rowdy and the group was now drawing attention from other guests in the lobby. Jamie began putting cheese up his nose and screaming the words of the British national anthem at the top of his voice with his arms in the air. The others joined in, including Jerome. The large woman with the flowery frock and glasses fell off her chair onto the marble floor, giggling as she struggled to get up. Wine bottles were toppling and cutlery crashing to the floor. I couldn't help feeling incredibly embarrassed as the disgusted onlookers shook their heads at us. What was meant to be a civilised evening had somehow descended into farce, and I felt quite ashamed to be part of it. It wasn't long before the hotel manager approached us, looking extremely distressed.

'Ladies and gentlemen, I am afraid I am going to have to ask you to keep the noise down.'

'Fuck off!' replied Jamie, an exclamation that was met with a roar of applause from the table. The manager turned white with embarrassment. I saw it as a perfect opportunity to escape and make a dash for the men's room.

I took a deep breath of relief as I locked the door behind me. The silent sanctuary of the cubicle provided a huge relief from the commotion outside. But as I began to unzip my trousers, I was startled by the sound of an ecstatic female voice in the cubicle next to mine.

'Oh, Colin!' she screamed.

'That's my name,' replied a familiar voice.

'Colin, you tiger!'

'That I am, darling. That I am.'

I quickly gathered what I was disturbing and made a swift exit before the situation could get any more awkward.

Back at the table, the group had struggled to their feet and were stumbling out of the hotel like a clan of intoxicated football hooligans, much to the relief of the manager. They scrambled into taxis waiting outside, still singing all the way.

'Oi, Jerome! You comin', yeah?' shouted Colin, who had now finished his business in the bathroom and rejoined the group, oblivious that the zipper on his trousers was still wide open.

'Where are you guys going?' asked Jerome.

'Barasti, my man! It's ladies' night tonight. So many women, so little time!'

The female colleagues in the back of Colin's taxi found this particularly funny.

'Okay, cool, I might see you guys there in a bit.'

'Suit yourself,' said Colin before jumping into his cab. "More women for me!"

'What's Barasti?' I asked Jerome.

'Hmm, difficult to explain. Think about it this way: imagine your old school disco. Now add a bunch of drunken English expats, cheesy 80s music and a beach. That's Barasti. It's chav heaven in Dubai.' I shuddered at the thought.

Jerome handed the valet attendant his ticket and within minutes a convertible black Mercedes SLK with the roof lowered appeared before us.

'Is this your ride?' I asked.

'Sure is.' He jumped into the driver's seat before lighting a cigarette. 'Let's roll, dude!'

I hesitated. 'Haven't you been drinking, Jerome?'

'Don't worry, *habibi*, I'm fine!'

'What if you get pulled over?'

'Trust me, bro, I've been a lot drunker than this in the past and had absolutely no issues. I'm totally fine. Jump in!'

I was quite alarmed by his blasé attitude to the country's strict legal code, which employed a zero-tolerance approach to drink driving. If caught, an immediate jail sentence followed by deportation was certain. But for some inexplicable reason I sat in the passenger seat anyway. Jerome put a CD into the stereo and the speakers began to blast out the heavy bass of a hip-hop track. With a mighty roar of the engine, we drove off into the night.

My heart was in my mouth for most of the journey. Jerome weaved carelessly between the six lanes of the Sheikh Zayed Road, missing the speeding cars around him by inches as they honked at us in protest. As we sped past the bright lights of the skyscrapers, my heart was pounding in sync with the music. Jerome kept the convertible hood down despite the punishing humidity and dusty breeze, as we charged towards the Trade Centre roundabout and the old part of the city.

To my horror, Jerome pulled out his mobile phone and began to dial. I almost grabbed the wheel as he took his eyes off the road to make the call. Using a mobile while driving was the second law I had seen him break in less than ten minutes, and again he didn't seem to care.

'Hey babe, it's Jerome, we're on our way now. Keep a table warm. *Ciao.*'

We eventually pulled up outside the lobby entrance of The Raffles, one of Dubai's newest and most exclusive five-star hotels, and not a moment too soon. Jerome tossed his keys to the Filipino valet attendant and we strolled in like a couple of high rollers.

From the outside the hotel looked like a giant pyramid of glass and concrete, forming the new centrepiece of the Egyptian-themed Wafi Mall. Inside, the lobby oozed opulence, with large velvet sofas, marble pillars and a stunning indoor waterfall.

'Welcome to The Raffles, gentlemen,' said a beautiful Oriental woman dressed like a china doll. She offered us a hot towel scented with jasmine before ushering us into the gold-plated elevators.

'Where are we going, Jerome?'

'You'll see,' he smiled.

As the elevator doors opened, we found ourselves at the foot of a large staircase in a dark room surrounded by huge floor-to-ceiling windows.

'Good evening and welcome to the China Moon bar,' said the tall, exotic hostess who greeted us. She had flawless olive skin and sleek black hair, and would not have looked out of place on the catwalk in Paris fashion week.

'Thanks, babe. The name's Jerome. We're guests of Chantal.'

'Yes, we were expecting you. Please follow me.' As she strutted up the glass staircase to the upper floor, Jerome kept his eyes fixed on her toned behind. I realised we were now in the very tip of the pyramid, and the view of the old city skyline below us was stunning.

'She's smoking hot! Remind me to get her number when we leave,' said Jerome as the hostess glided away after showing us to the table.

'Oh, so the girl you were sitting with at the Shangri La is not your girlfriend?' I asked.

'Lucy? Hell no, she's nobody!'

'Really? She didn't look like nobody to me.'

'She's our office secretary. Lucy and I have just been fooling around. It's nothing serious. To tell you the truth, I'm completely bored and I have no idea how to get rid of her. The more I keep my distance, the more she keeps clinging on.'

I could see that Jerome was getting uncomfortable talking about it, so I decided not to probe further. 'So, what brought you to Dubai, Jerome?'

'Three words: Money. Dough. Peso. I'm going to make five million in the next couple of years here, and I'm getting the fuck out. I'm gonna buy a home in Kensington and a flat in Cannes, and sit back and live the good life.'

'Just five million?' I laughed. 'Hell, why not push it to a billion?'

He failed to see the humour. 'I think that should be the very least considering where we are right now. Think about it, this is the fastest-growing city in the world and it's an untapped goldmine. It's the Wild West and we're the first cowboys to get our share.'

His words struck an immediate chord with me. 'Yes, I totally agree.'

'People like you and me are pioneers. We're among the few who have the balls to come and take this opportunity. Yeah, others will be

58

here after us, but they will be too late. The time is now and we have to grab it!'

I could feel the passion in his every word. 'You're right, Jerome. But are you really going to make your millions through recruitment? There are only so many jobs and people looking for them, right?'

'No, recruitment is only a time-filler for me. It pays the bills. Just like I don't think you're planning to be a banker for ever. It's a means to an end, that's all. I'm working on a few other things that are going to make me the real money.'

'Like what?' I asked, intrigued.

'Well, unfortunately I'm not at liberty to say right now.' His caginess was both frustrating and enticing.

'Come on, man, who am I going to tell? I only just met you!'

Jerome paused and stared at me deeply for a moment, as if he was assessing whether I could be trusted. 'I don't know, mate, it's kind of confidential.'

I felt like he was toying with me; if he was, it was working. 'Jerome, come on, you can trust me, I swear!'

He sighed. 'Well, I guess you are a friend of my brother, and he's the best freakin' judge of character I know.' He paused again. 'Okay, I will let you in on something, but you have to promise to keep it very confidential. This is some seriously sensitive shit.'

'Of course!' I said reassuringly. 'It doesn't leave this bar, promise.'

The intensity in his green eyes was making me a little uncomfortable. He moved closer and began to whisper. 'Well, there is a prime piece of land in Dubai that I have direct access to. Very few people know about it, but it's in a very attractive location. I'm talking grade A prime location.'

'Okay, so where is it?'

'I can't say just yet. But take my word for it, it's the best location in the city,' he replied. 'I've been given a mandate to sell it on behalf of the seller. If you can help me find a buyer, we can make a fortune that we'll split between us.'

'Okay, but how do you have access to it?'

'Let's just say I'm connected with people who know people in the corridors of power.'

'How powerful are we talking exactly?'

'I'm talking all the way to the top.'

Jerome was certainly persuasive, but something didn't sound right and I began to smell the bullshit. How could a young, cocky recruitment consultant who had barely been in the country for a year be so well connected?

'Jerome if you don't mind me asking, how did you get to know these people?'

Jerome suddenly recoiled. 'Mate, if you don't want to be involved then I don't mind. I'm quite capable of finding a buyer on my own.'

'Okay, okay, I'm sorry. I just want to know if it's a credible source. That's all. I gotta protect my reputation too, you know.'

He shook his head and calmed down. 'Listen. I'm not allowed to say too much, but trust me, this deal is coming through somebody who knows the big daddy Sheikh Mohammed himself. That's all I can say right now. You find me a buyer and we split the fees fifty-fifty. I can't say fairer than that.'

'So let's say hypothetically I did have a buyer. How much money can we actually make on this deal?'

Jerome sat back in his chair and smiled. It seemed I was finally speaking his language. 'Look at it this way. A plot like this is worth at least half a billion dirhams, which is around seventy-five million pounds. If we're working on a minimum 2 per cent commission, you do the math.'

I punched in the numbers on my mobile phone calculator. The figure that appeared almost made me fall off my chair.

'Are you honestly saying we could make 10 million dirhams if we close this?'

'Yep,' said Jerome, sipping on his cocktail. 'So are you in?'

'Of course I am! But I need some more details, location, price, plans...'

'Listen. You find me a serious buyer and I will provide you with everything you need. You have my word. If we can close this quickly, we will both make a lot of money. And there are plenty more where this is coming from, believe me. Do we have a deal?'

As he put out his hand I looked into his eyes and grabbed it. 'Deal!'

There were all sorts of thoughts rushing through my mind. Why had Jerome decided to trust me so easily? Why hadn't he found a buyer on his own? Was the deal even for real? But despite my doubts, at that moment the opportunity sounded just too good to miss. I sat back and took a long, deep pull of my cigar. If Jerome was for real, this was my chance to become the person I had always dreamed of being. A true player in a land of opportunity.

***

The next morning I woke up to the worrying reality that I still had not found an apartment. Imperial Bank had agreed to pay my expenses for a month, after which I was out on the street, so I had to move fast. Over breakfast I grabbed a copy of the property section of the *Gulf News* to assess my options. I ploughed through three chunky property supplements before I finally got to the lettings section. It was not a pretty sight. Every single studio or one-bedroom apartment was at least two thousand dirhams outside my budget, including those in the older parts of town like Satwa and Bur Dubai. It seemed my dream of beachside living was further away than I had imagined.

Finding a reasonably priced apartment in Dubai in late 2004 was virtually impossible. With the huge influx of immigrant workers who had converged on the city, there was simply not enough property to cater for the sudden increase in demand. Unscrupulous landlords had seized the opportunity to inflate their rates to extortionate levels and so even property in the city's less affluent neighbourhoods had become completely unaffordable.

To make matters worse, most rent cheques in Dubai were required as a single up-front payment for the year. More merciful landlords agreed to divide this into two, but this was always at the cost of an increment on the total rent due for the year. If you refused, there was a waiting list of ten others who were just as desperate for somewhere to live. As a result, rent had become by far the largest expense for Dubai residents. Flat shares and sublets were common, even though they were officially illegal. It was not unusual for low-income workers to share single rooms with ten or even twelve others, and many were forced to accept the most intolerable living conditions to retain something to survive on from their humble salaries.

The rock-bottom scenario for every Western Dubai expat was being priced out of the market and having to consider living in the neighbouring Emirate of Sharjah, where rents were much more affordable. But Sharjah was not Dubai. There was no booze, no poolside lounges and certainly no brunches. Life there was conservative and chaotic, the roads were dusty and barren, and the residents cold and unfriendly. Moving to Sharjah from Dubai was not just downgrading your location; it was downgrading your identity. To tell people in Dubai that you lived in Sharjah was like pulling out a gun and committing social suicide. But sadly, it seemed that for me, Sharjah was becoming an ever-looming possibility.

Studio apartment near Burjuman shopping centre. Bachelor wanted. AED 5,500 PCM.

It was the only one that vaguely matched my price range, so I rang up immediately to book a viewing.

'Yes?' shouted an angry voice down the phone.

'Erm, hello, I'm calling about the advertisement about a room near the Burjuman Centre.'

There was a pause, followed by some offline shouting in Arabic. 'Where you from?'

'Do you mean which country am I from?'

'Yes, where you from, where you from?' he shouted again.

'Erm, I'm British.'

'British! Very nice, welcome to Dubai! Yes, of course my friend, we have a very good room, just for you.' His tone seemed to have changed suddenly. 'Come to the apartment at six tonight. I will show you a very nice room.'

So after work I took a taxi to Bur Dubai, the older quarter of the city. The cab dropped me at the entrance of the Bab Al Shams building, which translated in Arabic as the 'Gateway to Sunshine'. But as I stood outside the crumbling structure, it seemed clear that the building had not seen a sunny day for years. It was one of the older buildings in Bur Dubai and it certainly showed its age. The bricks were crumbling and the windows were filthy with sand and mud. I cautiously walked into the dark, unlit lobby and pushed the dirty elevator button to the third floor. A series of ominous screeching noises followed, which sounded strangely like a cat was stuck in the lift shaft. After a few nervous minutes the lift arrived, but I decided at the last moment not to take the risk and climbed the stairs instead.

The long hallway of the third floor smelt like baked beans and sick, and I had no choice but to cover my nose. After three knocks on the faded wooden door of apartment seven, a hairy, overweight Egyptian man with a ponytail and a food-stained vest opened it.

'Yes, what you want?' he sneered at me. I recognised his voice from the telephone.

'I made an appointment to see the room for rent. I'm the British guy.'

The fat man paused for a moment and a change came over his demeanour. 'Ah yes, my friend! How are you? Come in, come in!' He opened the door and welcomed me inside. His body odour was unbearable. 'You don't look like British, you look Arab.'

'Yes, I get that a lot.'

'The room is this way. You will like it.' As we walked through the dusty hallway there were odd noises of crashing pots and voices from the other rooms. 'Come, come, follow me.'

I followed him into the bedroom and he switched on the light. It was a tiny box room with cracking walls and broken floorboards, and it smelt of detergent. A dim light bulb swinging from an unhealthy chord struggled to provide some illumination, and the small window looked out onto the brick wall of the adjacent building. The only piece of furniture was a single bunk bed in the corner that had clearly seen better days.

'Is this the only furniture I would get?' I enquired with concern.

'My friend, what furniture you want?'

'Well, a decent bed perhaps. And maybe a desk and a wardrobe?'

63

'No problem, my friend, I get you a new bed, and desk and anything else you want.' Considering his forthcoming manner, I was compelled to throw in a request for a snooker table and a Jacuzzi, but I held back out of politeness.

'Who else lives here? I heard some noises from the other rooms as we walked in,' I asked.

A nervous expression came over his face. 'It's just some friends of mine. They will be leaving very soon. You don't worry!'

As we walked back through the hall towards the kitchen, I noticed that one bedroom door was left ajar. I peered curiously inside and saw at least fifteen men lying in rows on the floor on worn mattresses. They were mostly of South Asian origin, although a couple of them looked like Filipinos. A makeshift partition made of unfolded cardboard boxes had been erected to divide the tiny room into two crude areas. I made eye contact with one of the men, an emaciated Indian who looked worryingly malnourished and exhausted. He stared at me with forlorn eyes, although he didn't say a word. I quickly gathered that I had walked into some kind of makeshift labour camp for Dubai's labouring underclass. But before I could say anything, the fat Egyptian slammed the door shut and ushered me towards the lobby, annoyed by my curiosity.

'So, my friend, you want to sign the contract?' he asked assertively, clearly worried that what I had just witnessed may change my mind.

'Erm, I need to have a little think.'

He groaned. 'You know, I have four other people who have given me a cheque. If you don't want the room, I will give it to somebody else.' When I didn't reply, he quickly reined in his anger and changed his manner again. 'But I like your face, so I want you to live here, because you look like Arab, so I will wait until tomorrow for you. Okay?'

'I appreciate that.'

'Okay, my friend. I will wait for your call,' he smiled.

I thanked him for his time and rushed down the stairs and out of the building as fast I could without looking back once.

64

6

Bullshit Talks

Since meeting Jerome, I could think of nothing else but closing the deal. It was for opportunities like these that I had gambled on Dubai in the first place, and if I wasn't going to reach out and grab them I may as well have been back in my dreary job in London. But there remained just one obstacle in the way of unspeakable riches: I didn't have a buyer, and neither did I have a clue where to begin looking for one.

I thought about blasting out an email to friends and colleagues back in London, but it was unlikely anybody I knew would be looking for a plot of land in Dubai. I considered putting an advertisement in the local press, but with the huge number of property classifieds in the daily newspapers, mine was certain to be swamped and unnoticed. Who was I kidding? I had no price, no idea of the location and no leads. It was a lost cause. After an agonising week of racking my brain, I decided to join Hani and his friend Sami over a bite and a *shisha* in the Dubai Marina to clear my mind.

The Marina was a popular spot for Dubai's residents to spend their evenings at its many restaurants and *shisha* lounges. Less than five years ago, the vast site on which the Marina sat had been a barren wasteland. Today it was a sprawling community of condominiums and skyscrapers, housing much of Dubai's affluent migrant community; a bastion of the city's aspirational lifestyle. We met at an outdoor Lebanese restaurant in the heart of the promenade, surrounded by a multitude of residential apartment blocks, palm trees and luxury yachts. The Marina was buzzing as usual tonight with families, groups of friends and young couples grabbing a bite or having a stroll along the walkway under the star-filled sky.

'So how is life in banking, buddy? Are you making the big dough?' asked Hani as my strawberry-flavoured *shisha* arrived.

'Not yet, I'm still working on it. You know, things take a lot longer in Dubai than I thought.'

'Welcome to the real Dubai, my friend! From the outside this place looks like the perfect city. But Dubai is not the West and many people forget that. This is a new city with all the teething problems of an emerging market,' said Hani. Sami nodded in agreement. 'You know what Dubai is?' Hani continued. 'It's a third-world country with a first-world face.'

'I guess you're right and I'm learning it the hard way,' I replied with a sigh. 'Sami, how's everything in the website design world?'

'Things are good, *habibi*. Work is crazy busy at the moment. There are new businesses starting in this city every day and they all need a website, so I am working flat out.'

'What types of businesses?' I asked.

'You name it. Recruitment firms, PR agencies, events management companies, luxury yacht brokers... Everybody believes they can start a company and get rich in Dubai.'

'Wow...'

'And that's not including all the property related business! I would still say 80 per cent of our work is real estate related. I spend most of my time designing websites for new property agents, developers or other real estate service providers. Actually, just this morning I was in a meeting with the CEO of a new developer called Darius Developments. Very impressive guy. They are planning to launch five new projects in Dubai by the end of the year and are actively looking for plots. We are helping them build their corporate identity and brand.'

I almost choked on my pipe. 'Did they say where?'

'Where?' Sami looked confused.

'Where they are looking for plots?' I repeated impatiently.

'No, not specifically, but they said something about building a land bank in prime locations across the city. The CEO is called Saff Haque, a British Pakistani guy. He seems like he's on the ball. You know, I think they will soon be a serious player in the development market.'

I jumped out of my seat, threw a hundred dirhams on the table and ran for the taxi stand.

'Where the hell are you going?' shouted Hani.

'I gotta rush home. I'll explain later.'

I ran out of the taxi and into my hotel room. I immediately googled 'Darius Developments Dubai' and an article popped up entitled 'Dubai's New Kid on the Block'. And there it was, an interview with the CEO Saff Haque about how the company planned to build five landmark commercial and residential towers in the city's best locations, and was actively in the market for plots of land. Saff looked impressive in the picture, a well-groomed, middle-aged man in a sharp pinstriped suit. Surely he was the buyer I had been looking for. I simply had to speak to him.

So the following morning while at work, I found an unused meeting room and made the call.

'Good afternoon, Darius Developments,' answered the female operator in a nasal Arabic accent.

'Good afternoon. May I speak with Saff Haque please?'

'I'm afraid Saff is in a meeting.'

'Ah, do you know when he may be available?'

'I'm sorry, he has a full schedule today.'

'I see. And tomorrow?'

'He is completely booked tomorrow too.'

I was rattled by her blunt responses. 'Okay. Well, can you perhaps suggest when may be a good time to catch him?'

'No sorry, I can't.'

'I see, well I guess I'll call back another...' She hung up before I could finish, and just like that my chance had disappeared into thin air.

I felt like a total loser. My single lead had disappeared in a puff of smoke because I couldn't even get past the gatekeeper. Pathetic. I had blown my only shot and I was back firmly at square one.

But it couldn't be over, not like this. There was just too much at stake to give up so easily. Any other day, I would have quit, but not today. After a few moments of moping, something made me pick myself up and try again.

'Good morning, Darius Developments,' answered the same monotonal voice.

'Gooood morning, who am I speaking with please?'

'This is Norah. How can I help?'

'Good morning, Norah. Wow, Norah, that's a lovely name! Where are you from, if you don't mind me asking?'

There was a pause. 'I am Lebanese, actually.'

'Wow, really? You're so lucky! Lebanon is such a beautiful country. I love the food, the music, the history.'

'Thanks! Yes, it's a beautiful country. Have you been there?'

'Not yet. But I'm dying to go. I really am. I just don't know anybody there to show me around.'

'Well, if you're going I can connect you to some of my friends who live there if you like. They can show you a good time.'

'Wow, you would do that for me?'

'Of course, my pleasure!'

'You're too kind, thank you. I'm so glad we spoke today, Norah.'

'No problem.'

'By the way, Norah, is Saff Haque around? I am a business associate of Mr Haque and he asked me to call him back. It's quite urgent.'

'Sure. Just give me a second, I will put you right through.'

I punched the air in triumph. 'Hello, Saff speaking,' a voice eventually said in a crisp British accent.

'Good morning, Saff. My name is Adam and I am an employee of Imperial Bank. I apologise for the unsolicited call, I know you're a busy man so I won't take too much of your time. I have heard from a senior colleague that your firm is looking to purchase plots in Dubai?'

'Yes, that's correct.'

'Great. I may have exactly what you are looking for.'

'I'm listening.'

'Well, through one of our affiliates we have access to a prime piece of land that has come directly from government sources. It is in a key location and has not been exposed to the market.'

'Okay, can you tell me where the plot is?' asked Saff. It was the question I had been dreading.

'I'm afraid I can't divulge that information at this stage. But can I ask which locations you would be looking for?'

'Well, there are two areas on our radar currently: the Business Bay and the Marina. Can you at least tell me if it is in one of these?'

'I'm afraid I can't on the phone, but I suggest we meet up to discuss what we have and I can share some further details then. How does that sound?'

There was a pause. 'Okay, sure, how about tomorrow evening? Say, nine at the Montgomerie golf club?'

'Erm, that's perfect. See you tomorrow at nine.'

'Who's the man!' I screamed the second I hung up. I had just engineered a meeting with the CEO of one of the city's new property developers from nothing! Sure, I didn't have the location, the plans or the price, but it was a start. I was tempted to call Jerome right way and tell him the good news, but I held back. I wanted to be completely sure that Saff was in a position to buy first, so I decided it was best to tell Jerome after the meeting. The following evening, I jumped in a cab and made my way to meet Saff as agreed.

En route, I got talking to my driver about life in the city. I always enjoyed my conversations with taxi drivers; they were the real ears and eyes in Dubai and their stories and observations often exposed hidden truths never mentioned in the newspapers and travel guides. Their claims were usually unsubstantiated, of course. But like so many other aspects of life in Dubai, the fine line between reality and fantasy was blurred, which made their stories even more intriguing.

'Can I ask you something, buddy?' I asked my driver.

'Please sir, tell me,' he replied willingly.

'Is there really no crime in Dubai?' It was a question I had been burning to ask for a while and I was looking forward to his view.

'Sir, there is many crime in Dubai! But you will never hear of it,' he replied.

'Can you give me an example?' I asked, curious.

'Do you know the story of the Russian businessman at Burj Al Arab?'

'No, I haven't heard that one.'

An ominous look came over his face. 'Oh sir, very bad story.'

'I would love to hear it.' It sounded like a thriller; I couldn't wait.

'Sir, only two months ago, a big Russian businessman was staying in Burj Al Arab hotel. Very rich and powerful man. He was in Dubai for one week only. So he wanted to buy some beautiful jewels for his wife, you know, because he want to impress her.'

'As you do,' I said with a smile.

'Yes, sir. So he called one big Indian jewellery company in Dubai to bring his best jewels to show him in his room. He said money is no problem. He will pay anything. Thinking he will make a big profit, the Indian jeweller took his very best diamonds, rubies, gold, silver and sapphires in his suitcase to Burj Al Arab hotel. He takes $4.5 million worth of jewels to show to Russian businessman. He is thinking he will make the biggest sale of his life. Big money.'

This was getting juicy. 'Okay, so what happened?'

'So he travels to Burj Al Arab hotel, to show his jewels. And then he never comes home. He completely disappeared. The jeweller's wife is going crazy, his family is worried. He just vanished.'

'What happened to him?'

'After a few days, there is a bad, how you say, smell in Burj Al Arab. It is coming from Russian man's room. The police come to the hotel and break open the door. They find Indian jeweller's body hanging in the bedroom cupboard. He is stabbed to death, and Russian and jewels is gone. Nobody ever see Russian man again.' I was speechless. 'So you see there is many crimes in Dubai, sir.'

'Is that a true story?' I asked.

'Yes, sir, true story.'

70

'How do you know that?'

'My cousin is the bell boy at Burj Al Arab hotel. He saw everything. And my cousin never told a lie in his life.'

We took our exit off the Sheikh Zayed Road and entered the Emirates Hills development. Nicknamed 'Millionaire's Row', it was considered the most exclusive neighbourhood in Dubai due to its high concentration of ultra-wealthy residents. The Montgomerie Golf Club was nestled in the centre of the Hills, and many of the villas looked out onto its groomed world-class fairways. I remembered how Cameron had described it to me back in London months ago. It was just as idyllic as he had said, with countless palm trees, dancing fountains and meandering lakes. As we passed the ostentatious villas, I wondered which of them was Cameron's.

I arrived at the clubhouse a little earlier than nine, so I ordered a cappuccino and waited for Saff inside. Observing the tables around me, it was obvious that the Montgomerie was the preferred social haunt of well-to-do Western expats. Groups of European men shared a round of pints after eighteen holes and expat wives sipped on expensive red wine while their husbands finished up on the floodlit driving range outside. The only non-white faces in the club were the Indian waiters, who were rushing around tirelessly to serve and please.

I recognised Saff instantly from his picture. He was tall, slim and immaculately dressed in an elegant tailor-made suit with a matching salmon tie and handkerchief. I stood up to welcome him.

'Glad to meet you,' he said in a polished English accent as he shook my hand firmly.

'Likewise, thanks for taking the time,' I replied. 'I know you're a busy man.'

'No, not at all. It's always a pleasure to meet a fellow British Pakistani.'

I froze, surprised. 'How did you know I was British Pakistani?'

'Well, I'm the same, so I guess I could tell as soon as I saw you. We seem to be a rare breed over here, right?'

71

'Wow, Saff, you're the first person I have come across in this city who has worked that out. Most people think I'm an Arab until they hear me speak. Then they're completely confused.'

'Ha-ha, I'm not surprised to hear that. I'm sure you've also noticed that we "Brit-Paks" somewhat disturb the ethnic hierarchy of this crazy place.'

'Yes, exactly!'

'I grapple with it every day. We are a bit of a mystery to the Emiratis. We're not white Western guys, but we speak with their accents and are just as educated. So there's a dilemma. Do they pay us the same as an Englishman, or treat us like the labourers and house servants from the subcontinent? Personally I would prefer it if everybody was compensated on merit. But that's just me and my revolutionary ideas.'

'Well Saff, It's refreshing to know that I'm not the only one who feels like that.'

Saff told me he had trained as an accountant in London before spending the past five years as a financial controller for a large multinational company in Jeddah, Saudi Arabia. He was relatively young, but had a sophistication beyond his years. His professionalism and experience were rare qualities in this part of the world, and I couldn't help thinking he was perhaps wasting his talents dealing with cowboys and freewheelers.

'So are you here alone or with the family?' I asked.

'With the wife and three kids. They absolutely love it here. My wife has the help of a maid around the house. My kids are in the best private school in the city. And I get to squeeze in a round of golf every week.' He smiled. 'You know, my 5 year old learned to ski at Ski Dubai, of all places. Not in Austria or Switzerland, but in Dubai. It's insane.'

'Only in Dubai,' I laughed.

'So, shall we get down to business?'

'Sure,' I replied.

'Great. Well, I'm not too sure how much you know about our company, so let me give you some background. Darius is a new developer here in Dubai, although we have a lot of property investment experience in London and the Far East. Our chairman is a wealthy Iranian businessman who has interests in the technology and energy sectors, and is now looking to diversify into the Dubai property market. We have significant capital behind us, and once we have found the right locations we are ready to start building immediately.'

'Great. As I mentioned to you on the phone, Saff, I have access to this plot through one of my key contacts who prefers to remain anonymous at this point. I can tell you, however, that the plot is in a very exclusive location and I am certain would meet your requirements.'

'Is it so exclusive you can't tell me where it is?' he asked.

I suddenly froze. It was a reasonable request, but I still didn't have the answer. 'Yes, I'm afraid so. I will gladly reveal all of that information once you express your firm interest.'

Saff frowned. 'Okay, that seems very strange, but I guess I understand that you want to keep it confidential for now.'

'Exactly. I'm glad you understand.'

'Well, as I said to you there are two locations that we are very serious about right now: the Dubai Marina and the Business Bay. If it is in either of these locations and it's for real, then I can tell you confidentially that the deal is as good as done. But of course, before we can take this any further, I will need some more information to discuss with my chairman, like the plans, proof of ownership and so on.'

I was struggling to contain my excitement. 'I understand your position and I appreciate your openness, Saff. I will be sure to get back to you this week with more details.'

'I look forward to it. Now, I must be making a move.'

**

'Jerome, we need to talk,' I shouted down the phone.

'Hey, no need to bite my head off! What's up, buddy?'

'I have some news about the deal.'

'Okay, that's great. I'm meeting some Emirati friends of mine later tonight for drinks at the Crown Plaza hotel. Why don't you join us and we can speak then?'

'Emiratis? Okay, sure. Who are they?'

'Just a local friend of mine called Abdallah. He's a very influential young Arab. I've actually been meaning to introduce him to you. It's always good to build a bit of *wasta*. See you at ten thirty?'

'See you there.'

Since arriving in Dubai, I still hadn't had a proper conversation with a real Emirati. It was not that I didn't want to, rather that I hadn't really had an opportunity. Most Emiratis didn't mingle in expat circles and instead seemed to prefer living parallel lives in which their paths seldom crossed with foreigners. But there was one overarching reason for expats to pounce on any opportunity to meet and socialise with the Arabs if it should ever present itself: to build *wasta*.

Wasta was an old Arab expression that loosely translated as 'influence' or 'connections'. It had its origins in tribal customs and remained deeply ingrained in the fabric of modern Arab society. Strong *wasta* was crucial in Dubai if you wanted to get anything done. It was like the force in *Star Wars*, a ubiquitous energy that held society together and made the impossible magically real. *Wasta* could make traffic fines disappear overnight, get you a table in a fully booked restaurant, secure a constant flow of fresh coal for your *shisha* or make a toilet roll appear under the door when you had run out. It was also crucial in the workplace, as it could secure a pay rise or ensure that a well-deserved promotion was not overlooked. Many international companies employed Emiratis for the sole purpose of providing *wasta*. Whether you saw it as networking on speed or modern-day magic, it was the key to success in Dubai. As a mere novice in its mysterious ways, I was keen to learn and Jerome's invitation to meet with his Emirati friend could be the opportunity I was waiting for.

'Piano Bar at ten' read Jerome's text message. I made my way there. The Piano Bar was an intimate little joint that looked straight out of an 1980s episode of *Miami Vice*. The ceilings were padded and the walls were mirrored, with crystal chandeliers hanging ostentatiously from the dark ceilings. The clientele were mainly groups of Emirati men in traditional dress, all sipping on malt whisky or beer and puffing

74

away on heavy Cuban cigars. In the corner of the room was a black piano where a large African man was smashing away on the ivories, and beside him stood a tall, dark brunette in a ball gown singing a seductive cover version of Stevie Wonder's 'Superstitious'. A row of scantily clad Eastern European woman sat at the bar, smoking cigarettes while scanning for potential clients.

'How you doing, bro? Glad you made it!' said Jerome's voice through the dense air. 'Come and take a seat. Let me introduce you to Abdallah Al Joom of the Al Joom family.'

'Welcome, my friend, you are most welcome!' said Abdallah, a young Emirati of no more than 30, with long, curly hair and big, beady brown eyes. He was dressed in a traditional white *dishdasha* and sandals.

'Thanks. It's a pleasure to meet you too Abdallah.'

The small table in front of us was full of bottles of whisky, rum and vodka; it was clear that a fair amount had already been consumed. Next to Abdallah sat an obese Emirati man who seemed too distracted to notice me. 'This is my brother Ahmed. He doesn't speak any English.' I extended my hand, but he didn't reciprocate. 'Don't mind Ahmed,' said Abdallah. 'He is very sad because it is his big trial tomorrow.'

'Trial?' I asked, curious.

'Yes, trial. He smashed his Ferrari up. He was drunk and hit some Australian bitch's rented Ford. Can you believe it? The car was totally fucked up! Now his trial is tomorrow.' Abdallah laughed heartily as he spoke. 'Ahmed, you will go to jail tomorrow, so drink up and enjoy your last day of freedom,' he said mockingly, as he filled his brother's glass with whisky to toast him.

'Come on, Ahmed, you may as well enjoy tonight. Have a drink,' insisted Jerome.

Suddenly, Ahmed burst out crying. He looked inconsolable as his tears soaked his chubby hands. I felt bad for the poor guy, but Abdallah just laughed at him ruthlessly.

'Ha-ha, okay, Ahmed, okay! I give up. I cannot see you so sad. I will tell you something now.' Abdallah proceeded to say something in

Arabic and Ahmed eventually wiped the tears from his face, looking stunned. 'I told Ahmed, I have already spoken to somebody at the courts. They delete the file, *khalaas*, finished! I got him off scot free with my connections. There is no trial now.'

Abdallah almost fell on the floor in a fit of hysterical laughter and I gathered that he had played some kind of twisted practical joke on his poor brother. We all reluctantly joined in, except Ahmed, who merely looked relieved. I didn't know what was worse, the cruel nature of the joke or the fact that a drink-driving offence could be erased with such a lack of due legal procedure. I was sure we had just seen an example of *wasta* in action.

The singer was now in the middle of an awful rendition of Sinatra's 'Fly Me to the Moon'. I was furious at how she was murdering a classic, but the Emirati audience seemed to love it. Two of the Russian women at the bar had left and been replaced by two others who looked almost identical.

'Please excuse me, I need the bathroom,' mumbled Abdallah, stumbling away. This was my chance to grab Jerome.

'Jerome, I have some news about the plot, we need to talk.'

'Sure, dude, but let's speak a bit later on, okay? We are Abdallah's guests tonight and I don't want to seem rude.'

'But Jerome, you don't understand, I met the CEO of a...'

'Dude, we will chat later. Now have a drink and enjoy yourself!' I sat back sulkily.

Abdallah returned to the table and poured himself a vodka and tonic. 'So, my friend, Jerome tells me you like the party scene in Dubai.'

'Yes, I have been out a few times. I went to 360 and The Boudoir. Both very cool places.'

'Ah, but those places are for tourists! The real party in Dubai is a secret. They are private parties in villas in the desert, maybe two or three hours' drive from Dubai.'

I was intrigued. 'And what happens there?'

'Ha-ha, my friend, the correct question is what doesn't happen. I was at one party two days ago at my friend's villa in Liwa. Honest to God, he brought in bus loads of models. Bus loads! From Russia, Croatia, Brazil, even England. All beautiful, like virgins, I swear to God. You know how many women I sleep with at this party?'

'How many?' Jerome asked.

'How many hair I have on my head? That's how many!' Once again, Abdallah fell into a fit of laughter. He was now drunk beyond reason.

'Are you serious? How do I get an invite?' said Jerome.

'I tell you, Jerome, these parties are like heaven on earth. You think there is no cocaine in Dubai? Bullshit! In this party there is mountains of cocaine,' he gestured with his hands. 'Fucking mountains!'

I was shocked by Abdallah's sordid revelations. He went on to speak of underground illegal street-racing events where Emirati kids would race their five-hundred-thousand-dollar modified sports cars in secret locations in the desert until daybreak. He told of orgies and swingers' parties and even gay clubs. I had learned more in this hour about the dark underbelly of Dubai than most would hear in their lifetime. I had no idea if his stories were true, of course. But they added to the mystique of the city, a mysterious place where reality was cloaked in fantasy and truth depended on folklore.

'So, guys, I would like to invite you tomorrow to be my guests at the Dubai Polo Club to watch me play,' said Abdallah as the bizarre evening drew to an end.

'I didn't know you played polo,' said Jerome.

'I don't really, I just pay people to tell me I'm good! My wife will be there, so be careful what you say, okay?'

'You're married?' I asked with surprise.

'Yes, of course! Just because I screw doesn't mean I cannot be married, my friend. My family life and personal life do not mix. Everybody is happy like this.'

Jerome raised his glass to toast him. 'You have the best life in the world, Abdallah! Money, cocaine, virgins and a beautiful wife. What more could a man ask for?'

'Ha-ha. So you guys will come?'

'Of course!' replied Jerome and looked at me. I nodded and smiled politely.

'Great! Be at the polo fields for two o'clock sharp. Now, I must leave or I will be too drunk to win the match tomorrow.' As he got up he almost fell onto the table.

'Steady on there, buddy,' said Jerome, helping Abdallah steady himself.

'I'm okay, I'm okay.'

Jerome and I left shortly after. Jerome was also now very drunk, so I helped him into a taxi home before jumping in another myself. I was still bursting to tell him my news and I couldn't wait for a moment alone with him. One more day couldn't hurt.

***

The following morning, Jerome picked me up from the Emirates Towers and we made our way over to the Dubai Polo Club. As I got into his car I noticed that he didn't look his usual vibrant self, hiding his hung-over eyes behind dark shades and shielding himself from the sun with a baseball cap.

'Jerome, I've been meaning to ask you about the plot deal we discussed at The Raffles.'

'I see.'

'Did you get any more details as we discussed?'

He paused. 'Not yet, I'm afraid. I should have them in the next week. Why, do you have a buyer?' he asked, keeping his eyes fixed on the road.

'Well, I have had a few serious conversations. But I can't take it any further without plans, prices and so on. Can you tell me the location at least?'

'I'm afraid I can't just yet!' he snapped. 'Can't it wait until the end of the week?'

'I need some details, just to help me back up what I'm offering, that's all.'

Jerome lost his temper. 'Am I not getting through to you? I said the end of the week! Is it so hard to wait just a few more days? Let's enjoy ourselves at this polo match today and chat about business later. I will get you all the details you need in a few days. Is that cool?'

'Sure,' I replied. I seemed to have touched a nerve. It was obvious Jerome was not in the best of moods, so I backed off for now. 'No problem.'

The weekly Saturday afternoon polo meeting was one of the quintessential highlights of Dubai socialites' events calendar, and they came in droves in their Land Cruisers and Range Rovers to watch. It was a worthy pretext for the *nouveaux riches* to congregate in a grand display of keeping up with the Joneses. Many smug expatriates equated a day at the polo with their newly acquired social status, an affirmation that they had somehow arrived and were now firmly perched on a rung of the social ladder that they could only have dreamed of reaching in their home countries. Few knew the difference between a chucker and a check and turn, but that was beside the point. This day was really about being fabulous and being seen.

Pretty girls with dark shades and excessive tans dressed in their finest dresses and hats as they tittle-tattled and hobnobbed through the crowds, sipping suggestively from ever-brimming champagne flutes. Red-faced men with pot bellies and overflowing pint glasses stood by the sideboards, pretending to understand the intricacies of the game. They set up picnics and feasted on sandwiches, cakes and biscuits from hampers arranged by their overworked maids the night before. And as the game began, the air was filled with the constant din of popping corks and tinny laughs in a shameless celebration of the good life.

Today, Abdallah's team was squaring off against the mighty Habtoor polo club, and we arrived just in time for the beginning of the first chucker. Abdallah was already padded up and ready to play and he came over to greet us before he went onto the field.

79

'Welcome, guys! Glad you could make it.' He stood proudly beside his horse, a beautiful black stallion with glistening skin, its every muscle perfectly toned. He stroked it lovingly before beckoning a beautiful European woman over to meet us.

'Meet Alice, my wife. Alice, these are the two guys from the UK I was telling you about yesterday.'

Alice shook our hands without saying a word and wearing a forced smile. I had expected Abdallah's wife to be an Emirati like him, so I was slightly taken aback. She was very pretty and dressed elegantly in jeans, a chemise and dark Chanel sunglasses. Their 3-year-old son Zaid wandered around on the grass as his father mounted his horse and prepared to enter the field. This Abdallah was a different man to the womanising fiend with a twisted sense of humour from the night before. Today he was a devoted husband, loving father and disciplined sportsman. The seamless change of persona baffled me.

As the game began, Jerome and I were ushered to a small marquee erected on the edge of the polo field, which suitably sheltered us from the mid-afternoon sun. We took our seats on the cushioned deckchairs as an Indian butler appeared with cups of mint tea, a plate of luscious dates and *shisha*. We snacked on meticulously prepared sandwiches and cakes, and the mint- and grape-flavoured *shisha* was the smoothest I had had so far.

My attention began to wander around the field as I puffed out larger and larger billows of smoke from my pipe. Next to our tent was Abdallah's navy-blue convertible Aston Martin, its roof temptingly lowered to reveal its delicious cream upholstery. The two digit number plate '23' was a symbol of high status in the Emirati hierarchy; it was probably even worth more than the car itself. To the right of the fields beyond a line of palm trees were a dozen unfinished mansions surrounded by flags bearing the unmistakable symbol of property developer Emaar. These concrete shells, looking out directly onto the field, were eventually to become exclusive luxury homes for discerning polo enthusiasts. Each was already worth a small fortune, even though they were still years away from completion.

'I'm going to check out the talent on the other side of the field. Back shortly,' said Jerome, before disappearing for a while. I was perfectly content where I was and continued to puff and enjoy the game.

'So how long have you been in Dubai?' asked a soothing Irish voice to my left. Alice had taken her seat beside me. She sipped on a glass of red wine, keeping her eyes firmly on the field through her sunglasses.

'A few months now,' I replied hesitantly.

'And do you like it here?'

'Yeah, it's an interesting place.'

'Interesting?' She smiled wryly. 'That it is. That it certainly is.' There was a distinct sadness in her voice that I couldn't ignore.

'Have you and Abdallah been married long?' I asked.

'Eight years. Although it seems like a lifetime now.'

'Wow, so I guess you've seen Dubai go from camels to Cadillacs, as they say!'

'Yes, and a whole lot more. Dubai is not all that it seems, believe me. But I'm sure you're enjoying yourself too much to care. Am I right?'

'Yes, I think I'm settling in okay.'

'I'm sure. Dubai is like Neverland for a young, good-looking guy like you,' she smiled, still refusing to look away from the game. I was flattered, and if I wasn't mistaken I was sure she was flirting with me. Considering her husband was the son of one of the wealthiest locals in the country, all I could think of was the unthinkable punishment if somebody was watching us.

'So I get the impression you don't like Dubai very much?'

'I used to, once upon a time.' She took off her glasses, revealing her stunning green eyes. 'It's not quite the same any more. You know, Dubai used to be a romantic place. Like a fairytale. The people were good and friendly. People cared about each other more, and you felt part of something amazing, like a family.'

'And is it different now?'

81

'Now...' she smiled again. 'Well, now it's all about money and greed and sex. It's sad, you know.' There was a beautiful sense of tragedy in her words.

She told me how she and Abdallah had met in Dublin when he was travelling through Ireland as a young man. She was 19 at the time and he had wooed her with his boyish charm and persistent romantic gestures. She had actually believed that he was an Arabian prince who had come to whisk her away to an exotic land. They married in a humble Christian ceremony in Dublin, followed by a much larger Muslim affair in Dubai, to which over three thousand guests were invited. Today she was living in a ten-bedroom mansion with an army of servants catering to her every whim, and had every luxury she could dream of at her fingertips. But there was an emptiness in her voice, as if her dream to become a princess had turned into a horrible nightmare.

'But it's never too late, you know. We all make mistakes. How else would we learn?'

'What do you mean?' I was a little confused.

'I have access to money. A lot of money. I could disappear and nobody would care.' I assumed she was taking about leaving Abdallah. 'If I asked you, would you come with me?' She laughed wickedly as I tried to decipher whether there was a hidden meaning to her words. Before I could answer her, half-time approached.

'I would like to ask our spectators to come onto the field and help replace the divots, if you would be so kind,' said the announcer over the tannoy. The crowd rushed onto the grass, champagne flutes and pint glasses in hand, and began to stomp away frantically. It seemed that few of them actually knew the reasons for stomping the divots, except that it was what posh people did at polo matches.

'Come on, let's do it!' Alice jumped up and grabbed my hand to lead me onto the field. I looked around quickly to see if anybody was watching before following her. She was like a possessed child as she ran around, playfully stepping on every displaced piece of turf she could see, laughing wildly all the way. It looked like the most fun she had had for a long time. Suddenly she tripped, and I managed to catch her before she fell embarrassingly to the ground. And then something happened that I couldn't really explain. As I held her in my arms, she paused and stared into my eyes. It didn't last long, but I was sure we both felt the connection. She stood up and stumbled off the field. Alice didn't say another word to me for the rest of the game, and I worried that I had upset her somehow.

Abdallah trotted over on his horse to speak to us at the end of the match.

'Great game, Abdallah!' I said as he approached, although in truth I had watched very little of it.

'Thanks, guys. You know, I only took up polo when I got bored of shooting. Look how much I am sweating now! I should go back to shooting, I think,' he joked and we all laughed. Alice wasn't paying attention.

'Abdallah, thank you for the invitation today, but I'm afraid we have to make a move,' said Jerome.

'No problem, thanks for coming, guys.' He looked around to check the coast was clear before whispering, 'Let's party soon.' He winked before riding back towards the field.

'Let's get out of here, dude,' said Jerome and began to walk to the car.

'You go on ahead, I'll catch up with you in a sec.'

'Where the hell are you going?'

'I forgot something! I'll meet you at the car.'

I rushed over to Alice, who was preparing a plate of sandwiches and cakes for Zaid.

'I'm leaving, Alice. It was really nice to meet you. I just wanted to say goodbye.'

'You're sweating. Here, wipe your brow with this.' She handed me a folded white napkin, which I used and put in my pocket. 'It was nice to meet you too. Perhaps I will see you around.' She kissed my cheek, smiled and walked away.

'What was that about?' asked Jerome as I got into the car.

'Nothing. I didn't get a chance to say goodbye, that's all.'

'Yes, I'm sure you didn't. Listen, mate, here is some advice: don't do anything stupid! You don't want to get your balls chopped off now, do you?'

'I don't know what you're talking about. I was just being nice.'

'Yeah, sure you were. I saw how you two were getting friendly. Are you a fucking idiot?'

'Jerome, it's nothing like that. We were just talking, that's all.'

'I hope so,' he replied. 'For your sake.'

As Jerome drove away, I reached into my pocket for the napkin Alice had given me. I noticed a pink smear on the inside and opened it up to investigate. The smear was in fact a full imprint of a kiss. Below it was a phone number, followed by the words 'call me x'.

I held onto it for the rest of the journey, carefully hiding it from Jerome, and spent the rest of the drive deep in thought. But as we finally pulled into the Emirates Towers, I rolled down the window and threw the napkin out of the window.

'What was that?'

'Nothing.'

'Okay, whatever, mate. Let's catch up tomorrow to talk some business. *Ciao.*'

As I walked into the hotel lobby, I thought about what I had just done. I had certainly felt the chemistry with Alice, and her note was proof that she had too. It was obvious that she was looking to escape from Abdallah and Dubai, and she had money at her disposal. Romantic ideas of running away with her to some far corner of the world had passed through my mind during the drive back. She was beautiful, intelligent and rich. But who was I kidding? Even if we did elope, Abdallah would find us in no time and use his *wasta* to have my head chopped off, or worse.

I had more important things on my plate right now than saving damsels in distress and risking my life in the process. I needed to stay focused. I had my fortune to make, and there was not a moment more to waste on frivolous distractions.

84

7

Bullshit Walks

It was a good time in history to be an Emirati. The Bedouin ancestors of today's Arabs had lived in simple Barasti huts made from mud and palm fronds. After a long day of trading on the docks or diving for pearls, they pumped water from the communal well before skinning a goat and roasting it over an open fire to be shared among the tribe.

Today, the 4x4 had replaced the camel and mud huts had made way for mansions. Young Emiratis cruised in fully loaded Range Rovers, sipped skinny cappuccinos, and feasted on American cheese burgers and milkshakes after a spot of skiing at the mall. Endless hours were passed in spas, nail salons and beauty parlours, and money was never a concern. Life for the modern Arab was a breeze.

In a rigidly hierarchical social order, the Emiratis sat comfortably unchallenged at its peak. They constituted a special 'leisure class', a unique position of privilege that the expatriate workforce could only aspire for, but never reach. Emiratis were granted subsidised homes and allowances for their children, the state paid for their education up to PhD level, and they enjoyed unlimited access to free healthcare. Every Emirati household had an army of maids, nannies and drivers to service their every need and desire.

While the majority of expats worked tirelessly to maintain their lifestyle, Emiratis lived luxurious lives of endless pampering and indulgence. Such were the benefits of an unspoken contract of convenience whereby the Maktoum dynasty consolidated its rule and governed unchallenged. In exchange for a generous list of privileges, Sheikh Mohammed had effectively bought the loyalty of the clan. This was the way tribal rule had been organised for centuries, and it was the only form of rule the Emiratis had ever known.

With disposable income and time, it was no surprise that the national pastime of Emirati society was shopping. The epicentre of Emirati social life in Dubai was the mall, to which they would flock in their hundreds every day to shop tirelessly at the mainstream designer

85

outlets. Retailers were fully aware of the indulgent tastes and bulging wallets of their brand-obsessed customers, and many even created exclusive products catering to their specific preferences. Dior made headscarves for the Emirati woman and Armani offered traditional Bedouin-style men's sandals with the designer label slapped across them in full view.

But aside from the unbridled consumerism, the malls also provided a fertile hunting ground for testosterone-charged young Arab men to scope the local talent discreetly. Dating in the Western sense among young Emiratis was not permitted by Islamic tradition, which dictated that only married couples could be seen together without a chaperone. But that didn't stop sexually charged Arabs from bending the rules and conjuring up creative ways to make contact with the opposite sex.

Among the most popular tactics was dropping a scrap of paper with their phone number at the feet of an attractive woman as they walked past, or throwing a note through the passenger seat window as a local girl stopped at a traffic light. But as exhilarating as this sounded, it was also extremely risky. If the father or older brother of the target became aware, the consequences could be fatal. Honour was paramount in an Emirati's household and any challenge had to be dealt with severely.

Perhaps it was these restrictions that drove many young local men to begin chasing expats for their kicks instead. They were spoilt for choice in modern Dubai, which offered an assortment of single women from every nationality and ethnicity, many of them seeking their own Prince Charming to whisk them away to a desert palace. Emirati charmers would offer lavish gifts of designer bags, expensive jewellery and even fast cars to woo their foreign sweethearts. But there was a sinister side to this chivalrous game. Disturbing stories became increasingly common of young Western women being followed home by a group of horny local men or forced off the road by an Emirati stranger and harassed for a phone number. As sexual deviance and infidelity increased, it was no surprise that divorce rates among Emirati couples were the highest in the Gulf.

With all of these distractions, it seemed that a nine-to-five job was a frightful inconvenience for most young Emiratis, and many avoided the hassle. Those who did opt to work usually took a low-key position in the public sector. A government post offered a job for life with convenient working hours, a steadily increasing salary and insulation from the horrors of private enterprise. Nevertheless, it was soon apparent that there were simply not enough public-sector jobs for the growing Emirati population, and fear of mass unemployment among locals motivated the government to take action.

The 'Emiratisation' policy was implemented amid concerns that an escalating expatriate workforce was taking over the leadership of the main economic sectors. It was effectively a policy of affirmative action through a quota system for the private sector to take on a predetermined number of UAE nationals in key areas such as banking, engineering, construction and services. There were harsh penalties for private-sector firms that did not comply, so many were forced to cooperate against their will.

In reality, Emiratisation was positive discrimination on steroids. In one case, a semi-governmental telecommunications company laid off about a hundred and fifty of its largely Asian workforce so it could increase its required level of Emirati workers from 43 per cent to 50 per cent to meet the quota. While workers in the West were living in fear of losing their jobs to cheaper Asian labour, Asians in Dubai were losing out to more expensive and less skilled Emiratis.

Although some private-sector firms welcomed Emirati employees for their contacts and knowledge of local customs and *wasta*, many were not so optimistic. Most UAE nationals were unskilled for private-sector jobs and were simply not willing to take entry-level positions and work their way up. Many preferred to remain unemployed than accept demeaning work as a taxi driver or a waiter. In their eyes such menial jobs were reserved for foreigners alone, and to accept such a lowly position would only encourage unspeakable dishonour and shame from the community.

***

There was no denying it. The display on my bedside alarm clock was indisputable proof: the outside temperature had now reached a scorching fifty degrees Celsius! Curiously, official statistics still never seemed to top forty-nine, and there were a number of conspiracies about why this may be the case. Dubai's authorities didn't want to put off the tourists with official statistics indicating the true extent of the heat; and as the law stated that labourers had to stop working if the temperature hit fifty degrees, it was obvious why the government preferred to keep it quiet.

But the heat was the least of my worries right now. The extremes of the Dubai lifestyle were finally catching up with me in other ways, and I was beginning to notice the devastating effects. As I brushed my teeth, I was mortified when I could no longer see my toes under my ever-expanding belly and my once-chiselled jaw line was slowly disappearing under a layer of fat. The weekly brunches and midnight cheeseburgers had taken their toll on my formerly athletic physique. It seemed I was the latest victim of an epidemic that was claiming unsuspecting Dubai expats every day – a condition widely known as the 'Dubai stone'. Its causes were simple: a deadly cocktail of late nights, all-you-can-eat buffets and a lack of physical exercise. I was horrified with myself, although I couldn't say I hadn't been warned. It was said that every new Dubai resident would be an eventual casualty, so it was only a matter of time.

I was also succumbing to the fact that expat life in Dubai was not as comfortable as I had been led to believe. Endless traffic jams, laborious bureaucracy and backward processes were all beginning to eat away at my patience. Simple tasks like getting a mobile phone or an internet connection required a plethora of unnecessary paperwork. Home comforts like my favourite breakfast cereal and chocolate biscuits were seldom available at the local Dubai supermarket, and if they were it was for triple the price which meant I often had to do without. And calling my family back home meant departing with a small fortune, as the city's only network operator held a tight monopoly on all international calls, meaning an extortionate per-minute rate that was taking a toll on my bank balance.

The only vaguely good news was that I had finally found a place to live, although it was hardly my dream apartment. A friend of Jerome's had told him about a small studio in a run-down villa in Jumeirah that was soon to be vacated by a British teacher who was relocating to Qatar. It was a far cry from the luxury, sea-facing duplex I had hoped for, but considering my lack of options and the ever-looming fear of having to relocate to Sharjah, I had no choice but to take it.

The room was on the ground floor of an old house and it just about fell into my price range. It was only big enough for a bed and a wardrobe, but it had an en-suite bathroom and didn't smell too bad. I managed to negotiate with the landlord to pay the year's rent in three cheques, which was unheard of in most cases, so I counted myself lucky. Besides, it was only a temporary solution, as I was certain my big break was right around the corner. It wasn't a matter of if, but when.

Things at work weren't too rosy either. As a junior salesman, my job was to sell the bank's financial products to wealthy clients in Dubai. Asim had given me a list of his weakest relationships that I was expected to cold call and generate business from, but so far I had hit brick wall after brick wall. Clients didn't want the exotic derivatives or bonds we were trying to peddle, and as hard as I tried to push the merits of an interest-rate swap or a call option, there was only one question that kept cropping up in response: 'What do you have in property?'

In 2005, there were few investments in the world that were generating returns like Dubai real estate, and investors simply didn't want to look at anything else. I was facing an uphill task and my team and boss were hardly the support network I desperately needed. I had been right to presume the lack of interaction with my colleagues, and my conversation with them failed to extend beyond 'good morning' on most days.

I soon gathered, however, that it was nothing personal against me, but a matter of money. By virtue of the very fact that I was British, I was probably earning at least twice what my Indian colleagues were. Of course it was unfair; many of them were older and more experienced than I was, and there was no rational reason for me to be paid more. But Dubai's pay structure was not based on merit – British passport holders were almost always paid more than Indians or Pakistanis, based on an unsubstantiated perception that Western labour was always more valuable. Through no fault of my own, I was an outsider to their world and they didn't try to hide it.

And then just three months into my career at Imperial Bank, things got even worse when Asim called me into his office for a chat.

'Yes, Asim, you wanted to speak to me?' I asked as I nervously stepped inside his corner office.

'Yes, take a seat.' I did as I was told. 'I have some news.'

'Okay...'

'I'm not sure how to break it to you. This will be my last week at Imperial Bank.'

'Excuse me?'

'I have decided to take up an offer as a director of capital markets with a US investment bank that recently opened a Dubai office. They head-hunted me for my experience and contacts. It was too good to turn down.'

'But what about me? I've only just joined!'

'Don't worry. The guys will help you out until they find a replacement for me. I'm sure you will be fine.'

If by the 'guys' he was referring to Deepak, Ram and Sanjay, I knew I was screwed. There was no way in hell these guys were going to watch my back. I wished him good luck and went back to my desk almost in tears. I couldn't blame Asim for taking the offer; it was a big deal for a young Pakistani banker to get headhunted by a top-tier American bank, and he would probably be paid at least triple his current salary. But the fact that he hadn't even considered his responsibility to mentor and train me was deeply upsetting. My banking career was quickly going down the toilet and I needed a back-up fast.

It had been over a week since Jerome and I had been to watch Abdallah at the polo club, and we still hadn't met up as he had promised. I was getting anxious that Saff would figure I was a fraud and drop his interest in the plot. And with the way things were going at work, there was more riding on the deal now than ever. I had to act fast if I was going to salvage my future. I called him immediately.

'Jerome, where have you been?'

'Dude, work has been a nightmare.'

'Okay, but we were meant to meet last week!'

'Can you meet me in thirty minutes at the Mall of the Emirates?'

I was taken aback by hi response. 'Erm, okay, sure. See you there.'

The Mall of the Emirates was packed every Saturday afternoon, and today was no different. It was by far the most grandiose of Dubai's super-malls, boasting luxury fashion boutiques, cutting-edge furniture shops and international department stores combining the best of Bond Street, Fifth Avenue and the Rue de la Paix under one giant roof of retail indulgence. Locals and expats alike would spend endless hours browsing the hundreds of boutiques and megastores until late into the night.

The undisputed centrepiece of the giant MOE was the incredible Ski Dubai, an indoor winter wonderland boasting a life-size ski slope complete with chair lifts, snow-dusted trees and real snowmen. In a region where the annual recorded snowfall was zero, Ski Dubai was something of a miracle boasting five impressive slopes, including the world's first indoor black run. While temperatures hit a scorching forty-five degrees outside, avid skiers and snowboarders could pretend they were on the slopes of Chamonix in sub-zero temperatures in the planet's largest refrigerator. For many, it was the closest they would get to real snow in their lives.

We met at Après, a trendy restaurant and bar at the bottom of the Ski Dubai slopes with a ringside view of crashing snowboarders and tumbling skiers through its giant glass windows. It was always entertaining watching the *burka*-clad ski bunnies and *dishdasha* daredevils flying down the slopes. As we ordered and tucked into our pizzas, I was dying to get down to business, but as usual Jerome was distracted.

'Jerome, look mate, we need to speak about the plot.'

'Yes, I know we do.'

'As I said to you at the polo field, I think I have a buyer.'

'That's great!'

'Yes, but I desperately need some concrete information. I need the plans, pricing, location map...'

I noticed Jerome's eyes wandering. 'Man, that waitress is cute.'

'What?'

'The blondie over there. Check out her ass. Wowsers!'

'Jerome, can you just focus for a moment?'

'Okay, okay, buddy. Listen, I will have everything you need in the next few days. There's been a slight delay. Now just keep your guy on ice and manage his expectations. If he's serious, he will understand. Okay?'

His was testing my patience. 'But you said that last week!'

'I know, but I need two, maybe three more days, tops.'

'And what the hell should I tell my buyer in the meantime?'

'Tell him that the price is being revised and it will mean a better deal for him. Trust me, he won't mind.'

I was at my wits end. 'Jerome, you better have something by the middle of next week. I'm beginning to look like an idiot. I am giving you until next Thursday or this deal is off.'

'Okay. You have my word. I can't say more than that. Cool?' I nodded reluctantly. 'Good. Now, come with me. I have a challenge for you.'

I followed him to a costume store close by and he scoured the shop as if he was searching for something.

'What are you looking for?' I asked.

He didn't answer, but whatever it was he found it moments later. I walked over to see exactly what he was so excited about. Jerome was holding a box with the label 'the mother of all afros' and had the look of a man with a crazy plan. It scared the hell out of me.

'I have a dare for you.'

'What kind of dare?'

'I dare you to wear this afro through the mall for the rest of the day.'

'Jerome, how old are you, 5? Stop messing around, man, let's get outta here.'

An earnest look overcame his boyish face. 'You think I'm joking? Well, I'm not. Let's see just how big your balls really are!'

'Are you insane? I'm not going to make a compete fool of myself!'

'You chicken shit. You think you're gonna be a deal maker with little balls like that?'

I sighed. 'Come on, Jerome, are you freakin' serious?'

He wasn't backing down, and put on the afro himself. He looked ridiculous. 'Yaa, maan. I am totally serious, maan'.

'Okay, I'll only do it if you do it too. Deal?'

'No problemo.'

And so we both put on the 'mother of all afros' and walked through the mall in one of the world's most conservative societies. British kids pointed at us with delight and Indian women giggled as two nonchalant idiots strolled causally through the mall like members of the Jackson 5. Tourists took pictures with us and men looked over their shoulders for a hidden camera. But the locals were not amused by our juvenile antics. Expressionless Emirati men shook their head as they walked past and women in black *abayas* looked at the floor in embarrassment. Even the Emirati kids stared us down with disapproval. It seemed we were disrupting a social order that did not look kindly on such childish frivolity.

It was fun, but deep down Jerome's unpredictable personality was beginning to worry me. He was alarmingly erratic and I was concerned that he just didn't understand the seriousness of this deal to my future. All sorts of doubts were creeping into my mind and I was losing hope in his ability to deliver. I decided that this was the last straw – if he didn't come through this week as we had agreed, I would know the deal was dead in the water.

***

Exactly a week later, Jerome called me.

'As promised, I have the full details of the plot. I suggest we meet in thirty minutes at the Shakespeare café on the Sheikh Zayed Road.'

I nearly fell off of my chair. 'See you there.'

I spotted Jerome sitting in the corner and puffing on a *shisha* pipe as I entered the café. 'This has come directly from the daughter of the Sheikh of Abu Dhabi's private office,' he said, tossing a file of papers in my direction. I opened it and scanned the plans as he spoke. 'The plot is in Business Bay and nobody else has access to it. These are the plans and the location map.'

'How did you get access to this?'

'One of my clients works directly with the private office and managed to obtain exclusivity to sell it before it became public knowledge. It was gifted to the sheikha by her father, and she is now looking to sell it for a profit.'

'I see.' It seemed that everything Saff had requested was there in front of me.

'So now tell me about your buyer,' said Jerome.

'Well, I met with the CEO of a new company called Darius Developments a couple of weeks ago. They are actively looking for plots in key locations. He mentioned that Business Bay is a target, so I think this could be exactly what they are looking for.'

'That's excellent news! But we can't afford to fuck this up, so we need to approach it properly.'

He was right. Despite my good relationship with Saff, the firm's chairman would simply not consider signing contracts with a couple of twenty-something chancers like us. We desperately needed credibility if we had any chance of closing this deal. Jerome and I sat for a while considering all the angles. Eventually he clapped his hands and smiled like he'd had a revelation.

'Okay, I got it. My uncle runs a small property company back in the UK called Empire Realtors. I can pretend to act as the Dubai representative for the company and tell him that we have been managing some properties in London on behalf of the Abu Dhabi royals. So through our connections with the royals, Empire has been granted access to some exclusive deals. You are the representative from Imperial Bank who is acting as introducer and simply bringing the parties together. What do you think?'

'Yes, I guess it could work.'

'Great, let's do it!'

And so a meeting was arranged the following Saturday afternoon between Saff, the CEO of Darius Developments, and Jerome, the newly appointed Middle East Director of Empire Realtors, to discuss

94

the commercial terms of the Business Bay plot. We agreed to meet in the lobby of the Emirates Towers. It was rumoured that hundreds of millions of dirhams worth of transactions were closed there every week, so this was sure to be a good omen.

Despite it being a weekend, I wore a suit and tie for the meeting. If this was to be my first deal in Dubai, I wanted to look the part. I arrived twenty minutes early and scanned the room for an empty table. The lobby was as thriving as ever with groups of would-be deal makers pushing to close. I noticed a free table in the corner near the piano and seized it immediately.

Saff arrived before Jerome. He was dressed in a crisp grey suit and a tie, as expected. We greeted each other and he took a seat. But after almost twenty minutes of small talk, we could no longer ignore that Jerome was late. It was not a great start.

'So will your colleague be joining us soon?'

'He should be here any moment. He's never usually late.' I scrambled for my phone to call him. There was no answer. I tried again ten minutes later, but again no answer. My palms were sweating now and I began to think of the worst-case scenario. What if he didn't show at all? What would Saff think of me? How would I ever save face? Almost an entire hour later, Jerome strolled nonchalantly into the lobby.

'Sorry I'm late, guys, the traffic is a killer today.' His lack of punctuality was not the worst of it. Jerome had turned up to the most businesslike meeting of our lives in ripped jeans, a cap and sneakers, like he had just stepped out of a boy-band video. I could have killed him right there, but somehow I composed myself. Was he deliberately trying to screw this up for both of us?

'Saff, meet Jerome, the Middle East Director of Empire Realtors,' I said, through gritted teeth.

'Pleased to meet you, Jerome. I didn't realise this meeting was so casual,' said Saff, 'I feel so overdressed.'

I looked at Jerome with a piercing stare, which he noticed but ignored.

'No, it's fine, Saff. You look great,' replied Jerome with a cheeky grin.

'So, let's get down to business. We have heard a lot about the plot of land you are offering,' said Saff. 'We are very interested. But can you now give us some further details, beginning with where it is?'

'Well, I'm glad to tell you that the plot is in Business Bay.' Saff's eyes lit up as Jerome showed him the plans. 'It's a prime location as you can see, between the Al Khail and Emirates Road. There is no better location in the development.'

'And may I ask how Empire came across this plot?' asked Saff.

'Well, I can't reveal too much, but I can tell you that Empire has very intimate links with the Abu Dhabi royal office, as we have managed a substantial portion of their assets in the UK for over twenty years. It is the exceptional level of trust that we have developed over the years with the office of His Royal Highness that has led to the privilege of being informed about this exclusive plot.' It was the best spiel of bullshit I had ever heard, and Jerome was so convincing that even I believed him. Saff looked assured.

'Well, we have been looking at acquiring a plot in the Business Bay for a while, and if this piece of land is exactly where you say it is, we can confirm that we would like to make an offer.' His words were like sweet music to my ears. 'I will communicate this to my chairman today and we will send you through the offer tomorrow morning. Once agreed, we will ask our lawyers to draft the MOU.'

'That works for me. I look forward to hearing from you,' replied Jerome, before Saff shook our hands.

'I look forward to doing business with you both,' he said, and left.

Somehow, our charade had worked. It was one of the greatest feelings of my life.

The next morning, Saff sent through a formal offer for the plot to my email account as promised. I forwarded it on to Jerome and waited for his response. But he didn't reply. I called, but he didn't answer. I waited for his call, but it never came. Jerome had disappeared off the face of the planet and I began to fear the worst.

A few days later, Saff rang. 'Adam, what the hell is going on? Are we doing this deal or not?'

A lump formed in my throat. 'Yes, of course we are, Saff. There's just been a slight delay.'

'What kind of delay? My chairman is asking me when we are signing. It's making me look quite stupid. Get back to me soon!'

'Sure, will do.'

I was irate. Jerome was not only jeopardising the deal, he was costing me my credibility. Another week went by without a word and I finally accepted that the deal was dead.

Breaking the news to Saff was one of the hardest things I had ever done. I made up a story about how the seller had changed his mind at the last moment and had withdrawn the selling agreement. It was a massive blow to my ego and I almost burst into tears as I put down the phone. Saff had taken a chance and trusted me, and I had let him down. I couldn't help but blame myself, although deep down I knew it wasn't really my fault at all.

***

The next week I received a text out of the blue from Jerome's number: 'Meet me in 30 minutes at Falafal Hut. J.'

In a small Lebanese café on the Sheikh Zayed Road the ugly truth finally emerged.

'I have some bad news, I'm afraid. This deal is not going to happen.'

I don't know how I refrained from punching him in the face, but somehow I used all of my strength to muster up the patience to stay quiet and hear his explanation. It materialised that Jerome had never had access to the plot in the first place. His apparent relationship with the royal office was not a direct connection at all. Rather, he had been introduced to the deal by a broker who claimed to have known somebody who worked for the royal office. The broker had told Jerome there may be a chance to access the plot if he could find a buyer, and that's where I came in.

'Did you have anything signed?' I asked.

'Well, that's where the problem kinda was.'

'Jerome, did you have anything signed?'

He sighed and looked out of the window, avoiding eye contact. 'No.'

Once I had informed him of Saff's interest, Jerome had told his broker to convince his private office contact that there was a buyer. But once Jerome shared the formal offer from Saff with his broker, who in turn shared it with his royal office contact, he was told that they no longer wanted to sell.

At first this didn't make sense to me. Why would the royal office reject a formal offer if they were seriously planning to sell? There were two reasons. One was that Jerome, the broker and his royal office contact could not agree on fees. They all wanted a cut that was too large, and considering Jerome would also have to share a fee with me, there wasn't enough left to split four ways.

The second reason was that the royal office had never really wanted to sell in the first place. The process of soliciting an offer was simply a benchmarking exercise so they could get an idea of what the plot was worth in the market. Now they knew what somebody in the market was willing to pay for it, they would be more likely sell it to another royal office or prominent Emirati family for an inflated value over and above the benchmark market price.

As Jerome broke the news to me, I sat and listened without saying a word. I was past anger. As soon as he finished speaking, I simply got up and walked out of the café.

We never spoke again after that meeting. I never called him, and I guessed he was too embarrassed to get in touch with me. It wasn't the collapse of the deal that upset me so much; I was more hurt that Jerome had not been open with me from the beginning. He cared so little about our friendship that he had allowed me to risk my reputation without considering how I would look if the deal went sour, and the impact that would have on my relationship with Saff.

I had always heard the old adage about the perils of mixing business and friendship, but this was my first lesson in why it was so true. And so I had lost not only a potential business partner but a close friend too. I was angry with myself for not seeing the signs: the lack of clear information, Jerome's reluctance to discuss the deal and the unexplained delays. I promised myself that I would not be so naive and trusting in the future, and that next time I would smell the bullshit early on.

But despite the painful lesson I had learned, one good thing had come out of all of this. I had proved to myself that I was credible, I was professional and I could make things happen. All I needed was a break and I would surely be on my way to earning some real money.

I was more determined than ever to make my mark on this city, and I vowed that nothing would stand in my way now.

8

A Grand Affair

Few things thrilled Sheikh Mohammed as much as his horses. As a boy the young prince would often share his breakfast with his favourite thoroughbred on the way to school; and riding in his first race aged just 12, the future sheikh quickly earned a reputation for his impressive ability to tame wild stallions. While at Cambridge, Mohammed lodged with an English family where horse-racing heritage was often discussed at the dinner table. He was proud to tell his hosts that the most influential sire in British racing was an Arabian horse known as Godolphin, a name that would stay close to his heart. Away from his public duties as crown prince, Mohammed continued to invest in bloodstock. It wasn't long before the famous maroon and white colours of his Godolphin stable were carried to countless victories, earning great praise and adoration across the racing world.

But just as the sheikh's stallions competed for his favour, so did his business investments. The state-backed property developers Nakheel and Emaar were the undisputed thoroughbreds of Dubai's property industry. They competed fiercely between 2002 and 2008 to create the biggest and most ambitious new projects, vying to outdo each other to grab the headlines and transform the Emirate's skyline for ever. Together they became the bellwethers of the booming real estate industry, and as they battled ferociously to win the favour of the demanding sheikh, a new city emerged in their wake.

Under the leadership of the charismatic Mohammed Ali Alabbar, the US-educated son of an illiterate *dhow* captain and one of the sheikh's most trusted young companions, Emaar was launched as a publicly listed company in 1997. Success did not come easy for the development company, as its first major villa project, the Emirates Hills, struggled to sell many units the following year owing to its limited leasehold status. It was only after the freehold property law of 2002 that matters quickly turned around. As soon as the Emirates Hills was relaunched as a freehold project, the properties were snapped up in a matter of hours by investors and expatriates looking to take early advantage of the city's promising investment prospects. A real estate success story was born.

Emaar ploughed ahead with plans to build the world's largest manmade marina surrounded by dozens of high-rise luxury condominiums. This was to become the Dubai Marina, and would eventually house forty thousand new residents. Emaar quickly followed up with villa communities the Springs, the Greens and the Meadows, which catered for every budget of Dubai's rising expat population. The launch of the second phase of the Meadows saw a queue of a thousand people at the ballroom of the Emirates Towers and all seven hundred villas were sold in a matter of hours. Emaar had initiated a modern land grab as keen speculators saw the opportunity to flip their investments on the back of growing demand, and foreigners sought to buy a piece of the desert to call home.

But if Emaar was the reliable workhorse of the Maktoum stable, Nakheel was undoubtedly its wild stallion. Translated from Arabic simply as 'Palm', Nakheel was created by royal decree in 2002 and soon became known for some of the more ambitious and outrageous projects in Dubai. The reins of the company were entrusted to Sultan Bin Sulayem, the CEO of Dubai World and one of Sheikh Mohammed's closest confidants. His brief was simple: to make the impossible possible and to turn the sheikh's wildest dreams into reality. With an estimated portfolio of thirty billion dollars' worth of projects under development at its peak, Nakheel perfectly personified the dynamic spirit of the city.

The first of its grand projects was the iconic Palm Jumeirah, a $1.6 billion manmade palm-shaped island of reclaimed land off the coast of the city. It was rumoured that Sheikh Mohammed had sketched the original idea for the Palm on a napkin, which he had presented to Bin Sulayem with a direct order to build it no matter what. Nicknamed the Eighth Wonder of the World, the Palm emerged a few years later and became a global symbol of Dubai's lofty ambitions. As word of this unprecedented feat of human endeavour reverberated along the newswires, it was no surprise that its seven thousand beachfront villas were sold out in days. Nakheel soon announced a second island, the Palm Jebel Ali, planned to be 50 per cent larger than the first, with six marinas, a water theme park and boardwalks that would circle the 'fronds'. The ultimate showpiece of the Palm Jebel Ali would be an Arabic poem written in sand by Sheikh Mohammed himself in the ocean surrounding the island. It would read:

Take wisdom from the wise

It takes a man of vision to write on water

Not everyone who rides a horse is a jockey

Great men rise to greater challenges.

Nakheel's obsession with reclaimed islands was only just beginning. In 2004 it announced a third island, the Palm Deira, which would be eight times larger than the Palm Jumeirah and five times larger than the Palm Jebel Ali, housing one million new residents. Together this 'Palm Trilogy' would add a total of 520 kilometres of coastline to the city of Dubai. The mega-projects kept on coming. Later in 2004, Nakheel announced the launch of The World, an archipelago of three hundred islands constructed in the crude shape of a map of the landmasses of the earth. The company promoted the islands as 'a blank canvas', providing investors with the freedom to create their own vision of utopia where the globe could literally revolve around them.

Nakheel's legacy was a tough act to follow, but Emaar came back strongly with the launch of Downtown Dubai, a mega-district that would become the new epicentre of the city and would feature as its centrepiece the planet's tallest building, the mighty Burj Dubai. Downtown Dubai offered an unprecedented standard of living to future residents in what was promised to be the 'most valuable square mile in the world'. The clamour for Emaar's property launches in the Downtown district was so great that the developer was forced to resort to a lottery system just to allow investors to gain access to the projects and put down a deposit. With demand at fever pitch, a secondary market for these lottery tickets soon emerged and investors were paying small fortunes just for the privilege of attending the launch event, before a penny had even been spent.

On the back of the great success of these two titans, a plethora of new private developers flooded into the market to compete for a piece of the frenzy. But despite the competition, Emaar and Nakheel remained the undisputed leviathans of the industry, and as prices spiralled to dizzying heights, they commanded higher and higher premiums for their properties.

The pace for the great race had been set and as the punters placed their bets, a clear leader was yet to emerge.

***

'Good morning, folks, you're listening to Dubai FM 94.5 and it's finally here, the one you've been waiting for, day one of Cityscape Dubai! Make sure you have your chequebooks ready to snap up those property bargains, because it's going to be a fish market in there today...'

The hype around Cityscape had reached fever pitch. Newspapers, radio shows and billboards had been building up to the exhibition for weeks and investors were rubbing their hands eagerly as opening day approached. Staged at the colossal Dubai International Convention and Exhibition Centre, Cityscape provided a platform for Dubai's plethora of real estate developers to showcase their newest projects. Since the first show in 2002, the exhibition had grown from strength to strength to become an annual marker of the health of the city's real estate industry. At last year's show a total of $160 billion of transactions had been completed, and this year was expected to shatter that record.

I arrived at the Exhibition Centre soon after the doors opened and things were already in full swing. The enormous atrium was brimming with punters, all itching to get inside and grab a piece of paradise. After collecting my wrist tag from the front desk, I walked into the main exhibition hall like an awestruck child entering the gates of Disneyland. I was dwarfed by giant property stands of different shapes and sizes, all vying for my attention. There was pandemonium in the halls as hundreds of punters rushed through the aisles, grabbing brochures and any other freebies they could get their hands on. Dozens huddled around intricate miniature models of skyscrapers and villas, each crafted to microscopic detail with trees, street lamps, boats and sunbathing bikini babes. Over a thousand exhibitors were present, competing aggressively to push their awe-inspiring projects as the biggest, newest and most groundbreaking investment opportunity, and the punters couldn't get enough.

The press had reported that a staggering $200 billion of new real estate projects were set to be launched at Cityscape this year alone. It

103

was impossible to keep track of all the stands. I passed a luxury villa development called Flamingo Creek within the $80 billion Lagoons district that boasted 'stunning views of the Ras Al-Khor bird sanctuary'. The Manhattan luxury apartment complex within the Jumeirah Village development was inspired by the 'urban residences of 1930s New York'. And the four-billion-dirham Bay Square presented a 'new age community project offering a stress-free lifestyle'.

But I soon gathered that not everybody was at Cityscape to buy. The crowds could be divided into two broad categories – the browsers and the investors – and each developer's sales teams were well trained to tell the difference. The browsers were here to soak in the atmosphere, marvel at the spectacle and collect free pens and brochures. They had not come with any serious intention to buy, but could always be swayed to make a small investment if a sales agent managed to pitch them right. Developers didn't care too much for the browsers, who they saw as making up the numbers and building the hype. The investors, on the other hand, were a different breed completely.

Oblivious to the pomp and paraphernalia, investors were here for one reason and one reason alone: to buy low and flip high. Armed with chequebooks and suitcases of cash, investors didn't care for small talk and giveaways. All that mattered to them were the numbers: the price per square foot at which they were buying, and the premium at which they could sell. For them, Cityscape was nothing but a marketplace, an exchange where buyers and sellers could meet and trade. They knew what they wanted and they were there to buy big.

The biggest deals at Cityscape were closed out of view from the crowds. Each property developer's stand had a VIP section that could only be accessed by an inconspicuous staircase protected by muscular bouncers and velvet ropes. This was the 'closing room', a private area where the real business happened. While salespeople battled with indecisive browsers over the merits of purchasing a studio flat, multimillion-dollar transactions were taking place confidentially upstairs in the closing room, and nobody knew anything about them.

The important investors were usually wealthy Saudis, Kuwaitis and Emiratis, as well as some Russians and Africans. Trays full of stuffed dates, Belgian chocolates and the finest baklava were ushered in for

104

their enjoyment as they put their feet up and sunk into the soft leather sofas in the closing room. Senior sales executives flattered and massaged their already inflated egos while subtly communicating the merits of their offerings. And as their targets sipped on fresh mint tea and freshly squeezed fruit juices, the sales team stealthily moved in for the kill.

I had already wandered around for hours when I spotted a familiar name ahead of me. Darius Developments was launching a brand new project in the Business Bay, and a crowd had developed around a scale model of the tower. It seemed they had found their plot after all, which made me a little upset. I spotted Saff in the closing room upstairs, engaged in conversation with two important-looking Arab men. I decided it probably wasn't appropriate to say hello so hurried quickly past the stand, hiding my face and avoiding making eye contact despite the desperate attempts of the eager salespeople to hand me a brochure. 'He's probably just browsing anyway,' I heard one of the girls say as I rushed past.

As hard as Dubai's developers pushed their new projects, it seemed that Cityscape was not just a competition for who had the biggest tower. It was impossible to ignore the fact that every stand I passed was brimming with beautiful women. Most of them wore revealing outfits that tested the limits of decency, much to the delight of the salivating male visitors. A developer called Faraz Properties was leading the race so far with an army of a dozen six-foot blondes sporting hotpants and red stilettos. The stand was more like a party at the Playboy mansion than a sales effort, but the tactic was certainly working, as crowds of curious men loitered aimlessly to get a decent eyeful. As I walked past, I spotted one of the girls standing alone and looking rather bored, so I took the opportunity to give her some company.

'Hi, I have a question. Can you help me?' I asked.

'Of course, sir,' she replied in a seductive European accent.

'What is the completion date for this project?'

'I think it is expected to be handed over in 2012, sir. But I will need to check...'

'No, that's fine! What's your name, by the way?'

105

'Anastasia,' she replied with a smile.

'Anastasia. That's a nice name.' I shook her hand. 'Where are you from, Anastasia?'

'I'm from the Ukraine.'

'I see. And your friends?' I asked, pointing at the other models.

'We are all from the same modelling agency in Ukraine. We were flown here together by private jet a few days ago for the show.'

'Private jet?'

'Yes, Faraz Properties brought us over for Cityscape. We are all staying in a penthouse suite at the Jumeirah Beach Hotel.'

The thought of twelve Ukrainian models in a single suite blew my mind.

'So, is this your first time in Dubai, Anastasia?'

'Yes, and I just love it here! Only last night we were at a pool party in a villa in the desert. There was champagne and great food and a Jacuzzi tub! I will definitely come back here soon. So what were you going to ask me?'

I was suddenly blinded by the random flash of a camera lens. Rubbing my eyes, I looked up and saw a young Emirati man in a *dishdasha* and cap carrying a camera. He began circling us curiously, as if he was listening to our conversation while pretending to be interested in the nearby miniature model. I ignored him at first, but he was making me a little nervous.

'So Anastasia, what are you doing on Friday night?'

Another flash. The Emirati now had his back to us, although his camera was pointing in our direction. I was certain he had taken a picture, but as I was about to walk up to him to ask, I was distracted by a commotion behind me. Anastasia disappeared to get a better view as I turned around to see what all the fuss was about.

'Can you see him?' whispered an Egyptian women on her tiptoes.

'Not yet! Are you sure it's him?' replied her Lebanese colleague.

An army of photographers took their spots and reporters gathered around them in anticipation of something big. In the distance at the far end of the gangway, I saw a sea of white figures coming my way. As they slowly got closer, I noticed that the group was actually as many as a hundred Emirati men, dressed in identical white spotless *dishdashas*. They walked in my direction in a triangular formation led by a single figure, whose casual pace the pack followed obediently. He was certainly in no hurry. He strolled through the hall, observing the stands to his left and right, while nervous salespeople and promotional girls stood silent and smiled, and the cameras flashed frantically with his every step.

This was clearly somebody very important, perhaps an ambassador or a royal, but it wasn't until he was a hundred metres away from me that his identity became clear. It was the big cheese himself. The top dog. The big kahuna. It was Sheikh Mohammed, the ruler of Dubai.

He was less regal than his portrait in the flesh. He looked older and was much shorter than I had expected. There was no hint of the great visionary, businessman and leader. In his place was a somewhat frail and reserved man, as if he was carrying a great responsibility on his weary shoulders. It was understandable, of course. The entire fortunes of investors from across the world depended on his every decision and whim. It was a tough burden to carry.

I didn't move until he was a stone's throw away, and for some reason I wanted him to notice me. He didn't. The entourage eventually walked past me and into the distance and the hall quickly got back to business.

'Are you looking for something?'

I turned around to see a beautiful pair of big brown eyes staring into mine. Standing before me was a stunning woman with olive skin and tightly curled hair. She was dressed in a tight-fitting white blouse, black pencil skirt and stilettos. Her black-framed glasses sat perfectly on her button nose, like the secretary from every man's fantasy.

'Perhaps,' I replied. 'There is so much going on, I really don't know where to start.'

'Well, do you need me to hold your hand?' she asked playfully.

'Well, if you're offering,' I smiled.

She smiled back. 'But first you have to tell me what you're looking for.'

I didn't want to come across as a hopeless browser, so I decided to fib a little to keep her interested.

'Well, I'm after a floor or even a building in a good location for an investment.' Her eyes lit up. 'Maybe you can show me some options?'

'I would love to! I'm Alesia, by the way.' I looked at her badge and noticed she worked for a firm called Milestone Properties.

'It's a pleasure to meet you, Alesia.'

'So what's your budget?'

'Budget?'

'Yes, how much do you want to spend?'

'Well, I would say… a few million?'

'Wow, I should take you to my closing room.' I smiled at the very thought of it. 'How about I suggest something? It's a bit crazy in here right now, so why don't we meet tomorrow, one on one?'

It was a difficult offer to refuse. 'Sure.'

'Great, shall we say dinner at eight?'

'Dinner? Yes, dinner sounds perfect.'

'I'll show you everything I have then.' She gave me her business card. 'Here's my number. See you tomorrow night.' She winked seductively before returning to her duties on the Milestone stand.

I felt like the luckiest man at Cityscape. Alesia was more beautiful than any of the models on the other stands, and I couldn't believe that I had just arranged to have dinner with her tomorrow night without even having to ask.

I suddenly was brought crashing back to reality by a large African man who ran into my shoulder and almost knocked me off my feet. Before I could turn around to confront him, I noticed that a huge crowd had developed at the Emaar stand behind me and dozens more were rushing to join it. People were pushing to get to the front of the crowd, and I ran over to get the scoop.

'What's all the fuss about?' I asked an Indian sales representative on the stand opposite.

'Emaar have just announced a new tower in Downtown Dubai, next to the Burj Dubai. They're selling units on a first come, first served basis. Everybody wants to buy at launch price to ensure they can flip it at a good premium.'

It wasn't long before the uproar turned aggressive. An Indian man put his hand on an Arab man's face as he struggled to get to the front, and the Arab retaliated by punching him in the mouth. Soon everybody was shoving viciously amid a chorus of swear words and shouting. The girls on the Emaar stand froze with fear as the sales team attempted to calm the crowd, with little effect. As security guards piled into the halls from all directions, the crowd finally began to settle. This was the ugly face of the real estate market, a winner-takes-all shoot-out where men were willing to sacrifice their dignity and respect in the pursuit of a quick profit.

I had seen enough and decided it was time to leave. Cityscape had been a huge eye-opener for me. It was not so surprising that banking had failed to live up to my expectations; real estate was where the action was in Dubai! It was here that the real money was flowing, the big deals were closing and the serious money was being made. Property was the engine that was fuelling the Dubai growth story and anything else was just peripheral. I left the exhibition hall with a renewed sense of purpose. I needed to get out of my dreary job and immerse myself in this once-in-a-lifetime opportunity.

In the cafés outside the halls, yet more business meetings were in progress, small coffee tables becoming makeshift boardrooms for hungry salespeople to take yet more cash from greedy investors. I decided to grab a coffee before taking a taxi, but as I waited in the queue I noticed a familiar face sitting alone at a table beside me. It was the Emirati man who had been loitering on the Faraz Properties stand. He was looking through the pictures on his digital camera and I watched from the corner of my eye. This young voyeur had spent his day shooting photos of the unsuspecting promotional girls. Every single picture he had taken featured a close-up shot of a different woman's thighs or cleavage. It explained the flashes while I was speaking with Anastasia. I shuddered at the thought of what this pervert had in store for his day's work.

109

'Sir, sir! Can I have a word?' An Indian man had rushed in from the hall to get my attention and was panting for air as he spoke.

'Sure.'

'I am Vijay from Milestone Properties. I have an offer which I am certain you will find difficult to turn down.'

We stepped to the side as Vijay filled me in.

'My colleague tells me you put a deposit down on a floor in the Victory Tower in Business Bay at the launch price. I have an investor on the phone right now who will offer you a 15 per cent premium today if you want to sell. Think about it: you will make 15 per cent in just two hours, minus our brokerage fee. You can't get a better deal than this! If this is interesting for you, we can go to my car and do the paperwork in a few minutes. What do you say?'

His offer was compelling, and I hesitated for a moment before having to break the unfortunate news that he had mistaken me for somebody else. He looked disappointed when I told him, but he apologised and rushed back towards the hall to grab his next victim. Milestone clearly had a slick operation in progress. While their keen salespeople sold property to investors in the main hall, this was a secondary operation where reps were under orders to grab those investors and compel them to sell immediately at an attractive premium. No stone was left unturned in this crazy game.

***

The next morning, I was awoken by the bleep of an incoming text message:

Looking forward to dinner tonight at Pier Chic. Meet me in the lobby of the Al Qasr Hotel at eight. Alesia xx

I was ecstatic that dinner was on, but I still wasn't sure if it was a business meeting or a date. This was Dubai, after all; if business and pleasure were seamlessly intertwined anywhere in the world, it was here. That evening I decided to dress for both eventualities in a suit and casual shirt, and made my way to the hotel.

Nestled in the grand Madinat Jumeirah complex, the Al Qasr was one of Dubai's finest five-star hotels. It was fashioned around the sheikh's own summer residences; a stunning tribute to the grand palaces of old. As my taxi drove up the palm tree-lined ramp towards the lobby entrance, it certainly felt more discreet and exclusive than other hotels in the city. A fleet of super-cars were parked around an impressive sculpture of wild stallions and dancing fountains. The lobby was bustling with affluent tourists and local Arabs, and my attention was immediately drawn towards the majestic chandelier that lit every crevice of the magnificent lounge.

There was no sign of Alesia yet, so I took a seat on one of the delicious oversized sofas and waited. On the table next to mine sat a well-groomed European man dressed in a sharp dark blue suit, engaged in conversation with two young Emirati men. He spotted me as I sat down and I noticed him glance over a couple of times. He certainly didn't look familiar, but then again I had never been too good with faces. A few moments later he got up with his Emirati colleagues and they prepared to leave. Once again, he turned around to glance at me before disappearing through the revolving doors.

'Sir, the gentlemen left this for you,' said the waiter a few moments later. He handed me a business card.

'Which gentleman?'

He pointed at the vacant sofa next to me. 'The European gentleman who was sitting over here.'

I glanced at the card: *Jonas Nielson, General Manager, Al Danana Group*. His name didn't ring any bells. There was a mobile number, but before I could think about calling it, Alesia strolled into the lobby. She was dressed in a breath-taking red cocktail dress, an elegant pink shawl and the highest stilettos I had ever seen. It was the type of dress that caused the entire room to stand and stare. She looked simply stunning.

'I'm sorry I'm a little late,' she said and kissed my cheek.

'Wow, Alesia, you look absolutely incredible!'

'Why thank you. You look pretty handsome yourself.' She winked. 'Shall we?'

She wrapped her arm around mine and we made our way down the staircase, which led us to the outdoor area at the rear of the hotel. It was a beautiful evening, the stars were out in force and the moon

111

shone prominently in the distance. We followed the landscaped pathway that meandered towards the beach, and with each step the seductive sound of the waves got tantalisingly closer. I felt like I was in a dream. I was in one of the most opulent hotels in the world, on my way to dine in one of the finest restaurants in the city, with a beautiful woman on my arm. Could life get any better than this?

We strolled towards the giant pier that extended into the ocean, and I could now see the flickering lights of the restaurant at the end of it. The magnificent Burj Al Arab towered over us and its bright purple, white and blue lights helped light our path along the wooden pier.

Another couple approached us from the opposite direction. They were a little tipsy and the gentleman was struggling to keep his female companion from toppling over.

'Wow, what a stunning couple you are!' said the woman as they walked past. A sense of pride overwhelmed me and I couldn't help but smile. But Alesia wasn't my girlfriend; in fact, she wasn't even a friend. She was my property agent, and as I had no intention of buying anything, she wasn't even that. I had no idea what our relationship was, although at that moment I didn't really care.

I glanced around the candlelit tables as we walked into the restaurant. Most of them were occupied by affluent-looking older men with their younger, surgically enhanced dates, drenched in designer labels and brilliant jewellery. Few of the couples seemed to be engaged in any meaningful conversation. Most of the men were preoccupied by their mobile phones while their lady friends were more interested in the shoes, watches and handbags of the women surrounding them. It seemed that even dating was a business transaction in Dubai.

We were shown to our corner table facing the beach and made ourselves comfortable.

'So, Alesia, I really appreciate your time to give me your views on the property market, and perhaps help me with a decision to invest.'

'My pleasure. You just tell me exactly what you want and I'll do what I can to give it to you.' I almost choked on my water. 'But why don't we get to know each other a little first?'

'Erm, okay, sure.'

'I can see you look good, you dress well and you obviously have money. So what's your story?'

'Well, I'm from London. My father made his money in construction and I joined the family business two years ago.' It wasn't the best on-the-spot lie I had ever told, but I was sure it was what she wanted to hear.

'Wow. Lucky boy.'

'Now my father wants to diversify his investments into Dubai and that's why I'm here. And what's your story, Alesia?'

She suddenly looked uncomfortable. 'I don't think you want to know my story.'

'No, I do!' I insisted.

'It's not as rosy as yours, believe me.'

'I would really love to hear it.'

She sighed. 'Well, I am from Kazakhstan. I grew up very poor in a one-room apartment with my four sisters and my mother. My father died before I was born, so we grew up with barely enough to eat. I hardly went to school and worked in a bottle factory from the age of 14 just to put food on the table. I left my family alone for Dubai two years ago to make a better life for myself. I somehow got involved in property, and now I'm living on the Palm, driving a Mercedes and making $50,000 a month in commissions. How life changes... Shall we order?'

I was speechless. As we tucked into our delicious starters, I brought the conversation back to business again. 'So how long do you think the market can keep going up for?'

'I'm sure it will keep on rising.' She caressed her wine glass with her blood-red lips and stared at me seductively with her bed-me-now eyes. The more I studied her, the more I wanted her.

'But where will it peak?'

'You mean climax?'

I blushed. 'Yes, exactly, there has to be a point where it comes to a head.'

113

'Maybe. But that won't happen any time soon. There's too much fun to have yet.' I felt a foot begin to caress my leg under the table, which almost made me jump out of my seat.

'Alesia, can you excuse me for a moment please?'

'Of course. Is everything okay?' she asked with a naughty grin.

'Fine. Just fine.'

I rushed to the bathroom and locked the door behind me.

'Pull yourself together, man! It's just a business meeting!' I washed my hands with cold water and patted my face to cool down. After a few deep breathes, I made my way back to the table and sat down.

'What do you say we get out of here?' said Alesia in a commanding tone.

'But you haven't finished your risotto.'

'Fuck the risotto.'

We rushed out over the pier and through the hotel lobby to jump in a taxi.

'Take us to the 400 Club,' she ordered the driver. I felt a hand creep up my thigh as she began to caress my earlobe with her tongue. I closed my eyes, but I was annoyingly interrupted by the continuous coughing of the Pakistani taxi driver, who looked nervous at the debauchery that was unfolding in the back seat of his cab. Alesia ignored him and jumped onto my lap as I began to kiss her neck.

'400 Club, we are here!' shouted the taxi driver with a sigh of relief. I threw a hundred dirhams on the passenger seat as Alesia grabbed my hand and we ran towards the club. There was a huge crowd outside desperate to get in, but the bouncer opened the velvet rope for us as soon as he saw Alesia approaching.

'Thanks, darling,' she said as we strolled in.

'You know him?' I asked.

'Yeah, kinda. I sold him an apartment in JBR last week. He has a portfolio of ten now.'

We walked down an opulent staircase into the packed club below. The party was in full swing as the revellers swayed to the funky house music. The crowd was beautiful; everybody here looked like a model. Yet the entire club paused the moment Alesia arrived. Every man wanted her, and every woman despised her because of it. We walked over to the bar and Alesia started to dance seductively against my thigh.

'What do you want?' I shouted over the music.

'A chocolate martini.'

As I ordered, Alesia put my hands on her toned hips and began to grind me seductively. I could feel her every curve against my groin and my head almost exploded.

'I need the bathroom, be right back!' she said.

I grabbed the drinks and waited for her outside. As soon as she emerged, she stared into my eyes and kissed my lips passionately.

'Take me home now,' she whispered into my ear. It was an offer I couldn't refuse. I took her hand and we ran up the stairs.

'Your place or mine?' I asked as we got into the taxi.

'Mine.'

'Palm Jumeirah, please, driver,' I shouted.

I wanted her now more than anything and I couldn't wait to get her home. We pulled up outside her apartment block not a moment too soon. I had to button up my shirt just to make myself look decent before preparing to get out. I paid the driver and we stepped out of the taxi together. But as I grabbed Alesia's hand to guide her upstairs, she resisted.

'Wait,' she said.

'What is it?'

'Wait, we need to agree first.'

'Agree what?'

'Agree the price.'

'What price?'

'Three thousand dirhams for the whole night. Is that okay?'

I was completely confused. 'I don't understand.'

'It's a special price for you, I promise. I usually ask for more. Just three thousand dirhams and as many times as you like.'

Suddenly, the penny dropped and my heart sank into my stomach. I let go of her hand and got back into the taxi, slamming the passenger door shut. Alesia looked stunned.

'Driver, take me home, please,' I said. 'Now.'

'Yes, sir.' The driver was clearly confused, but he did as he was told.

As we began to pull away, I looked through the rear-view window and saw Alesia standing alone in the street in complete shock. She had probably never been rejected for her services before in her life.

It was about time she had a taste of how it felt.

9

Other People's Money

The irritating sound of hammering on steel was driving me insane! The secret preparations for the DIFC anniversary ball had been going on for weeks, and most of it seemed to be happening outside my office window. It was billed as one of the most exclusive social events of the year: a gala celebration to commemorate the growth of the DIFC and its vision to become the world's fastest-growing financial centre. The guest list was expected to run like a 'Who's Who' of Dubai's elite: royalty, dignitaries, senior government figures and CEOs. It was sure be the networking event of the century, an opportunity I couldn't afford to miss.

But as a lowly junior banker I also knew there was no chance in hell I would be getting a formal invitation in the mail. I needed to think outside the box if I was going to have any chance of getting in. It was time to pick up the phone and harness some *wasta*.

'Hani, how's it going?'

'Hey, I'm good bro. Where have you been?'

'I'm sorry for not being in touch, things have been a bit crazy lately. Listen, I need a huge favour.'

'Sure, what's up?'

'Do you know anybody who can get me a ticket for the DIFC ball next week?'

He burst out laughing. 'Let me get this straight, the banker is asking me to get him into a banking event?'

'Yes, something like that.'

'That's priceless! Okay, listen, I think LBC is covering the event for the ten o'clock news. I might be able to get you a press pass if you can pretend to be an LBC journalist.'

'I think I can manage that. Obviously I would need to dress down a little...'

'You rascal!' snapped Hani.

'Can you look into it for me?'

'Sure. Let me see what I can do!'

As promised, Hani came through a couple of days later with a press invitation. On the night of the party I pulled out my old beer-stained Oxford tuxedo and jumped into a taxi to attend the event of the year.

As I pulled up to the DIFC, the grounds were unrecognisable. The financial centre had been transformed into an impressive outdoor wonderland. There were ice sculptures, acrobats fire breathers and human mannequins. Scattered across the vast grounds were hundreds of senior bankers in expensive black tuxedos, with their much younger and more glamorous 'plus ones' in their elegant designer ball gowns and sexy cocktail dresses. There were also dozens of Emirati men in traditional *thobes*, although their wives were notably absent. A four-piece orchestra set a sophisticated mood as the distinguished guests hobnobbed and busy waitresses precariously hoisted trays of cocktails and fruit juices as they weaved through the crowds.

I walked around eagerly searching for important-looking people to schmooze with. As I picked up snippets of conversations, there was little talk of finance. Instead, everybody was discussing property!

'I just flipped a floor in the Business Bay,' boasted an older British man while puffing on a cigar. 'Picked it up at twelve hundred dirhams per square foot and flipped it at eighteen.'

'That's great. I was in a couple of floors in the Jumeirah Lake Towers,' replied a slightly younger man with thick glasses and a French accent. 'I managed to get out of both in a month. The developer won't start construction for a couple of years and I've already made my money!'

'The developer has reserved ten units for me at the pre-launch of their new project tomorrow. He says I can sell it within a week at the official launch party when some fool thinks he's actually paying launch price. As they say, it's all about who you know in this city,' added another Asian man.

Eventually the orchestra stopped and the crowds were ushered towards a giant grandstand erected in front of buildings three and four. I scanned the area for a vacant seat and spotted an older man with a bushy moustache and shock of grey hair sitting alone. He looked suitably important, so I rushed over to take the empty seat next to him before anybody else could claim it. But to my annoyance, his lady friend arrived seconds before I did and sat down leaving me stranded.

The grandstand was filling up fast and as I scuttled back towards the aisle still seeking a good spot, a scruffy looking man abruptly crashed his behind into the seat next to where I was standing, blocking my exit route.

'Ladies and gentlemen, please be seated as the show will be beginning shortly,' said the announcer.

As the lights began to go down, I had no choice but to take the empty seat beside the bedraggled man. My plan had failed miserably; he certainly didn't look very useful to my grand networking plan. Just moments after I reluctantly sat down, his constant fidgeting was already beginning to drive me crazy.

'What the hell do these bloody Arabs know about putting on a decent show?' he proclaimed in an American accent, moments before the show began. I wasn't entirely sure whether he was talking to me directly, so I smiled back politely. 'You know, I won't be surprised if they start doing a bloody sword dance for the next couple of hours. If they do, please freaking shoot me now!' An Emirati couple in the row in front looked offended by his direct comments, and shook their heads in disgust. 'You know, it's all smoke and mirrors, this place,' he continued. 'Don't believe the hype! Just because you build a few nice buildings doesn't mean shit. It's a mirage. These people are as savage as they have been for a thousand years, chopping each other's heads off and shit. I swear to God...'

Another appalled European couple beside me couldn't believe their ears and stared at him with a look of shock, but he didn't seem to care. Yet as rude as he seemed, I was somewhat intrigued by this uncouth stranger. It was the first time since arriving in Dubai that I had heard somebody speak so negatively about the city, and I was interested to know why. But before I could think about introducing myself, the lights went down and the crowd fell silent. The show was starting.

A small Emirati man dressed in a *dishdasha* stumbled onto the stage, nervously clasping his script. He approached the microphone stand and there was awkward pause before he began to speak. 'Your R-r-royal Highnesses, la-la-ladies and gentlemen, friends and, and, and... distinguished guests. I would like to welcome you to this wonderful event... this evening.' His English wasn't perfect and his nerves were clearly getting the better of him.

'This is the guy Sheikh Mohammed has hand-picked to lead the financial centre?' whispered the scruffy man to me and rolled his eyes. 'God help us!'

After mumbling the rest of his monotonous speech, the Emirati finally plodded off the stage as unimpressively as he had arrived, to the sound of muted applause. If his dreary delivery was a sign of things to come, we were certainly in for a bore. Suddnly, the seating stands shook and the ground rumbled. A giant kabuki dropped to reveal a three-hundred-piece choir suspended high between buildings three and four singing a haunting rendition of Ravel's Balero. Finally, the reason for the long painful weeks of construction work outside my office made sense, and the awesome spectacle seemed worth it. And so began an impressive performance of Arabic opera singers, classical dancers and theatre. The entire audience was captivated from the start, except the scruffy man, who looked disdainfully unimpressed.

Throughout the show, he continued to fidget constantly and huff with disapproval. And just half an hour in, it seemed he had had enough and pushed his way to the exit, to a chorus of sighs and huffs from the audience behind him. I decided to follow him. I excused myself, rushed down the steps and headed towards the grounds outside, where I spotted him helping himself to the grand buffet.

'Buddy, you gotta try these prawns,' he said as I approached. 'Fuckin' awesome. Only reason I came tonight was for these prawns.' His plate was piled precariously high already, but it didn't stop him from piling on more.

'So was the show as bad as you thought?' I asked, tucking into some tuna sashimi and chicken dumplings.

'I told you, man, these guys have no fucking clue. I'm surprised they know how to wipe their own asses in the morning. What the hell could Arabs know about opera? What they can't get through their stupid heads is you can't buy culture and class! Good taste takes years to refine. They should stick to camels and falconry, I swear to God.' I noticed a drop of ketchup on his chin, but I decided not to point it out and embarrass him. 'So what are you, a journalist?'

'No, I'm actually a banker.'

'So why the hell are you wearing that LBC press pass?'

'Oh, I forgot about that.' I tucked it away into my shirt.

'Come on, dude, you can't fool me! You crashed this party, right?'

'Well, yes, kind of,' I replied sheepishly.

'Nice! Good for you. Worth it just for the free dinner, I say. That's the only reason I'm here. It's a decent spread, too. Glad to say they got something right.' He was certainly correct about that. It seemed that no expense had been spared on the endless buffet of food in front of us, which featured delights from almost every cuisine imaginable. 'So which bank do you work for?'

'I work for Imperial Bank, in building one behind you,' I replied and pointed at my office.

'Ah, so we're neighbours. I'm the CEO of DubCap Investments in building two, right next door. The name's Jamal.' He wiped his filthy hand on his trousers before offering to shake mine.

'Great to meet you, Jamal, I'm Adam.'

'Listen, I'm done here. Like I said, I only came for the food. You know what, you got some balls, kid. Here's my card. Maybe we can grab lunch some time.'

'Thanks. That would be great!'

A rapturous round of applause erupted in the grandstand behind us to mark the end of the night's performances. Jamal licked his fingers and released a giant burp.

'That's my cue to leave. See ya later. Call me!'

As he made his way towards the taxis, a giant fireworks display lit up the night sky behind me as hundreds of guests converged on the buffet, which was now out of prawns.

***

121

Getting out of bed the following morning was no easy feat. I was tired and grumpy, and in desperate need of coffee. I somehow stumbled into a taxi to Starbucks wearing dark shades and a cap to get my caffeine fix as inconspicuously as possible.

'Hello, sir, howwww arrrreeee youuuuu!' screamed the bright-eyed barista. Great, the last thing I needed right now was a high-on-life Filipino.

'Erm, yeah, I'm good. Can I get a black Americano, extra hot?' I said in a croaky voice.

'Of course! What size, sirrrrrr?' His loud, whiny voice ricocheted against every corner of my skull.

'Small. Just small is fine,' I mumbled.

'Small, sirrrrr?'

'Yes. Small.'

'Sorry, sir, smallllll?'

That was the last straw and I totally lost it. 'Didn't you fucking hear me the first time?' I screamed. 'Yes, I said small! What's wrong with you people? I said small! SMALL!'

The barista froze and turned white with fear. 'Sorry, sirrrr,' he whispered under his breath, trying desperately to hold back his tears. 'I thought you said tall...'

A wave of guilt suddenly overcame me as I began to calm down. 'It's okay. Look, I didn't mean to shout at you like that.'

'It's ok, sirr,' he whispered, his bottom lip quivering uncontrollably. But I could see it wasn't really okay at all.

I had no idea why I snapped like that. It was out of character for me; the poor barista was only doing his job. Perhaps my frustration had finally boiled over; a reaction to the recent setbacks I had faced that were now finding an outlet. Or maybe the real reason was something much more terrifying. Could I be becoming the obnoxious and self-obsessed Western expat I had always dreaded? Was I finally buying into the ethnic hierarchy of Dubai that I had found so abhorrent? The thought alone terrified me. I paid for my coffee and took a seat in the furthest corner, out of sight.

As I was putting my change back in my wallet, Jamal's business card fell onto the table. I picked it up and thought about our conversation at the ball last night. I felt guilty that I had judged him a little unfairly; I had actually enjoyed our brief chat. He was, after all, the CEO of a financial institution and he could surely be a useful contact for me. I didn't have any plans for the rest of the day, so I decided to see if he was free to meet.

'Yeah?' he answered.

'Hey, Jamal? I'm not sure if you remember me. It's Adam, the guy with the press pass you met at the party last night.'

'Who?'

'We met at the DIFC event. You told me to try the prawns?'

There was a pause. 'Oh yeah, the party crasher. How you doing, dude? Listen, I'm caught up in a meeting right now. How about I call you back in an hour?'

'Sure, that would be fine...'

Three and a half hours later, he called me back as promised.

'Hey, buddy, you wanna grab a bite?'

'Sure!' I replied.

'Let's meet at Chilli's restaurant at the Mall of the Emirates in half an hour.'

'Sounds good, I'll see you there.'

I left my apartment and jumped into a passing cab.

'One thousand dirhams per square foot! Very good price, I close deal today!' shouted the taxi driver at his phone. It seemed he hadn't even noticed me get in.

I feigned a cough to get his attention. 'Mall of the Emirates, please.' There was no response.

'You tell me seven hundred, I tell you one thousand! This is my best price. Okay, we close deal today!'

'Excuse me!' I shouted. The driver turned around and stared at me angrily.

123

'Can't you see I am closing a deal? Please get other cab, okay?'

'Are you serious?'

He went back to his call. 'No, no, no, one thousand dirham only!'

There was no use. It seemed the entrepreneurial driver was moonlighting as a realtor, which clearly took precedence over his taxi duties. I shook my head in disbelief as I got out and flagged down another cab.

I eventually arrived at the MOE a little earlier than planned, so I decided to grab a coffee while I waited for Jamal. It was still early in the day and the mall was quieter than I had seen it before. I noticed there were a peculiarly disproportionate number of women here at this time of day, all dressed immaculately in designer labels, with perfect tans and blow-dried hair. As I watched them stroll from boutique to boutique, it hit me that I was lucky enough to be witnessing the gathering of a rare species in Dubai. It was an exciting moment and I observed with great interest, albeit from a distance. I had heard stories of their existence, but I had never actually seen a real one in the flesh before. In all their superficial glory, these were the infamous Jumeirah Janes.

Jumeirah Jane was a popular term to describe the hopelessly materialistic wives of wealthy Western expats. They were ladies of leisure unleashed onto the city with oodles of free time and endless pocket money to squander. The Janes were real-life 'Desperate Housewives'. They lived in large rented villas near the beach, drove gas-guzzling 4x4s and had few goals in life except collecting designer handbags and looking fabulous. Their often absent husbands were engineers, bankers, lawyers and project managers on overweight tax-free salaries whose only means of keeping their demanding wives happy was to bankroll their lavish lifestyles and excessive spending habits while they slaved away in the office to maintain the expat lifestyle.

A typical day for a Jumeirah Jane followed a predictable pattern of dropping off the kids at their $20,000-a-year private school, followed by a three-hour, gossip-fuelled champagne brunch or coffee morning with fellow Janes. They would then head to the mall for a spot of retail therapy, before a personal training session at the gym and a manicure at the Ladies' Club. After a swim and a massage, they picked up the

124

kids then looked forward to a leisurely evening on the couch watching reruns of *Sex in the City* to unwind after a demanding day. Tomorrow's schedule was much the same.

The Janes all employed help around the house, often a Filipina or Indian maid (the least attractive they could find) who would take care of all the menial domestic chores that could ruin the French manicure. Yet the stroppy Janes still constantly complained about being overworked and unappreciated. In truth they were purposeless, spoilt brats whose only quantifiable contribution to the expat community was making love to their hard-working husbands. By doing so, their husbands would be happier at work hence more productive, and thus add more value to the company's bottom line and the economy at large. Dubai therefore needed the Janes and their service to the country was invaluable.

Jamal showed up an hour late. I spotted him immediately as he plodded towards me dressed in a crumpled shirt, slacks and sandals. He looked more like a hobo than the CEO of an investment bank.

'Sorry I'm late, I got caught up in a meeting with a couple of dumb-as-shit Saudi investors who, as usual, didn't understand a fucking word I was saying. Shall we order? The cheeseburgers here are pretty special.'

'No problem. Good to see you again, Jamal. Yes let's order...'

'So did you stick around long at that party the other night?' Jamal asked.

'No, not much longer after you left.'

'It was a fucking waste of time anyway. Just like most things in this stupid city. Waiter!'

'So what's your story, Jamal? What brings you out here?' I asked.

'Well, I graduated from Harvard and joined one of the big consultancy firms. They posted me out here for a while to work on a big telecoms project. I made some connections with some of the big families, so I started consulting for them privately. Once I was in, I used my *wasta* and managed to get them to back DubCap Investments, which I run now. I actually have no real background in finance, but they still went for it. An American accent and a bit of chutzpah is all you need to get them to dance on the table.'

'Jamal, please don't take this the wrong way, but I get the impression that you're not actually a huge fan of Dubai.'

'No, no, Dubai is okay. I don't mind this city. It's just the fucking idiots that run the place that piss me off.'

'Do you mean the Emiratis?'

'I mean the Arabs in general. They're a bunch of lazy, arrogant fools with more money than sense. Don't get me wrong, I think the previous generations of Arabs were very smart. Before oil, they were great merchants and traders. But the money has turned their brain to mush. They have just gotten too used to having everything done for them. Today they're more concerned with buying a new handbag or getting their Bentley gold-plated.'

I shook my head in disagreement. 'Come on, Jamal, that's a bit of a sweeping generalisation.'

'Oh yeah? Okay, let me give you an example. Last year I was teaching a course in entrepreneurship at the American University of Dubai. You know, just for the hell of it. My students were mainly young Emiratis who were being groomed to become the future business leaders of the country. They were the sons and daughters of wealthy industrial families and diplomats. It was like trying to teach Satanism to the freaking Pope! They just didn't give a shit. Most of them were more interested in fucking around on their BlackBerrys and booking tables at the Boudoir club on Friday night. Some of them even used to leave the engines of their Ferraris and Range Rovers running while they were in my class. Can you believe that? It sums up the modern Arab mentality perfectly. If these kids are the future, this place is truly fucked.'

'Jamal, you can't tell me you're not impressed by what they've done here. They've built an incredible city from nothing. It's amazing!'

'You really think these guys did any of this by themselves? No freaking way! They just bring in the best architects and engineers from Britain and the States, pay them a shitload of money and sit back and watch. Any dumb idiot with bottomless pockets could do that. These

126

shepherds can't even wipe their own asses, let alone build a fucking city.'

I couldn't believe what I was hearing, but I also couldn't doubt much of what Jamal was saying. I had seen very few Emiratis working since I had been in Dubai. The economy depended on the foreign migrant workforce for everything from serving customers to cleaning the streets to running entire conglomerates. It was no wonder that many Arabs spent their days cruising around in their fast cars and smoking *shisha*.

It was also obvious that Jamal had an ambiguous relationship with the Arabs. Despite spending much of his professional career in the Middle East, he had little respect for their ability to do business and he didn't hide it. But he also knew exactly how to work them to his advantage. Where others would suck up to the Emiratis, buy them gifts and pay them empty compliments to gain their favour, Jamal told them exactly what he thought. If they were making mistakes, he didn't mince his words and they loved it. He was like the mean boyfriend telling his girlfriend she was overweight. He was a straight talker in a land of bullshit, and this won him their respect. As much as his comments hurt, his brutal honesty made them even more desperate to win his affection.

'So what are you long term plans, Jamal?' I asked. 'I guess you're not looking to stay here too long?'

He stared into my eyes. 'Look, as much as I dislike this place, even I can't deny there's a massive opportunity to make money here right now. You and I are smart guys with professional backgrounds, but there are some pretty dumb nobodys making a lot of cash in this city right now. I don't know about you, but I'm looking to get a piece of this pie and make a run for it'.

In a way, Jamal and I were birds of a feather: we were both frustrated professionals who had worked hard for a good education to get ahead, only to witness cowboys and hustlers become overnight millionaires in Dubai before our very eyes. A degree from a top-class university had no value here. To get ahead in this city you needed balls, bullshit and *wasta*. And as frustrating as it was, we both wanted a piece of that pie. So Jamal became something of a mentor to me and

127

we began to meet regularly to brainstorm ways we could make our fortune in the city.

***

We agreed to meet one evening at Cin Cin, a swanky bar at the Fairmont Hotel on Sheikh Zayed Road, best known for its great cigar collection and attractive female clientele. After ogling the exotic beauties taking their seats at the bar, Jamal pulled himself together and we began today's lesson.

'So tell me a couple of entrepreneurs you admire. Who are your idols?' Jamal asked.

'I don't know, Branson, Trump, Gates...'

'Okay, good. There is one thing all of these guys have in common. Do you know what it is?'

'They all signed a pact with Satan?'

'No, one word, my friend: leverage.'

'Leverage?'

'Yes, leverage. They borrowed money, multiplied it, gave back what they borrowed and kept the rest. And then they repeated the process. They used a magical principle called OPM.'

'OPM? Isn't that what the Beatles famously did in the bathroom at Buckingham Palace?'

He ignored my silly joke. 'It stands for 'Other People's Money'. It's what leverage is all about. The smart people use other people's money to invest and it's what we need to be thinking about too.'

It made perfect sense. OPM was the universal principle on which most serious wealth was created. Everybody knew you needed to have money to make money, but the smart people weren't using their own. Great empires in business, real estate and finance were built on the foundations of OPM and it was time we did the same.

Jamal continued his sermon. 'There are two ways to use OPM: debt and equity. And you know where we are sitting right now? The Mecca of OPM! Considering we are in one of the most cash-rich regions on the planet, I have the perfect idea for us to use the immense capital around us to get rich!'

128

'And how would we do that?'

'Two words, my friend: private equity. We should set up a private equity fund to invest in the real estate market. It's a vehicle investors put their money into and we manage it by investing in real estate assets on their behalf. That way when they make money, we make money. We both have credible profiles as Western-educated professionals, which is a rare quality here, so we can use that to sell the fund. And you work with high net worth investors in the region, so we can utilise your client database. Once we've raised the capital, we extract a 2.5 per cent management fee and a 20 per cent performance fee and sit back while the money rolls in. It's foolproof!'

It was one of those rare 'eureka' moments. Until now the Dubai real estate market had been fuelled by private investors, but in the context of global capital flows they were small fry. The serious capital was controlled by the institutions: banks, pension funds, insurance companies, hedge funds and asset managers. Often referred to as the 'smart money', these global institutional investors were usually managing billions of dollars of OPM and were the largest investors in the world, but none of them had invested in Dubai yet. With the sheer pace of development and returns that the market was offering, it was surely only a matter of time before the institutions would be looking to participate in the growth story. If we could structure a credible investment fund that offered risk-adjusted access, we could potentially pioneer a new phase in the evolution of the market and make a fortune in the process.

Within days, Jamal had the analysts at his bank working on the prospectus, while I began speaking discreetly about the idea to potential investors from my database at work. Jamal had suggested that we would need about three-quarters of a million dollars in set-up costs to cover legal expenses and working capital. I certainly didn't have the money and it was unlikely that Jamal would put up all the cash himself, so we both agreed that we needed an anchor investor to whom we would be willing to give up part of the General Partnership in exchange for some working capital to get things off the ground.

A week later, he called me while I was at work. 'Hey, buddy, can you talk?'

129

'Just a minute.' I rushed into a nearby meeting room. 'Yeah, go ahead.'

'I'm with somebody I think you should meet. He could be a key player in our project. Can you come to the Burjuman shopping centre right away?'

'You mean right now?'

'Yes, he's with me now.'

It was the middle of the day at work so it wasn't easy for me to leave the office without anybody noticing, but this was too important. I quietly slipped away and made my way there.

Jamal was sitting at a café near the food court with a balding, overweight Indian man dressed in a polo shirt and chinos.

'Glad you could come at short notice,' said Jamal as I took a seat at the table. 'This is Lucky Chanda, an associate of mine from India.' The fat man looked me up and down, making me feel a little uncomfortable. 'I have been talking to him about our fund idea and he is quite interested to know more.'

'Nice to meet you, Lucky,' I said and shook his hand.

'Good to meet you too. Jamal tells me great things about you.' His voice was deep and bellowing.

'All good things, I hope.'

'Of course! He told you me that you are a graduate of Oxford University and that you are working for Imperial Bank. Very impressive.'

'So, Lucky, why don't you tell Adam a little about what you do?' said Jamal.

'Well, I am a real estate developer here in Dubai. We specialise in residential projects around Jebel Ali. Most of our investors are wealthy Russian statesmen and prominent businessmen.' As he reached for his coffee cup, I noticed that his solid gold watch was studded with at least a hundred gleaming diamonds.

'I have told Lucky about the fund and he is interested in becoming a seed investor. He will also bring us investors through his own

130

contacts, and can provide us with a pipeline of projects that we can invest in once it's up and running.'

'I would like you guys to come and pitch the idea to my team at our offices later this week. I think we can do a deal quickly,' said the Indian.

'I told Lucky that we are looking to begin with a fund size of $100 million,' said Jamal. 'We have discussed a deal for working capital of $1.5 million in exchange for a 5 per cent stake in the General Partnership.'

It sounded too good to be true. Was this wealthy stranger willing to bankroll our project and find us investors without having looked at a pitch book or a prospectus? We still hadn't even formalised the strategy for the fund, how much we wanted to raise, nor where we would invest. As much as I trusted Jamal's judgement, there was something untoward about Lucky, although I couldn't put my finger on it.

The following week, Jamal and I made our way to Lucky's offices on the Sheikh Zayed Road to make the pitch. As we walked into the small lobby of the thirty-second-floor office, we were greeted by an attractive Moroccan receptionist who led us down a long corridor and towards a large oak door. After a knock, a familiar voice shouted 'Enter!' and we followed the receptionist in.

It felt like I had just walked into a scene from *The Godfather*. The room was dark with oak panels and mahogany sofas, as the streams of light shone through the slits in the half-shut blinds over the windows. I noticed Lucky first, sitting in the corner on an old brown leather sofa. Behind an oak desk sat an older Emirati man with silver, slicked-back hair and a goatee, who watched us intently through the smoke billowing from the fat cigar he puffed. To his right was a younger Indian man, wearing thick glasses and an ill-fitting suit.

'Welcome, gentlemen,' said Lucky, as he stood up to greet us. I shook his hand and scanned the other figures in the room.

'Let me introduce you to everybody: this is Mohammed, our chairman, and Niraj, our accountant.'

'Nice to meet you all,' said Jamal on behalf of both of us.

'So, Lucky tells me that you are both bankers,' said Mohammed, staring at Jamal with beady yellow eyes.

'Yes, that's right.'

'Very good. I'm looking for a loan, can you help me out?' He started to laugh but Jamal failed to see the humour.

'I'm not that kind of banker I'm afraid,' replied Jamal, and Mohammed took the hint.

'As you know,' Lucky continued, 'these gentlemen are here to present the fund idea that we have discussed. Jamal, please begin when you are ready.'

Jamal handed out copies of a pitch book that his analysts had created for the meeting. 'As you know, we are setting up a new real estate private equity vehicle that will revolutionise the property industry here in Dubai. Please turn to page one...'

He immediately launched into the most impressive sales pitch I had ever heard. He explained how the fund would work, how it would be structured and ultimately how we would make money.

'...The vehicle will be structured as an offshore Cayman Limited Partnership, which will ensure limited liability and complete confidentiality for institutional investors...'

His presentation was as slick as any investment banker on Wall Street. He used graphs, figures and charts, and he threw in the right financial terminology to confuse, amaze and intrigue his captivated audience.

'...Our unique origination capabilities and diverse capital base will ensure inherent value in our portfolio, which will be realised at attractive multiples and projected IRRs...'

He wasn't just selling an investment opportunity. He was making a solid case for why missing this opportunity would be committing financial suicide. Jamal was like a masterful hypnotist, except he was using financial jargon instead of a swinging pocket watch to captivate his audience and gain access to their chequebooks.

'Any questions?' asked Jamal as he finished. The room was silent. Lucky slowly got up and walked over to whisper something in Mohammed's ear. Mohammed whispered back and nodded.

'Bravo. Very good, Jamal. An excellent presentation indeed,' said Mohammed. 'I think we have all the information we need to make a decision. Lucky will be in touch with you shortly.'

Nothing more was said. We shook their hands and were shown out of the building by Lucky. Jamal didn't say a word until we got into his car outside, but I was dying to get his view on how he felt the meeting had gone.

'So what do you think?' I asked eagerly as we drove away.

Jamal looked at me and smiled. 'We've got them by the freaking balls, dude!' He revved his engine as we darted towards the Sheikh Zayed Road. 'We've got them!'

10

Something to Celebrate

Jamal called me after midnight with some urgent news. 'I just got a call from Lucky. He has invited us to join him for dinner tomorrow tonight.'

I jumped up from my bed and rubbed the weariness from my eyes. 'Okay, great, I'll be there. Do you know if there is any news yet?'

'No idea. He didn't say. He just told us to be at the Burj Al Arab at nine sharp. See you there and don't be late.'

The Burj Al Arab! I couldn't contain my excitement. Mere mortals were seldom considered worthy to enter Dubai's most exclusive hotel, so an invite like this was a rare privilege. At last, I was no longer destined to be among the curious tourists vying for a glimpse of its mysterious opulence from a distance. For one night only, I would be elevated to privileged status to dine with Dubai's social elite. Lucky sent a car to pick me up from my apartment, and as I jumped into the back seat I could hardly contain my excitement.

The magnificent sail-like structure of the Burj Al Arab could be seen for miles along Jumeirah Beach. Translated as 'Tower of the Arab', the Burj was Dubai's answer to the Eiffel Tower or Sydney Opera House: a tribute to the Emirate's maritime heritage and an unmistakable symbol of Brand Dubai. The hotel boasted world-class opulence and seven-star service, and its five-thousand-dollar-a-night rooms were strictly reserved for its exclusive clientele of Russian oligarchs, world leaders and rock stars. As our car pulled up to the entrance, a huge gush of water shot up from the fountain to indicate the arrival of a VIP guest. I was playing in the big league now, and it felt great.

I entered the hotel lobby through the giant revolving glass doors and was warmly greeted by three striking-looking Oriental women with hot towels, Arabian perfume and rose-petal finger bowls.

'Welcome to the Burj Al Arab, sir,' said each of them with a smile.

Refreshed and smelling fabulous, I thanked them and ventured inside. The striking lobby lounge was an instant onslaught on my vulnerable senses. Like the inside of a kaleidoscope, a multitude of colours and textures clashed to create a striking explosion of bright reds, blues and golds, merging in a psychedelic tapestry of patterns and shapes. The walls on either side of me were giant aquariums full of exotic fish, and a dancing water fountain leapt all the way up to the mezzanine floor. It was gaudy and excessive, but unquestionably spectacular. I stepped onto the escalator and looked up at the huge canvas atrium above. Floor by floor, it went on and on, until I had to steady myself as it made me a little dizzy.

A text message came through on my phone. It was Jamal:

We are at the Al Mahara restaurant. About to start. Where are you?

I looked at my watch and remembered he had specifically asked me not to be late. It was time to get a move on.

'Good evening, I am a guest at Lucky Chanda's table,' I said to the maître d' at the entrance to the restaurant. His bulging muscles, tight-fitting suit and no-nonsense demeanour made him look more like a henchman in a James Bond movie.

He checked his list carefully. 'Of course, sir. Please follow me to the submarine.'

I hesitated. 'Sorry, did you say submarine?'

'Yes, submarine, sir. You have to take a submarine ride to the restaurant.'

'Is it a real submarine?' I asked, curious.

He rolled his eyes. 'No, sir, it's just pretend,' he whispered, so as not to ruin the illusion for the other guests.

'So can't I just take the stairs?'

'No, sir. I'm afraid you have to take the submarine.'

I reluctantly did as I was told and stepped into the small chamber of the 'submarine'. As I made myself comfortable, I greeted my crew mates, a Russian man with two surgically enhanced blondes dressed in mini-skirts and stilettos. As the chamber door closed, we were suddenly 'plunged' twenty thousand leagues into the 'ocean', past sharks, blowfish and octopi. It was a little cheesy but enjoyable, although, considering I was now running quite late, slightly inconvenient. Finally, as the capsule door opened at the bottom, a tall woman greeted me to usher me to the table.

'Welcome to Al Mahara. Please come with me, sir.' I followed her through a giant gold tunnel into the main dining room. There were dozens of tables arranged in a circle around a massive aquarium whose brilliant blue waters illuminated the room. Thousands of tropical fish swam frantically around inside as their less fortunate brethren were devoured on the plates of the elite clientele.

'Glad you could make it,' said Lucky as I approached the table. 'Let me guess, you got stuck in the submarine, right?'

'Yes, something like that,' I replied.

'Ha-ha, happens every time!'

To Lucky's left sat Niraj, who I remembered from the meeting at their offices. Jamal sat to his right, already tucking into the breadsticks, and opposite the men were three Eastern European-looking models dressed in tiny cocktail dresses, all appearing rather bored.

'Meet Christina, Natasha and...' Lucky pointed at the best-looking and most scantily dressed of the three and paused. 'What was your name again, darling?'

'Veronica,' she replied, rolling her eyes and refusing to unfold her arms like an insolent child.

'Veronica, yes. How could I forget? But something tells me I will remember your name by the morning.' He laughed, but she wasn't amused. 'Why don't we order?'

The Michelin-starred menu consisted of an impressive selection of the finest seafood dishes from around the world. I couldn't pronounce most of them, but decided to go for the fresh Fine de Claire oysters baked in the shell with champagne sabayon. It was the most impressive-sounding dish on the menu and I assumed, perhaps naively, that I wouldn't be paying. As I made myself comfortable, I glanced at the surrounding tables. The Russian man and his two glamour-model

136

friends from the submarine were now sitting at the next table. The women competed for his attention as he poured oysters into their mouths one by one, washed down with a bottle of Dom Pérignon champagne.

Lucky stood up and raised his glass. 'Now that we are all here, I would like to propose a toast to our new business partners.' Jamal's eyes lit up. 'I am glad to confirm that we will be making a seed investment into your real estate fund of a million dollars.'

I couldn't believe my ears.

'Wow, that's great news, Lucky,' said Jamal, who looked overjoyed by the good news. 'We won't let you down.'

'Of course you won't, or I will come and find you and break your legs,' said Lucky with a stern look. Jamal turned white and the table fell into an awkward silence, until Lucky burst into uncontrollable laughter. 'I had you there, didn't I?' Jamal nodded sheepishly. 'May we make shitloads of money together, all buy huge yachts and sail around the world with beautiful topless supermodels. *Salut!*'

'Cheers!' We raised our glasses.

'Now, let's tuck into our amazing, overpriced, unpronounceable food. Enjoy!'

I began my beautifully crafted dish, keeping one eye on the fierce stingray that seemed to be watching my every mouthful from the tank above, making me a little uncomfortable. I glanced over at Jamal who was completely engrossed by his sea bass and truffle main course.

'Jamal, this is the first time you have shut your mouth since I've known you,' said Lucky. The table erupted with laughter, except Veronica, who didn't seem to get the joke.

Lucky turned to confront her. 'What, you don't find my jokes funny?' he asked her. She stared at him nervously like a remorseful schoolgirl. 'You are not having a good time?' Still no reply. 'When everybody smiles, you smile!' The tables around us fell silent as many of the diners turned around to see what the commotion was about. 'I am paying you enough for the night, so the very least you can do is smile!' shouted Lucky, jumping to his feet in anger. 'Now smile, you bitch! Smile for my friends!'

137

Veronica was almost in tears, but out of fear she forced her mouth into the faintest of smiles. As the tears began rolling down her cheeks, I felt sorry for the poor girl, but I had no intention of crossing Lucky, who looked possessed with rage. Her compliance seemed to placate him and he began to calm down. 'Good. Now finish your soup,' he said, and sat back down to finish his meal.

As the restaurant slowly returned to normal, I tried to ease the tension. 'So Lucky, how is business going for you at the moment?'

He smiled before he answered. 'Adam, I drive a customised Aston Martin DB9, I have a fifty-metre yacht in the marina, and I live in a ten-bedroom mansion. How good do you think business is, my friend?' He laughed. 'This city is a fucking cash cow.'

'Point taken. But what is the secret, Lucky? What are you doing right that others aren't?'

He put down his cutlery and looked directly into my eyes. 'I am a successful real estate developer in the fastest-growing market in the world. It's really that simple.'

'Come on, Lucky. Surely there's a lot more to your success than being in the right place at the right time?'

He noticed the hidden compliment and smiled. 'Okay, let me explain how this game works. If I want to construct a building, what is the first thing I need? Land, right? So I approach the master developer, Nakheel for example, and tell him I want a plot for let's say a thirty-storey residential building. I will make an offer, put down a 10 per cent deposit on the plot, and I'm ready to start selling my project. Then I hire an architect, design some nice brochures and DVDs and I am ready to sell. Make sense?'

'So far, yes,' I said.

'To sell my building, I just need to call up a few of my closest customers to a buy a floor each. They put down 10 per cent each as a deposit, and within a couple of weeks my building is sold out and I now have enough money to start construction. If I like, I can buy back from my investors and resell to the broader market by throwing a launch party or using a property agent. Every few months I collect another 10 per cent from my investors, and they fund the construction without me having to put in any more money. In the meantime, I can launch my next building and repeat the process. It's like taking candy from a baby.' Lucky had just made Dubai property development sound as easy as baking a cake.

'Okay, that makes sense,' I said. 'But let's put some numbers on this: how much money are you guys actually making per project?' The mere mention of money made the girls play close attention.

'Well, I can pick up a plot in a second-tier location like Jumeirah Village South directly from Nakheel for, say, a hundred dirhams per square foot, or about thirty dollars. Add another three hundred dirhams for construction and another hundred for marketing costs, so total costs of five hundred dirhams per square foot. Before even laying a brick, I can sell that building in this market for twelve hundred dirhams per square foot with my eyes closed. But for argument's sake, let's say I sell for a thousand. Just to be conservative. That's still 100 per cent profit margin. Not too bad, I think.'

It seemed the key to the success of Dubai's developers was off-plan sales. They could sell an entire building based purely on the sales brochure years before any development was scheduled to begin. Their initial outlay was a simple deposit to purchase the land and the marketing costs to create the sales materials. As the actual construction costs would be financed by the investors on a phased payment schedule until completion, developers could make huge margins for minimal risk in a market where demand was far outstripping supply and prices were going through the roof. It was the ultimate example of OPM.

We finished our meal and to my relief Lucky took care of the bill. He didn't even glance at the number, which was certainly substantial considering the amount of food and champagne we had consumed. He simply pulled out his American Express Centurion card and handed it to the hovering waitress who gladly took care of it. It was getting late now, and after a great meal I was looking forward to crashing in my bed. But Lucky, it seemed, had other plans.

'So, are you guys ready to party?'

'What do you have in mind?' asked Jamal.

'It's a surprise. Just wait and see!' He was clearly excited by what was in store. As we made our way out of the restaurant and the Burj, we were ushered into two pearl-white, chauffeur-driven Rolls-Royce Phantoms waiting outside. I got into one of the cars with Lucky, Veronica and Christina, and Jamal and Natasha stepped in the other with Niraj. Our convoy sped down the Sheikh Zayed Road, through Bur Dubai and the Shindinga tunnel into the heart of Deira, the old part of the city. We eventually pulled up at an old, inconspicuous hotel called the Carlton Towers. It hardly looked like a party hotspot, but I had a feeling there was something big in store for us.

'You like Indian music?' asked Lucky as we got out of the car.

'Sure, why not?' I replied.

'And do you like Indian girls?'

'Erm, I guess so.'

'Good! Then you're gonna love this place. It's owned by my good friend and we are his personal guests tonight.'

We followed Lucky into the dated lobby and down a staircase towards the basement. The fading wallpaper and cracked marble floors were a far cry from the grand lobby at the Burj. Unsavoury-looking Indian men with side partings and moustaches were sitting on filthy sofas smoking cigarettes and staring at us through their boozy eyes. Veronica was now rather tipsy and struggling to walk in a straight line, oblivious to the groups of men gawping at her every stumble. We arrived at a large door with the words 'Hollywood, Bollywood' in pink neon lights above. Muffled Indian pop music could be heard inside.

The room was vast and dark. The air was dense with smoke and the floor was crowded with captivated spectators, all men, with waiters rushing around serving jugs of beer and bottles of spirits. The attention of the crowd was directed towards a makeshift stage where four overweight Indian girls in skimpy clothes gyrating unenthusiastically to the live Indian music from the live band behind them.

Lucky was spotted by the hostess, a hideous old woman known as the 'aunty', and she greeted him fondly, before leading us to a reserved table directly in front of the stage. It was by far the best table in the house, and as we sat down an army of waiters were there to attend to our every command. Within seconds, there were a dozen bottles of vodka, rum, whisky and champagne on our table, as well as six stacks of white cards, each around a hundred high.

'What is this place?' I shouted at Niraj over the thumping music.

'It's called a *mujra*!' He shouted back. 'An Indian dance bar!'

'You mean like a strip club?'

'Not exactly. The women do not get naked here.'

'So what's the appeal then?' I asked, confused.

'The thrill is of a beautiful woman dancing for you. She will tease you with her smiles, and the more you pay the more attention she will give you.'

'That's it?'

'Yes, that is all.'

It seemed that the *mujra* was Dubai's answer to a gentleman's club, only there were no clothes removed, nor were there any lap dances. Here men paid vast sums for the exclusive privilege of having a scantily clothed, chubby woman dance in front of them. If they were lucky, they would at best catch a slight wink or a smile. The entire concept baffled me, but the boisterous audience couldn't get enough as they clapped and wolf-whistled at the peculiar spectacle on the stage.

The origins of the *mujra* dated to the days of the Mogul Empire, when beautiful dancers would entertain the emperors in the grand palace courtyards. It was an ancient Indian art form and the performers would train for years to perfect their craft. It was said that men would become so captivated by the beauty of the women that they would lose all sense of the material world and submit themselves completely to their charms.

However, Dubai's take on the *mujra* was a far cry from the romantic ideal. Here the beautiful and talented dancers were replaced by overweight and disinterested girls who oscillated apathetically to the repetitive music. Their audience was not emperors and courtiers, but perverted old Indian men, sleazy sheikhs and dodgy labourers, many of whom had left their families at home to come and watch these girls shake their superfluous stuff.

'Lucky mentioned this place is owned by a friend of his,' I said to Niraj.

141

'Yes,' he replied as he took a sip of his whisky. 'This is one of Mustafa Edris's joints.'

'Who?'

Niraj froze. 'You have never heard of Mustafa Edris?'

'Should I have?' I answered sheepishly.

'Mustafa Edris is one of the wealthiest men in the world.'

'Really? I haven't heard of him, what line of business is he in?'

Niraj leaned in close and whispered, 'Keep this between us, okay?' I could smell the alcohol on his breath.

'Sure...'

'Edris is the godfather of the Indian underworld. He runs the biggest weapons and drugs cartel in India. He practically bankrolls the Indian film industry and has hundreds of politicians in his back pocket. Lucky and Mr Edris do a lot of business together, so we are invited as his personal guests tonight.'

'So are you telling me Lucky is connected with the Indian underworld?'

Niraj put his hand over his mouth as if he had crossed a forbidden line. 'I can't officially answer that question. I thought you knew already.'

Just then, Lucky picked up one of the stacks of cards on the table and threw it at one of the dancing girls as she gyrated provocatively in front of him. The girl joined her hands in gratitude and Lucky nodded in acknowledgement. A small Indian man in a waistcoat with a broom appeared on stage from nowhere and swept up the cards from around the girl's feet until they were all gone. Lucky's cards were swiftly followed by cards from another Indian man who was sitting at the table next to us. As he threw his stack at the same girl, one hit her square in the face but again she smiled with appreciation. And again the little Indian came in and swept up until the stage was clean. It was the most bizarre thing I had ever seen.

'What does the card throwing represent?' I asked Niraj.

'It's a way of showing his appreciation for her,' he shouted back, his eyes firmly on the stage.

142

'But he just slapped her in the face with some cards. How is that a gesture of appreciation?'

'No, you don't understand. Lucky bought the cards for a thousand dirhams a stack. Throwing actual money at her is considered disrespectful, so the cards are like a symbol of money.'

As I tried to get my head around it all, a card-throwing war had broken out between Lucky and the other man, and hundreds of cards were flying at the girls from both directions. It was like a grand test of masculinity, and considering that the reward was at most a grin, this surely rivalled Mona Lisa's as the world's most expensive smile.

Suddenly, Lucky's arch-rival got up on the table and began to dance like a man possessed. As the music got louder, he jumped onto the stage like an embarrassing drunken uncle at a wedding. The girls ran for cover as two bouncers rushed in and escorted him out of the club. The entire audience erupted with laughter, but Lucky was more pleased that he had emerged triumphant in the card-throwing war.

Veronica kicked off her shoes and jumped on the stage, where she began to dance with the Indian women. The crowd loved it; men cheered and wolf-whistled at the show they were being given. Lucky threw more cards at the stage, now joined by an Emirati man who had come to the stage from the back of the room with hundreds more cards in his arms. The poor Indian with the broom was finding it impossible to keep up with the sweeping, and eventually just gave up. It was soon raining cards and I was stunned by the sheer amount of money that had been thrown away in the last ten testosterone-fuelled minutes alone.

But just as things were getting out of control, the music was cut and the lights came on, to a groan from the disappointed crowd.

'What happened?' I asked Niraj.

'It's three in the morning,' said Niraj. 'The law says all entertainment venues have to stop at three.'

Lucky wasn't pleased. He tried shouting at the band and ordering them to play, but they refused and he accepted that the performance was over. As we stumbled out of the hotel, our white Rolls-Royces were still waiting for us at the entrance. Lucky carried Veronica in his arms while the other girls followed with their shoes in their hands. He threw her into the back seat of one of the cars before jumping in after her.

'Driver, take us back to the Burj Al Arab!' he shouted.

I saw this as my chance to excuse myself politely. 'Lucky, I really should be going.'

'Nonsense!' he shouted. 'This was just a warm-up. Now the night really begins. Get in.'

I sighed but reluctantly obliged, and once again we were on our way to the Burj.

The early rays of dawn were now piercing the dark desert night as our convoy sped down the ramp of the hotel entrance and back towards new Dubai. We passed the open waters of the creek, where dozens of dock workers were already unloading boxes and crates containing televisions, dates and car parts from the dozens of *dhows* lining the banks. Their day was just beginning, but our night was far from over yet. As we headed back up the Sheikh Zayed Road, I began to hear noises from the back seat. It seemed Lucky and Veronica had taken their relationship to a new level of intimacy. I assumed they wanted a little privacy, so I refrained from turning around to watch. Fortunately the rear windows of the Rolls were blacked out, so the passing cars were none the wiser. After eventually pulling up outside the hotel, we headed through the lobby to a private elevator, which took us to the twenty-fifth-floor penthouse.

The penthouse suite at the Burj was more opulent than my wildest imagination. A long hallway with orange and black marble walls led to a gold staircase with leopard-print tufted carpets. The room itself was split across two floors with a dining area, an Arabic-style *majlis* or seating area, and a library. There was a fully loaded bar and a stunning jacuzzi terrace that looked out onto the vast waters of the Persian Gulf. In the centre of the living room an impressive array of fruits, sweets and dates had been laid out, ready for our arrival.

'Please come in, guys, make yourselves comfortable,' said Lucky as he ushered us into the suite. 'What do you think of the room?'

'It's quite amazing,' I replied.

'Isn't it? It has its own private cinema, state-of-the-art sound system and a master bedroom with a revolving four-poster canopy bed.' He went over to the bar area to mix us some drinks.

'Not bad at all, Lucky,' said Jamal, walking around in awe.

We were joined by two other Indian men I had not met before. They were both dressed in jeans and blazers with their shirts buttoned down low. One of them rested his sunglasses above his gel-drenched hair.

'Let me introduce you guys,' said Lucky. 'These are my good friends Sanjay and Salman. Guys, meet my new business partners, Adam and Jamal.'

I shook their hands, but they made little eye contact, which I found rather rude.

'Hey, you look quite familiar. Do I know you?' asked Jamal as he greeted Salman.

'Are you serious?' shouted Lucky, grabbing Salman's cheeks. 'This is one of the most famous faces in India.'

'No, Lucky, please,' replied Salman bashfully.

'This is Salman Aziz, the most famous actor in Bollywood. And this is the world-famous Indian cricketer Sanjay Patel. Please take a seat, gentlemen, we will be beginning soon.'

'Beginning what?' I asked, but Lucky didn't answer.

Just then, the doorbell rang.

'Ah, right on time,' smiled Lucky. He walked over and opened the door. A group of thirty dark figures floated eerily into the room. They were dressed from head to toe in black *abayas*, hiding every part of their body except their manicured hands. Keeping their heads lowered to the ground, one by one they lined up with impressive precision. Once all thirty were in place, the tallest figure clapped its hands and all at once they dropped their *abayas* to the ground. There before us stood the most stunningly beautiful women I had ever seen, completely naked. They all looked different, some dark and some fairer, some tall and others petite, but each a perfect woman in her own unique, angelic way. The eyes of everyone in the room lit up, including Veronica and the girls. I was in a state of shock.

145

'Gentlemen, before you is my gift to you as my new business partners. You may take your pick as you wish. Enjoy!'

Lucky was the first to make his choice, a dark-skinned exotic beauty with sleek black hair and endless legs. He took her by the hand and led her upstairs. One by one the men took their pick, some two at a time, and led their women away in different directions. But as my turn approached, I hesitated. I had enjoyed the night's celebrations up to this point, but I had no intention of partaking in a mass orgy! I decided this was my chance to make a swift exit, so as soon as the other guys had gone, I rushed past the remaining naked girls and out of the front door as fast as I could.

I thought about the evening's outrageous events in the cab home: Lucky's outburst at Veronica, the revelations of his underworld connections and the orgy that was in progress right now at the penthouse. I began to worry whether I was making the right decision by going into business with him. Was he everything he appeared to be? Was his commitment to the fund legitimate? Was I making a colossal mistake? All sorts of doubts were entering my mind; I was extremely confused and I needed to clear my head.

The sun had fully risen by the time I approached my apartment, but I couldn't sleep. It was almost nine in the morning, so I took a shower and lay on my bed. As I reached for my phone on my bedside table, I suddenly noticed the business card of the blond blue-eyed man who had been sitting beside me at the Al Qasr hotel the night I met Alesia. I remembered he had left his card with the waiter to give to me, and I still had not got to the bottom of who he was. I decided it was a good time to call him and solve the mystery for good.

The phone rang at least ten times before a voice with a Scandinavian accent finally answered. 'Hello, Jonas speaking.'

'Hi, Jonas. I'm not sure if you remember me, but I'm the guy who was sitting next to you in the lobby at the Al Qasr a few days ago. You left me your business card.'

'Oh, hi. Of course I remember. How are you? I didn't think you would call back.'

'I'm great, thanks. How are you?'

'I'm very well.'

'Great. Listen, I'm sorry if I didn't recognise you, but do we know each other?'

'No, we don't. Well, not yet anyway. I thought maybe we could have a chat.'

'Erm, sure. About what exactly?'

'Well, what kind of scene are you into?'

'Scene? I'm sorry, I don't know what you mean.'

'What's your thing?'

I paused for a moment as I tried to decipher his meaning. 'Well, I enjoy nice restaurants and I've been to a couple of clubs here, if that's what you mean'.

'Not exactly. I don't think you're getting me.'

'I'm sorry, Jonas, I'm really confused.'

'You want me to spell it out for you?'

'Yes please, if you don't mind.'

'Are you gay?'

I almost fell off the bed. 'What?'

'You know, gay?'

'No, I'm not gay!'

'I see. So I guess we're not into the same scene.'

'No, not at all!'

'Well, nice to hear from you. Call me if you ever change your mind,' he said before hanging up.

11

Passing the Grenade

The suave image of Benito Valli dressed to the nines in a tailored blue pinstriped suit and smoking a fat Cuban cigar featured on every magazine cover in the city. 'Meet Mr Property', 'Dubai's property wunderkind', 'the self-made property tycoon' read the flattering headlines. Benito played the part of the archetypal millionaire playboy perfectly with his slicked-back hair, sharp suits and debonair demeanour. He certainly seemed to have it all: looks, style, wealth, success and gravitas. There were rumours that he was a prince or the descendant of Italian aristocracy, or even the son of a movie star, which he neither confirmed nor denied, serving only to perpetuate the mystique of Benito Valli.

The unlikely poster boy of the Dubai property success story, Benito was a young, smooth-talking Italian of 30 who arrived in Dubai in 2003. A former investment banker, he spotted an opportunity to exploit the dynamic UAE property market early. In 2004 he established the DCA Real Estate Group, a new asset management vehicle that would invest on behalf of celebrities, high net worth individuals and family offices into the incredible growth of the Dubai property market. And an overnight success story was born.

After a few lucrative early investments for his investors, Benito set his aim higher. By 2005, DCA began purchasing entire buildings directly from developers, rebranding and selling them to its private investors as individual units and even whole floors. DCA would then buy them back and resell the properties to the wider market at a hefty premium. It was a flawless business model in an ever-rising market, and it was reported that within four years of beginning operations, DCA was turning over a billion dollars in revenue.

It was no wonder that stories of Benito's extravagances bordered on the obscene. There were widespread rumours that he owned seven luxury Bentley Continental GTs in different colours, one for each day of the week, as well as a fleet of private jets, and that he was dating four leading Hollywood actresses at once. As a rising young star in the fastest-growing property market in the world, it seemed that anything was possible for Benito Valli.

***

Between 2002 and 2008, an estimated $64.9 billion in foreign direct investment flowed into the UAE from Europe, Asia, Russia, Africa and the Gulf, and most of it went into Dubai's booming property market. During the same period, oil prices quadrupled, reaching a peak in 2008 of $140 per barrel. The city became a haven for surplus petrodollars from across the region flowing into its real estate sector and multiplying many times over, creating new millionaires every day in the process.

Dubai redefined real estate as an asset class when property became nothing but a vehicle to recycle cash for remarkable returns. Investors were spoilt for choice, with dozens of new property developments launched daily across the city by both the government-backed and private developers. Once a deposit had been paid, the investor was free to sell or flip their new purchase to a secondary buyer at whatever premium they could fetch. The new buyer would be responsible for outstanding payments to the developer, and the original owner could then reinvest his profits by doubling down and repeating the process again, and again. It was a foolproof path to a fortune.

Most real estate in Dubai was sold off-plan, which meant that a buyer could purchase the deed on a property before a brick had even been laid. Investors didn't need to waste their time being shown around by enthusiastic agents, evaluating finishings or assessing the merits of the neighbourhood. Property was nothing but an instrument to trade, and only two things mattered to Dubai's cash-hungry investors: the price they were paying and the premium they could obtain. The Dubai real estate market was unrestricted by the regulation and red tape of more developed markets. It was growing too fast for legislation to keep up, and surveying or conveyancing was considered an unnecessary inconvenience. Instead, property values were determined purely by the raw forces of supply and demand, and profits depended entirely on what the market was willing to pay.

The other great advantage was the ability to buy on margin. Investors could put down a 10 or even 5 per cent deposit and resell their investment within a matter of days. This mitigated the risk to the investor and allowed him to turn around a quick profit with little money down. It also meant that even a small increase in the market value of the property could translate into a huge return on investment. In many cases this deposit was borrowed or placed on a credit card, making it the ultimate no-money-down investment.

Nevertheless, huge returns were not without substantial risk and early investors in Dubai took a great leap of faith. Few performed any meaningful due diligence, as the market moved too quickly for such time-consuming checks and balances. They gave their money to unproven developers and invested in projects they had no guarantees would ever be built. Their money was not placed into escrow accounts until much later when the escrow law was passed, and there was little legislation or legal framework protecting their interests. They committed to aggressive payment schedules unlinked to construction milestones, and most of them didn't think beyond financing the first one or two payments. This was a high risk, high reward game which was attracting new gamblers daily.

The key to making money in the Dubai property game was to find the greater fool. The fool was the next buyer in the chain who believed that he was buying at a low enough price to lock in a profit to the next purchaser. The ultimate fool would be the final investor, or end user, who would have no choice but to hold the proverbial hot potato. Therefore the most important principle in churning a profit was to buy low and sell high. The best way to lock in a premium was to buy as close to the launch price as possible, and the best way to ensure the best price was to build close relationships with the developers.

With such low barriers to entry, competition between the developers quickly turned fierce. There was only so much they could do to differentiate their luxury tower from the next one, so many developers began to offer sweeteners to investors to make their project that little bit more enticing. Some offered luxury cars to their biggest investors with every purchase, while others threw in a yacht-club membership or a free holiday. Soon investors were buying to claim the incentive as much as the property itself.

Eventually, the government cottoned on to the success of such gimmicks and offered the ultimate incentive to overseas investors: a residency visa with every property purchase. Previously, visas had been reserved for expats working in the Emirate, but now for the first time investors were given the privilege of residing in the tax haven if they purchased property. The exact conditions of this new law were yet to be ironed out, but the promise was enough to send investors into a frenzy as sales rocketed on the news.

In addition to the flurry of developers entering the market, around two and a half thousand new real estate brokerage firms were also set up from 2003. The role of the brokers was to act as a conduit between the developers and buyers. They were market makers who created a secondary market for investors and much-needed liquidity for speculators seeking to flip. The brokers were big winners in the property game. They saw themselves as the 'big swinging dicks' of Dubai, and their huge monthly commissions justified the hype. They took a fee of between 2 and 5 per cent from every transaction and were exposed to none of the risks. Billions of dollars worth of real estate was soon passing through the brokers, earning them millions in commissions and making many young realtors very wealthy in the process.

Most real estate agencies hired an army of realtors to generate business and close deals. In addition to competing with other brokerage companies, they also competed with hundreds of freelance brokers who maintained day jobs as taxi drivers or delivery boys. The market was a free-for-all. Freelancers didn't need the overhead of an office, a marketing budget or a trade licence; they simply needed a phone and some balls. Many worked from hotel lobbies and malls, and some of the more successful freelancers made more money in a day than most registered agencies were making in a month.

As investors made more money, their eyes became beadier and the prize became greater. Investors went from buying a few units in a building to entire floors, and then to half buildings, and eventually entire buildings, giving rise to a process that became known as underwriting. Buying entire buildings from developers at a wholesale price and selling individual units to their clients at inflated premiums was the quickest way to generate massive returns that only the most cash rich could afford to do. In reality, it was flipping on a huge scale.

Between 2002 and 2008, market analysts tried to predict the moment when supply would finally overtake demand, but it never seemed to materialise. Hours after the announcement of a new project, units were snapped up by the pent-up demand. And as more and more property changed hands, prices continued to spiral upwards at breakneck speed. And with ever-increasing liquidity in the market, developers were encouraged to launch bigger projects to meet the insatiable demand from investors, which again drove up values, adding yet more fuel to the roaring real estate furnace.

***

The launch party for DCA's Business Bay project was a grand affair. A giant marquee was erected on Jumeirah Beach under the Burj Al Arab, and the event was attended by investors from across the globe, many of whom had flown in just for the night. Once the crowds were seated, the lights went down and the proceedings began. There was a fanfare of trumpets and a dramatic drum roll before the giant yacht rolled slowly into the hall to the delight of the crowd. And there on the bow stood Benito Valli, dressed in a fine black tuxedo and sailor hat, like Caesar entering Rome to rapturous applause. On his arms were a stunning blonde and a brunette dressed in tight-fitting swimwear, smiling ear to ear while posing for the army of photographers.

Within minutes, units and floors in the new tower were already oversubscribed. Cheques were flying around the room as DCA's eager representatives scuttled between the tables to take down the details of greedy investors who were certain that buying at the launch price would guarantee a profit when they flipped to the secondary market. Little did they know that the building's units had already been bought and sold numerous times by DCA's elite investors, and DCA had made a fortune each time in the process.

It was no wonder that Benito held the huge grin on his smug face for the rest of the night.

12

Driven to Decision

'So your father told me that you're in Doo-bai. What on earth are you doing out there? Why didn't you tell me you wanted to work abroad? I could have connected you with some people here in the States.'

'But uncle, this city is really going places.'

'Yes, I've heard. But the question is, is it for real or just another bubble?'

'Of course it's for real, uncle. This is one of the fastest-growing cities in the world. People are arriving here in their hundreds every day and they are all looking for property.'

'Yeah, but just remember one thing: what goes up usually comes down just as quickly.'

I rolled my eyes. 'Sure, I'll remember that.'

'And listen, if you hear of any good deals out there, be sure to keep me posted, okay?'

'Will do, uncle.'

In a way, Uncle Ali's scepticism was reflective of most outsiders' suspicions of Dubai. My father's brother was always thought of as the success story of the family, having moved to the US early on in his career and done rather well for himself. Like most Americans, Ali saw the Middle East as a backward, third-world region and he simply couldn't understand why I had made the move here. But Ali was still a capitalist at heart and the wealth opportunities of Dubai were impossible to ignore. Despite his reservations, he was itching not to miss the action and even to get a share of the spoils.

'By the way, while you're out there you should meet up with an old buddy of mine. We used to work together years ago in London. I hear he's some real estate bigwig in Dubai now. He may be a useful contact for you.'

'Sure, that would be great.'

'His name is Tariq Sharaf. I haven't seen him in years, but I think he's doing pretty well for himself. I'll email you his phone number.'

'Thanks uncle.'

'And just promise me one thing, okay? Make sure you don't get your manhood chopped off for chatting up some sheikh's daughter.'

'Okay, uncle, I'll try to behave myself.'

Moments after hanging up, Ali emailed me Tariq's number and I called him right away.

'Hello, Tariq speaking,' answered a man in an English accent.

'Hi, Tariq, I was given your number by my uncle Ali in San Francisco. I'm his nephew Adam, and I'm living here in Dubai now.'

There was a pause. 'Ali?'

'Yes.'

'How is that old bastard? Is he still hiding in the US?'

'Yep, he still lives in the US.'

'Great. Well, as you're Ali's nephew, why don't you come over to our house for tea? Get in a taxi over to the Jumeirah Islands, cluster twenty-three, villa seven. Tell the driver it's near Jebel Ali. See you at nine?'

'That would be perfect, see you then.'

I freshened up and jumped in a taxi to make my way over for dinner.

'Yes, sir?' said the Indian taxi driver.

'Do you know the Jumeirah Islands?'

'Jumeirah Eye-lun, sir?'

'Yes, the Jumeirah Islands, do you know it?'

'Okay, sir.'

'Well, is that a yes or a no?'

'Okay, sir. Tell me which place is close by.'

'It's near Jebel Ali.'

154

'Okay, sir. No problem.'

'So do you know it?' I was still unsure.

'No problem.'

I wasn't completely convinced he knew where we were going, but I gave him the benefit of the doubt, and we were on our way.

'Where you from, sir?'

It was an all too familiar question. 'I'm from London.'

'London? You look like Arab.'

'Yes, I've heard that before.'

'London good, Dubai bad,' he smiled.

'Hmm, that depends.'

'Depends?'

'It depends what you do, I guess. Would you rather be in London?' I asked.

'Oh yes, sir. I wish I go London. It is my dream!' he said with a huge grin.

He wasn't alone. It was the ultimate aspiration of most taxi drivers I had met to live in the West. Most of them couldn't understand why anybody with a British passport would come to the Middle East to work. This contradicted every ideal they had about the West as the perfect society, where salaries were high, life was easy and the streets were paved with gold. Theirs was a world far from the Friday brunches, BBQs and dinner parties. They didn't see the benefits of a tax-free salary and the beach clubs that ungrateful Western expatriates took for granted. The sole purpose of every low-paid worker was to make and save money, so that their children could eat at least a meal a day, and their families could hang on to some poor excuse for shelter back in their poverty-stricken home countries. While they spent up to eighteen hours a day working for a measly wage in Dubai, often to the detriment of their health and safety, the Western world offered the prospect of that little bit more to earn and send back home.

Distracted by our conversation, I suddenly realised we had been circling the same block for over ten minutes. Clearly, we were lost. It

155

didn't help that there was no formal system of addresses in Dubai. Without a significant landmark close to the destination, one could be circling a neighbourhood for days and still not find the place. The added challenge of the ever-changing road network that reinvented itself daily to accommodate the massive amount of construction activity didn't help. Some routes seemed to disappear and reappear out of nowhere overnight.

'Do you actually know where we are?' I finally asked the driver.

'Yes, sir.'

'So are we close?'

'Close sir, no problem.' I wasn't convinced.

He nervously pulled out his mobile phone and began to shout at it in Urdu. The only phrase I vaguely understood was 'Jumeirah Eye-lun', which he repeated at least fifty times. Eventually, he seemed satisfied enough to hang up.

'Okay, sir, I know Jumeirah Eye-lun now.'

'But I thought you said we weren't lost?'

'No problem, sir.'

As we finally pulled up to the gate, an Indian man in a beret and blue uniform came out of a small security hut. I told him the cluster and the villa number and he opened the barrier. As we drove into the Islands, it felt like entering the pages of a property brochure. There were beautifully landscaped gardens, small wooden bridges and dancing water features. Young children rode past us on bicycles amid fountains and palm trees, and Lycra-clad expats jogged past us by the dozen. It was eerily perfect and my taxi driver looked as astonished as I was as we absorbed the idyllic scenery. I was astonished at the sheer size of some of the villas ahead, each with its own unique identity and character. 'I think this is it,' I said as we drove into cluster twenty-three. The driver parked up outside.

'Seventy-two dirhams, please.' I gave him a two-hundred-dirham note and waited for my change. It didn't come.

'Can I have my change, please?' I asked assertively.

'Sir, you want change?'

'Yes!'

'Okay, sir.'

He reluctantly obliged and handed me the cash, perhaps assuming that my high-end destination was somehow a reflection of my own financial well-being.

The taxi sped away and I strolled up to the house. Villa seven was the largest on the block by far. I walked up the cobbled path past the perfectly mown front lawn and rose beds. A fountain gushed gently in the centre of the courtyard, breaking the silence of the sleepy neighbourhood. I strolled up to giant oak doors, tucked in my shirt and rang the door bell. After a few moments, the door opened and there stood a tall Asian man with a bushy moustache and oily hair.

'Good evening. It's a pleasure to meet you, Tariq. I'm Adam.' I handed him the box of chocolates I had picked up on the way and shook his hand enthusiastically. He didn't say a word and looked confused. 'I really want to apologise for being so late, we got completely lost and my taxi driver didn't really know his way around too well.'

The man just stared at me, and I feared that my lack of punctuality had caused offence. 'Sir will be down in a short while.'

I froze with embarrassment. 'Ah, so you're not Tariq?'

He shook his head. I smiled sheepishly and followed him into the living room. 'Please,' he said, pointing at the inviting couch. I took a seat and waited patiently for my real host.

'So you made it!' I turned around and saw a small, unassuming man in a loose-fitting shirt and slacks. The little hair he had left was short and spiky, and he wore spectacles on the tip of his broad, flattish nose. I stood up to shake his hand.

'Good evening, Tariq, it's a pleasure to meet you.'

'So you're Ali's nephew, huh?'

'Yes I am. I'm sorry I'm a little late. I brought some chocolates. I left them with...'

'Akbar? Yes, he's our help. He makes a great curry, you know. Make yourself at home. Are you hungry?'

157

Akbar emerged from the kitchen and laid the coffee table with tea and strawberry cheesecake.

'Looks amazing,' I said, as I eyeballed the cake.

'Your uncle and I go back a long way. We used to chase girls together back in school, the rascal! I bet he never told you that.'

'No, he didn't. Do you guys still keep in contact?'

'Not really. He went out to the US and I came out here to the Gulf, so we lost touch recently. He never liked the Middle East much. He thought it was a mirage. But I always told him that if you know the right people, there's more money to be made out here than anywhere in the world. It's still an untapped goldmine as far as I'm concerned. So tell me, how have you settled in Dubai?'

'Pretty well, I think. There have been some up and downs, but I think I'm finding my feet now.'

'Ha-ha, ups and downs. There are certainly a lot of those. Dubai can be a very difficult place to live if you don't know the right people. Somebody needs to be watching your back all of the time in this place, if you know what I mean.' He was alluding to *wasta*.

'So my uncle mentioned you're in real estate,' I said as I took a bite of the delicious cake.

'That's right.'

'I was at Cityscape recently. It totally blew me away!'

'Yes, it's a great time for Dubai. But it wasn't always like this. I've been here for almost twenty years now and trust me, I've seen the ups and downs.'

'So do you work for one of the developers or agencies?' I asked.

He smiled. 'Well, technically I don't work for anybody. I sort of run my own thing.'

'Oh, great. Would I have heard of your company?'

'Possibly. We are called Milestone Properties.'

I almost choked on my cheesecake.

'Are you okay?' asked Tariq, with concern.

'I'm fine, thanks,' I replied as I coughed the piece of cake out of my throat. 'Yes, the name Milestone rings a bell. You guys are one of the bigger names in the market, if I'm not mistaken.'

It was an understatement of gargantuan proportions. Milestone was one of two premier real estate agencies in Dubai, probably the biggest. The name featured on every newspaper and billboard across the city, with branches in prime locations, a 500-strong workforce and a reputation others could only dream of. And here I was sitting with the founder, sipping his tea and eating his cheesecake! I tried to keep calm and not look intimidated.

'So, Tariq, how long do you think this real estate boom can realistically go on for?' I asked, attempting to sound credible.

'That's a very good question,' he replied. 'What we see happening today is a once-in-a-lifetime event. But this is just the beginning of the Dubai success story, in my opinion.'

'How so?' I probed.

'Well, just look around you. The economy is booming. Dubai has a clean slate to build a city from scratch, and it's taking advantage of the opportunity.'

'Yes, but there is just so much property being built here. Can the city really absorb all of this supply?'

'That's true, but thousands of people are also arriving here every day, and they will all need somewhere to live eventually. What we're seeing is a massive population shift from Asia, India, Africa and the West. We're actually just scratching the surface.'

'But prices can't keep going up for ever, can they? They have to stop somewhere, surely.'

'No, they can't. But prices in Dubai are still very reasonable compared to the rest of the developed world. Compare Dubai to the UK, for instance: prices here are still around a third of those in London, yet salaries in Dubai are at least on par with if not higher than UK post-tax salaries. This suggests that prices still have a long, long way to go.'

I paused to absorb his convincing argument. 'I didn't look at it that way.'

'Look, there will always be sceptics and pessimists who stand on the sidelines and look for reasons why people shouldn't be making money. Most of the time, they're just angry with themselves because they missed the boat. Waiting for a crash to happen is like waiting to win the lottery – it may never happen and you waste a lot of time in the process.'

I wasn't sure whether Tariq really believed what he was saying, or whether he was just the best salesman I had ever met. Either way, it was just what I needed to hear. A positive view on the market from a man with his pedigree and experience was enough to instil confidence in even the most pessimistic observer. It also vindicated my confidence in the fund Jamal and I were planning. I began to ponder whether Tariq's involvement could be the final ingredient to ensure its success.

'Tariq, do you mind if I get your opinion on something?' I asked, after some thought.

'Not at all,' he said.

'It's an idea that I've been working on which will offer a totally new brand of investors access the real estate market in Dubai.'

He looked interested. 'I see. Tell me more.'

And so I told him the whole story of how Jamal and I had come up with the idea, Lucky's involvement, the meeting at his offices, and Lucky's subsequent investment. I told him how the fund would be structured, the fee model and who we would target as investors. Tariq didn't say a word. Instead, he listened attentively until I stopped speaking.

'Interesting. Very interesting indeed. Between you and me, we have also been looking to set up an investment division within Milestone for a while now, so I can see the rationale. Let me have a think about this. I think there may be a way for us to work together.'

We didn't talk about real estate for the rest of the evening. Tariq told me stories of the old days in London with my uncle Ali, many of which were quite amusing. I ate more cheesecake and sipped more tea, until I looked at my watch and realised it was getting rather late.

'Well thank you Tariq for a very pleasant evening. It's been a pleasure.'

'Absolutely', said Tariq. 'I will give your fund idea some thought. Do keep in touch.'

He ordered me a cab and I made my way home.

***

The next morning, Jamal called me at work and he sounded anxious. 'I have some news. There's been a slight hiccup with the fund.'

'What kind of hiccup?'

'Well, it's Lucky and his people. They have changed their mind about seeding the fund.'

My heart sank. 'What? They don't want to go ahead?'

'No, they do. But they want to do things differently to what we originally agreed. They now want to seed the fund with assets rather than cash.'

I was starting to panic. 'What assets do they have in mind?'

'Well, apparently they own four plots in Ras Al Khaimah. They want to use them as seed assets for the fund. It shouldn't be a big problem.'

But it was. Plots of land in Ras Al Khaimah were not exactly the most sought-after, and replacing capital with dead assets was not exactly the ideal start for our new project. I was getting suspicious that Lucky was using the fund as a vehicle to offload bad investments that his group had no hope of selling for a profit. And if it was unlikely that these assets would ever rise in value, it was also unlikely that they would ever generate a return for our investors.

'Jamal, I need to think about this. Let me...' Call waiting buzzed with a number I didn't recognise. 'Jamal, I'm getting another call, I'm going to have to call you back.'

'Ok, sure.'

I answered the waiting number. 'Hello?'

161

'Good morning,' said a gruff Indian voice. 'This is Rav Singh, the Chief Financial Officer of Milestone Properties. Can you speak for a moment?'

I jumped up suddenly. 'Yes, sure, go ahead.'

'I have discussed the proposal that you made to Tariq Sharaf. I would like to meet you to discuss how Milestone can add value to this project. Are you free to meet tonight?'

'Erm, yes, sure.'

'Very good. See you in the lobby at the Dhow Palace at eight pm.' He hung up. I tried to call Jamal back but he didn't answer.

***

That evening after work, I made my way to the Dhow Palace hotel in Bur Dubai. In the small lobby, a large Indian man sat alone, sipping on a cappuccino as he waited. He looked more like a professor than a property executive, with a grey beard and big bushy hair, and dressed in a tweed jacket and brown baggy trousers.

'Rav?'

'Yes, nice to meet you, Adam,' he replied in a quasi-Indian accent. 'Please take a seat. Can I get you anything?'

'No, I'm fine, thanks.'

'Okay. So let's get down to business. Tariq has asked me to tell you that he was very impressed with your fund idea. We have discussed it and we agree it makes a lot of sense. So Tariq has asked me to put a proposal to you.'

'A proposal?'

'Yes, a proposal. Tariq would like you to set up this fund under the Milestone brand. He wants to bring you into the company and will give you a salary and a housing allowance. He will also give you equity in the fund and a share of the management fee. We will provide a pipeline of deals to the fund and act as its exclusive broker. But you must set this up as a *Milestone* fund.'

I was speechless. 'Wow, I really wasn't expecting this. I had only just asked for his opinion. I really need to talk this over with my business partner before I can agree to anything.'

'But there is a condition,' added Rav.

'What kind of condition?'

'Tariq doesn't want anybody else to be involved in this project. He only wants you.' Rav spoke in a robotic tone, devoid of emotion.

'You mean he doesn't want Jamal to be involved?'

'That is correct. Tariq feels that Jamal's participation is not necessary.'

I began to lose my cool. 'But Jamal is my partner and this is our idea!'

'I'm sorry, but this is the proposal I have been asked to put to you.'

'Look, tell Tariq I'm going to have to think about this.'

'Please take your time, but Tariq would like to know this week or the deal is off.' He got up to leave. 'Goodnight.'

Rav left and I sat alone in the lobby in disbelief. Tariq had made me an offer I couldn't really refuse, but in return I was being asked to betray my business partner and mentor. Turning my back on Jamal was going against every shred of conscience I possessed. He had taught me everything I knew about private equity and encouraged me to take this risk in the first place. However, considering that Lucky's involvement was now in jeopardy, there also was a real risk of losing both opportunities. Without Lucky there was no fund, which meant that if I didn't take Tariq's offer I could be missing out on a chance to work with one of the biggest names in the market.

I spent most of the night thinking about it, and by the time the early streaks of morning sunlight were shining through my curtains, I had made a decision. I had to speak to Tariq himself.

'Hey, how are you doing?' asked Tariq after answering my call early that morning.

'I'm okay, thanks. Listen, Tariq, I met up with Rav yesterday, as you know, and I need to discuss...'

Tariq interrupted. 'Why don't you come over to the house so we can have a chat?'

It was too important an offer to pass up. 'I'm on my way.'

The moment I arrived at the house, Akbar was loading up the white Range Rover in the drive with a picnic hamper.

'Hi, Akbar, where is Mr Tariq?'

'Sir is in the kitchen,' he replied.

'Hey, glad you could make it,' said Tariq as I walked inside. 'I want to introduce you to the family.' A pretty middle-aged lady dressed in a chemise and sandals came in behind me.

'Hey, Ayesha, this is Ali's nephew I told you about. Handsome boy, don't you think?'

'Oh hello, it's nice to meet you finally,' said Tariq's wife, Ayesha. 'Are you joining us for lunch today?'

'Yes, if that's okay.'

'Of course! I hope you like strawberry cheesecake.'

'Yes, very much.'

Two little kids rushed into the kitchen screaming with joy. 'And this is little Sabah and Salim.' Tariq picked up Sabah as she struggled to break free. 'Behave, young lady, we have a guest.'

'Okay, daddy,' she replied with the cutest smile.

'Good girl. Now get in the car. We're ready to go.'

'Go where?' I asked.

'We're having lunch at our villa on the Palm. I was hoping you could join us.'

It was an unexpected invitation, but I was no position to turn it down. 'Erm, okay, sure. That would be lovely.'

'Great. Let's go.'

We climbed into the 4x4 one by one. Tariq decided to drive himself, while Akbar sat next to him and I got in the back with Ayesha and the kids. I was secretly quite excited, as I had never actually been on the Palm Jumeirah before. We drove across an intricate network of winding highways and twisting roads towards the marina and the coast. Eventually, the road straightened and I could see the beach disappear below us before we were surrounded by the clear blue ocean.

A warning alarm began to sound in the car: 'Please turn around, please turn around!'

'What's going on? What's that noise?' I asked in a panic.

'Don't worry, it's just the satellite navigation system,' replied Tariq calmly. 'It thinks we're driving into the middle of the ocean. Remember, only a couple of years ago there was no landmass here. It was only the open sea.'

As we continued up the trunk of the palm, it was difficult to believe that this was actually a manmade island. It felt like any other street in Dubai, with palm trees, traffic lights and zebra crossings. Apartment blocks lined the six-lane road on either side, yet there was considerable construction in progress, suggesting that the island was far from finished still. As the 'trunk' ended, we drove towards the fronds of the palm and the villas. And as we entered Frond H, the road became eerily quiet. The giant villas on either side looked deserted, although many boasted gleaming sports cars in their large driveways.

We pulled up at Tariq's villa and there it was, the object of my desires: a beautiful black Porsche 911 Turbo.

'That's my baby,' said Tariq when he noticed me drooling.

'She's beautiful!'

'Yeah, she's a beast. Maybe we can go for a spin if we have time later.'

'Really? That would be amazing!'

'Sure. Come inside. Let me give you the grand tour.'

The villa was enormous. The lounge was infinitely spacious, with a two-storey window that looked out onto the private beach outside the patio. A double spiral staircase ascended high above the marble-floored atrium, and the kitchen was the biggest I had ever seen.

By the time we finished the tour of the house, Akbar had already set out the picnic on the outdoor terrace and we sat down for lunch. To our right was a panoramic view of the Dubai coastline and the towers of the Marina. In the distance ahead I could see the emerging structure of the Atlantis hotel on the outer rim of the Palm, which was now less than a year away from its grand opening.

'What do you say we step out for a spin in the Porsche?' asked Tariq when we had finished lunch.

It was the offer I had been waiting for from the moment I had laid eyes on it. 'Sure, that would be amazing!' I replied immediately.

'Boys and their toys,' said Ayesha, rolling her eyes affectionately.

'Great. We'll be back soon.'

'I haven't taken this baby out for a while,' added Tariq as he started the engine with a mighty roar, which brought an instant smile to my face. We slowly pulled out of the driveway and drove back onto the trunk of the Palm. 'She's a beauty, isn't she?' he asked, hardly accelerating beyond 40 kilometres an hour. I nodded, too excited to speak.

'So tell me, what do you want from your life?' he asked as we left the Palm and headed towards the Jumeirah Beach Road. It was a rather broad question and I wasn't quite sure what he was getting at.

'Well, I want to be successful and wealthy, I guess,' I answered hesitantly.

'Do you believe in the importance of family?'

'Of course,' I said confidently. 'Family is very important in keeping a man grounded.'

He smiled and put his foot down on the accelerator a little more. 'And what is your definition of success?'

'Well, to be good at what you do, I guess.'

'Why? What is the point?'

'Erm, I'm not sure what you mean.'

'What do you want, man?' he asked again, aggressively, and went a little faster.

'A nice house, I guess, and...'

'And what? Tell me!' The speedometer had hit a hundred kilometres an hour and I was starting to get nervous.

166

'A nice car and a good lifestyle?' I shouted, holding on to my seat.

'What car do you want? Be specific!' We hit one twenty.

'A Porsche 911 Turbo like this one! It's the car I always wanted. Can we slow down please, Tariq?'

Tariq ignored my plea. 'Say it like you mean it!' he shouted as we reached a hundred and forty.

'I want a Porsche 911 Turbo!'

'Louder!' screamed Tariq at one sixty-five.

'I want a Porsche 911 Turbo!'

Two hundred. 'Say it with conviction, man!'

'I want a Porsche 911 Turboooooooo!'

'Yes!' said Jamal, finally bringing an end to the scary ordeal. I was almost in tears. We turned around at the next junction and headed back to the Palm. I was shaking for the rest of the journey. I had seen a crazy side of the otherwise calm and collected Tariq, and it totally confused me. But as we parked up at the villa, he acted as if nothing had happened.

'The offer stands,' he whispered before we went back into the house. 'Please let me know by tomorrow afternoon.' I nodded as I tried to recapture my breath.

That night I went home and chewed over the day's insane events. I was still confused about whether I was any closer to making a decision. All I had really learnt was that Tariq was a potential psychopath under the façade of a calm and collected family man. Or had I missed the point completely? Perhaps he had actually done all the talking he wanted to without actually saying a word. He had dangled all of the elements of the good life in front of me and shown me that it was only touching distance away: the house, the loving family and the dream car. I merely needed to reach out and grab it. He had persuaded me that a life in real estate had handed him these luxuries, and he was now indirectly showing me that I, too, could have the trappings of great success if I simply joined him and his empire. Maybe it was the most convincing sales pitch in history.

And so there was only one thing left to do. The following day, I bit my tongue and made the call.

'Good afternoon, Milestone Properties,' answered the receptionist.

'Hi, could I speak with Tariq please?'

'I'm afraid he's not in the office. Can I take a message?'

'Erm, yes please. Can you tell him Adam called? I've thought about the offer and I would like to accept it. He will know what I mean.'

'Of course. I'll pass on the message, sir.'

13

The Property Tour Bus

I had never been as popular at Imperial Bank as the day I announced I was leaving. I suddenly received dozens of 'keep in touch' emails from colleagues I had never even spoken to before; and I was approached at the water cooler by nosy Indians and curious Emiratis, asking me where I was going. I knew what they really wanted to know was whether I was leaving for a higher salary, and, if so, whether I could put in a good word for them too. Company loyalty was a rare thing in the Middle East and even the slightest salary increment was often an incentive to move. But I didn't give them what they wanted. Instead, I decided to keep my new plans a secret, revealing only that I was moving on to bigger and better things. It didn't go down well, but I didn't care.

Since Asim's departure, I had known that my days at Imperial Bank were numbered, so deciding to leave wasn't too difficult. Ever since my eye-opening experience at Cityscape, I had seen the massive potential of Dubai's property market and had desperately wanted a piece of this exciting world. Tariq had presented me with an opportunity to make money with the biggest name in the market behind me, and despite the fact that the Indian mafia would probably soon be out for my head, I was sure I had done the right thing.

The hardest part, of course, would be breaking the news to Jamal. I had been dreading it from the moment I had accepted Tariq's offer, but as much as I tried to avoid it, I knew I would eventually have to man up and tell him. I owed him that much at least. So Jamal and I agreed to meet for a coffee, where I planned to fill him in.

Jamal was uncharacteristically early, which made me even more nervous. I shook his hand and sat down.

'Hey, buddy! What's been going on? You've not been an easy guy to get hold of recently.'

'Yeah, I guess I haven't. Listen, Jamal, I need to tell you something you may not want to hear.'

'Okay, sure. But before you tell me your news, I have some too.'

'Well, do you want to go first?' I asked, buying time.

'Are you sure? You sounded pretty keen to tell me yours.'

'No, please. Go ahead.'

'Okay. Well, it's regarding our fund project,' he sighed. 'I may have to take a back seat in the whole thing, I'm afraid. I met some guys from Silicon Valley a few days ago and they are very keen to set up a technology fund in the Middle East. As my background is in technology, it just seems natural for me to get involved and spend more time on that. I'm perfectly happy to continue giving you support for a real estate fund, but you will have to run the show alone. Otherwise, we could just abandon the whole idea. It's really up to you.'

I couldn't believe it; Jamal had done the deed for me! 'Well, I don't want to move forward without you. This was our project and if you can't be involved, I would rather go and do something else,' I replied decisively.

'I see. Well, if you're comfortable with that, then I think that makes sense.'

'Absolutely. It's no problem at all. I'm sure something new will come my way. But what will you tell Lucky?'

'Don't worry about Lucky, I'll handle him. After that night out at the dance bar, I started having a funny feeling about that guy. Great guy to party with, but I'm not sure he's all clean on the business front, if you know what I mean.'

'I was thinking exactly that, Jamal. I'm glad we're on the same page. You go ahead and run with this tech thing.'

'Thanks, I hope you're not pissed off about this.'

'No, not at all,' I smiled.

'Well, thanks for being so understanding. So tell me, what was your news?'

I paused and smiled. 'You know, Jamal, it doesn't matter that much. It's really not important at all.'

We shook hands and agreed to stay in touch. I left the cafe with a renewed sense of freedom. It was as if a huge burden had been lifted from my shoulders. There was nothing standing in my way now.

***

Lying in bed on the night before my first day at Milestone, I thought about why Tariq had been so eager to hire me. I had no real property or fund management experience, so it wasn't that. Perhaps it was my Oxford education or my investment banking pedigree, which he felt would rub off positively on the culture at Milestone. Or could it have been the vague family connection, which somehow meant I could be trusted in a city of backstabbers and cowboys? But I convinced myself that Tariq had seen something in me that reminded him of a young version of himself, an entrepreneurial flair and a burning ambition to achieve great things. Whatever the real reason was, one thing was certain: he had taken a gamble on me and it was up to me to prove him right.

As part of our deal, I was offered a generous benefits package, including a housing allowance on top of my basic salary. Considering the sky-high cost of renting in the city, the allowance was hefty, and although it was unlikely, we agreed that any residual amount would be given to me as a cash sum. The sensible move would have been to find an apartment in a mid-range neighbourhood outside the popular areas and then pocket the rest as cash. But I wasn't in a sensible mood. I had been waiting for my bachelor pad from the moment I landed in Dubai and I was finally in a position to live the dream. It was time to climb to the top of the social ladder.

In Dubai's social hierarchy, where you lived said everything about who you were and how well you were doing. It was the benchmark of your value and status, and was often among the first questions asked at parties, along with 'What have you flipped recently?' I wanted to be sharing elevators with Russian oligarchs and Bollywood movie stars, not computer engineers from Chennai. I yearned to be a member of Dubai's dynamic young elite and I wouldn't settle for anything less.

So I began a whirlwind tour of the most exclusive neighbourhoods in search of the ultimate bachelor pad. My guide was Nick Edwards, a young Brit who was one of Milestone's best rental agents. Together we looked at apartments in Downtown Dubai, the Jumeirah Lake

Towers and the Greens. Although they were all brand spanking new, nothing I looked at screamed out at me as 'the one'. Many of the apartments were awkwardly shaped or poorly finished, with exposed wires and missing tiles. Others looked out onto a ghastly view of construction sites, or could only be accessed through a perilous maze of sandpits and scaffolding. The thought of risking my life to get home after work every day didn't appeal to me much, so the search went on, and on. After an exhausting day of back-to-back viewings, I had still not decided and Nick was getting frustrated.

'So none of the apartments we've seen today is even a maybe?' he asked desperately as we drove along the Beach Road.

'No, not really, Nick. None of them felt like home.'

Nick looked worried. 'I understand, but I'm kind of running out of options.' He paused to think. 'Okay, listen, I've got one more I want to show you. I'm hoping this one may finally change your mind.'

Our final stop for the day was the mammoth Jumeirah Beach Residences in the Marina. This was a recently completed luxury complex of forty-eight towers that occupied a mile-long stretch of land across the far side of the Marina, overlooking the coast. Billed as the world's largest single-phase residential development, JBR offered a unique cocktail of all of the finest elements of the Dubai lifestyle: beachside living, al fresco dining and a Who's Who of A-list neighbours.

As soon as I walked into the thirtieth-floor apartment, it felt right. There was a huge lounge, two king-size bedrooms and a state-of-the-art kitchen, which alone was the size of my old apartment in London.

'As you can see, it's wonderfully spacious,' said Nick, who could see that I was smitten. 'But I think the real selling point of the apartment is the amazing view.'

I followed him out onto the balcony and the breathtaking sight of the entire Jumeirah Beach and the endless ocean beyond. To our right was the grand Palm Jumeirah in all its glory, and directly below was a poolside terrace where a host of bikini-clad beauties were roasting under the desert sun. Directly below us a Miami Beach-style, kilometre-long stretch of shops, cafés and restaurants ran the length of the complex. Just as the sun began to set gloriously over the Gulf, its rays caused the water to shimmer like a million fireflies, and it wasn't hard for me to say the three important words: 'I'll take it!'

'Great,' said Nick, with a sigh of relief. 'You're lucky, because it's the last one we have in JBR. These apartments are going like hot cakes. I'll get the paperwork ready.'

Nevertheless, my dream apartment came at a substantial cost. On a square-foot basis, I was paying something in the same range as uptown Manhattan or London's Kensington. Unlike those densely populated cities, however, the JBR was in the middle of the desert and it was unlikely that sand would be running out any time soon. But value was a relative term in Dubai. Rents were determined by supply and demand, and considering the waiting list for JBR apartments, prices were likely to rocket higher still in the next few months.

Back in London, I had always been cautious about spending beyond my means. I was a strong believer in luxury as the reward for achievement, and I began to feel guilty that I was sabotaging my values. In Dubai things were different: everybody was spending beyond their means. It was the Mecca of 'buy now, pay later'. And so for the first time in my life, I ditched my financial discipline and went with my gut. Like everybody else, I was sucked in by the lure of the Dubai lifestyle, and was certain that I too would be making millions in no time.

As soon as I received the keys, I spent an entire weekend decking out my new home with the latest and trendiest furniture and toys I could find. I bought a pool table, a fussball table, a basketball hoop and a giant flat-screen television with state-of-the-art surround-sound speakers. I bought funky lamps and chairs and ornaments. I indulged in every must-have gadget on the market, from an iPod to a PlayStation to a remote-controlled helicopter. I couldn't actually afford any of it yet, of course, but having been offered four credit cards on the back of my new salary, that didn't matter much. After a busy weekend of retail indulgence, my bachelor pad was finally ready.

But there was still one important element missing. After putting together the finishing touches on the apartment, I jumped in a taxi and made my way towards the flagship Porsche showroom on the Sheikh Zayed Road. Walking through the garage was like taking a stroll through paradise. For me, a Porsche was more than just a flash car to

173

pick up chicks; it represented the last missing piece in the jigsaw to propel me to the elite of the Dubai social pyramid. Every car gleamed brilliantly under the intense spotlights, calling out to be admired and caressed. Carreras, Boxsters and Cayennes competed fiercely for my affection. However, I had only had eyes for one ever since I could remember, and there it was, teasing me as I approached: a stunning white Porsche 911 Turbo. I stared at it longingly for a while, before I began gently to run my finger along the smooth contours of its body – until I was rudely interrupted.

'Can I help you?' asked the skinny salesman in an Australian accent.

'No, thank you. I'm just looking,' I replied sheepishly.

'I see. Just looking.' He rolled his eyes sarcastically. 'If I could only have a dirham for every time I have heard that one.'

'Excuse me?'

'Oh, nothing, sir. Please do keep *looking*. I'll be over here with a *real* customer in case you need anything.'

I couldn't believe my ears. 'How do you know I'm not a real customer?'

'You just told me you are only looking, sir.' The sarcasm in his tone was starting to annoy me.

'Well, "looking" often leads to buying, in case you didn't know,' I huffed.

'Sir, how I wish it did. But from my experience, lookers and buyers are quite different species.'

That was the final straw. 'If you don't mind me saying, I think you're a bit out of order treating your customers this way.'

He grinned annoyingly. 'Do you know where you are, sir?'

'What?'

'I asked if you knew where you were, sir?'

'I'm in a bloody Porsche garage!'

'Not just any Porsche garage, sir. You are in the busiest Porsche garage in the world. These cars are almost flying out of the doors

174

every day. And as a result of this wonderful fact, my wife has a collection of the latest Louis Vuitton handbags and a wardrobe full of Jimmy Choo shoes in every colour of the rainbow. My kids have a Nintendo, an Xbox and a PlayStation – the grand slam of games consoles. I live in a five-bedroom villa overlooking the beach. So tell me, sir. Do you really think I need your business?'

'I don't believe this!'

'Believe it, sir.'

'Well, what if I gave you a cheque today? Something tells me you would still gladly take it.'

'Perhaps I would, sir. But you still wouldn't get a car.'

'Why not?'

'Because there is a three-month waiting list, sir. Like I said, this is the busiest garage in the world. There's only so many cars our facility can produce, so I'm afraid you would have to wait. So will sir be putting a deposit down today?'

I hesitated. As tempted as I was to teach this cocky salesman a lesson, I allowed reason to prevail and refrained from doing something I might regret. 'No. I won't.'

'I didn't think so. Now if you will excuse me, I believe a *buyer* is looking for me.'

As he strolled away, I composed myself and touched the car once last time.

'I'll be back, my love. I'll be back…'

***

My first day at Milestone was to be an official induction to the Dubai property market. Tariq believed it was important for all joiners to gain a first-hand look at the city's developments to touch and feel what they would be selling. I was looking forward to it. I knew of most of the new projects already, as they were plastered across newspapers and billboards every day, but I had not been into the heart of the construction sites to see the progress close up. This would surely be an eye-opener.

I was joined on the day by six other people who had been recently recruited into the sales team. We piled into the Milestone minibus and started our adventure. Our tour guides were Sharon and Amy, two bubbly blondes from Liverpool who worked as business development managers in the Milestone projects team. They looked like sisters, except that Sharon was much shorter and larger than the skinny and rather lanky Amy. Together they put on a well-rehearsed double act straight out of a British seaside holiday camp.

'Gooood morning! How is everybody today?' asked Sharon on the speakerphone in her thick Northern accent. 'Welcome to the Milestone tour bus! I'm Sharon and this is my colleague Amy, and we will be your guides on a whirlwind tour of three of Dubai's most iconic developments. Feel free to ask questions, and if you need the bathroom I would ask you to wait until we alight. Let's have a great day!'

I sat next to the window at the back of the bus to get the best view. Next to me was a young, pasty Englishman dressed in a baggy suit and a pink necktie, with an oversized knot.

'This is quite exciting, isn't it?' he said in a Cockney accent.

'Yes, it is,' I replied politely.

'I'm Paul Potters.' He extended his hand. 'I'll be working in the commercial sales team.'

'Nice to meet you, Paul,' I replied and shook his hand. 'So are you joining Milestone from another property firm?'

'Nope. I have no property experience whatsoever,' he replied smugly.

'Are you serious?'

'I swear, none at all. This all quite new to me.'

I was quite confused. 'So what were you doing before this?'

'Believe it or not, I was a golf coach at the Dubai Golf Club. I never even thought about property as a career,' he chuckled.

'So how on earth did you get this job?'

'Well, Tariq is an avid golfer and we met in the club house one afternoon. We started talking, and he asked me if I wanted to make some real money. After chatting for about an hour I was offered the job. I couldn't believe it!'

I couldn't believe it either. Why on earth would Tariq hire a former golf coach? Surely somebody with experience of real estate in the region would have been a more sensible candidate. I began to question whether Tariq was the shrewd businessman I thought he was after all.

I probed a little further. 'So, Paul, what kind of people were you coaching?'

'Mainly very senior guys: CEOs of multinational firms, chairmen of property companies, lawyers, consultants, bankers, and even some sheikhs. You name it, I've taught them to swing. A lot of them are good friends and I can still freelance at the weekends. So happy days!'

The penny dropped. Paul brought something valuable to Milestone that few salespeople could. It was an old business adage that the best contacts were made on the golf course. By recruiting Paul, Tariq had effectively bought direct access to a database of high-profile contacts and potential customers. Paul's Rolodex was the cream of wealthy expats and Emiratis. And a man who could improve your golf swing could always be trusted, so even though Paul knew little about property, his relationships now belonged to Milestone. It was a stroke of business genius.

We drove into the centre of an enormous construction site with hundreds of cranes and dump trucks working actively around the growing foundations of dozens of towers, all at varying stages in the construction process. This was the beginnings of the Downtown Dubai district, a five-hundred-acre development that was to become the most valuable square kilometre of real estate in the world. We parked outside the modern sales centre, the only completed building on the site.

As we entered, we were greeted by Noura, a pretty young Emirati woman dressed in a traditional *abaya*. She asked us to gather round a full-scale model of the development before beginning her presentation.

'As you can see, the development will include the Dubai Mall, the planet's largest shopping and entertainment complex; The Residences, a series of high-rise apartment towers; and the Old Town, a low-rise traditional residences community...'

Her pitch was flawless and she spoke excellent English with a distinctive Californian accent.

'...When it's finished, it will boast nine world-class hotels, nineteen residential towers and thirty thousand homes...'

She pointed at the centre of the model, where a giant silver, needle-like structure protruded high into the air.

'...The grand centrepiece of the development will be the incredible Burj Dubai, or 'Dubai Tower', which will be the tallest building in the world. This mighty skyscraper will be surrounded by restaurants and cafés, and will feature the globe's largest dancing fountain...'

The height of the Burj Dubai model compared to the surrounding buildings was astonishing. It looked like a futuristic icicle, pointing at the heavens as if to make God aware that Dubai had arrived.

'If you turn around, you will see the building is already in progress.' We looked through the giant windows to see the skeleton of a giant structure. The foundations of the actual Burj Dubai had been laid and even at this early stage, it looked colossal. 'Once it is finished, on a clear day you will be able to see Iran from the observation deck,' smiled Noura.

'I have a question,' said Paul, interrupting her in full flow.

She paused. 'Sure, please go ahead.'

'What if I feel like a pizza?'

Noura looked baffled. 'Excuse me?'

'You know, pizza. What if I lived right at the very top of the building? High up, way up there.' He pointed at the tip of the model.

'Yes...'

'How could the pizza possibly stay warm? Surely it will take ages for the pizza guy to get all the way up there!' Despite the giggle that rippled through the crowd, Noura was stumped for an answer.

'I'm not sure if the architects had thought about pizza guys,' she smiled.

'Well, they should have. And not just pizza. Burgers, coffees, heck, even fried chicken.' We all erupted with laughter. In his own

178

way, Paul had exposed an important design flaw. Building a tower as tall as the Burj came with a plethora of new and complicated logistical challenges. Although cold pizza was not the highest priority, the fact that Noura didn't have a constructive reply was perhaps a worrying sign that certain details had been overlooked.

We eventually drove out of the emerging Downtown district to our next destination. Our minivan passed a large queue of South Asian labourers in blue overalls and yellow hard hats, waiting for a bus to take them back to their labour camps after an all-night work shift. Construction in Dubai was around the clock, and these poor men would soon be replaced by a fresh batch who would continue where they left off in a seamless, never-ending ordeal. They looked empty and soulless, as if their monotonous lives had sucked dry every last drop of their humanity. Some of them held hands, desperate for some companionship and assurance in their otherwise meaningless and dispensable existence.

I remembered reading an article back in London about the unspeakable trials these men had gone through to get to the Emirates. They were made to live in horrific conditions at the behest of their unscrupulous employers, who confiscated their passports and withheld their pay without warning. They were desperate and powerless, and often their only escape was suicide. Stories of blue-collar workers jumping from building sites or slashing their wrists were increasingly common, although allegedly hushed up by the authorities. Such was the cost of earning a little extra money to feed their poverty-stricken families at home, many of whom they did not see or hear from for years at a time.

Glimpsing their forlorn faces so close up, my heart sank and I swallowed hard to get rid of the lump which suddenly formed in my throat. It was easy to forget that these were the men who were building Dubai, brick by brick with their bare hands. Without them, there would be no city. I had never been so close to their world before; most expats in the city went about their daily business without crossing paths with these labourers. But as they watched us pass them through their tired eyes, for the first time I saw them as real human beings with needs and dreams like the rest of us.

'So how did everybody enjoy that?' asked Sharon as we hit the Sheikh Zayed Road. 'That Burj Dubai is going to be something special when it's complete. Don't you guys think?' We all nodded in agreement, except Paul, who had made his stance quite clear.

Our next stop was the Dubailand sales centre on the Emirates Road.

'Dubailand will be the biggest theme park in the world: a theme park of theme parks,' said the Emirati representative as we walked through the showroom. 'Within Dubailand will be forty-five world-class projects, which will include golf courses, super-hero worlds, eco-tourism districts, autodromes, an Andalusian spa complex, a Las Vegas-style strip, a snow mountain, art galleries, the largest zoo in the Middle East and the Mall of Arabia – the largest mall ever built.'

The sheer scale of the Dubailand project was mind-boggling, and the miniature model of the development was the largest and most intricate I had ever seen. There were dozens of mini-projects within the complex. The Falcon City of Wonders featured life-size replicas of the planet's most iconic buildings, including the Taj Mahal, the Eiffel Tower and Big Ben. Bawadi was a fifty-five billion dollar strip with fifty-one themed hotels offering sixty thousand new rooms. US theme park and entertainment giants like Universal and Marvel had already signed up to build their own parks within Dubailand. There were full-size dinosaurs, indoor mountain ranges and giant roller-coasters. When it was finished in 2012, this mighty pleasure park would make Disneyland look like a kindergarten playpen.

While I walked around the enormous scale model, it suddenly struck me how important Dubailand was to the future of Dubai. The city's tourism sector was critical to its sustainability over the coming years, and Dubailand was the cornerstone of this strategy. If Dubai was going to fulfil its lofty ambitions of attracting 15 million overseas visitors, three times as many as New York City, it needed something spectacular to bring them in. This larger-than-life pleasure dome was the key to Dubai's aim to be the world's leading tourist destination, and there was little doubt from what I had seen today that it would claim that crown in no time.

'Psst, over here!' said a voice behind me. 'Psst, here, here!' I peered around my shoulder curiously.

'Yes?'

'So is it true?' asked a small, unassuming Indian woman. She was a member of our party but we hadn't formally met.

'Is what true?'

'Is what everybody is saying true? That you are Tariq's son.'

'Pardon?'

'Somebody told me you were his son. That's how you got the best-paying job in Milestone.'

'No, I'm not his son. Who told you that? And how do you know what I'm being paid?'

'Everybody is saying you are being paid more than anybody and you have been given an apartment.'

'Well, that's none of your business!' I said assertively.

'Okay. But can you do something for me, please?'

'What?'

'Can you tell Tariq that the salary is a bit low? If he can give me extra one thousand dirhams then that will be better. Okay?'

I couldn't believe her cheek. 'No, I won't tell him that!'

'But he will listen to you. You are his son.'

'I'm not his son!' She shrugged her shoulders and scuttled off to join the rest of the group.

The final stop on the journey was the upcoming Culture Village project, towards the older part of the city. The Culture Village was modelled around the old architecture of Arabia, offering a rustic experience with traditional wind towers, cobbled stone walkways and creek-side souks. In a city often accused of submitting to soulless modernity, the Culture Village aimed to instil some much-needed history and heritage to redress the balance.

'The centrepiece of Culture Village will be Palazzo Versace, a decadent condominium resort with two hundred and sixteen hotel rooms and one hundred and eighty-eight apartments decorated completely in Versace opulence.' Our guide this time was a chubby Emirati man of no more than 20. 'The Palazzo Versace will also feature the world's first refrigerated beach, so visitors will always remain cool.'

'Sorry, I'm confused,' I interrupted. 'What has Palazzo Versace got to do with Culture Village?'

'The architecture of the Palazzo Versace is like an old Roman palace, which fits in with the cultural heritage of the master project,' he replied, in what seemed like an off-the-cuff response.

'Yes, but doesn't that dilute the Arabian theme? I thought the point of Culture Village is to promote Arabian culture.'

He started to look rather nervous. 'I'm afraid I will have to get back to you on that.'

The truth was that Culture Village was yet another example of 'faux Arabia' – a modern attempt to recreate the Middle East of yesterday, albeit with air conditioning and Starbucks. It wasn't particularly convincing.

'I have a question about the refrigerated beach,' said Brenda, a red-haired woman in her fifties who would be joining the residential sales team.

'Erm, sure,' the guide replied nervously.

'It's a great idea, but it doesn't sound very environmentally friendly.'

'Well, we will surely do whatever we can to ensure that the process is efficient and no energy is wasted.'

'Can you explain how exactly this will be done?'

'I don't know the exact dynamics. I will need to come back to you on that, if that's okay.'

In a few embarrassing minutes, we had already poked a number of holes in the plans, and our poor guide looked out of his depth. It wasn't his fault, of course. His role was simply to mesmerise and impress visitors with the grandeur of the project. Just like a magician astounding his audience, we were being drawn into the dream. And like every great magic trick, knowing how it was done would only ruin the illusion. Nobody ever asked 'How?' in Dubai; this was a question for the overpaid expat engineers and architects to worry about. What mattered was the mirage, and our niggling questions were certainly not going down well.

As we made our way back to the office that evening, I bumped into Tariq, who was leaving for the day.

'Have you enjoyed the induction so far?' he asked with a smile.

'Yes, it's certainly been very interesting to see these projects close up.'

'Good. So, I am assuming that you are now an expert on the Dubai property market?'

'Well, I wouldn't say an expert, but I'm certainly more familiar.'

'Which means you are ready to make some money. By the way, I have a surprise for you tomorrow before you officially start here at Milestone.'

I was intrigued. 'Really, what is that?'

'You'll see tomorrow. Good night.'

***

The next morning, Rav was waiting for me outside the office next to one of the Milestone company cars. 'Good morning. Are you ready to go?'

'Yes, but where are we going?' I asked.

'Tariq didn't tell you?'

'No, he didn't.'

'Ah, well then, let me just say if you think you have seen Dubai, you haven't seen anything yet.'

I got into the car and we headed towards the Marina. We finally turned off the Beach Road and down a long driveway to the Nakheel head office. A tall Emirati man greeted us at the entrance and led Rav and me down a long corridor towards the back of the building. And there waiting for us was the biggest helicopter I had ever seen.

'Bon voyage!' said Rav as I strapped myself into the passenger seat. The pilot was a middle-aged American with a bushy grey moustache, sporting a cap and flying jacket.

'Hi, I'm Chuck and I'll be your pilot today. Are you ready for the ride?' he asked and I responded with a thumbs up. Within moments we were away.

The chopper rose high up above the buildings of the Dubai Marina and headed downtown along the Jumeirah Beach and past the villas of Umm Sequim and Jumeirah. It was a glorious day as the sun's brilliant rays shimmered off the glass panes of the luxury towers below us. We hovered past the sail-like Burj Al Arab, a glowing white apparition on the horizon. I could see the tiny white Rolls-Royces scuttling across the mini-causeway from the hotel to the mainland. We passed over the Burj's famous helipad, where Tiger Woods had stood three years before to promote Brand Dubai. Directly below us passed hundreds of mansions with swimming pools and tennis courts, separated by an intricate network of streets and alleys. We then bore right, across the Sheikh Zayed Road and into the emerging Downtown and Business Bay developments. The early foundations of the Burj Dubai sat uncontested in the centre of the massive construction site as hundreds of cranes worked fastidiously to erect Dubai's proudest monument.

We turned around and continued back up towards the completed towers of the Marina. From this vantage point, it was nothing but a chaotic urban jungle of skyscrapers, huddled together within touching distance of each other. On the waters below nestled dozens of yachts and speedboats, a few making their way to the open expanse of the Persian Gulf. We continued towards the coast and flew directly over the JBR, where I spotted my own apartment; one of thousands of tiny black windows above the mile-long stretch of beach, where clusters of sunbathers lay soaking up the rays.

We then flew out over the coast and above the trunk of the mighty Palm Jumeirah. From this unique perspective the sheer grandeur of the manmade wonder was astonishing, the tree shape of the island unmistakable and dozens of sprouting towers rising out of the reclaimed land below. The pilot took us further still into the ocean beyond the palm, where a random scattering of patches of sand appeared. They looked like the pieces of an unfinished jigsaw puzzle, scattered across the surface of the clear blue waters.

'What is that below us?' I asked Chuck over my headset.

'Welcome to The World!'

He pulled back and we darted upwards. As we rose higher and higher, I saw something quite amazing. The little patches below somehow magically came together to create a crude outline of the countries of the Earth. They were all undeveloped as yet, except one between 'northern Europe' and 'the USA'. On it sat a beautiful mansion surrounded by luscious palm trees, flawless green lawns and a giant swimming pool. It looked the hidden lair of a Bond villain.

Hovering three thousand feet above the city was strangely liberating. I felt calmer and more composed than I had for a long time, unperturbed by the maddening crowds below me. As we passed every project vying to defy the limitations of the harsh desert environment, the gargantuan scale of the Dubai project was fully evident for the first time. I was astonished at first, but I began to think about things I hadn't considered before. Was any of this really necessary? Could Dubai really swallow all this construction? Was there actually any method to the madness? Was it ever going to end?

Sheikh Mohammed had surely made his point; there was nothing left to prove. From up here it was clear that the fine line between ambition and insanity had been crossed. What was once awe-inspiring had now turned into a crazy obsession; the experiment was out of control. Dubai had always justified its building frenzy on the premise of 'if you build it, they will come', and so far it had worked, with new residents arriving every day to seek their own piece of the dream. But it was a fickle premise. What if they stopped coming? Dubai's grand plan relied on the faith of the punters, and faith couldn't last for ever. All it would take was a single event for this place to tumble like a house of cards.

For the first time, I saw that Dubai was not invincible. I desperately hoped that I was wrong and that my scepticism was unfounded. But something in the back of my mind convinced me that I wasn't. And it scared the hell out of me.

185

14

Boiler Room

Tariq was an old-school businessman in a brave new world. Having started Milestone from humble beginnings, he had single-handedly built the company into the property powerhouse it was today. He had learnt his trade in the school of hard knocks and through years of sweat and graft, which had made him shrewd and highly respected. He remained a firm believer in mitigating risk and keeping costs low. While his competitors took lavish office space, spent generously on state-of-the-art technology and hired an army of salespeople and assistants, Milestone remained largely unchanged from the company it was before the boom. Its head office was a modest space in an office block on the Sheikh Zayed Road. The computers were outdated and barely functional, and the phones were basic. Tariq was not distracted by technology or expensive gimmicks; instead, he remained focused on one thing alone – closing the deal.

The sales room at Milestone felt much like the trading floor at Goldman Sachs. It was a tense boiler room where focused salespeople spent their entire day glued to the phones, selling hard and closing deals. As space in the office was limited, the sales team sat packed together like sardines in a tin. Some joiners even had to share desks until they proved themselves with a sale. The phones rang constantly from eight in the morning until late in the evening and each time they rang, hungry salespeople jumped on them like cheetahs on a wildebeest, hoping desperately it was a floor buyer or investor looking for a whole building to flip. The level of property experience amongst the team varied substantially, from the hungry novice to the seasoned realtor, but they were united by one overarching purpose: a burning desire to make money.

Successful selling at Milestone was often about picking up the phone first, as nine times out of ten there was a deal waiting at the other end. It was a game of reflexes over substance, although few admitted this publicly. Salespeople wanted all the credit they could get for their brilliance and ability to bring in business whenever they closed a deal. The prize was not only a nice commission but bragging rights over their jealous colleagues.

With such fierce competition and high expectations, salespeople were expected to stay at their desks every waking hour and sell, sell, sell. In Tariq's view, coffee breaks and lunch hours were a sign of weakness, so salespeople would often have to conjure up excuses just to pop out to grab a sandwich or use the toilet. One of the most common and amusing red herrings for a cheeky cigarette was that a big client was waiting outside in his car to hand over a cheque. But soon enough everybody was using it, and when nobody ever came back with a cheque, the excuse quickly lost any shred of credibility. Soon the sales team stopped taking breaks altogether, and it wasn't unusual to see a salesperson collapse at his desk out of dehydration or malnourishment – to the delight of his colleagues, as it meant one less person to compete with when the phone rang.

A large array of nationalities was represented on the sales floor at Milestone. Each salesperson was like an ambassador for his or her respective nation, navigating fellow countryfolk through the rocky waters of the Dubai property market. Tariq pushed for his salespeople to be considered as consultants to their clients, as opposed to merely sales reps. This implied complete trust and was the best way to secure repeat business, since confused clients became dependent on the wisdom of their Milestone guru. It seemed to work well, each of Milestone's salespeople developing a loyal client base who believed that the firm was working in their best interest to make them a fortune.

Rav introduced me to each member of the team on my first day. There were two young Lebanese men, both called George, who looked almost identical with slicked-back hair, crotch-hugging trousers and perfectly manicured facial hair. They spoke with a strong Arabic accent, starting most sentences with *yaani* or *yalla*, and had gained a reputation in the office as a double act, often working on deals together. Their clients were a cross-section of the Arabic-speaking world and although they knew very little about real estate, they were doing rather well by virtue of their mother tongue and tireless work ethic.

Next to them sat Omid from Iran, a tall, slim, understated man in his mid-thirties. He didn't speak much English, but spent all of his day glued to his phone with his mysterious Iranian clients. Nobody knew who they were, but there were rumours at Milestone that he had sold property to President Ahmadinejad and Ayatollah Khomeini; rumours that he never refuted or denied. It was well known that Iranians were among the biggest buyers of property in Dubai, so Omid was sure to be making a fortune despite his modest and unassuming demeanour.

Emma was a tall, blonde English girl from Shropshire who spoke with a seductive upper-class accent. She was the daughter of a lord and had come to Dubai after her degree at Cambridge to 'expand her horizons'. She had fallen into real estate sales by sheer coincidence, but she was now the preferred conduit for middle-class British couples looking for holiday homes and Western expats searching for somewhere to invest for retirement. She would often be invited to brunches and dinners, and hobnobbed with the cream of British expatriate society. She hoped to marry one day and breed horses on her own farm, and with the amount of money she had already made, her dream surely wasn't too far away.

Ashan was an older man from a small village in Southern India who wore the same grey, ill-fitting suit to the office every day. He had spent most of his career as an IT consultant, but had lost his job and seen an opportunity in property. His clients today were wealthy Indian industrialists and Bollywood actors, all of whom he called 'sir'. Ashan was a consistent top biller at Milestone, pulling in the sales numbers and making himself a nice fortune in the process. He saved most of what he earned and sent much of it back home to his parents in India, where they were enjoying their status as the richest peasants in the village.

The director and dreaded overlord of the sales team was an obnoxious Brit called Edward Quirk. A middle-aged man from London with boozy eyes and bony fingers, he was divorced and lived alone, and the stories around the office suggested his penchant was to pay for companionship. He spoke in a cold, patronising tone and broke down his sentences into monosyllabic words, as if his audience were morons. However, his impressive sales record was indisputable, and few clients saw through the fake smiles and feigned belly laughs as he played the role of the slimy estate agent to perfection. Perhaps this was because his clients, as most buyers in Dubai, were in fact stupid and needed a pushy salesman to make the buying decisions on their behalf.

Edward simply smelled their vulnerability and took advantage, making himself a tidy fortune in the process.

But when he was not closing a sale, the glossy exterior faded away to reveal a grumpy, detestable monster who became the bane of anybody who dared to step in his path. Edward knew how to wind up just about everybody in the company. He would sit in team meetings though uninvited, interrupt a client meeting just as a cheque was being signed, and generally hassle and annoy anybody who was trying to get some real work done. His management technique revolved around taking every opportunity to belittle his minions. In his opinion, this was the best way to keep them in line and win their loyalty. It didn't always work. Despite the bitter rivalry and competitiveness between salespeople, there was one common thread that acted as a universal binding force across the sales floor: a loathing of Edward Quirk.

Of course, not everybody showed it to his face. Out of fear, many gave him the respect and importance he demanded. They laughed at his crude and often sexually explicit jokes and succumbed to his scolding, while others just tried to stay out of his way. Edward could smell fear, and if you showed too much weakness he would come down on you like a meteor shower of disparagement. I quickly learned that the best way to handle him was to treat him as an equal at all costs, and to avoid showing even the slightest sign of vulnerability. This way he only ever approached me for work-related matters, or avoided speaking to me at all.

All that divided the savagery of the sales floor from the more humane environment of the business development team was a single glass wall, and fortunately my desk was on the safer side of this battle line. The head of the team was Rav Singh, Tariq's CFO and all-round nice guy. As a member of senior management, Rav was a mirror image of the obnoxious Edward. He was approachable and helpful, and was well respected as a father figure by his team. I reported to Rav and he would be my guide and mentor as I toiled the muddy waters of Dubai's real estate quagmire.

The role of business development was to source good inventory for the sales team to sell. This required building strong relationships with developers so that they would offer their best stock, preferably on an exclusive basis. Considering that Milestone was one of the biggest names in the brokerage market and every developer's aim was to sell inventory as fast as possible, business development was hardly the most challenging job. This explained the more relaxed atmosphere on this side of the glass partition, as working hours were often broken up with random games of I Spy and the occasional singsong, much to the disdain of the ever-busy sales team.

Your overall standing in the Milestone hierarchy depended on one variable alone: how much money you were bringing in the door. There was no hiding from the numbers. Every deal closed was listed on a giant whiteboard on the sales floor, and each salesperson was ranked monthly according to the commissions they had earned for the company. But it was not always just the sales team's names on the board; anybody could sell at Milestone. It was not unusual for the ranking board to feature the name of somebody from IT or admin who had known someone who wanted a floor in a tower in the Marina and had closed a deal. Indeed, to see a non-sales employee ranked higher was the ultimate insult to a struggling salesperson. Milestone fostered a cut-throat environment where only the fittest survived.

The sales team was divided into two: the commercial team and the residential team. The residential team generally sold to less sophisticated retail or 'mom and pop' investors who invested small sums into studios or one-bedroom apartments. Their sales were slow and steady, small fry compared to the mighty commercial team. Dubai's self-confessed Masters of the Universe, every broker's aspiration was to work in commercial sales. As most floor or building buyers were investors in commercial property, they naturally worked on the biggest deals and earned the highest commissions.

The director of the commercial sales team was Connor McQueen, a six-foot-seven American from Michigan. He was nicknamed the 'human skyscraper' for obvious reasons, and the irony that a man this size was selling multi-storey towers was always amusing. Connor looked like the archetypal jock – the kind of guy who was the captain of the college football team and slept with all the cheerleaders. His charm and sheer size were enough to make him unforgettable to his clients. A white face and a North American accent always went down well in this part of the world, and Connor milked both to his advantage. He was doing more business than anybody else at Milestone and was consistently the company's number one performer.

On my first day in the office, Tariq asked me to spend some time with Connor to get a feel for the business and learn the ropes.

'Look, buddy, it's not rocket science. Let me put it this way, we're basically glorified drug dealers,' said Connor with a straight face.

'Did you say drug dealers?'

'Yeah, man. We're street hustlers, lookin' to make a quick buck.' He smiled.

'I'm sorry, Connor, I'm completely lost.'

'Look, what's the key to being a good drug dealer?'

'I'm not sure. I've never been one.'

'Rule number one: get your client hooked. You have to give a little to get a lot. You know, just give them a taste of the good stuff. Right? It's the same with selling real estate in Dubai. You sell the client something small, like a studio apartment, and promise him a quick exit. You know, just enough to get him high. He buys, you help him flip it, he makes some money. Bada bing, bada bang. He's fucking jumping with joy. You made him money for nothing. He's over the fuckin' moon and he loves you like a son. But the most important thing is he's hooked.'

It was starting to make sense.

'So now you got him by the balls. He sees easy money. He smells it. So you up-sell him, maybe a one- or two-bedroom apartment. You do the same again, get him an exit and make him some more quick returns. Now he's fucking jumping over mountains! So now you tell him to buy three apartments, ten, twenty, a floor, a building. Do you get where I'm going with this?'

'Yeah, I think so.'

'And the wonder of it all is that we make money on every transaction. So the more he buys and sells, the more commission we make. It's a beautiful thing.'

I decided to play devil's advocate. 'Okay, but tell me, Connor, what if you can't get him an exit? What if there are no buyers and the investor can't sell and gets stuck?'

191

Connor demeanour changed as if I had said the unthinkable. 'Then the salesperson is not doing their job. We link buyers with sellers. We create a secondary market. Right? If there is no demand, we make the demand. There's always somebody out there who's willing to buy something a seller is selling. We just gotta find him and make him buy it. Simple.'

So a salesperson's job was to find the next fool and convince him to buy at any cost. I think I had the hang of it. That afternoon, Connor and I headed out for lunch at a nearby café on the Sheikh Zayed Road, where I decided to find out a little more about him.

'So, Connor, tell me how you ended up here at Milestone. It's a long way from home for you, isn't it?'

'Fuckin' long way. I was in a dead-end job as an encyclopedia salesman. I decided to pack it in and travel across the Middle East on my own a few years ago, you know, trying to find myself or some shit. So I ended up in Dubai and bumped into Tariq at a friend's barbeque. We got talking about Dubai property, and he tells me "Dubai is like Rome". I'm like "how?". So he's like "It's going to be the greatest city in the world". Next thing I know he's offered me a job. I needed the money, so I thought, what have I got to lose? And boom, here I am.'

'Connor, can I ask you something?'

'Sure, buddy, shoot.'

'Is there a girl called Alesia who works at Milestone?'

'Hot Alesia with the sexy legs?'

I assumed we were talking about the same girl. 'Yeah, I guess that's her.'

'There was, yeah. She left recently. The rumour was she was a bit of an entrepreneur and had a few other projects on the side. Some say she even had another job. Beats me. All I know is she was freakin' gorgeous, a real knockout. Do you know her?'

'No, I just met her once. Very briefly.'

'Lucky you!' he winked. 'Anyway, listen, I gotta get back to work, but I hope with my pearls of wisdom you'll be closing that Marina plot in no time.'

'What Marina plot?' I asked as he got up to leave.

Connor froze. 'What? Nobody has told you about the Marina plot yet? Jeez, that should have been the first thing you learned here. The Marina plot is the Holy Grail!'

I was intrigued. 'What do you mean?'

Connor sat back down and lowered his voice. 'It's the last prime piece of land available in the Dubai Marina. The best damn plot looking over the Persian Gulf. Don't ask how we got it, but between you and me, it came through Tariq's connections at the highest level.' He winked.

'You mean from the sheikh?' I whispered.

'My lips are sealed.'

I read between the lines. 'So what's the deal with it?'

'Well, whoever finds a buyer will make at least a million dollars in commission. Everybody at Milestone is secretly working on it, whether they tell you so or not. It's like a bank vault waiting to get robbed. You sell this plot, you're made, buddy. Good luck!'

I salivated at the thought and thanked him for the tip.

My desk at Milestone was tucked away in a cosy corner near the business development team. It wasn't a separate office as I had hoped for, but a deliciously soft leather swivel chair and a panoramic view of the Sheikh Zayed Road made up for that. Directly behind my desk was a giant panoramic map of the city, which covered the breadth of the back wall. It featured all the existing communities like Emirates Living, the Marina and Jumeirah, as well as most of Dubai's up-and-coming developments. As I stood in front of it, my eye was immediately drawn to the palm trilogy that dominated much of the vast coastline. The Palm Jumeirah was dwarfed by the Palm Jebel Ali and the even larger protruding Palm Deira. Hovering between the Palms was the cluster of World islands, and to the far left of the map another peculiar landmass extended outwards and around the Palm Jebel Ali like a giant dinosaur claw. This was the newly announced Waterfront, which was planned to house a further 1.5 million people, the largest manmade development in the world. There was hardly any open desert remaining on the map, and it was only a matter of time before the little that did remain was transformed into the next mega-project.

My business cards were waiting for me on my desk as soon as I arrived. I took one out of the box and stared proudly at my new title: *Head of Investments*. It oozed status and importance. I smiled at how far I had come. Less than three years ago, I was a humble analyst at the bottom of a steep and slippery career ladder. Today, I was the head of a business division in the leading company in the globe's fastest-growing market. In Dubai, it didn't matter that I had no property experience. At the age of 27, I was at the peak of my career and it felt incredible.

After my induction and a lesson in sales from Connor, I was raring to go. As a first step, I decided that developing close relationships with developers would be a crucial element for the success of the fund, as they would provide the important pipeline of projects to invest in once I had raised the capital. Milestone's most intimate business relationship was with a developer called Signature Properties. Tariq was a tennis partner with the CEO, who in turn had offered Milestone exclusivity to sell three buildings, so I thought a meeting with Signature would be a good place to start. But apart from business, Signature Properties was the talk of the Milestone office for another reason too.

'I heard you have an appointment with Signature Properties tomorrow,' said Sharon one morning. 'Is that true?'

'Yep, at eleven am tomorrow,' I replied as I typed up an email.

'Who are you meeting with there?'

'Erm, some salesperson I think.'

'Do you have a name?'

I stopped typing and looked at Sharon curiously. 'Is it important?'

'I was just asking, that's all.'

I ruffled through my papers to find the name, in the hope that she would let me work in peace. 'Farishta Hijazi. Do you know her?'

'Farishta! I see.'

'Ooh, Farishta!' echoed Amy, who sat beside her.

'Well, just be careful,' warned Sharon.

'Careful? What do you mean?'

'Farishta is the head of sales at Signature. She also has something of a reputation.'

'What kind of reputation?' I asked sternly.

'Face of an angel, heart of a devil. She will eat you alive if you're not careful.'

'Eat you alive she will,' added Amy.

'Ladies, I'm going to meet her to discuss business, not to ask her out on a date!'

'Ah yes, that's how it always starts,' said Sharon. '"Just business" they all say. But soon enough she will have you eating out of her little palm.'

'Out of her palm, yes,' added Amy again.

'Surely you guys are having me on,' I said dismissively.

'Do you know what Farishta means in Arabic?' asked Sharon.

'No, I don't,' I replied, rolling my eyes.

'It means angel. And she's the angel of broken hearts, is what she is.'

'Broken hearts, yes,' said Amy.

The routine was starting to irritate me. 'And how do you know all this?'

Sharon looked around to see if anybody was listening. 'She used be Connor's girlfriend,' she whispered under her breath. 'I shouldn't be telling you this, but they were together for a year. He's never been the same man since.'

I lost my temper. 'Well, I'm not Connor. I appreciate the advice, but I'm meeting her strictly for business, so there's no need to be worried, thanks.'

Both Sharon and Amy looked a little hurt by my outburst. 'Okay. Don't say we didn't warn you.'

On the day of the meeting, I shaved with a fresh blade and dressed in my finest suit, tie and shirt. If this Farishta was the heartless man-eater she was being made out to be, I was going to show her I wasn't the type to fall so easily. I strolled into Signature's plush offices with the swagger of Hugh Hefner and the self-belief of Evil Knievel. I was shown into the boardroom and waited patiently for at least twenty minutes. She was late and I began to lose my patience. It didn't matter how much of a heartless goddess this woman was, her punctuality sucked.

Just then there was a knock on the door. It opened slowly and in she walked.

'Hi, I'm Farishta. I'm so sorry I'm late. We're in the middle of a very large deal and I got a little tied up.'

The first thing I noticed were her gorgeous big green eyes, followed by her flawless olive skin and perfect physique. She was one of the most beautiful women I had ever laid eyes on.

'N-n-n-no problem at all. I was actually hoping you would be late.' I wasn't making any sense. I needed to pull myself together fast.

'So you're the new guy at Milestone I have heard so much about,' she said seductively, sitting down elegantly in the leather chair in front of me. Her voice was soft and soothing, like music.

'Erm, yes, I guess I am.' I smiled like a smitten schoolboy as she flicked her silky golden hair.

'How is Connor, by the way?'

'He's, er, great. Do you know him?'

'Yes, I do. We used to do a lot of business together. And we kind of dated for a while too.' I caught a glimpse of her left hand. There wasn't a ring. 'So what do you think we can do together?'

As she leaned forward, I couldn't help gawping at her tight white blouse, which clung to her shapely physique. My mind was going into overdrive and I was struggling to keep my composure.

'Well, you may have heard that I am setting up a Milestone Property fund, so we will be investing large sums for our investors into new projects. Considering the strong relationship Milestone already has with Signature, I think we can build on this and work on much bigger deals together.'

Her beautiful eyes lit up with delight at my suggestion. 'Oh certainly, that sounds great! I would be more than happy to keep you updated on our new launches.'

'That would be fantastic'.

She spent some time talking about Signature's up-and-coming projects and plans. I couldn't keep my eyes off her the whole time she spoke, and I didn't remember much of what she said.

'Farishta, can I ask you a question?' I said as she finished speaking.

'Sure,' she replied.

'It's not exactly business related.'

She smiled coyly. 'Okay...'

'Well, I hear a beautiful French accent, but you look so exotic. May I ask where you are from, Farishta?'

'I'm French, actually. But originally from Morocco. My family moved to Paris when I was a child.'

'Ah, I see. That explains your exotic beauty,' I smiled.

She blushed. 'You're too kind.'

'Well, thanks for your time. It's been an absolute pleasure,' I said and prepared to leave.

'No, thank you. I look forward to working together.'

'So do I.' I almost walked into the glass door before realising I needed to open it first, and I looked back sheepishly, hoping she hadn't noticed. She just smiled as I walked out of the building with a giant grin on my face.

***

'So how did it go?' asked Sharon as I got back to my desk.

'It went fine. You know, I can't believe you both. You built this woman up as some dangerous femme fatale, but she's one of the nicest, most sincere people I have ever met. I really don't understand

197

how anybody can say a single bad word about her. She's an absolute angel.'

'Oh no, it looks like she's got him,' cried Sharon.

'Yep, he's fallen into the trap,' repeated Amy, shaking her head.

'What trap?'

'That's exactly what Connor said after the first meeting. It's how she gets her way. She's just playing her game and spinning her web.'

'Spinning her web, yes,' said Amy.

'But what the hell could she possibly want from me?' I said angrily.

'Are you blind? You're setting up an investment fund, so she sees you as a client to buy buildings and floors from her. She can make a lot of money out of you.'

And then I lost it completely. 'Will you two just stop it? I've had enough! I think you have this woman all wrong and I feel sorry for her. You know what, I think you are just jealous.'

The women looked shocked by my outrage. 'Adam, we are just looking out for you,' said Sharon. 'We genuinely care about you and don't want to see you get hurt.'

'Well, thanks, but if I want two guardian angels, I'll be sure to let you know. Now please let me do some bloody work.'

Sharon sighed before coming to sit on the empty chair next to me. 'Do you want to know the full story about her and Connor?'

'Not really,' I said. 'But I know you're going to tell me anyway.'

'They met at a property launch and there was instant attraction. They started dating shortly after and it all looked very good. It was around the time that Milestone and Signature started doing more and more business, so they were working together closely too. They were making money and looked great, a real power couple. Connor fell completely in love with her and after almost a year of dating he asked her to marry him. She agreed and he was over the moon.'

'Okay, go on.'

'And then a month before the wedding, she completely disappeared. Connor was searching everywhere for her. She didn't come home or turn up to work. He even called the police. Two weeks later she rang and told him she was in Paris. She said she was pregnant. And he wasn't the father.'

'What? So who was the father?'

'Nobody really knows. There are rumours that she was a mistress of one of the Abu Dhabi sheikhs, but obviously we will never know the truth behind that. Some say he was funding her extravagant lifestyle in exchange for favours. Others say it's the CEO of Signature's child.'

'So what happened to Connor?'

'He hasn't mentioned her since. He broke off the engagement and refuses to discuss it. She eventually came back to Dubai after the birth of her son, and Connor won't work with Signature. If I were you I wouldn't even tell him you met her today.'

I was baffled. 'I don't believe it. It can't be true! She seemed so sweet and innocent.'

'Of course it's true!' insisted Sharon. 'Connor told me the whole story. There's more to this woman than meets the eye, Adam. She is only motivated by money and power. If you're going to deal with her, keep your relationship at arm's length, or avoid her completely. I'm certain the real truth about her will come out one day and it won't be pretty.'

Despite Sharon's warning, I didn't avoid Farishta. I just couldn't accept that this elegant woman could be so callous. Over the next few months I started to spend more and more time with her, discussing Signature's upcoming projects and exploring ways we could work together. Every time we met, Farishta surprised me. She was always beautifully dressed, effortlessly graceful and softly spoken; a world away from the manipulative she-devil Sharon and Amy had made her out to be. I wasn't sure if Connor was aware of our meetings, but I decided it was best not to let him know. I couldn't deny I was attracted to her, but I was careful that our relationship never strayed out of a strictly professional context. That was until one evening exactly a month after we first met, when everything changed.

199

As Farishta and I were wrapping up a late meeting at her offices, we decided to have a casual drink before calling it a night. In a bar overlooking the Marina, the conversation turned to our lives in Dubai.

'So, do you live alone, Farishta?'

'No, actually I don't.'

'Oh, so you're married?'

'No. But I do live with a man,' she winked. 'My 3-year-old son, Zack.'

'Wow, I can't believe you're a mother!'

'You're too kind,' she replied bashfully. 'So what about you, mister? Is there is a Ms Right in your life?'

'I'm afraid not. Unfortunately she hasn't arrived yet.'

'Well, do you know what she will look like?'

I laughed. 'Well, she will probably have olive skin and big green eyes. Her hair will be blonde and she will dress elegantly and always look fabulous.' I took a sip of my drink. 'A bit like you, perhaps.'

Farishta began to blush. As the bill arrived, we both reached for it at once and our hands touched, like a scene from an old romantic movie. It was subtle, but she didn't withdraw her hand immediately and I knew it was a sign.

'Farishta, we've been spending a lot of time together recently and I need to tell you something.'

'Okay,' she replied shyly.

'I think I'm falling for you. Every time I see you, I feel it. And I hope you feel the same way too. Will you join me for dinner tomorrow night? And I don't mean as business associates.'

She was speechless for a moment and looked away. 'I would love to.'

The ecstatic feeling that overcame me was difficult to describe. I smiled and kissed the smooth skin on the back of her hand. She then kissed me goodnight and left, while I sat alone for a little longer, sipping my cocktail and thinking about her. It seemed Ms Right had arrived in my life after all.

The next morning, I strolled into the office with a spring in my step. I was planning on breaking the news to Sharon and Amy, and was adamant about proving to them that I was the man who was going to tame their seductress for ever. But there was an unusual stir on the sales floor, as most of the team were huddled around one of the desks.

'What's going on?' I asked Emma.

'Haven't you seen the news?'

'What news?'

Amy put the newspaper under my nose. The bold headline read 'Moroccan Mata Hari Arrested at Dubai Airport'.

'Who are they referring to?'

'Farishta Hijazi at Signature. Apparently she's been up to no good.'

I snatched a copy of the newspaper from a nearby desk and scanned the news:

'Farishta Hijazi, sales executive at Signature Properties, was arrested yesterday on charges of money laundering, arms dealing and fraud worth millions of dollars. She has been accused of being a modern-day Mata Hari. Hijazi had worked for the French secret service in 2004 and was sent to Dubai late in 2006 to investigate terrorist financing and money laundering in the UAE. However, while in Dubai under the cover of a real estate agent, Hijazi had become involved in high-profile drug deals and the illegal sale of arms, and is accused of funnelling millions of dollars of illegal funds into the Dubai property market. She has also been accused of counter-espionage for the Egyptian government. Hijazi was caught at Dubai International Airport in the late hours of last night by the Secret Police as she tried to leave the country with over two hundred thousand euros. She is currently in the custody of the UAE authorities and is facing a jail sentence if convicted.'

I felt a pain in my chest I had never experienced before, and I had to sit down.

'Are you okay, Adam?' asked Sharon, who had spotted me collapse in my chair.

'Yes... I'm fine...' I was actually finding it difficult to breathe.

'I told you there was something funny about this girl, didn't I?' said Sharon.

'Funny,' replied Amy. 'Very funny indeed.'

15

A Tale of Two Cities

By 2006, Dubai was beginning to show the symptoms of a severe identity crisis. Like the popular kid running for class president, the Emirate aimed to please by offering something for everybody: tax-free status, a family environment, a booming nightlife, luxury, security, hope, a future. But this catch-all approval came at a cost. By trying to be all things to all people, the city was struggling with its own identity.

Ostensibly, the overarching Muslim values of the region still pervaded most aspects of society. The *azaan* or call to prayer could be heard five times a day in the streets and the malls at prayer times. Beautiful mosques could be seen every hundred metres, brimming with weekly worshippers for Friday prayers. And all the latest Hollywood movies were censored for sexual content before the cinemas could play them. But behind this slim Islamic veil, there was a darker and more sinister Dubai, and many began to accuse the city of contradictions and double standards.

Nevertheless, Dubai revelled in its duplicity. A city of contrasts, it was both religious and debauched, tolerant and oppressive, modern and medieval. In the malls, Russian beauties in hotpants and boob tubes walked side by side with *burka*-clad Emiratis. A public display of affection like a simple kiss was an arrestable offence, yet the excesses of the wild nightlife were conveniently ignored. Expats consumed copious quantities of alcohol within the havens of the hotels, but any public drunken antics were punishable with prison and deportation. Was this a city succeeding at being all things to all people? Was it a place in transition from tradition to modernity? Or was it simply a land tolerant of hypocrisy? While some celebrated the diversity as a balance of Eastern and Western values, others warned that the Emirate was fast becoming the battleground of two civilisations on a collision course; a time bomb waiting to erupt.

Despite the growing voices of conservatism, Dubai stayed true to its business spirit. While many of its reactionary Arab neighbours looked on with disdain, it cleverly used its liberalism to monetise Islam's vices. A case in point was the open sale of alcohol in Dubai, which was something of a revolution in the conservative Middle East. While the Saudis only drank in the privacy of their homes, Dubai opened the floodgates, making alcohol freely available in bars, restaurants and nightclubs. It was not unusual to see an Emirati in a swanky city bar dressed in a *dishdasha* enjoying a cold beer. But freedom came at a cost. Alcohol was sold at a huge premium, which the government collected as an indirect tax on *haram* activity, prohibited by Islam. Vice, it seemed, was a lucrative luxury in Dubai.

Sex was even bigger business and there was something for every price range. Most of the city's trendiest bars and clubs were swarming with high-class prostitutes, while testosterone-fuelled labourers piled into seedy joints and drinking holes, desperately seeking female companionship for the lonely night ahead. Yet there was no government clampdown on prostitution. There were even rumours of a state-regulated racket whereby new girls were brought in regularly on sponsored visas to provide their services to wealthy businessmen. Sex, after all, was good for business, and Dubai's authorities didn't want to deprive wealthy customers if it ensured closing the deal.

The Dubai authorities maintained a delicate balance and operated on the precarious principle of 'don't ask, don't tell'. The law was the law, but if it was broken in private without affecting the greater social harmony, they would generally turn a blind eye. This applied to everything from subletting property to cohabitation by unmarried couples, and even homosexuality. Same-sex relationships were illegal according to Islamic law, yet there was a thriving underground gay scene in Dubai and cohabiting gay couples stayed under the radar. What people did in the privacy of their bedrooms was not the concern of the authorities, unless it became public and a potential source of embarrassment and reputational damage. The authorities could not be put in a position to be tolerating *haram* actions and a response was then needed to save face. In these instances, the full force of the law would clamp down in the name of morality and Islam, and the consequences were severe.

Many Emiratis disapproved of their country's hypocrisy and blamed the expats for the moral decay. They were at best ambivalent and at worst opposed to the swarm of foreigners that had engulfed their country. Although many understood the skills and expertise they brought with them, the voices of dissent among the Arabs were daily becoming louder. They lamented the alien morals and questionable intentions of young Westerners to corrupt their traditional way of life. The locals felt threatened and outnumbered by foreigners, and as their numbers dwindled to a mere 5 per cent of the country's population, many saw their identity and heritage being swept away by an alien invasion that brought more harm than good.

The debate as to whether Dubai society was experiencing a reformation or a moral decline raged on, but for one month every year the city unmistakably cleaned up its act. The Islamic holy month of Ramadan was like an annual stint at rehab, the city transforming into a serene, peaceful and spiritual place. Restaurants were closed during daylight hours and the malls were deserted. The radio advertisements for beach and foam parties stopped, and working hours were significantly reduced to promote family values. There was no question during Ramadan that Islam was Dubai's prevalent ideology, and for a month at least the liberal voices were silenced.

***

It was the week before Ramadan and things were falling into place for me. The fund formation process was well underway. I had finalised the investor presentations and the brochures, which had been submitted for printing. I had also started building close relationships with a number of developers to build a pipeline of investments, and Tariq had even told me he had some people lined up ready to invest once we were up and running.

My social life was also better than ever. With my sexy new apartment and high-profile job, I was now a qualified member of Dubai's social elite. I was regularly attending private parties, BBQs, garden parties, art openings and property launches, and schmoozing with movers and shakers and the cream of Gulf society. My wardrobe was dominated with designer brands and I became more conscious than ever of where and with whom I was seen. I had regular facials, manicures and banana-leaf massages. Perhaps I was selling out a bit, but this was what I had wanted since I had touched down in the city. Finally, I was living the elusive Dubai Dream and I felt vindicated.

A few days before my hectic calendar took a breather for Ramadan, I got an unexpected email from an old school buddy from London called Aziz, who was passing through Dubai on his way back from Malaysia. I hadn't seen him for years, so I was looking forward to catching up and showing him around the city. Aziz was that kid who had a fake ID made to buy cheap beer from the liquor store so he could get drunk in the park, before sobering up and going home to his unsuspecting parents. He had given me my first cigarette at the age of 12 and my first joint at 15; although drugs were illegal here, I was looking forward to reliving some of the old days. I had even put together a list of clubs we would hit and had ranked them on a spreadsheet into categories like music type, location and hotness of women.

We agreed to meet at the Royal Mirage hotel for tea and *shisha* before heading out. I dressed to party and reserved a great table in the courtyard overlooking the fountain. It was packed as usual with groups of young locals and some expats lounging under the traditional gazebos and puffing away on pipes.

Two tall figures approached me dressed in long white traditional *thobes*. One had a short trimmed goatee, the other a big bushy beard.

'*Assalamualaikum*, brother, how are you?' said the bushy-bearded man in a familiar English voice as he prepared to sit down beside me.

'Sorry, this table is reserved,' I said angrily.

'Adam, it's me, Aziz!'

I couldn't believe my eyes. 'Aziz? Is that you? What the hell is that thing on your face?'

'It's a beard, bro.'

'I can see that, but you look like a freakin' Taliban! Is this some kind of twisted fashion statement? I thought I told you to dress for clubbing?'

'Sorry bro, I don't go clubbing any more.' He sat down and smiled.

'What?'

'I have changed my ways, Adam. I have devoted my life to God.'

'You gotta be freaking kidding me.'

206

'No brother, I'm not kidding. I finally found the light.'

'I see.' I sighed. 'So I guess there's no partying tonight.'

'I'm afraid not.'

'Well, that's just fabulous,' I muttered resentfully.

'Come on, don't be upset. You should be pleased for me,' said Aziz.

'I'm overjoyed,' I replied sarcastically.

'By the way, I want you to meet a friend of mine.' He beckoned over the tall man with the goatee. 'This is Sharaz. He has recently moved to Dubai from the UK like you.'

Sharaz was a handsome, dark-haired British Pakistani man in his late twenties. He shook my hand enthusiastically.

'Aziz has told me a lot about you,' he said in a Northern English accent.

'What, that I'm an infidel who's going to hell?'

He laughed out loud. 'No, bro, that you're one of his oldest and best friends.'

'As you both moved to Dubai around the same time, I thought it would be good for you guys to meet and socialise together,' said Aziz.

'Yeah, sure, sounds great'. I imagined a day out with Sharaz, praying and reading religious books with a spot of jihad training. So what do you do here in Dubai, Sharaz?'

'I work for the Dubai Department of Transport as a project manager. I used to be a management consultant back in Birmingham, but I wanted a change, so I thought Dubai might be a good place to go. Bit of sun and tax-free cash can't hurt.' It was an all too familiar story. 'So what do you usually get up to in your spare time?' he asked me.

'Erm, you know, this and that. Go to the mosque, pray and stuff.' He was oblivious to the sarcasm. 'What about you? Have you made some friends in Dubai?' I was desperately hoping he had so I would be rid of the burden of having to befriend him.

'Well, I have met a group of expats who call themselves the "Dubai Brotherhood". Have you heard of them?'

'The Dubai Brotherhood? Sounds like a dodgy suicide cult to me.'
I cracked up, but they weren't amused.

'No, not at all. They're a bunch of expat Muslims, mainly from the UK. They get together at least a couple of times a week for religious circles and family dinners. They're great guys and even my wife has made some good friends among their wives. It's a tight-knit community.'

'You're married?' I asked.

'Yes, of course,' he replied, pointing at his wedding ring. 'I have a 2-year-old son too.'

That was the nail in the coffin. I was young, free and single, at the peak of my sexual prowess. Going out with Sharaz would be like taking my disapproving dad on a pub crawl. There was no way we were going to be best friends, but as I began to plot my escape, things got even worse.

'In fact, the brothers are having a dinner event tomorrow evening. Why don't you join me? I can introduce you to the guys.'

I began to panic. 'Erm, well, tomorrow may be...'

'Come on, man, I'll book you a place,' he insisted.

'I'm afraid I...'

'I think it will be good for you to meet these guys. Maybe they'll be a good influence on you,' added Aziz.

'It's at the BBQ Delights restaurant in Bur Dubai,' said Sharaz. 'Get there for eight?'

I accepted there was no chance of getting out of this without being rude, so I reluctantly accepted. 'Okay, well, maybe I can pop in for a bit.'

'Good man! I wish I could join you guys too, but I'm flying out tomorrow morning,' said Aziz. 'It's a shame.'

Yes, a shame indeed, the lucky sod. And so just like that, the precious final Friday-night party slot before Ramadan was occupied by dinner with a bunch of bearded fundamentalists. I was not pleased.

'I'm so glad I introduced you guys,' smiled Aziz.

'So am I, Aziz,' I replied through gritted teeth. 'So am I.'

***

On the night of the dinner, my strategy was clear. I would stay for a short while and then make an inconspicuous exit without Sharaz noticing. Hani had a table booked at the Casbar club for later, so I dressed in preparation for a night on the town after the ordeal. The one vague positive in this annoying situation was that the BBQ Delights was considered one of the best Pakistani restaurants in Dubai, so I was actually looking forward to a good meal before a heavy night of clubbing.

I arrived at the restaurant a little late and everybody had already taken their seats. In the middle of the restaurant was a huge table with around twenty bearded men chatting away. I felt frightfully overdressed. Most of the other men were dressed in tracksuits and sandals, while I was ready to rave in ripped jeans and tight t-shirt. Sharaz spotted me from the other end of the restaurant and rushed over to greet me.

'Hey, buddy, glad you could make it. Let me introduce you to some of the guys.'

He went around the table one by one. There was Akbar the accountant, Ali the project manager, Haytham the recruitment consultant and Shaqeel the investment banker. They were all educated professionals working for various international firms across the city, and they all seemed genuinely glad to meet me. I took my place at the table and we ordered a tantalising selection of chicken curry, lamb chops, biryani, Indian mince and BBQ fish. The delicious food appeared minutes later, and as we tucked in the conversation started flowing.

'So it seems most of you guys are from the UK,' I said.

'Yes, I would say so. A couple of Americans too,' replied Shaqeel, a short, fat middle-aged man with a beard that consumed most of his face.

'And do you enjoy the lifestyle out here in Dubai?'

'It's great, especially for our families,' replied Akbar, a gaunt-looking man in his mid-forties.

'Yes, there's a good British expat community out here,' I said.

'True, there is, but we only care to spend time with the British Muslims. We are a close community.'

'Oh, so you only socialise with other British Muslims?' I asked.

'Of course. The other Brits spend their time getting drunk and partying. Why would we have left the evils of the UK to come and seek it here?' said Shaqeel. There was a roar of laughter from the table.

'Life is so easy for Muslims in Dubai. We don't have to worry about finding halal meat to eat or avoiding drunken people on the streets,' said Akbar.

'That's the benefit of living in a Muslim country,' added Shaqeel, as he bit into his chicken breast.

'It's the main reason I moved here,' replied a third man to my right.

'Yes, not to mention the fantastic tax-free salary and lifestyle, right?' I joked, tucking into my naan bread.

Nobody seemed to find my off-the-cuff remark amusing. 'No, not really. Those are secondary concerns to me. I actually left the UK because I no longer felt welcome there,' said Akbar to a chorus of agreement.

'Really, why wouldn't you feel welcome? It's your home country,' I asked, genuinely interested.

'Well, things are changing for us Muslims in the West, particularly after 9/11. We are becoming increasingly victimised by the media and judged by society. I think it's just going to get worse. So I decided it was best for me and my family to leave for Muslim lands.'

'Do you think you are more welcome here than in the UK?' I asked.

'Of course. This is an Islamic country. I feel more at home here than anywhere.'

'Even though you have no rights here? You will always be a second-class citizen and you would have to leave straight away if you lost your job. How can you possibly call this place more welcoming than Britain?'

'Because it's a Muslim country and we will never be victimised for our faith,' said Shaqeel adamantly.

'So you decided to turn your back on the country that gave you the opportunity to come here in the first place.' I was beginning to lose my cool.

'Well, I'm in a better place now.'

'But you are not a citizen here and you never will be. You're a commodity. You're only worth something in Dubai as long as you have a job that a local Arab has not yet learnt to do himself.'

'I'm not sure about that. This country allows me to earn a good wage and be who I want to be.'

'Yes, but only because of your Western education, British passport and UK work experience!' I was visibly heated now. 'You're only valuable here as long as you're contributing to the economy. As soon as you stop adding value, all of that goes out of the window and you're out of here like yesterday's newspaper.'

Akbar was also becoming emotional. 'I came to Dubai so that I could bring my family up in an Islamic environment. The crime rate in the UK is getting out of control and I don't want my children growing up surrounded by junkies, alcoholics and criminals.'

'Do you honestly believe that Dubai is a crime-free society?' I asked, remembering the shocking story of the Russian and the jeweller.

'Yes, of course, it's a Muslim country. There are stricter punishments here.'

'Have you even driven down the backstreets of Bur Dubai on a Friday night?' I asked him frankly.

'No.'

'Have you heard of places like the Cyclone or the Rattlesnake?'

'No, I haven't.'

'Have you heard the story about the Russian and the Indian jeweller?'

'No.'

'Well, I don't mean to be rude, but I think the Dubai you live in is a very different place from the one I know.'

I was interrupted by a text message on my mobile phone. It was Hani:

We are going to Club Casbar now. See you there. H

It was my cue to leave, but just as I was about to slip away, Sharaz came over.

'So are you enjoying yourself?' he asked.

'Yes, they're certainly an interesting bunch.'

'Great. Listen, I have to make a move. The wife is home alone, so I need to get back.'

'Yes, I actually need to go too. Thanks for inviting me, Sharaz, it's been a real eye-opener,' I said while I shook his hand.

'My pleasure. Let's meet again soon.'

I politely agreed, knowing full well that I had no intention of seeing Sharaz or the Brotherhood again. He was nice enough, but his religious and family-oriented lifestyle was a world apart from mine, and I just couldn't see us being friends. I wished him goodnight, jumped in a taxi and headed to the Casbar for the real night's events to begin.

***

On the way, I thought about the discussion at the table tonight. The Dubai Brotherhood were not the crazed fundamentalists I had expected them to be. They were in fact a great bunch of guys and had actually made me feel very welcome. But their disdain for Western values disturbed me. They seemed oddly oblivious to the fact that every vice they abhorred was readily available here in Dubai, often on an even grander and more decadent scale. If it were not for their British or American passports, they would certainly not be earning the inflated salaries they were enjoying now, and I wondered if any of them would ever consider relinquishing their passports now that they were in so-called Muslim lands. It was unlikely. Instead, the Brotherhood were content to be a closed community, living in a bubble of self-deception in a country rife with contradictions.

It was already midnight and as all clubs had to shut by three, it didn't leave me much time. I rushed to the entrance of the Casbar, where a cute Lebanese girl in tight leather pants stood with a clipboard, accompanied by two huge African bouncers.

'Hi, I'm on Hani's table.' She stared at me from head to toe, then scanned her clipboard before nodding her approval for the bouncer to open the velvet rope.

The strobe lighting was in full flow as house music blasted out onto the huge dance floor, where a giant crowd was raving to the beats. Above the main room was a balcony with a number of VIP enclosures where groups of guys and girls danced together in a more intimate setting. The crowd at the Casbar was different to the other clubs in the city: there were more locals and more Russian models than anywhere else, many of them high-class hookers. I spotted Hani on his table at the back of the dance floor and strolled over to join him. He was with at least a dozen girls, most of them Lebanese or Moroccan, and a giant magnum of champagne sat in the middle of the table, surrounded by bottles of vodka and whisky.

'You finally made it!' he shouted as he spotted me, and gave me a hug. 'Where were you all evening?'

'It's a long story. I got tied up at a dinner with some religious guys.'

'Religious guys? Wow, don't tell me you're going Taliban on me, buddy. Who the hell am I gonna share all these girls with? I'm getting too old to handle them all myself.' He laughed. 'By the way, there's somebody I want you to meet. He'll be joining us shortly.'

'Who?'

'He recently moved to Dubai from the UK actually. And I think he's an even bigger party animal than you. This guy is a beast! You're gonna love him.'

I poured myself a drink while Hani grabbed two of the girls and sandwiched himself between them. Everywhere I looked, there were women in tiny skirts or hotpants dancing provocatively to the music. The champagne and vodka were flowing and the crowd was out of control.

As I returned to the table from the bathroom, I noticed that Hani's friend had arrived with a Russian blonde who had the longest legs I had ever seen. I couldn't make out his face as Hani hugged him and poured him a drink.

'Hey, Adam, this is my new friend from the UK I was telling you about,' Hani said.

As the man turned to face me, I almost choked on my drink. Dressed in a crisp black shirt and jeans, it was Sharaz!

He looked as shocked as I was. 'Hey, man, how you doing?'

'Sharaz, what the hell are you doing here? I thought you were going home to your...'

'You gotta be shitting me?' interrupted Hani. 'You know each other?'

'Yeah, we do. Small world,' I said.

'Well, that's great! No need for formalities, so let's fucking party!' Hani jumped on the table and threw his hands in the air, which the girls all seemed to love.

'Sharaz, what are you doing here?' I asked again.

'Are you joking? This place is off the hook,' he smiled.

'But this isn't your scene! Besides, I thought you had to go home to your wife?'

'Nah, man, she's tucked up in bed with the kid. I told her I'm at an all-night Islamic study session. She'll never know.'

'But I thought you were...'

'You thought I was a good little religious boy, didn't you. Ha-ha, what can I say, I'm a social chameleon. I adapt to my surroundings. By the way, this is Anya. She's from Moscow. She's smoking hot, isn't she?'

'Do the Brotherhood guys know this?' I asked.

'The brothers? All they know is the way to the mosque. They're useful to know to recommend a plumber or to borrow some jump leads, so I keep them sweet.' Sharaz whispered in my ear. 'I think Anya really likes me. She gave me a huge discount for the night.'

'Congratulations...' I replied.

'So come on, let's party, dude!'

Sharaz led Anya to the dance floor while I returned to the table and sat down. This was all too surreal for me. I just couldn't get my head around how wrong I had been about him. Not only was he not the religious family man I had thought, he had lied to his wife and was dancing with a Russian prostitute. Even by my hazy moral principles, I knew this was wrong.

I spent the rest of the night watching Sharaz from the corner of my eye. For some reason, I felt strangely responsible for him, as if I needed to make sure that he didn't overstep the line any further. By now, he and Anya had been joined by a brunette, and Sharaz was rubbing against them both as they danced intimately. I felt helpless and rather guilty as he descended further into moral oblivion.

Sharaz eventually returned to the table with Anya on his right arm and the brunette on his left. He was now clearly drunk.

'Bro, what's wrong? Aren't you enjoying yourself?'

'I'm okay, I'm just a little tired,' I replied. 'Listen, I think I'm going to make a move.'

'Are you sure? The party is just starting.' He winked at Anya and she smiled back.

'Yeah, it's been a long day. You enjoy yourself, buddy, let's catch up another time.'

'Suit yourself, party pooper! He's missing out, isn't he, girls?' They nodded in agreement. I wished goodbye to Hani, who was now too drunk to care. Before leaving, I looked back at the table one last time and saw that Sharaz had his tongue down Anya's throat. It was clear his night was only just beginning.

16

Twisted Fate

To do business successfully with an Emirati, you must first win his favour and respect. You must spend hours with him sipping mint tea, or smoking *shisha* in his home or his *majlis*. You must indulge in a painful and tiring process of constant compliments, ego massaging and flattery. You must courteously listen to endless stories about how his children, cousins, brothers and nephews are excellent jockeys, falconers or sword dancers. You must bring him flamboyant gifts with shiny wrapping paper and huge bows, so that everybody around him will know he has been given a gift, which affirms his importance; although he will never open the gift in public in case he falls victim to the 'evil eye' of the jealous onlooker. You must laugh at his every joke, no matter how ridiculous and unamusing, and you must listen attentively to his laborious stories of how he has recently customised his sports car with the most hideously ostentatious trimmings.

The Arabs are a nation of procrastinators, often oblivious to the importance of deadlines, so you must accommodate his timelines and rules. He will have no qualms about sending you on a wild goose-chase around town in exchange for the privilege of his ear. And even after all of your great effort he will often continue to string you along without a concrete answer, simply answering *Insh'Allah* ('God willing'), placing the all important outcome firmly in the hands of God.

The most successful businesspeople in Dubai were those who studied the idiosyncrasies of conducting business with the Emiratis, and had developed the patience to persevere. The rewards were substantial. Not only were they the biggest potential clients, but a good rapport with an Emirati could open doors to *wasta* and unspeakable riches. The most astute businesspeople knew that there were two things that excited the passions of Emirati men more than anything else – horses and beautiful women – and both were used to great effect as marketing tools by Dubai's property firms. The most astute brokers and developers used images of stallions in their logos and marketing materials, and ramped up their sales teams with leggy blondes, brunettes and redheads from Latvia to Brazil.

Like modern-day Geishas, these girls entertained their clients with flirtation and playful innuendo, sometimes more. They knew exactly how to play directly to the ego of the wealthy Arab. They would compliment his expensive watch, laugh at his jokes and respond to his advances to make him feel like he was simply irresistible – an Emirati sex god who could do no wrong with the ladies. And when he was at his most vulnerable and helpless, a brochure for a fifty-storey building would be subtly placed in front of him with a contract to purchase five floors in cash.

***

'Cameron? Is that you?'

He looked up before getting into the taxi. 'Adam?'

'Yes, it's me!'

'How the hell are you buddy?'

'I'm great!' I rushed over and gave him a hug.

'What are you doing in Dubai?' he asked.

'I live out here now. I moved here a couple of years ago.'

'Fantastic! So you took my advice.' He winked.

'I did indeed.'

'And isn't this place everything I said it would be?'

'It's amazing, Cameron. I gotta hand it to you, you were right. Do you have time to catch up now over a coffee?'

Cameron looked at his watch. 'For you, I make time.' He tipped the driver for the inconvenience and we headed to Starbucks, which was only a short walk away.

'So have you made any serious money yet?' asked Cameron as he sipped on his skinny cappuccino.

'I'm getting there,' I smiled. 'There have been a few false starts, but I'm definitely on the right road now.'

'Great! *Insha'Allah*, as they say.'

'*Insha'Allah*, indeed.'

'Well, Dubai has become a lot more competitive since we last spoke back in London, that's for sure. There were a lot fewer cowboys then, believe me. Now every man and his dog is trying to make a quick buck in the property game. But that's not to say there aren't still some big opportunities to make money. So who are you working with?'

'I work for Milestone Properties.'

He stared at me. '*The* Milestone?'

'Yep. I'm Head of Investments there,' I said proudly.

'Well done, old boy! You really did land on your feet, didn't you?'

'Thanks, I guess so. So what brings you here? Did you finally make the move yourself?' I asked.

'Not yet, buddy. But I'm doing a lot more out here now than before. I made a killing on those villas in the Emirates Hills. I went on to buy and flip a few more things in the Marina and the Waterfront, and did well on that too. At the moment advising with a developer I know to help them find a plot for their project.'

'Can you tell me any more?' I asked, curious.

'Not really. It's all a bit top secret; I'm sworn to secrecy.'

'I see. Well, just so you know, Milestone has access to a number of plots across Dubai. If I can help in any way, I would be glad to.'

'I appreciate that. I'm really seeking an iconic plot, perhaps something on the beachfront in the Marina. Although I know such plots are virtually non-existent these days.'

My eyes lit up. 'Cameron, I think we may have just the one! It's a Marina plot directly overlooking the beachfront. It's the last of its kind and we have direct access to it from Emaar.'

Cameron stared at me intensely. I could see he was smelling a deal, just as I was. 'Are you serious?'

'Yes, of course. If you want me to get you the details, it's only a phone call away.'

Cameron leaned in close to whisper. 'Okay, Adam. What I'm about to tell you is highly confidential. Do you understand?'

'Of course, Cam.'

He looked around and over both his shoulders before continuing. 'Have you heard of the Revolving Tower?'

'No, I can't say I have.'

'Few people have – yet. It will be the world's first fully rotating building, a truly groundbreaking concept. Each floor will rotate a full three hundred and sixty degrees in a single month. So today you could be looking down the Sheikh Zayed Road and tomorrow watching the sunset over the waters of the Gulf. Each floor will rotate at a different starting point, so the building will also physically change shape as it moves over time. Just imagine, an entire building in motion! Incredible.'

'Are you serious? Is that even possible?' I asked.

'You better believe it is. The architect who has designed it is a British man named Robert Hopkins. He is planning to build one of these here, and in Moscow, London and New York. Dubai will be the first. Robert is collaborating closely with a local developer called Escape Investments. They have won the contract to build it, and I am working with them directly to find the right plot for this project. If you're telling me you have exclusive access to a unique plot in the Marina that nobody else knows of, I think we may have a deal.'

'Cameron, let me go back tomorrow and check the details, and I will let you know immediately.'

'Do that. This is a landmark project and could make us both a load of cash. Let's move as quickly as we can. I will be waiting for your call.'

'Understood.'

'The CEO of Escape Investments is an Emirati gentleman called Karim Al Fasi. He trusts me and he is ready to move straight away.'

***

As soon as I got into the office the following morning, I rushed over to Rav's desk.

'Rav, do we still have access to the plot in the Marina from Emaar?'

'Yes, we do,' he replied while typing up an email. 'There have been a few enquiries from some of the sales guys, but nothing serious yet. Why do you ask?'

'I think I have a buyer!'

Rav stopped what he was doing. 'A serious buyer?'

'As serious as serious can be.'

'Okay, if you're sure, we can set up a meeting with Emaar as soon as possible.'

It was the good news I was desperate to hear and I made the call to Cameron. 'Cam, we have the plot. It's direct to us and we can meet Emaar when you're ready.'

'You beauty! I'm coming over to your offices with Karim this afternoon.'

Karim and Cameron arrived at the Milestone offices together soon after lunch. Karim was a middle-aged Emirati with a pot belly and a receding hairline. He didn't look like an Arab despite dressing in the traditional *dishdasha*, as he was fairer than most with more European-looking features. He was what was known as an *Ajam*, a descendant of Iranian merchants who relocated to the Emirates in the 1920s. Although they were officially just as Emirati as any other Arabs, it was said that the *Ajam* were sometimes distrusted by the Bedouin Arabs, as they were not considered 'pure' *Khaliji* or Arabs of the 'Gulf'..

Cameron started with the introductions. 'Karim, this is the friend Adam from London I told you about. He is heading up the investments division here at Milestone.'

'It's good to meet ya, buddy,' said Karim, shaking my hand vigorously. His accent surprised me, reminding me of a Sicilian mob boss from Brooklyn.

'Pleasure to meet you, Karim. I have to say your accent doesn't sound very Arabic.'

'Yeah, I spent quite a few years out in New York when I was growin' up. I went to college at Stern and worked there for a while, too. People call me the Emirati from the East village. So you're from London, right?'

'Yes, born and bred.'

'Fantastic, I love London. It is my favourite city. I love to stay on Park Lane, shop in Harrods and party in China White.' I remembered the sheikhs from my days as a club promoter in London. Karim would have fit in with them perfectly. 'So, Cameron tells me you got this plot in the Marina. I'm listening.'

I put the plans in front of him. 'It's a G plus fifty plot with residential permission and a built-up area of a million square feet. The plot is situated on the edge of the Marina opposite the Grosvenor House hotel and offers unobstructed views of the ocean and the Palm Jumeirah.'

Karim scanned the plans eagerly. 'Nice. Very nice. Any indications on price?'

'Not yet. But we think it should be somewhere in the region of four and five hundred dirhams a square foot.'

'Not bad. What you tell me so far sounds promising. I like what I hear. Let's set up the meeting with Emaar next week. If this is what you say it is, we are ready to make an offer immediately.'

Rav set up the meeting with the CEO of Emaar for me the following Monday. Rav and I attended from Milestone, along with Karim and Cameron. The meeting couldn't have gone better. Emaar confirmed their interest in selling the plot, and Karim gave a soft commitment and agreed to sign the papers in a week, after getting approval from his board of directors. It was a far cry from my first sour plot deal with Jerome who claimed to 'know a guy'. This time I was sitting at the top table with Dubai property royalty, and the deal was as good as done.

As we left the Emaar offices I punched the air in triumph! There was only one thing on my mind now. I jumped into the back of a taxi and headed straight to the Porsche garage.

The Australian salesman spotted me immediately. 'So nice to see sir has returned. Still *looking*, are we?'

I didn't say a word and produced a cheque from my inside pocket. 'Oh what a joyous day, sir has finally become a man!' He snatched it from my fingertips with a huge smile. 'So which one do we want, sir?'

I pointed at the white 911 Turbo. 'That one.'

'Excellent choice, sir. As I said to you before, there is a three-month waiting list, and the deposit is fully refundable if sir happens to change his mind, but I assume that won't be happening?'

'No, that certainly won't be necessary. Unless I decide on a Ferrari instead, of course.'

'Oh, sir is in a funny mood today,' he said sarcastically as I signed the papers.

Leaving the garage that day was a turning point in my life. I had just ordered the car I had wanted since my earliest memories. I felt as if I had somehow arrived, and it brought a tear to my eye. Today was the last piece in the puzzle; my life was complete.

***

As I waited anxiously for the day of the contract signing, Rav came over to my desk with a suggestion.

'I have told Tariq about the meeting with Emaar. He is pleased it went well. I think while we are waiting for the contract to be signed, we need to keep Karim warm. Emiratis can be a little unpredictable, and we don't want any surprises.'

I nodded. 'Sure, what do you have in mind?'

'You should take Karim out on Friday night. Perhaps for a meal? Milestone will cover all expenses, as long as they're not too excessive...'

I agreed, and arranged to pick Karim up from his home in a rented chauffeur-driven black Mercedes to make a good impression. Karim's villa was on the Al Wasl road in Jumeirah, an exclusive community that was off limits for non-Emiratis and home to some of the most prominent Emirati families. On the way, we passed enormous villas, each with their own distinctive architecture and style, from Gothic to ultra-contemporary to mock Tudor. We finally pulled up at the gates of a mansion that looked like a Tuscan palace. In front of the house were perfectly kept lawns where two Indian gardeners were working away, sweating profusely in the desert heat. Parked ostentatiously in front of the house was a yellow Ford Mustang, a black Rolls-Royce Phantom and a white Range Rover. I manoeuvred my way around the cars and

222

climbed the steps to the huge oak front door before knocking. After some time, a tiny Filipina woman opened and peered outside.

'Good evening, I'm here for Mr Karim.'

'Are you Mr Adam?'

'I am indeed.'

'Come in, sirrrr. Mr Karim is waiting for you in the garden.'

As I followed her through the house, I felt like I had just stepped into the Palace of Versailles. There were columns and urns and tapestries everywhere, and the marble floors were polished to perfection. The housemaid led me out to the vast grounds at the rear of the mansion, where Karim was sitting in a gazebo watching the biggest television set I had ever seen. I assumed he hadn't noticed me, so I quietly took a seat and waited.

'...There is growing concern that the US housing market is overheating and a major correction is expected by analysts...' announced the news anchor.

'You know what the West's problem is?' Karim asked suddenly. It seems he had noticed me after all. 'They borrow too much freaking cash. They don't work hard any more, they don't make things. Instead they just consume and they get into debt. And you know what, now it's catching up with the bastards.'

'I guess you're right,' I answered.

'How are you, pal? Thanks for coming over.'

'No problem, Karim. Are you ready to leave?'

'Not yet. Give me half an hour, I'll be back shortly.'

Karim eventually emerged dressed in a white suit, dark shades and white slip-on shoes without socks. His hair had been blow-dried and he smelled like an Old Spice commercial, an Arabic John Travolta. I had never seen an Emirati wear anything other than the traditional *dishdasha*, so the transformation came as a shock.

'So where we goin', buddy?' he asked as our driver pulled out of the gates.

'Well, I thought we could perhaps grab a bite. I booked a table at a great steak restaurant in the Royal Mirage hotel.'

Karim looked unimpressed. 'Steak? C'mon man, it's Friday night. I don't wanna spend the night eating steak. I want to party!'

I wasn't sure what a man of Karim's age and position meant by 'party', but I was certain I was about to find out.

'Sure. Whatever you want to do,' I replied reluctantly. I was actually rather hungry. 'Where do you want to go?'

'There's only one place on a Friday night in Dubai, my friend.' He leaned forward and shouted at the driver. 'Hey, driver, turn around. We're going to Plastik.'

Located on a discreet stretch of beach around twenty minutes outside Dubai, Plastik was an ultra-chic beach club for the society elite. Modelled on the famous Nikki Beach in Miami, it was a self-proclaimed playground for the 'filthy rich and aesthetically perfect'. If Dubai was a city obsessed with its image, then Plastik was its epicentre – a temple for gold diggers and sugar daddies to worship at the shrine of vanity. The club was accessible by car, helicopter and yacht and its exclusive clientele was an eclectic mix of supermodels, rich kids and Russian and Arab playboys, with pockets full of cash and sex on their minds.

It was just before sunset and things were already in full swing. As we pulled up at the entrance, we passed a parade of Lamborghinis, Ferraris and Aston Martins. We strolled up the red carpet and into the club. Super-tanned Barbie-doll wannabes and muscular guys with signature six packs danced around the pools and on the beach as the DJ spun funky house tracks on his decks. There was a giant hot tub in the centre of the club, where girls in tiny bikinis sipped champagne, while guys posed at the neon-lit bar, competing for their attention.

'Now this is what I'm talking about, man,' said Karim, unable to contain his excitement. He danced up to the bar and began to eye up a cute, leggy blonde. He didn't waste any time and moved in for the kill.

'Hey, darling, you look like you're having a good time.' She responded with a seductive smile, although I was sure she was more interested in his solid gold Rolex. 'What's your name?'

'Alexa,' she replied in an Eastern European accent.

'Wow, Alexa, I would bet you are a model. I am correct?'

'Yes, you are correct. You want to buy me a drink?' she asked bluntly.

'Sure, what are you drinking?'

'I will have a zero cocktail.'

'A zero cocktail?'

'Yes.'

Karim looked baffled. 'What is a zero cocktail?'

'Zero calories.'

'I see. So that's how you keep that incredible body looking the way it is. Hey, barman, two zero cocktails right here. Buddy, you want a zero cocktail too?'

'Sure,' I replied.

'Barman, make that three zero cocktails. We are all looking after our weight!'

Soon after the drinks arrived, Alexa took Karim by the hand and led him to a sun lounger so they could be alone; I decided to keep my distance and stay by the bar. As they sat flirting and chatting, Karim began caressing her thigh, which she didn't seem to mind. They were clearly getting on swimmingly.

The moon was in full view now and the atmosphere had changed from a chilled-out beach lounge to a full-on rave. The music became louder and the crowd was getting more intoxicated. Many of the revellers were crowded around a group of Russian businessmen at a table in the centre of the club. The men, all dressed in white trousers, loafers and designer shirts, handed out glasses of champagne to the girls who danced seductively around them in tiny string bikinis.

Karim suddenly jumped up. 'Let's get the party started!' he shouted, rushing towards the empty table next to the Russians with Alexa on his arm. 'Waiter, bring us a jeroboam of champagne!'

The giant bottle required two huge barmen to bring it to the table, and immediately beautiful girls crowded around us, like moths to a flame. Suddenly, our table had become the focal point of the club, and Karim was revelling in the attention. Some of the girls from the Russians' table defected to ours, and they didn't seem too pleased with this shift in the balance of power.

As they looked on with disdain, Karim stood on the table and began to dance while the growing crowd around us released a giant roar. The tribal house music felt like a cult-like chant and Karim looked down like a deity, revered by the adoring worshippers below. He lifted the jeroboam over his head and began to shake it vigorously as the crowd screamed their approval. With a twist of his fist, the giant cork flew high into the night sky, followed by a gush of champagne that drenched everyone within a five-metre radius. Some of the spray caught the Russian men and they got up in anger. One of them grabbed an unopened bottle of champagne and shook it violently, before spraying it in Karim's direction in revenge. His aim was lousy, instead drenching three bikini girls who screamed in disapproval.

'You bastard!' shouted one of the girls in a shrill voice. She picked up one of the other bottles and took her revenge by soaking him back, until his shirt was dripping wet and clinging to his torso.

And so began an all-out war. Everybody below Karim tried to get their hands on any bottle they could find to spray the Russians, who found themselves defenceless against the onslaught. In a matter of moments the club was eclipsed by a champagne blizzard, as thousands of dirhams worth of alcohol was deployed as ammunition in the Battle of Plastik. They fought on the beaches and on the sun loungers and in the hot tub, and as the waiters struggled to keep up with supplies, many were caught in the crossfire. I even joined in myself, spraying an entire bottle at a Moroccan girl who seemed to enjoy the soaking and retaliated by pouring half a bottle over my head. It was pandemonium; a shamefully enjoyable display of excess, crossing all known boundaries of decency and decorum. But one thing was for sure – it was the most fun I had had in a long time.

Eventually the bar ran out of supplies and things slowly calmed down. Most of the crowd headed to the beach to wash themselves off and continue the party, but Karim had other plans.

'Let's get out of here, buddy.'

'Where now?' I asked.

'I'm feeling a little frisky and I know just the place.'

'But what about Alexa?' I asked.

'Her? No way. She won't come home with me until I buy her a freakin' Prada handbag and a Ferrari. I've met a million girls like her. I need some real action tonight. Let's go.'

As he stumbled out towards the car park, I was stopped in my tracks by a tap on the shoulder. I turned around to see a small Filipino water staring at me.

'Sir, the check?' he said, handing me a black wallet. I opened it and nearly collapsed. They were charging us for thirty bottles and a jeroboam of champagne, which came to a staggering twenty thousand dirhams, over three thousand pounds! Karim was already in the car park, so I reluctantly pulled out my corporate card and settled the damage. I had not exceeded Rav's spending limit, I had obliterated it. And the night was not over yet.

We got into the Mercedes reeking of booze and headed back towards the Sheikh Zayed Road.

'So where are we going now?' I asked Karim nervously.

'The Cyclone!'

Masquerading as a sports bar in Bur Dubai, the Cyclone was famous for a more sinister reason, as the seediest pick-up joint in the city. It was like the United Nations of hookers, a candy store for the sexually starved to choose among to their delight. Cyclone functioned as a free market for horny expats and promiscuous locals to proposition friendly women from dozens of nationalities looking for a good time. It astonished me how a place like that could escape the wrath of the Dubai authorities. There were rumours that its proprietor was a certain Mustafa Edris, the untouchable king of the Indian underworld, who enjoyed immunity status owing to his close connections to the upper echelons of power.

We paid our entrance fee and strolled into the bar. It looked like a forgotten drinking hole for bikers off Route 66. There was a small stage at the far end where an awful Filipino band fronted by a chubby woman who was belting out 'Sweet Home Alabama'. There were women of all shapes, sizes and ethnicities, desperately competing for

227

the attention of the sex-hungry male punters. As we strolled towards the bar, two women tried to grab my hand and my buttocks were pinched at least three times. In here, a virile young man was like a lamb in a slaughterhouse. I was terrified.

'Hey, sexy. You want to have some fun tonight?' said a redhead in skinny jeans and a sequined blouse sitting at the bar. Her cheesy opening line was an instant turn-off, and besides I'd never been too fond of redheads.

'No, thank you, but I appreciate the kind offer,' I replied politely.

She moved in closer. 'Come on, baby. I don't bite.' Her hand began to caress my leg and I pushed her away nervously.

'Sorry, please excuse me for a moment; I'm looking for my friend.'

Karim had already been escorted into a quiet corner by two identical-looking Russian blondes. I could see that a financial negotiation had started and Karim was shaking his head as if he was driving a hard bargain. After a while, a deal was reached and he put his arm around them both while they made their way to the exit together.

'Buddy, meet Tanya and Aria. They're going to put on a private show for me,' he mumbled in a drunken stupor.

'How nice of them. Are we leaving now, Karim?'

'Damn right we are!'

As we made our way out, I felt a hand grab mine from behind. It was the redhead from the bar again.

'Sexy boy, you are leaving without me?'

'Yes, I'm afraid so. Listen, I'm quite flattered, but I'm not really looking for a relationship right now.' She looked annoyed and muttered something derogatory in Russian before heading back to her bar stool.

Outside, Tanya and Aria were helping Karim into the back of the Mercedes.

'You comin'?' he shouted at me.

'No, I don't think so, Karim. I think I'm going to call it a night.'

'Okay, suit yourself. But I suggest you go back inside and get yourself a little something too. I spotted a redhead who really liked you in there.'

'Thanks, Karim, I might just do that. You gonna be okay?'

'Buddy, I'm in a car with two gorgeous blondes. Why the hell would I not be okay?'

'Gotcha,' I smiled.

Karim lowered his voice and leaned out of the car. 'Listen, these girls like to get paid up front and I don't have any cash with me, do you mind?'

I sighed and pulled out my wallet. 'Sure. How much do you need?'

'Three thousand should do it.' I counted out the notes and handed him the cash.

'Thanks, bud. Have a good night. I know I will!'

'Wait, Karim, before you go, can you tell me if the deal is on course for next week?'

'*Insha'Allah.*'

'Sorry, is that a yes or a no?'

'*Insha'Allah*. It means God willing. Let's speak soon, my friend.'

It was a frustratingly inadequate answer. But then, getting a straight answer from an Arab was often like drawing blood from a stone. After a painstaking ordeal of satisfying his every demand, I still didn't have a firm answer. Instead, the final decision rested in the hands of God; a God who surely wouldn't approve of champagne spraying and prostitutes. Karim's answer made me a little uneasy, but I kept my hopes up nonetheless.

***

It was two days before the contract signing date, and I was nervous. It dawned on me that I had done very little background research of my own on Karim and his firm. I trusted Cameron completely, but it wouldn't hurt to check him out myself, for my own piece of mind. So that evening, I sat at my laptop for a little detective work. I started by doing some research on the project. I looked up the website of the

229

Rotating Tower. There it was, a perfectly rendered artist's image of the building in all its glory. I looked up the plans and the background to the idea, and everything checked out.

Then I decided to research the architect Robert Hopkins. There were various links to his name, mostly interviews he had done in which he spoke of his confidence in Dubai and his hope to design something in the city. I found a biography, which stated he had graduated from the University of Leicester in 1972 and had developed hotels in New York in the mid-1990s. So far, so good. The biography also stated that he had received an honorary doctorate from the Halo Institute at Columbia University. I googled the Halo Institute; nothing came up. I looked up the Columbia website for a reference to the Institute; there was nothing. I was baffled, so I called the university directly.

'Hello, is this Columbia University?'

'Yes it is.'

'I am wondering if you can put me through to the Halo Institute. It's part of the architecture faculty.'

'Do you mind if I put you on hold, sir?'

'Not at all.'

After a long pause, the receptionist returned. 'I'm sorry, sir, there is no such institute.'

'I see. Perhaps I have spelled it incorrectly...'

'Sorry, sir, there is no such institute with any similar name.'

'Okay. Just one more question, do you have any records of a Robert Hopkins in your alumni?'

Again I was put on hold. 'Sorry, sir, there is no record of that name.'

'Thanks for your help today.'

'My pleasure. Have a nice day.'

I was confused. Could there be an error in Robert's official biography? Or had I made some kind of mistake? I immediately turned my attention to Karim and Escape Investments. There was no website and no mention of Escape or Karim anywhere on the net. My heart began to sink, but I calmed myself down. There was surely a rational explanation. Perhaps the project was so secretive that it would be unlikely to have any press coverage at this stage. I was probably getting worked up over nothing, so I decided to switch off my laptop and head to bed.

Rav pulled me into his office as soon as I arrived the next morning. 'I need to speak to you. Look at this!' He opened an email and turned his laptop to face me:

After conducting our due diligence on the prospective buyer of plot number 238 in the Dubai Marina, we have concluded that the buyer does not meet our minimum due diligence requirements, so we have regretfully decided to terminate the transaction.

Best regards,

CEO's Office

Emaar Properties

'What the hell does that mean?' I cried.

'It means your guys are not for real. The deal is off,' replied Rav.

My legs turned to jelly and I felt physically sick. This couldn't be happening. I tried to call Cameron, but his phone went straight to voicemail. I tried to call Karim too, but the same happened. What was the use? The deal was dead in the water and there was nothing I could do about it.

The full story broke a month later across the newswires. Hopkins had never received an honorary degree from Columbia and the Halo Institute was a fabricated institution. Worse still, Hopkins had not formally practised architecture for decades and had never designed a skyscraper before the Rotating Tower. When confronted by the media, he simply answered, 'I have not designed skyscrapers, but I feel I am ready to now.' Hopkins' choice of Dubai as the first destination for his unproven concept made perfect sense. Not only was it the only place that would take such an insane and untested idea seriously, it was also the only city that would fail to question whether it was possible at all.

The press also uncovered that Escape Investments had no track record in property. Karim had made his wealth importing used cars

231

and had been introduced to Hopkins by a mutual friend. Impressed by the concept, he took a punt and decided to make the Rotating Tower his first property venture. The fact that it was a no go was hardly a blow to his business interests, and he could simply go back to his philandering ways unscathed.

There was one last thing for me do. My heart sank at the very thought of it, but I had no choice. I had to make the call.

'Hi... I came in last week to put a deposit down on a Porsche... Yes... The white 911 Turbo... That's the one. I have some bad news, I'm afraid. I'm going to have to cancel it... Yes, I'll hold...'

17

The Laundry Business

Sheikh Mohammed was the first of a new breed of autocrat. He did not reign over his subjects from an ivory tower as did many of his Arab contemporaries. Mohammed was a much more hands-on and accessible leader, highly adored and respected among his countrymen. Affectionately named 'Sheikh Mo' by Dubai's residents, he was a symbol of strength, ambition and peace for modern Arabia. As he drove his white Mercedes G55 with the unmistakable '1' number plate along the Sheikh Zayed Road, he was greeted with fanatical admiration by every passer-by, Arab and expat alike. Mo was the super-hero sheikh, and at the turn of the twenty-first century his city was standing on the threshold of greatness.

Mohammed personified the great trading heritage of the Bedouins. He had taken the barren desert's only abundant commodity, sand, and sold it to the world as if it were gold. He was the ultimate merchant, and extended this innate business sense to his style of government. Sheikh Mohammed was not just a statesman; he was the chairman of a unique city-corporation aptly nicknamed 'Dubai Inc.'. This 'super-conglomerate' consisted of an intricate network of companies, investment funds and corporations under the umbrella of a centrally controlled holding company known as Dubai Holding. Its far-reaching tentacles spread across a plethora of business interests including aviation, leisure, real estate, hospitality, investments and logistics. The underlying principle of Dubai Inc.'s business model was simple: diversification backed by an unwavering ambition to be a leader in every field it entered.

Dubai's unique government structure was a critical ingredient in its sudden success. The absence of a cumbersome democratic process meant there was no time wasted on formulating manifestos, debating political ideas or canvassing for votes. Centralised decision making was opportunistic and nimble, and the government's constituents had complete confidence in the choices of its ruler, who ploughed ahead unchallenged. But neither did central administration equal central

233

planning; Dubai had no time for socialist models of wealth distribution. It was as capitalist as any Western administration, and there was no question that the overarching objective of its government-run entities was solely to make money.

From the outset, it seemed that Dubai Inc.'s business model was flawless. The economy was the fastest growing in the region, foreign investment was flowing into government coffers and Dubai's companies were fast becoming global leaders. And as the money rolled in, the sheikh went on a global shopping spree of trophy assets across the globe. Through its investment arms like Dubai International Capital and Istithmar, Dubai bought substantial stakes in blue-chip companies such as DaimlerChrysler, General Electric and US department store Barneys. With its new-found prominence, the city was beginning to flex its financial muscles on the global stage, and it was only a matter of time before its bold actions ruffled some powerful feathers.

When Dubai Ports World, the prized shipping and logistics conglomerate, placed a bid for British firm P&O's interest in a US port terminal, a full-scale political crisis erupted. In the post 9/11 world, Republican opponents raised fears over the security risks of allowing a Middle Eastern operator to control US ports. Similar concerns arose over Dubai's subsequent bid for Doncasters Group, a UK manufacturer of components for military aircraft. Suddenly, the Emirate was making enemies in high places and despite the government tactfully backing down to avoid sparking a full-scale diplomatic disaster, suspicions grew about its ulterior motives. Dubai, it seemed, was becoming as infamous as it was famous.

There were two main sticking points for Dubai's detractors. The first was its flourishing relationship with Iran. Dubai had historically closer links to Iran than other Arab states, and its trading ties today were unprecedented. Dubai's ports were a key transshipment point for both legal and illegal Western goods passing into the Islamic republic, and it was by far Tehran's biggest trading partner. Dubai was also the most popular destination for Iranian investment, as billions of dollars of capital found their way into the city's booming real estate sector. This 'special relationship' was not looked on fondly by Washington, and in the context of increasing political tensions over Iran's nuclear ambitions, Dubai was quickly demonised as an ally of the rogue regime.

The second concern was Dubai's alleged links with international terrorism. Since 9/11, a raft of investigative journalism had sought to expose the Emirate's role as a financial intermediary for terrorist funding and money laundering by militant Islamic groups. It was implied that the city's state-sponsored banks had been directly involved in facilitating the transfer of funds for illicit means, and that its unregulated gold and property markets provided a platform to convert the proceeds from opium rackets into US dollars. There were stories that Osama Bin Laden enjoyed a close personal relationship with the Maktoum dynasty, and that a CIA-ordered strike to assassinate him in 2006 was aborted when he was seen hunting with a prominent member of the Emirati royal family. Further questions were raised as to why Dubai itself had never been the victim of a terrorist attack despite its liberal values and ambiguous Islamic ethics.

Such allegations inevitably raised questions over the true source of funding for Dubai's booming property market, as the official story became increasingly dubious. They certainly went some way to explaining how projects worth in excess of two hundred billion dollars had emerged in less than five years. African warlords, Russian mafia and the Indian underworld were all believed to be washing their money in Dubai property, and providing the lifeblood for the industry's explosion. Thousands of empty apartment blocks and unoccupied villas across the city vindicated the allegation that they were simply instruments to launder dirty money. Of course this was officially denied, and in response to the allegations, the authorities implemented new legislation to combat any illegal movement of funds. But as Dubai's property ATM continued to spew out cash daily, changes were implemented *shway shway* and without urgency. It would, after all, be imprudent to rock the boat too much...

***

'Yes! Yes!!' I was startled by the sudden commotion on the sales floor. 'I don't believe it!'

I rushed over to see most of the team huddled around the desk of Syed, a young salesman from Pakistan who looked as if he had just won the lottery.

'What's going on?' screamed Edward as he stormed into the middle of the group.

'Syed has just closed a huge deal!' replied George, who was massaging Syed's shoulders.

'What did you close, Syed?' demanded Edward.

'Three buildings I think, sir,' Syed was struggling to compose his nerves.

'Three buildings?' echoed Edward. 'Well, who is the investor?'

'I don't know him. It was a cold call,' replied Syed, still shaking. 'He just said he wants to buy three buildings in International City for cash. He's coming in to close the deal tomorrow afternoon.'

Edward rushed straight to Tariq's office, while the sales team gathered around the hero of the day.

'Well done, Syed,' said Ashan with a high five. 'Let me know if you need any help in closing the deal.'

'Syed, great news!' echoed Omid.

Even Connor came over to offer his congratulations. If Syed completed, this deal would be the largest in Milestone's history and would trump him for the first time as the top biller.

'Thanks, guys,' Syed replied, relishing his moment in the sun. Having been with Milestone for over a year, the biggest deal he had closed before this was a three-bedroom apartment in Ajman. Shortly his name would be shooting up to the top of the Milestone sales board to occupy the coveted number one spot.

Edward emerged from Tariq's office. 'Syed, can you come inside for a moment? We would like to have a word.'

Syed did as he was told and disappeared from view as the speculation on the sales floor continued. Who was the mysterious buyer? Where was he from? Would he buy more buildings? And was there a way to muscle in on this deal? Syed was not seen for the rest of the day, and the murmurs continued until late. I was just as curious as the rest of the team about the mysterious investor. I asked Rav for the inside scoop.

'It seems the buyer is real,' Rav confirmed. 'He will apparently be coming into the office tomorrow to secure the buildings. Tariq wants you to be at that meeting too. We may be able to convince him to put some money into the fund.'

'Sure, of course I'll be there.'

The next morning, there was nervous anticipation in the Milestone office. The mysterious cash buyer was due to arrive at two, and every member of the team was intrigued to see who he was. The women dressed in their shortest skirts and highest stilettos in the hope of catching his attention for possible future transactions. Syed himself had bought a new suit for the occasion in anticipation of the biggest cheque of his life. He was set to make half a million dirhams in commission on the deal; a decent sum for answering a phone and taking down some details.

As the clock struck two, Rav picked up his phone, nodded and hung up. 'He's here. Let's go.'

We headed down towards the boardroom together. As we entered, Edward and Syed were already sitting at the table. To their left was a beast of a man dressed in a black leather jacket and a t-shirt. He had pale skin and short, crew-cut hair, and there was a distinctive scar along the length of his left cheek. He was sweating profusely and looked awkwardly restless. On the table in front of him was a black briefcase, which was attached to his wrist with a silver handcuff.

'So we are all here now?' he asked abruptly in a thick Russian accent.

'Yes, we are, sir,' replied Edward. 'Gentlemen, this is Mr Vladimir, Syed's investor. He would like to talk to us about his intention to buy three buildings in International City, which I am certain we can help him with.'

'I want to close the deal quickly and I want to pay all cash. And no bullshit,' mumbled Vladimir.

'Of course!' said Edward. 'Mr Vladimir. We will do everything in our power to close the deal as quickly as possible, I promise you that. Mr Rav Sidhu here heads up our business development team, and they have already identified three buildings in the France cluster of International City which we think would be an ideal location for your

237

requirements. Would you like to arrange a viewing of the buildings this week?'

'I don't care which buildings,' he growled. 'Any three buildings in International City are okay with me. I just want to close fast.'

'I assure you, Mr Vladimir, these are the best buildings we have available,' Edward insisted.

'Then I will take your word for it.' Vladimir pulled out a key from his jacket pocket and unlocked the wrist cuff. He opened the briefcase and turned it towards us to reveal its contents. I almost fell off my chair. It was full of perfectly arranged, crisp, one thousand dirham banknotes, just like in the movies. I had never seen so much money in my life. 'This is ten million dirhams in cash. I will give you this as a guarantee today and I will pay the rest on signing the contract.'

Edward was almost crying tears of joy. 'Of course, Mr Vladimir. We aim to please.'

'Good. I hope there will be no problems closing this deal. I want everything to go smoothly.'

Rav interjected, 'Mr Vladimir, I hope you understand that before we accept this money we need to conduct our internal compliance checks as a matter of protocol.' Edward did not look pleased.

'I am a businessman, Mr Sidhu,' insisted Vladimir. 'I am involved in oil and gas deals in Russia. I have done very well in the past few years and I would like to invest my wealth in Dubai. What more do you need to know?'

'Thank you, I appreciate your honesty,' replied Rav. 'But I'm afraid we still need to conduct our own due diligence before we can accept any funds from you. It's a matter of process. I hope you understand.'

Vladimir jumped out of his seat. 'What the hell is this? I am not here for a fucking interview! I have come to you to offer my business because I have heard you are the best brokerage company in Dubai. If you do not want my business, I will go somewhere else.' He slammed the briefcase shut and prepared to leave.

Edward leapt out of his chair to stop him. 'No, Mr Vladimir, we certainly don't want that at all. Mr Sidhu was simply asking out of protocol. If you do not wish to answer any questions, we completely understand.' He stared at Rav, who was shaking his head. 'Now, let's get back to business, please. We will draw up the paperwork and fax it to you first thing tomorrow. We can have the deal closed in three days.'

Vladimir paused and, looking into Edward's desperate eyes, began to calm down. 'Okay, I will leave this suitcase with you now, and the remaining funds will be with you when the contracts are ready.'

'Thank you, Mr Vladimir. Thank you so much.'

'I will be back to sign the contracts. Make sure they are ready.'

Before Vladimir left the room, I saw my chance to pitch the fund. 'Mr Vladimir, I head up the investment team here and I would also like to bring to your attention that Milestone is setting up a real estate fund that you may be interested in participating in. Provided everything goes smoothly with this deal first, of course.'

He paused and stared at me. 'Tell me more.' So I gave him the thirty-second elevator pitch I had prepared the night before and waited for his response. 'This sounds very interesting. If we can close this deal, I will consider putting some capital into this fund. Now, gentlemen, I need to leave. I will see you in three days.'

Syed escorted his client out while Edward, Rav and I stayed behind in the boardroom.

'Rav, what the fuck were you thinking?' screamed Edward as soon as the door was shut. 'We are about to close the biggest deal in our history and you're telling the guy we can't take his fucking money?'

'Edward, it is my job to ensure that proper process is followed,' replied Rav calmly. 'We can't just accept a suitcase full of cash from somebody we know nothing about. Tariq wouldn't allow it.'

'Why fucking not? He's giving it to us! The risk is with him. I cannot believe you sometimes, I swear to God!' He stormed out of the room.

Over the next two days, there was a desperate scramble to get everything in order for Vladimir's return. Tariq had been kept up to date on all the developments by Rav, but the onus was left to him and Edward to take care of the fine details and ensure that the deal closed

239

in a timely manner. On the sales floor, elaborate plans were already being forged to celebrate, including an all-day boat party around the Palm Jumeirah and an all-expenses-paid team weekend in St Tropez. Syed's name was now sitting proudly at the top of the Milestone sales board, and the entire team assumed that the deal was as good as done.

On the morning before Vladimir was due back in the office to sign, Edward, Rav and Tariq were locked in a meeting for most of the day. Nobody knew what was being discussed, but I assumed that Tariq was giving them a last-minute briefing for the big day.

'Is everything on course for tomorrow?' I asked Rav as he finally emerged from the boardroom.

'Yes. But there's been a small change to the venue. Tariq has suggested the yacht club in the Marina instead of here at the office. He prefers a more informal setting to ensure that Vladimir is fully relaxed.'

It was an odd decision, but I thought nothing of it. 'Okay, I don't see how that's a problem. What time are we leaving?'

Rav hesitated. 'Erm, that's the other thing. Tariq doesn't think it's necessary for you to attend this meeting.'

'But he was interested in the fund, Rav. I think this guy can be a big investor for us!'

'Yes, perhaps, but he will only be signing the papers for the buildings tomorrow. The fund discussion can wait until everything is finalised.'

I lost my cool. 'No, Rav! I have a vested interest in this meeting and I'm not going to lose this opportunity. I will be at that meeting whether you like it or not.'

Rav sighed and shook his head. 'It is against Tariq's wishes.'

'I don't care! Tariq wants me to find investors for the fund! We have a great lead here and I'm not going to let it slip away. I'm going to that meeting whether you like it or not!'

The next morning, Syed, Edward and I got into the Milestone minibus and made our way to the yacht club. Syed couldn't contain his excitement and wore a permanent smile all the way.

As we arrived, Vladimir was already waiting for us in the lounge. He was dressed in a shiny grey suit and a matching pink shirt, tie and handkerchief. He was joined by a small, unassuming Russian colleague wearing a pinstriped suit and thick glasses. Vladimir's gold-plated pen was ready on the table in front of him.

'Gentlemen, I am glad you made it. Please meet Boris, my lawyer,' he began. Boris nodded but remained expressionless. 'What are you all drinking?'

Edward took the lead. 'Nothing for us, Mr Vladimir, thank you. Is it okay if we get down to business? We have the contract here for you as promised. Please take a few minutes to review it.' Edward placed the document in front of the Russians and Boris scanned it eagerly. After a few minutes, he whispered something into Vladimir's ear; his client picked up the pen and signed the contract in three places.

'It's a pleasure to do business with you, gentlemen,' he said as he shook our hands one by one.

'You too, Mr Vladimir,' said Edward. 'Now, regarding the remaining funds...'

Boris immediately produced a suitcase, which he opened and discreetly showed us its contents. Again, it was full to the brim with brand new bank notes. He closed it and handed it over to Edward. 'It's all there. You can count it if you like.'

'No, I don't think that will be necessary, Mr Vladimir,' smiled Edward.

'Good.' Vladimir turned to face me. 'Now, about your fund idea...'

Suddenly there was a huge crashing sound, like a giant explosion.

'*Yalla, yalla*! Go, go, go!'

Twenty men in army uniforms armed with guns stormed into the bar from every direction. Within seconds we were completely surrounded.

'Put your hands on your heads!' We all did as we were told. 'You are under arrest for money laundering and human trafficking.'

'What is this? What is going on?' protested Vladimir as one of the soldiers cuffed his wrists. Another seized the suitcase of cash and a third escorted out Boris, who was almost in tears. Edward, Syed and I were also cuffed before being bundled into one of two vans outside.

'What the hell is going on?' screamed Edward.

'Don't talk,' said one of the armed men, slamming the doors of the van shut, leaving us in darkness. I heard the engine start and we began to move. The three of us didn't say a word to each other for the duration of the drive, which seemed like an eternity.

Finally, the van stopped and the doors swung open.

'Get out, get out!' cried the Emirati officer, waving a rifle in our direction. We did as we were told. 'You two go this way, you come with me,' he said, pointing to me. I noticed that we were in some kind of closed compound. There were dozens of huts to my left and right, and in the distance were acres of unspoilt desert. The officer began to frisk me aggressively, and confiscated my mobile phone and wallet from my inside blazer pocket. He then ushered me into one of the huts and down a long corridor. At the end of the hallway was a small makeshift cell, which he unlocked before shoving me in. 'You go in here.'

'But I haven't done anything!' I protested.

'Be quiet, don't talk!' The door slammed shut behind me.

The inside of the cell was filthy, with what looked like dried vomit and faeces splattered around the floor. It smelt like a rotting corpse, which made me gag a few times, but I somehow managed to prevent myself from throwing up. I wasn't alone in the cell. In the corner sat an emaciated Indian man with no shoes and ripped clothes. His hair was dishevelled and his beard unkempt. He had his head in his hands and didn't flinch, despite the commotion of my entrance.

I was terrified and took a seat on the dirty floor to try to calm my nerves. I wanted to cry, but I did my best not to show any emotion in case it was interpreted as a sign of guilt. It seemed like an age before I saw any movement outside when the officer who had escorted me into the cell reappeared and opened the cell door.

'You come with me. Come, come.' I followed him back down the long hallway, only this time we bore left and into a small, dimly lit room with a desk and chair at either end. 'Sit down, sit down.' My heart was racing uncontrollably now and a million questions were rushing through my head. What would happen next? How would I be punished? Would I be deported or imprisoned, or worse? Was I entitled to a lawyer? Would my family be told?

In walked a huge Emirati man in a spotless *dishdasha*, who sat on the vacant chair to face me.

'Mr Adam?' he said.

'Yes,' I replied nervously, still shaking.

'I am Mr Jassim from CID.'

'What's CID?'

'Let's say we are like a special police unit for Dubai. But I will be asking the questions from now on. Okay?'

'Okay.'

'First, where are you from and what are you doing in Dubai?'

'I'm from London in England. I work for Milestone Properties.'

'Where are you from originally?'

'You mean my parents?'

'Yes.'

'Well, they were born in Pakistan. But they live in London. They are both British citizens.'

'I see. You look like an Arab.'

I nodded.

'Have you always worked for Milestone?'

'No, I first came to Dubai to work for Imperial Bank. I left them a few months ago.'

'And why did you leave Imperial Bank?'

I sighed. 'Well, things weren't going so well there. And I decided I wanted to work in real estate.'

'Ah, you think real estate is better than banking? Why?'

I shook my head with embarrassment. 'I wanted to make more money I guess.'

'I see, more money.' He paused to scribble something on his notepad.

'Can you at least tell me what's going on here? Am I in trouble?'

'Please, Mr Adam, I said no questions.'

I nodded again in acknowledgement.

'How do you know Mr Vladimir?'

'I don't know him! He was a client of one of my colleagues.'

'So why were you at this meeting today?'

'I was in the process of setting up an investment fund for Milestone. I assumed he could be an investor.'

Again he scribbled away on his notepad. 'Mr Adam, am I correct to say that you were a student at Oxford University?' My heart sank suddenly. How could he possibly have known that? 'Mr Adam?'

'Yes, I was.'

'And am I correct to assume that when you were at Oxford, you were also working for an establishment in London called The Rooms?'

I couldn't believe my ears. 'Yes, I was. How did you know that?'

'That's not your concern. Mr Adam, do you know why you are here?'

'No, I don't.'

'Mr Tariq, your boss, called us to tell us about the deal happening today. He had some suspicions about Mr Vladimir and informed us immediately. According to our background checks, Mr Vladimir has been laundering funds from the Russian mafia for years and we have been watching him closely for some time.'

I couldn't believe it. 'Tariq knew about this?'

'Yes, he cooperated with us to set up this sting operation.'

'So why am I in trouble?'

'You're not. But we needed to check you out as a precautionary measure. You are free to go.'

'Wait, are you saying I can leave?'

'Yes.'

The guard waiting outside entered the room to escort me out of the building.

'Wait,' said the CID officer before I left the room. 'Regarding The Rooms in London...' He stared into my eyes. 'Let's just say I never forget a face.' He smiled for a split second before beckoning the guard to take me outside. '*Yalla!*'

I was led to where Syed and Edward were being ushered into a car by two other guards. One of them handed me back my mobile phone and my wallet before pushing me into the car with my colleagues.

'So what about the deal?' asked Syed, as the guard closed the door behind him. I could see the tears building in his eyes.

'It's off, Syed. The deal is off!' said Edward, shaking his head.

The car dropped us back at the Milestone offices and I immediately stormed into Rav's office.

'Do you know what the hell just happened, Rav? Did you know about this?' He looked up at me and nodded.

'Yes, I did. Tariq used his government contacts to do some background checks on Mr Vladimir. It turns out he is a point man for the Russian mafia in Dubai. The Dubai authorities have been watching him for months, and after Tariq's tip-off the CID decided to catch him with illegal funds. This deal was the perfect scenario for them to catch him red-handed.'

'So why the hell did they arrest all of us?'

'That I can't answer. The police do things as they wish to.'

'But if there was the risk of that, why didn't you tell me not to go?'

'I did try to warn you, Adam. You didn't listen.' I was irate, but Rav was right. He had tried to discourage me, and I had been too adamant to take his hint.

'So what happens with the money?'

245

'I guess it will be used as evidence. But we won't know that for sure. Anyway, that's not our concern. Milestone has a reputation and we are not willing to jeopardise it by any means. That's why Tariq remains so respected by the authorities.'

After discovering the questionable source of Vladimir's funds, Tariq had done something that most others in his position would not have dreamed of. He had tipped off the authorities to protect his firm's reputation. Most other real estate companies would have welcomed a suitcase full of crisp bills without question. They were taking hundreds of millions of dirhams from unsavoury characters like Vladimir every day; indeed, for many agents their entire business models were built around this kind of business. But Milestone was not like every other broker and Tariq stuck to his ethics.

After one of the most stressful and frightening days of my life, I couldn't wait to get home and put it all behind me. I left the office a little early and patiently waited in the nearby queue for a taxi. It was unusually humid and my sweaty back was making my shirt cling uncomfortably to my skin. A large Filipina woman behind me was carrying her child in her arms and the baby didn't stop bellowing for a moment. Excruciatingly slowly, the taxis arrived one by one and the queue inched forward a little more.

Out of the corner of my eye, I noticed an awkward-looking Indian man with a rucksack loitering a few metres to my right. He seemed like he was watching me at the same time as the approaching cars, although I couldn't immediately tell what he was up to. I was at the end of my patience when I finally found myself at the front of the line. As my taxi approached, I prepared to jump into the back, but something quite unexpected happened. The Indian on my right flagged it down before it had reached me and jumped in. It was the last straw. I lost every semblance of composure and exploded with rage. I ran up to the taxi before the driver had a chance to pull away and almost ripped the back door off.

'Oi, you little prick! Can't you see there is a fucking queue here? People have been waiting for a taxi for half an hour and you think you can just get in as you please, you bastard!'

The man didn't know what had hit him. 'Okay, okay,' he pleaded.

I grabbed him by the neck and manhandled him out of the taxi. 'Get the fuck out of the car, you piece of shit!' He clasped his hands together in a begging gesture, terrified for his life. 'Get the fuck out!' I threw him onto the concrete street.

'I am sorry, I didn't know!'

'Don't lie to me!' I took his place in the back seat and tossed his rucksack onto the road next to him. 'Don't you ever try anything like that again, motherfucker!' I screamed, pointing at his trembling face before I slammed the door.

It was a rage I had never experienced before. A shudder went down my spine and I found it hard to breathe. I was becoming somebody I didn't recognise, and it terrified the hell out of me.

Perhaps all the setbacks and stresses over the past few months had caught up with me all at once and I was venting my frustration. Perhaps this was a symptom that I was losing my soul in Dubai. Perhaps it was a sign to get out of this godforsaken city once and for all.

18

Buy Now, Pay Later

By late 2007, the UAE boasted one of the highest concentrations of millionaires in the world. It was no wonder that the Emirates were suddenly engulfed by a new wave of bankers from Europe and the US trying to get their hands on a piece of the ever expanding cash pile. Although much of the wealth was the old money of affluent local families, the country was also awash with a wave of new money, much of which had been created in the previous five years in Dubai's property sector. And so life in the Emirates became one big party as the good times rolled.

Every day, Dubai's super-malls were overflowing with brand-obsessed shopaholics. The city's residents dined in the finest five-star restaurants, drove the latest luxury cars and drenched themselves in designer couture. Self-obsessed Jumeirah Janes treated themselves to so-called diamond facials, in which actual diamonds were blended into their skin for a sparkling finish. New mothers purchased gold-plated pacifiers studded with jewels for their spoilt toddlers. And Dubai's locals quenched their thirst with Bling water, served in handmade bottles studded with real Swarovski crystals. Materialism was rampant and indulgence became a way of life, as Dubai's prosperous residents flashed their fortune in new and creative ways in a grand display of *la dolce vita*.

In addition to quick profits in the property casino, this insane spending spree was also fuelled by a typhoon of cheap debt from the banks, opening the floodgates to anybody willing to sign on the dotted line. Credit cards became a must-have accessory and many residents boasted a collection of plastic of all colours and limits. There was no need for the inconvenience of credit checks or proof of income. Instead, professionals across the city were hunted down by loan officers who stalked them daily at their offices, in the malls and even at their homes to coax them into taking a line of credit. One line led to another and another, until the addict was hooked and there was no turning back.

In a city consumed by vanity, nobody was exempt from a share of the good life. As Gucci, Chanel and Dior goods flew off the shelves in the malls, in a dark hidden room at the back of an inconspicuous clothing store in Karama, uncanny replica Rolex watches, Prada handbags and Ray-Ban sunglasses were snapped up by Filipina maids, Indian labourers and Pakistani taxi drivers desperate to look the part. It was usually close enough to the real thing; or 'same same', as the shopkeeper insisted, despite the odd missing G in 'Ucci' or misplaced D in 'Dom Ford'.

Now on a six-year run, Dubai's real estate market was showing no signs of letting up. Construction had become an addiction, with developers scrambling to launch new projects every week to keep up with the growing demand. Increases in property values of 10 per cent in a matter of days were not unheard of, and sales targets were frequently obliterated. New investors were arriving daily and Dubai was getting global coverage as the hottest and most foolproof investment destination in the world. It was only a matter of time before the titans of global real estate sat up and paid attention.

2008 was a landmark year for Dubai property, marking the exciting arrival of the biggest property brand on the planet. The announcement by Donald Trump that he would be building a six-hundred-million-dollar, forty-eight-storey tower as the new centrepiece of the Palm Jumeirah sent shockwaves through the newswires and propelled the name of Dubai onto the international stage. Trump's announcement that the site was the best location in the Middle East gave Dubai valuable bragging rights over its neighbours and cemented its position as a world-class destination. As glamorous star-studded parties commemorated the announcement of the Trump project in Los Angeles, Dubai became the buzz of Tinseltown. It was a great coup for Brand Dubai, ushering the city into an uncharted new era of global praise and recognition.

Dubai had finally cracked America. Actors, sports stars and fashion designers were queuing to put their name and brand on a skyscraper on the city skyline. Chanel creative director Karl Lagerfeld was appointed to create a Coco-inspired project on the new Fashion Island on the manmade archipelago The World. Boris Becker and Giorgio Armani unveiled their own master plans. Even actor Brad Pitt would design his own eighty-room hotel. It was said that Sheikhs

Mohammed's ambitious father, Sheikh Rashid had always dreamed that his city would one day be mentioned in the same breath as the great cities of the West. Now, that dream had become a reality and Dubai found fame and celebrity beyond its wildest dreams.

In 2008, Dubai was cruising. But under the glossy exterior, some early cracks were also emerging. Up to this point, 90 per cent of buyers in the market had been speculators looking to flip, who didn't care much for completion dates. But as delivery dates approached, reports of continuing delays by property developers were becoming increasingly common, with some units now over two years late. Issues were being raised over the ability of developers to deliver, and fears of investors losing their money became more pronounced. For the first time in the short history of Dubai property, the question was not *when* a building would be delivered, but *if*. There were muted calls for improved regulation and legislation as the government was chastised for not legally protecting the rights of individual investors. As the market entered unchartered territory, new challenges called for new strategies, and many people waited to see how the city would respond.

***

The giant map on the wall behind my desk had changed yet again. It was more crowded than before, and even the smallest unoccupied spaces had now been filled. The most conspicuous addition was a lizard-like sea creature that looked to be attacking the islands of The World. Its giant head had seven tentacles protruding from it and its tail snaked around the coast of the Palm. This was the so-called Universe development, a monstrosity of a manmade landmass planned for the already crowded coastline. The head of the beast represented the sun and the boils on its tail were the planets of the solar system. There was even a galaxy, a floating, misplaced swirl that hovered awkwardly next to Australia on The World.

Back on dry land, a meandering blue waterway now sliced open a huge section of the desert from Jebel Ali to the Dubai Waterfront. It was to be the new seventy-five-kilometre Arabian Canal, a sixty-one-billion-dollar undertaking that would effectively turn the Jebel Ali landmass into an island. Some of the existing developments had changed a little too; the protruding claw of the Waterfront development was a little smaller beside the Jebel Ali Palm it surrounded, and the design for the massive Palm Deira had altered

250

dramatically. Whether this was the hallmark of the evolution of a city in progress, or an admission that imagination had found its limits, was up for debate.

One of the best perks of my position as head of investments for the city's biggest broker was being invited to most of the property launch parties. They were usually grand affairs with little expense spared on food, drink and entertainment. In a fiercely competitive marketplace, the services of a good broker were invaluable, so a representative from Milestone was a useful addition to a developer's guest list. Yet there were a few developers who refused to work with agents. Their list of clients was so exceptional that they could confidently sell out their project with just a few phone calls, so their launch parties were strictly off limits to Milestone employees. Most annoyingly, these parties were also usually the best.

One such developer was Paradise City. Established in 2005, the company was the brainchild of two former nursing-home entrepreneurs from Bradford in the north of England called Tasneem and Irfan, or Taz and Iffi. With no background or experience in commercial real estate, the brothers had come to Dubai in 2004 after hearing about its potential from an uncle, and had immediately started selling properties to their friends and family. The business grew rapidly, and now with some sizable capital behind them they had moved into development, launching their first residential tower in the Dubai Marina in 2006. The project sold out in six days.

On the back of this early success, Taz and Iffi were now launching their second project, a mixed-use fifty-storey tower in the upcoming Waterfront development. The official launch party was expected to be the biggest in history. It was to be held in the ballroom at the Al Qasr hotel, and the entertainment line-up alone was enough to get the tongues of the city's social elite wagging. The headline act was the world's biggest pop star Fernando, which caught the attention of global media and stole headlines across the region. Fernando had never performed in the Middle East before, a fact that instantly propelled Paradise City's party to the coveted status of the hottest ticket in town. For three weeks before the event, Paradise City counted down to it on a double-page spread in *Gulf News*. I wasn't going to miss this party for anything, but as they weren't inviting any agents, I needed another way in.

251

Having worked with real estate agents for a while now, I knew exactly what made them tick. They were simple creatures who could be made to jump through hoops if the right carrot was dangled in front of their greedy little eyes. I had a plan that was sure to get me what I wanted.

'Sharon...'

'Yes, darling?'

'Do you have any contacts in the sales team at Paradise City?'

'As a matter of fact I do. Sean Gibbon. English guy, lovely lad. Do you want Sean's number?'

'Yes please.'

'Of course, here it is. But if you think he's going to give you tickets to the launch party, I would forget about it. I've already asked him. I would give my right arm to see Fernando live! He's gorgeous.'

'Sharon, I'm offended. Do you think I would use Milestone's contacts for personal gain? I'm a serious businessman, you know,' I said coyly, but she saw right through me.

'Of course you are,' she smiled. 'I'm just letting you know, that's all.'

I found a discreet corner away from Sharon's desk to make the call.

'Hello, this is Sean!' shouted a young man in a cockney English accent.

'Hi, Sean, this is Adam from Milestone Properties. I got your number from Sharon in the business development team. I'm the new head of investments at Milestone and I'm calling to introduce myself.'

He interrupted me mid-sentence. 'You're calling about tickets to the launch party, aren't you?'

'Well, I was going to ask you if you could possibly...'

'Listen, buddy, I don't mean to sound harsh, but the event is completely oversubscribed. We have a waiting list that is twice as long as the guest list. There's simply no chance.'

'Oh, I see. Well, that's a real shame, because I have this huge investor who is really interested in buying a few floors in the Waterfront development. I told him about your new project and he's really keen, so I thought I would bring him along to the event.'

There was a long pause. 'Investor? Who is he?'

'He is a businessman from Lebanon. One of our bigger clients. He usually doesn't mess around and can pull the trigger pretty quickly if he sees something he likes. But I guess if you're oversubscribed...'

There was another pause. 'Okay, let me see what I can do. But please tell him he will have to bring his chequebook and be ready to buy on the night. We are expecting this project to sell out in hours.'

'Sean, trust me, I know this guy well. He will even bring his own collection of pens so he doesn't have to waste time looking for one.'

Sean sighed deeply. 'I'm probably going to get in trouble for this, but if it translates into a sale then I guess it makes sense. I will put you down on the list plus one. But please come early, otherwise I can't guarantee you will get in.'

'Of course! See you tomorrow night.'

My plan had worked perfectly, and just like that I had scored two tickets to the biggest event in Dubai's history.

A few moments later, Rav came over to my desk.

'Have you heard about the Paradise City event?' he asked.

I feared that my plan had been exposed and hoped I wasn't in any trouble. 'Yes, of course. They're having a big launch next week,' I replied nervously.

'They are. We won't be able to get tickets because they have a no-broker policy, but I want you to go and meet them. They could be a useful contact for the fund.' He handed me a business card. 'Here is their CEO Taz's number. Give his secretary a call and set up a time to see him.'

'Sure, Rav.' I did as I was told and arranged a meeting with Taz the following afternoon. I decided to keep my conversation with Sean confidential. This was business now, and any hint that I was trying to score tickets to the party surely wouldn't help my reputation.

After announcing my arrival to the pretty receptionist at Paradise City's offices, I took a seat on the soft white leather sofa and waited for my host. In front of me was a large coffee table with dozens of lifestyle and property magazines. One glossy cover particularly caught my eye on a property publication called *Dubai Today*, which featured the headline 'When Will Dubai Say Enough Is Enough?' It got me thinking. Did Dubai have an end goal? Would there be a point where the city would be 'finished'? Or would the insane construction go on for ever? Nobody seemed to know the answers.

'Mr Tasneem will see you now,' said the receptionist eventually. I followed an Indian man in a waistcoat down a long corridor. We reached a large white door at the end, on which the man knocked three times.

'Come!' shouted a voice from within.

The first thing that struck me was how white the room was. The walls, carpets and ceilings were all one spotless colour. There was a white coffee table in the middle of the room sitting on a white fluffy rug. On the table sat a huge white vase with white orchids. And at the far end behind a glass desk on a white leather chair sat a small man speaking on a white phone. He was dressed in a white suit, white t-shirt and sneakers. His hair was short and spiky, and his sideburns merged seamlessly into his trimmed goatee. He gave me a thumbs up as I walked into the office, followed by a 'sit down' hand gesture towards the white sofa behind me.

'Please, sir, what would you like to drink?' asked the Indian man while I waited.

'Do you have green tea?' I asked.

'No, sir. Only white tea.'

'Okay, that will be fine.'

Taz hung up and swivelled around to face me. 'Sorry about that, brav. Welcome! So Rav tells me you're the new head of investments at Milestone. Nice to meet you.' His voice was high pitched and whiney, and his inner-city accent made him sound like a gangster from the streets of East London.

'Yes, I'm Adam. Rav suggested I come over and meet you, so thanks very much for taking the time to see me today.'

'Nah, brav, the pleasure's all mine. Milestone has done very well in this market. I have never met Tariq, but his reputation as a talented businessman is well known.'

'Thank you, I will pass on your kind words.' I looked around the room. 'So you like white, I see.'

'Yeah, brav, white symbolizes purity, innit. White is the colour of calm and peace, you get me? I like to be surrounded by pure things and that, hence the white.'

I couldn't help think that his explanation was profoundly shallow, but I pretended to look interested nonetheless. 'Very interesting.'

'So tell me, how can we do business together?'

'Well, as you know, Milestone is one of the biggest names in the industry, so I wanted to explore how we may be able to partner up on some things that I'm working on.'

'I'm afraid I'm going to have to stop you there. I don't know if anybody has told you, but we follow a strict policy of not working with any brokers. Frankly, we have enough investors of our own, so we don't need the services of an agent, whether that's Milestone or anybody else.'

'I am aware of that, Taz. But I wanted to let you know that Milestone is now looking to manage capital on behalf of investors. My responsibility as the head of investments is to create and manage this new vehicle, and we are looking to build relationships with a few leading developers to provide us with a strong pipeline of deals.'

Taz listened attentively, rubbing his palms together as I spoke. 'So I am assuming you will be managing a large pool of funds and will be looking to invest in floors, buildings, plots…'

'Exactly right.'

'And where will this vehicle be domiciled?'

'Well, it will be structured as an offshore vehicle in the Cayman Islands or the British Virgin Islands. We want to maintain our investors' confidentiality and protect their interests at all costs.'

Taz's eyes lit up and he stroked his beard gently. 'Interesting. Very interesting.' He stared at me and smiled. 'In that case, I think we can certainly work together. You may have heard that we are actually launching a new project tonight, and I would like to invite you as my guest.' He rummaged through some papers on his desk before handing me an envelope. I opened it to find two VIP tickets to the launch party.

'Taz, thank you, but I can't accept these. We haven't even done any business together yet!'

'Please, I insist.' He wasn't giving in. 'Listen, I like you. I think you are somebody I can trust. I am a very good judge of character, you know. I think we can have a long-lasting business relationship.'

'Well, thank you. That's very kind.'

'No worries, brav. But this invitation is on one condition. That we meet again the day after the party to talk business. I will have some options I would like you to consider then. Enjoy the party and I will see you in a couple of days. How does that sound?'

I agreed and left Paradise City's offices feeling like I had hit the jackpot. Just this morning, it looked as if I had no chance of attending the biggest launch in Dubai property history. Now I not only had guaranteed entry from Sean, but had also scored two VIP tickets from the CEO of the firm! Tonight was going to be great.

I didn't want to go alone, so I asked Hani to join me as a thank-you for all the favours he had done for me recently. He was over the moon and we agreed to meet at eight. We dressed up in tuxedos and made our way to the Al Qasr.

As we pulled up at the entrance to the ballroom, it felt as if we had gone back in time for a Hollywood movie premiere from the golden era. The dancing beams from giant spotlights illuminated the sky as dozens of people scrambled to get past the army of security officers to the barriers and secure their spot for a view of Fernando. There were lines of super-cars parked close by, among them a beautiful white Aston Martin with white interiors and wheel rims featuring the unmistakable number plate 'TAZ 1'. A long red carpet had been laid out for the invited guests and scores of paparazzi from the local glossy magazines huddled together, armed with microphones and camera lenses.

256

The inside of the ballroom had been transformed into a dream-like fantasia. Every wall was dotted with hundreds of lights, creating the surreal effect that the room was floating against the night's sky. On the stage a live orchestra played a Tchaikovsky overture as the exclusive guests poured in and took their seats.

'Find our seats, buddy. I gotta make a quick call. I'll be back shortly,' said Hani, before disappearing for a while.

'Sure.' I grabbed a drink from a passing waiter and tried to mingle a bit. A circle of older European men near the bar were discussing the state of the property market as I loitered inconspicuously to listen in.

'Gosh, these parties are getting more and more lavish, I must say.'

'Yes, but that doesn't justify prices getting out of control. Who is seriously going to buy this project at three and a half thousand dirhams per square foot? It's preposterous.'

'You're right. If they honestly think putting on a show and feeding me well is going to make me part with my money, they have another think coming.'

It was clear that the euphoria of previous property launches was waning and speculation was not the cash cow it once was. With so much supply now on the market, developers were finding it difficult to command ludicrously inflated prices. The old game of flipping a newly launched property for a premium was beginning to disappear, and many investors were even forced to sell their units at a zero premium, or worse, at a loss. Sellers were outnumbering buyers, which meant it was much more feasible for an investor to buy something in a similar location for up to half the price on the secondary market. A celebrity appearance and a gourmet buffet from a Michelin-starred chef were a last resort for desperate developers to entice investors into buying in a market where doing so was becoming increasingly illogical, and unprofitable.

Hani returned shortly after and we took our seats at our table moments before dinner was served. But just as I was about to tuck in to the gorgeous plate of food in front of me, I felt my phone vibrate inside my trouser pocket.

'Hello?' I answered.

'Hi, it's Sean.'

'Sean?'

'Yes, Sean, from Paradise City. We spoke yesterday, remember?'

'Oh, hi Sean.'

'So is he here?'

'Who?'

'Your Lebanese investor. Is he with you?'

I had to think fast. 'Well, the thing is...'

'He has his chequebook, right? Because this building is going to move fast, believe me.'

'Yes, I'm sure, but Sean...'

'What table are you at? Wait a minute, I think I see you, I'm coming over.'

I turned to Hani in desperation. 'Hani, you gotta do me a big favour. You have to pretend to be a big Lebanese investor.'

Hani looked baffled. 'What? What are you talking about?'

'Just listen to me. Act like you're a big-shot investor who is here to buy. Okay?' Before he could respond, Sean was standing behind me.

'Hi there. Good thing I spotted you!'

'Hey, Sean, good to meet you,' I said and shook his hand.

'How did you guys get on the VIP table?' he asked, scratching his head. 'I booked you on table seventeen.'

'Well...'

'Anyway, that doesn't matter right now. So this must be your investor?'

'Yes. This is my investor. Mr... Bin Laden.'

Sean grabbed Hani's hand. 'Hello, Mr Bin Laden! Thank you so much for coming tonight. I hear you're very interested in buying in the Waterfront.' Hani nodded nervously. 'That's fantastic, because this building has one of the best plots in the entire development.' Again

Hani nodded, while glancing at me curiously. 'So do you have any questions about the development that I can help with?'

I interjected. 'Sean, I don't think Mr Bin Laden is too keen right now to...'

'No, it's okay,' interrupted Hani in a mock Arabic accent, which almost made me fall off my chair. 'Sean, as a matter of fact I do have a couple of questions. What is the price per square foot you are offering?'

'We are selling it at two thousand seven hundred dirhams per square foot, sir.'

'Don't you think that is a massive premium to the market?' Hani was playing the part to perfection.

'Not at all, sir. The Waterfront will be the most exclusive community in Dubai once it is complete and ours is one of the best sea-facing plots on offer.'

'Yes, but Sean, here is my issue. I can buy something in, say, Business Bay today on the secondary market for half the price of a newly launched project. There is a glut of unsold properties available that have been flipped a number of times and are now struggling to find a buyer. It simply makes no sense for me to buy a new launch when I can pick something up for cheaper. What's to say that won't happen in the Waterfront?'

Sean was stumped. Hani's question had thrown him off balance and he didn't seem to have an answer. 'We don't believe Business Bay can be compared to the Waterfront, and we are certain it will hold its value.' It was a poor effort right out of the Dubai property agent's handbook.

'Okay. Well, Sean, why don't we enjoy our dinner and we can speak again later in the evening. How does that seem?'

'Absolutely, Mr Bin Laden. Please, enjoy your dinner. I'm only a short distance away if you need me.' Sean winked at me before disappearing back to his table.

'Wow, Hani, that was incredible! I didn't know you knew anything about real estate!'

'Buddy, I'm in the fastest-growing market in the world, most of my friends are property brokers and I'm Lebanese; making money is in my blood. Besides, I needed a way to get rid of him so we can enjoy our food in peace, *yaani*.'

As we tucked into our Michelin-starred meal, the evening's entertainment was just beginning. The lights went down and the room fell silent as a small man in a white suit came onto the stage.

'Ladies and gentleman, good evening. I am Taz, the CEO of Paradise City,' he said, staring intensely at the scrap of paper in his hand. 'Three years ago, I had a dream to build towers in the desert. I had a dream to be one of the biggest property developers. I had a dream to bring people together in harmony and peace. In Dubai, my dream became real!' There was a rapturous round of applause. 'Welcome to the launch of our second project, the Paradise Tower in the Dubai Waterfront. Tonight is your opportunity to own your own piece of Paradise!' Again, a round of applause. 'We have an A-list line-up of entertainment, so without further ado, let the night's enjoyment begin.'

He left the stage as the spotlights began to flash and a band appeared with a familiar looking voluptuous Lebanese pop star called Alina, who began a rendition of her greatest hit, 'Yalla, oh baby'.

I rushed to the bathroom before dessert arrived and bumped into Taz in the lobby.

'Taz, great speech earlier,' I said.

'Thanks, man. I'm glad you could make it. Are you enjoying yourself?'

'Yes, it's great. The food was excellent and I'm looking forward to seeing Fernando later, along with everybody else here.'

'You want to meet him?' he asked suddenly.

'Who?'

'Fernando.'

'Are you serious?'

'Sure. Come, I will introduce you.' Taz put his arm round my shoulder and led me backstage. In the large green room there he was,

260

Fernando, the biggest star in the world, smoking a cigarette while his band members tuned their guitars.

'He looks a bit busy, Taz. Why don't we do this another time?'

'Don't be silly. Fernando, my man! This is my good friend Adam. He wanted to say hi.'

Fernando looked up and gave me a high five. He was very handsome in the flesh and his ripped torso made me a little jealous. 'Hey, Fernando, good to meet you,' I said nervously. Every teenage girl in the world would have killed to be in my position right now.

'I want you guys to take care of Adam and show him a good time tonight,' said Taz, while massaging my shoulders.

'Taz, anything you want, buddy. Your friend can hang out with us as long as he wants,' replied Fernando. I was speechless.

'Enjoy the night, gentlemen,' said Taz.

'Wait, Taz, aren't you going to join us?' I asked.

'No, I'm afraid not,' he smiled. 'I have important people to entertain. Have fun. Just remember, you owe me a favour back.' With that, he winked and walked away.

I watched the rest of the show from backstage. Fernando's performance was incredible and got the entire audience on their feet to party the night away. Men in expensive tuxedos and women in impractical ball gowns danced on their chairs and on tables as he played his greatest hits.

'What a show, Fernando!' I said as he finally returned backstage, sweating profusely.

'Thanks, mate. But the night is only just beginning. There's a limo waiting for us outside to take us to my penthouse. Are you ready for the night of your life?'

The rest of the night was a haze. I had vague flashbacks of a hotel room, lots of booze and perhaps some drugs. There were women, dozens of them, all stunning and exotic, and a pool and some empty champagne bottles. I have no idea how I got home, but I was woken suddenly the following evening by an email on my BlackBerry. As I scrambled for my phone, I noticed through blurry eyes that it was from

Taz's assistant requesting a meeting. I replied before rushing to the bathroom to throw up.

***

'So did you enjoy the party?' asked Taz, leaning back in his white leather chair, puffing on a fat cigar.

'It was incredible, I think. I don't remember much after the show,' I said sheepishly.

Taz winked. 'Sounds like you had a crazy night!'

'Yes, it seems I did. But thanks so much again for the invitation, Taz.'

'It was my pleasure to have you as our guest,' he smiled. 'But as I mentioned to you before, we need to talk serious business now.'

'Yes, of course. What would you like to discuss?'

Taz sat back and stroked his chin for a moment. 'I have been thinking some more about your fund idea. I see us working together in two ways. First, you need investors, and I can bring you investors with serious money. And second, you are looking for a strong pipeline of properties, and I can also help you there.'

'Okay, I'm listening,' I replied.

'Let's just say I have friends who have substantial capital and I can convince them to invest with you. But like every business deal, I need something from you.'

'Like what?'

'On one side I will bring you investors for your fund. If they invest, you pay me a percentage as an introduction fee. On the other side, I will bring you deals for the fund. You will use their capital to invest in these deals, and I will pay you a fee for investing in my deals. This way, everybody wins.'

I was a little confused. 'But why don't you just sell your investors the real estate directly?'

'I could. But there is a small problem. These are, you could say, "special investors". You see, these investors cannot technically invest directly into Dubai property, even though they have hundreds of millions of dollars to do so.'

'Why not?'

'Because there are certain restrictions on these investors.'

'I'm sorry, Taz, I don't understand.'

He got up and strolled over to where I was sitting. He took a seat next to me and lowered his voice.

'Can you keep this strictly between us?'

'Of course.'

'My investors are Israeli.'

I still didn't get it. 'What does that mean?'

Taz shook his head. 'Are you telling me you don't know about the rules in the Gulf against doing business with Israel?'

'I'm sorry, I don't.'

He sighed. 'There is an official ban on it. Israel is the enemy. The countries of the Gulf do not even recognise its existence, so any business dealings are completely forbidden.'

'And do Israeli investors really want to invest in a country where their money is not wanted?'

'Brav, just look around you. Who is not making money in Dubai? Everything is turning to gold here. People are making faster returns on their capital than any other investment in the world. Which serious investor would not want a piece of this?'

'Okay, Taz, but I still don't see how this fits in with the Milestone fund.'

'My friend, your fund is an offshore investment vehicle. My investors keep their capital in offshore trusts and shell companies. Milestone is a good name in the market. I think this is a unique opportunity for us both.'

What Taz was asking was suddenly clear. He wanted to use the Milestone fund structure as a front to help move funds illegally from Israelis to Paradise City's projects. The offshore structure removed a

263

layer of scrutiny by the authorities, and with an established and respected name like Milestone behind it, it was unlikely to encourage too much investigation. In return, he was willing to share fees with me every time the fund invested in a Paradise City project, which was effectively a bribe.

I began to panic. 'This is against the law, Taz! What if the Dubai authorities were to find out who the investors in the fund are?'

'The important question is, do they really want to find out?' He began to get heated as he spoke. 'You think this city is where it is because of working-class people putting their life savings into studio apartments? Bullshit! Billions of dollars have flooded into this market in the past few years. And you think that is clean money? No, my friend. Most of it is dirty money. Laundered money. Blood money. The authorities don't care one bit where it comes from. They have never cared. Dubai has been a haven for arms dealers, terrorists and money launderers from the beginning. Today these same men are building the greatest city in the world. Too many important people are making too much money to care where the hell the money is coming from. But it has to be done a certain way for political reasons. They need to save face. Now do you understand?'

'Yes, but…'

'But nothing! I told you I wanted a favour and you agreed. I was very clear. Now I'm offering you an opportunity to make some serious money, and you're throwing it back in my face!'

'I-I-I...' He made me feel terrible, like I had betrayed him somehow.

'Let me tell you something about my story. I have no formal education; I was kicked out of school at 16 for doing drugs. I was down and out, brav, I didn't have a future. How do you think a guy like me got to where I am now? Do you think I did it by working my way up from the bottom? No, man. I saw an opportunity. Do you know why Paradise City has been so successful so quickly? Paradise City is a front for the Indian mafia. We launder funds for gangsters. There, I said it! Are you shocked? Well, don't be. Most companies in Dubai are built on the same dirty money, believe me. The only difference is I have the fucking balls to admit it. So what's your answer?'

264

'I can't give you an answer now, I'm afraid, Taz. I need to think about it.'

He stared into my eyes as if he was about to strike me. 'To think about what? I need a decision now!'

'Then the answer is no.'

He jumped at me like an enraged animal. I managed to push him off, but he picked up a white chair and came at me again. 'I treat you as my friend, I invite you to my event as my guest, I introduce you to the biggest star in the world and this is how you fucking repay me? Get the fuck out of my office!'

I happily obliged and ran towards the door, while he continued to shout at me. 'This is how you do business? I can't believe you fucking people!'

I was shaking in the cab back to the office, and I decided to tell Rav the whole story. With Tariq's *wasta* among government officials and based on what Taz had revealed, I was sure Paradise City could be investigated for money laundering and criminal activity. If I had known Taz's invitation to the party would be at such a high cost, I wouldn't have attended at all. A night with Fernando was not worth this insane price. But one thing was for sure, it was unlikely that Paradise City's no-broker policy would be changing any time soon.

***

That evening, as I relaxed alone in my apartment after a gruelling few days, I received a call from Sharaz, Aziz's friend from the Brotherhood. He had tried called me regularly since that night at the Casbar, but I had consciously avoided him. It was now time to give him a clear hint that I wasn't interested in being his friend, so this time I picked up expecting to brush him off for good.

'Adam, I really need to talk to you, man.' He was struggling to hold back his tears.

'What's wrong?'

'Can you meet me in an hour in the Old Town? I really need to speak to somebody right now.' His voice was quivering and I knew something serious had happened.

'Of course. I'll be there.'

When I arrived at the café, Sharaz was sitting alone in the corner with his head in his hands. He looked dishevelled and broken. I walked up to his table and sat down slowly.

'Thanks for coming. I really didn't know who else to call,' he said. His eyes were bloodshot and he was sniffing back his tears.

'No problem. What's happened?'

'Man, I fucked up. I really fucked up.'

'What happened, Sharaz?'

'She caught me, man! She caught me red-handed. The bitch told her everything. I totally fucked up.' He began to sob again. I had no idea what he was talking about, so I probed a little further.

'Sharaz, start at the top. I'm here to help you.'

'Okay, okay.' He wiped the tears from his face and composed himself. 'Remember that Russian girl I introduced you to at the Casbar? The blonde?'

I had seen so many Russian girls in the past few months that I struggled to recall at first. But the image of Sharaz kissing and caressing a woman's thigh on the dance floor eventually came to mind. 'Yes, I do.'

'Well, I was kind of seeing her a few times a week. We were just fooling around, going for drinks and stuff. One night, we got pretty drunk and went back to her place. One thing led to another...' He started to cry again.

'Okay and...'

'I didn't mean for it to happen, really, I didn't mean it.'

'Did you get her pregnant, Sharaz?' I asked. He nodded.

'It just happened, man. I didn't do it on purpose.'

'Shit. Okay, and then what?'

'She just kept texting me and calling me, like some crazy, possessed bitch. She threatened to tell my wife everything if I didn't agree to pay her a regular maintenance allowance when the child was born.'

'Did you agree?'

'Yes, I did. But a few days later she…'

'Did your wife find out, Sharaz?'

'She read my emails last night. She knows everything…' He shook his head. 'What the fuck am I gonna do? I've lost everything!'

My heart sank to my stomach. I had seen this on the cards that night in the Casbar, but I had been helpless to do anything about it. Sharaz's wife had already booked her flight home to London with his son. It was a tragic situation, and although he had only himself to blame for his stupidity, I couldn't help feel sorry for him as he helplessly watched his family crumble.

Like so many others, Sharaz had fallen victim to the dark side of the Dubai Dream. The city was a honey trap full of gold diggers looking for vulnerable men, and Sharaz had fallen right in. Hard-working family men were helplessly lured by the temptation of this Arabian fantasyland like moths to the flame. Friendly women were only a phone call away, and men across the city were caught in a web of self-deception and temptation every day. It made good men neglect their real responsibilities, and in a few tragic cases like Sharaz's they were left washed up and bereft.

In a land without limitations, many pushed too far and lost themselves in the process. Sharaz was not the first to fall into the pit, and he would certainly not be the last.

19

The Boy Who Cried Wolf

The famous 'Skyscraper Index' was the brainchild of economist Andrew Lawrence. In his 1999 note as the Research Director at German investment bank Dresdner Kleinwort Wasserstein, Lawrence suggested that there was a direct correlation between business cycles and tall buildings. The World Trade Center in New York opened just before the 1973–74 Wall Street Crash. The Petronas Towers in Kuala Lumpur were completed prior to the Asian financial crisis in 1998. London's Canary Wharf tower opened in 1990 before a major recession. It seemed that history was suggesting that mankind's penchant for architectural overreach was an eerily reliable omen of troubles ahead.

I was sitting at the Calabar, a swanky outdoor lounge at the base of the mighty Burj Dubai, on the day it was officially announced as the tallest building in the world. It was a proud moment. I had witnessed every step of its growth from humble foundations into the mammoth spire of steel, aluminium and glass it was today. I looked up at it floor by floor to the point where the distant tip of the mighty icicle finally met the sky, almost straining my neck in the process. There was no doubt that it was an architectural feat and a masterpiece of construction that aptly celebrated Dubai's 'can do' mindset.

It was also the week that shocking news broke of the collapse of US investment banking giant Lehman Brothers. On the flat-screen televisions mounted above the pool bar were distressing pictures of forlorn bankers escorted out of office blocks, carrying their possessions in brown cardboard boxes. Yet nobody around the pool seemed to care much. Dubai was a world away from the petty troubles of the West, and most Westerners were thankful to have escaped the toil of their home countries. Few Dubai residents had any idea how severe the growing financial crisis in the US and Europe really was, including me, until my old lawyer friend Anthony called from London to tell me.

'Mate, the West is falling apart!' I could hear the desperation in his voice. 'This Lehman thing has fucked everything up.'

'Yes, I was watching it on the news earlier. It looks pretty bad.'

'It's a freaking disaster! Everybody is scared shitless about their jobs. Half the people I know now want to move to Dubai.'

'Really, why Dubai?'

'Are you kidding me? Things are cruising over there, right? Haven't you heard the phrase?'

'What phrase?'

'Dubai, Shanghai, Mumbai or goodbye! While people are losing their jobs here, you guys are building the world's tallest tower and tree-shaped islands. Everybody in the West is looking East now as a safe haven from the crisis.'

Anthony was right. While the titans of Western capitalism were toppling, Dubai looked invincible to the outside world. There were more Porsches and Ferraris on the roads than ever before. The malls were packed, the restaurants were bustling and the clubs were buzzing. Tourists were still flooding into the city in droves and the hotels were at capacity. And so recruitment companies in Dubai were inundated with the CVs of senior professionals from London and New York, and many investment banks shifted their best people to their Dubai offices to escape the turmoil at home.

Financial analysts and experts from Dubai jumped on the bandwagon and regularly began to appear on Bloomberg and CNBC to offer elaborate ideas about why the Emirate was immune from the world's problems. They spoke of its unique political system and centrally controlled economy, which meant it was not exposed to the raw forces of global capitalism. They argued that the city was a safe haven for capital, that consumer confidence would remain high and inward investment would continue. This theory that its economy was somehow decoupled from the global system began to gain momentum, to the point that most Dubai businesses accepted it as an economic fact.

And on the back of this new vote of confidence in the city's fortunes, the property market continued to surge forward, and the latest

269

round of project launches were the most outrageous yet. There were proposals for buildings lookin like Coke cans, various animals and even one in the form of an Emirati man, complete with traditional headdress and *dishdasha*. One developer proposed a 'Chess City' with thirty-two skyscrapers built in the form of individual chess pieces on a giant back and white chess board. But perhaps the most far-fetched idea was the luxury underwater resort, Hydropolis. Shaped like a giant jellyfish, the Hydropolis would consist of two hundred luxury suites submerged sixty-six metres under the sea, offering spectacular views of the ocean bed and passing mermaids! This one-of-a-kind hotel would feature a cosmetic surgery facility and its very own missile defence system. It was due for completion in 2014.

Milestone Properties was also entering a new era of growth by the middle of 2008. After over ten years, the firm was finally moving out of its tired old offices and into a brand new, state-of-the-art sales centre in the Dubai Marina. Tariq had spent over a million dirhams equipping the new office with the latest Italian furniture, computers and phone lines. There was even a bar offering coffee and juices to clients in the waiting area. Tariq had spent his entire summer recruiting an elite team of experienced real estate agents from Europe to take the company into the next phase of growth. Many of them were experienced brokers from Spain and the UK who, in the face of the collapse of their respective markets, were now looking for the next big thing.

Business confidence in the city was at an all-time high and the property market was reaching new heights of ambition. And then in August, like a bolt out of the blue, came the ominous Morgan Stanley Report. Entitled 'Winners and Losers in MENA Property,' its ominous findings sent shockwaves throughout the market:

We expect oversupply to hit Dubai in 2009, leading to a period of price declines.

The report was the first credible projection ever of a decline in real estate values in Dubai, predicting that property prices could fall by as much as 10 per cent by 2010. It didn't help that it was written by one of the world's most credible financial institutions, making its findings more difficult to brush under the carpet. It was an unwelcome spanner in the cogs of the well-oiled Dubai money machine, and an inevitably fierce backlash followed from the heavyweights of the Emirate's property industry. They argued that the report's valuation methodology was flawed and that it ignored the simple fact that the fundamentals of the Dubai property market were unique and exclusive compared to other regions. Some developers even threatened legal action against the bank for the potential losses in revenue it could cause.

As I lay on my bed and read through the entire report, a shudder went down my spine. There was not a single point in it I could disagree with. It warned of the excessively speculative nature of the market, the unsustainable rate of increase in property prices, the threat of spiralling inflation, and the real risks of oversupply and correction. Its bold observations vindicated every concern I had been feeling, and I was glad that industry leaders would finally sit up and pay attention.

Given its groundbreaking revelations, I strongly believed that everybody at Milestone should be fully aware of its findings. It was important that everybody knew the state of the market and where we were heading as a business. So I sent it to the entire team at Milestone, including Tariq, Rav and Edward. By doing so, I was showing initiative which I was sure would impress Tariq.

As I got ready for work the following morning, I was expecting to be greeted as a hero in the office. But from the moment I arrived I knew something wasn't right. Nobody wished me good morning and it seemed that everybody was avoiding eye contact with me. Even the usually bubbly Sharon and Amy refused to acknowledge me. As I sat at my desk, Rav spotted me from across the room and rushed over.

'Can we have a chat?' he said.

'Sure,' I replied.

'Let's grab a coffee downstairs. Follow me.' Rav never usually had time for coffee, so I knew something was up.

'That was a very interesting email you sent around last night.'

'You mean the report?' I asked.

'Yes, the report. I read through it this morning. I must admit I didn't understand it all, but I think I got the gist.'

'Well, I found it quite enlightening! There's a lot of truth in its observations that we should probably discuss as a firm.'

271

'Perhaps. But I don't think it was such a good move to send something like that to the whole company. I would strongly suggest that you don't do anything like that again.' His tone was uncompromising.

'Why not, Rav? Don't you think it's important that everybody in this firm knows the experts' view on the market? You don't have to agree with what it says, but as real estate professionals, surely we need to know what's going on?'

Rav looked deep into my eyes before answering. 'Son, I understand that you come from an investment banking background and you have a banking mindset. But the way we run things here is very different to what you're used to. Our sales people are not bankers. Most of them have never even worked in real estate before. They're not educated, intelligent and well-informed like you. They are trained to say good things to the clients, take down details and close. And that's all we want them to do. Do you understand what I'm telling you?'

'No, I can't say that I do.'

He looked over his shoulder before continuing. 'We don't want them to think too much out of the box, and we certainly don't want them to start thinking negatively about what they are doing. They don't understand reports like this! Most of them have never heard of Morgan Stanley, and we would prefer to keep it that way.' He leaned back in his seat and sighed heavily. 'Look, things are going well right now. Better than ever, actually. We certainly don't want to rock the boat too much, and we simply can't afford any negativity to set in.'

I knew at that moment that this message was really from Tariq, not Rav. In a way it was a warning to me not to interfere in the running of the business. Tariq had trained his team to think and work in a certain way, and by sharing the report I was somehow challenging the status quo and encouraging them to think independently.

But brushing its findings under the carpet with such ease in favour of short-term financial gain concerned me deeply. In a way, the analyst who had compiled the report and I were in a similar boat. While I had been cautioned for sharing it, he was also berated every day by all those whose interests it threatened. There was no room for the voice of reason in this greedy, money-obsessed game. I had tried to be too clever for my own good and I was paying the price.

The bad taste left by the report was quickly forgotten as the preparations for Cityscape 2008 began in earnest. With so much negative news looming, the event could not have come any sooner to cleanse the air and bring everything back to normal. It was now a matter of pride, and this was Dubai's chance to show the world it was back to business as usual. Milestone expected this to be its biggest Cityscape yet. The sales team were already talking about the record commissions they would make, and some even booked luxury vacations and sports cars in anticipation of the buckets of cash coming their way.

Undoubtedly the stands were more jaw-dropping, the saleswomen more beautiful and the projects more outrageous than ever before. This year's launches were bigger than anybody's wildest dreams as the Dubai PR machine rolled on relentlessly. A new developer called Meraas, Sheikh Mohammed's own private company, launched the three hundred and fifty billion dirham Jumeirah Gardens development, located in the old Satwa area and planned to house up to sixty thousand residents. And Nakheel launched the Nakheel Harbour and Tower, an inland marina at the foot of what was set to be the world's new tallest tower, extending over a kilometre into the sky. Three times the height of the Eiffel Tower, the skyscraper would utterly dwarf the mighty Burj Dubai.

As I walked though the packed halls, I abruptly brushed shoulders with a man who almost made me tumble.

'Hey! Sorry buddy, are you okay?' I looked up to see a familiar face offering his hand. It was none other than Hollywood superstar Michael Douglas!

'Thanks. I'm fine...'

'No problem. I guess Dubai has blown you away too, huh?' He winked and walked on his way. But he was not the only celebrity I would brush against that day. Actor Antonio Banderas, boxing champion Amir Khan and Bollywood superstar Shah Rukh Khan were all drawing in the crowds to various stands whose developers had recruited them for the event as brand ambassadors. They smiled, posed for photographs and signed autographs for the adoring crowds, bringing a touch of glamour to the proceedings.

Nevertheless, as Dubai continued on its trajectory of unfettered expansion, it became more and more difficult to ignore the fact that the rest of the world was falling to pieces. On the very day Cityscape 2008 opened and the regional newspapers hailed Nakheel's new tower, the front page of the *New York Times* featured the ominous headline 'Financial Crisis Spreads in Europe'. The glitz, grandeur and glamour in the halls could not hide the nervous murmurs. The gloomy news from the West had indubitably dented the confidence of the punters who strolled around the stands with a distinct sense of caution, adopting a 'wait and see' stance instead of diving in blindly as they had before.

On the Milestone stand, the sales team were spending more time fighting fires than selling real estate. They were being bombarded with questions from every direction about the future of the market, and they struggled to keep up.

'When do you think supply will begin to outstrip demand?'

'How much of a correction do you think there will be?'

'What if I can't flip before my next payment is due?'

'What are your views on the Morgan Stanley report?'

Most of the team were completely unready for the intense interrogation. I couldn't help thinking that perhaps if they had taken the Morgan Stanley report more seriously, as I had suggested, they may have been better prepared for this somewhat inevitable eventuality.

Then things got even worse: somebody uttered the dreaded 'B' word for the first time causing an uneasiness never felt before. Up to that moment, everybody had been making far too much money for the thought to cross their mind. But at Cityscape that day, I heard the word being tossed around recklessly, and it scared the hell out of me – what if Dubai's real estate market really was a bubble? Of course, the most alarming thing about all bubbles was that they burst, and if the so-called Dubai bubble was to pop, the fallout would be apocalyptic.

274

Alarmingly few deal were struck at Cityscape 2008. Although nobody would admit it, the event had been a gigantic failure for both Milestone and brand Dubai, as immense fear began to take hold.

Like a stubborn child, Dubai ploughed ahead with its fingers in its ears. There was only one way the city really knew how to offset the negative rumours and keep everybody smiling – to throw a party! A good party was the ultimate distraction and it was needed now more than ever. But this was not to be any ordinary party. It would be the party to end all parties, the party of the century!

The launch of the billion-dollar Atlantis hotel was the most anticipated event of the year which no global economic crisis was going to dampen. This grand new luxury hotel resort was set to redefine opulence in Dubai. It was the brainchild of Israeli billionaire Sol Kerzner, one of the few Jews who had been given the privileged status of openly partnering in a business venture with a Gulf head of state. Swarovski-studded invitations were selectively distributed a few weeks in advance to an A-list group that included Hollywood stars, property CEOs and members of the royal family. Nearly two tons of lobster and caviar and thousands of bottles of champagne were flown in for the event, which dominated the front pages of every publication in the city.

A few days before the party, heavyweight celebrities and sports stars like Robert De Niro, Michael Jordan, Boris Becker, Quincy Jones and Charlize Theron jetted into town for the event of the century. There were rumours that Dubai had paid each of the stars a hefty sum to attend, with complimentary accommodation at the resort. Even Tariq and his wife Ayesha received an invitation to attend on behalf of Milestone. Tariq never usually went to any property launches, so his acceptance was an indication of the gravity of the event.

On the night of the party, there was an unusually strong wind for a summer night in the desert. I took a spot on the beach at the JBR with Hani and his friends in preparation for the firework display that was promised as the grand finale. We were joined by dozens of other keen spectators on the shores overlooking the Palm. As the event began, the muted sound of the live band in the distance could be heard over the waters as pop diva Kylie Minogue took to the stage. There was a great cheer from the crowd on the beach as her familiar voice echoed against the night. She was reportedly paid $4 million for the appearance, which lasted all of an hour.

I didn't care too much that I wasn't attending. On any other night I would have longed to be there, but tonight was not for me. It was more appropriate that the visionaries, entrepreneurs and pioneers who had made Dubai's property boom a reality were in attendance. Tonight was the city's thank-you party to these men and women who had taken great risks, sacrificed their efforts and believed so strongly in the Dubai story. Although it was officially billed as a launch event, I saw it rather as a farewell bash. I knew then that the game was over. Tonight was a fitting end to the biggest party of all. The Dubai property bonanza was tragically approaching a spectacular crescendo.

The grand finale was more remarkable than anybody had expected. In twenty breathtaking minutes, over twenty million dollars went up in smoke in the most magnificent fireworks display I had ever witnessed. Each colourful blast was bigger and more magnificent than the last as the darkness of the night's sky was magically illuminated. Television cameras from Mumbai to Tokyo broadcast the images, and the extravaganza could even be seen from space. Finally, as the party reached its spectacular climax, a gradual calm fell over the beach as the slowly crowd dispersed and made their way home. And then silence. Although few knew it, we had just witnessed Dubai's last great spectacle. The final curtain had fallen and there was to be no encore. Only darkness.

20

Paradise Lost

The city awoke with a ghastly hangover the morning after the Atlantis launch party. The very next day, Dubai's property market drew to a sudden and abrupt halt, confidence evaporating overnight. Nakheel announced that it was firing five hundred people, roughly 15 per cent of its global workforce, sending shockwaves through the market. Building sites stopped and cranes were motionless. Investors weren't making calls and transactions dried up. The market had suffered a devastating stroke and nobody seemed to have an answer.

By September 2008, most investors were holding the majority of their net worth in real estate assets, often on deals with 5 per cent down. Having made quick money in earlier transactions, speculators had reinvested their profits in an ever-expanding portfolio. In most cases, they had never intended to pay a second or third instalment, betting instead on being able to flip their investment in good time. But now that transactions had ceased, they became increasingly concerned by the lack of a viable exit before the next payments were due, and many began to panic.

In the absence of cash, investors and developers looked to the banks for mortgages and project financing to plug the gap. But faced with massive overexposure to property on their balance sheets and the potentially toxic wave of bad debts approaching, the banks shut their doors. To make matters worse, it emerged that many of the Gulf's larger finance houses had significant exposure to Lehman Brothers' assets via bonds, derivatives and structured investment products. And so with the banks bleeding, a lack of liquidity and mounting liabilities, the market went into a state of shock.

At Milestone's new offices, the phones had stopped ringing and leads began to evaporate into thin air. The sales team were left scratching their heads and nobody knew what had caused the breakdown of their miraculous cash cow, or how to fix it. In the absence of any inbound calls, the sales team desperately tried to phone everybody in their database to feed them a pre-rehearsed list of reasons

277

why the property market was still in good health, and how it was still a good time to buy:

'My boss had lunch with the CEO of Emaar last week, who said that prices will start rising again in a month.'

'One of our properties had seventeen viewings yesterday, which proves that the market is back to normal. If you don't buy in the next two days, you will miss the bottom of the market.'

'Our CEO is close to Sheikh Mohammed, who told him personally that it's a tactic to get rid of the speculators. He said prices will start rising again next week.'

It's no surprise that such bullshit fell on deaf ears. After a few weeks the phones at Milestone did start ringing again, but instead of a keen investor on the other end it was more likely to be a former customer hurling abuse for being mis-sold a property in which his money was now invariably stuck.

For the first time in Milestone's history, a customer service department was created to deal with the ever-increasing number of complaints. Emma was removed from the sales team and appointed as the new head of investor relations to handle the plethora of grievances. But within a week she was so inundated with calls and angry customers that she broke down in tears and resigned. Tariq also appointed a young lawyer from Australia called Brad to fend off the ever-increasing threats of legal action against the company. From the day he joined, Brad didn't leave the office once. He spent his ays beneath a pile of papers or on the phone. He never took a lunch break, and even slept under his desk most nights of the week. Within a month he was completely burned out and also resigned.

Faced with the growing uncertainty, Tariq tried desperately to calm his troops. We saw more of him around the office, and he began regularly attending team meetings and morning briefings, where he patted backs and massaged shoulders to boost morale. Although he didn't say a great deal, his presence alone was enough to instil some confidence within the firm. It wasn't long before the inevitable happened and a Milestone management meeting to address the crisis was called. Everybody was ordered to attend.

'My message to you is don't worry,' said Tariq confidently to his anxious audience. 'This is just a temporary blip and is nothing to worry about. The West is going through a recession right now, but we are in Dubai. We do not share the same problems as the rest of the world, and it is only a matter of time before things are back to normal.'

His reassuring words and confident tone caused a sigh of relief across the room. But I wasn't entirely convinced. Much of what he said was mere wishful thinking and lacking any firm foundations, although much of the team failed to see through his words. As Tariq spoke I glanced over at Wasim, the company accountant, who was standing alone at the back of the room with his arms folded. He stared at the ground throughout the meeting; a forlorn figure with the weight of the world on his brittle shoulders.

But things didn't get back to normal as Tariq had promised. In fact, they only got worse. Confusion turned to desperation, desperation turned to anger, and the team began to point fingers at the only people they could: each other. Salespeople blamed the business development team for bringing them projects they couldn't sell. The business development team blamed the salespeople for not selling their projects. Senior management blamed the IT department for slow computers. The IT department blamed senior management for making them a scapegoat for poor sales. And the administration assistants just kept quiet so they wouldn't get fired.

As the threat of redundancies loomed, everybody at Milestone strangely became extremely busy. Salespeople started arriving in the office an hour earlier and leaving much later to create the impression they were working hard. In private, many of them began calculating how much they had earned for the company in commissions since joining, to constitute a benchmark of their value and to build a case for why they shouldn't be fired. This worried the new joiners particularly, who were afraid that if the cuts came, they would be first in the firing line.

Helpless, I watched my own pipeline dry up one by one. My prospective investors had stopped answering my calls and emails, and I spent my days leaving messages on answering machines or with secretaries who were under strict orders to keep the exact whereabouts of their bosses a secret. In the few rare cases where I did get replies, I

279

was given awkward excuses for avoiding meetings, ranging from illnesses to travel plans and in one case a fabricated death!

I also noticed a marked change in my relationship with Tariq, and I got the impression he was avoiding me. He never once came over to my desk to speak to me, and in the rare event our paths crossed he simply nodded without saying a word. I didn't take it too personally. Tariq had poured his blood and guts into building a successful business and he was now facing the threat of oblivion. Just a couple of weeks after his rallying speech, his confident facade appeared to wane and he began to look as worried as the rest of us.

As all business activity drew to a standstill, an air of foreboding suffused the office and we all feared the worst. Rumours spread throughout Milestone that rival real estate companies were responding to the lack of revenues by cutting staff salaries, or in some cases scrapping salaries completely in favour of a commission-based pay structure. Every salesperson in the company panicked, fearing that Milestone would follow suit. In the heyday of the boom, most salespeople had not even noticed their measly salary come into their account as it was eclipsed by their massive commissions. But since the market had turned, what was once extra beer money had become a critical lifeline for survival. To lose it would surely mean the end.

I certainly did not feel immune from what was to come. In a sharp market downturn, a highly paid investment manager was a luxury to a small business like Milestone. I was by far the most highly paid employee and I had still not produced a penny for the firm in commission so far. If excessive costs needed to be cut to save the company, I would surely be first in the firing line.

Yet more bad news surfaced. Investigations into financial irregularities had begun as early as April 2008, but it wasn't until after the crisis had hit that the extent of the corruption in Dubai became apparent. A staggering nine hundred and fifty million dollars had either been stolen or taken in bribes by executives at real estate and financial services firms during the property boom. From heads of departments to CEOs and board members and even former ministers, bribery and embezzlement were rife. One prominent Emirati businessman was reported to have defrauded investors out of two hundred and thirty million dollars. The case went all the way to the top, and Sheikh Mohammed himself ordered the seizure and liquidation of all assets related to the company.

And so with the collapse of confidence, absence of bank financing and allegations of deep-rooted corruption, the market suffered a heart attack. Although most people were still in a state of denial, the dream was over and the game had ended. Now it was nothing but a fight for survival.

21

Faulty Towers

The warnings of an approaching sandstorm were plastered across the city's newspapers for days before it arrived. All residents were advised to stay indoors until it had passed and encouraged to avoid driving at all costs. On the day it finally came, I watched the tempest develop from the sanctuary of my apartment window. The cloudless blue skies were quickly engulfed by an ominous dark-grey swathe, and the winds battered callously against my fragile living-room windows. It felt alarmingly apocalyptic and I was certainly a little frightened.

But not everybody heeded the warnings. Although most stayed clear, a few reckless folk ignored the cautions and drove into its path without fear. Some called them brave, others foolish, but these naysayers didn't care for the consequences, preferring to leave their fate in the hands of God.

***

'I haven't been paid this month, have you?'

'No, I haven't. What the hell is going on? I didn't come to Dubai to work for free!'

There was pandemonium at Milestone. It was payday and nobody's salary had hit their account. Most of the team had rent due and payments on 4x4s and sports cars to make. After four months of zero sales on the board, it seemed that Tariq was feeling the pinch. He had expanded his staff by over 50 per cent and spent a fortune on the new offices. Paying salaries without any returns was bleeding the company dry, and Milestone's cash-flow problems were becoming increasingly acute.

Rav called a meeting a day later, at which he blamed the late salaries on a technical glitch, promising that everybody would be paid within a week. It calmed the mood a little, but I knew it was just a temporary solution to a more serious emerging cancer.

282

And then came the news that everybody had been dreading. The email was sent to every member of the sales and business development team, and simply read as follows:

Dear Milestone employee

You have been called to a face-to-face meeting with your respective manager for a private appraisal. Please prepare a summary of your sales figures to date to bring with you. Your time slot will be sent to you shortly.

Milestone Senior Management

There were no further details about what was to be discussed, so the rumour mill began to churn once again. What was the purpose of the meeting? Were we all being fired? Was the company being sold? Were salaries being cut after all? Every possible option was discussed and dissected as the fear took hold.

My meeting was arranged with Rav. So on Thursday morning an hour before lunchtime, I nervously marched into his office to face my fate.

'Come in, please take a seat.' I had a sudden flashback of being summoned to the headmaster's room at school. 'Okay, Adam, listen, I'm not going to bullshit you. I think you know that the company is going through a difficult time at the moment. You're an intelligent young man, so I'm not going to go through the reasons why.'

'Of course,' I replied earnestly.

'We are currently speaking to every employee to understand where they see themselves in the current market, and what they think they can contribute to help Milestone get through this difficult time.'

I saw right through what Rav was trying to tell me. This was not a performance review; it was a battle for survival! It was obvious by now that firings were on the cards. The real purpose of the meetings was to understand who to get rid of and when. I quickly realised that in the next twenty minutes I would have to pull up my sleeves and fight for my job, and I prepared myself for the challenge.

'So, do you think you will be doing any business in the next six months?' asked Rav.

'Absolutely!' I replied assertively. 'My pipeline of deals has actually been growing and all of my clients still seem to be very keen.'

Rav looked confused. 'Really? But you don't think that as the market is changing your prospects will decrease?'

'Oh, not at all. Quite the opposite, in fact. That may be the case for retail customers, but I think sophisticated investors have nothing to worry about. As the market softens a little, investors will start to look at yields rather than pure capital appreciation, and yields in Dubai are still better than anywhere else. Also, without mortgages fewer people will be able to buy property, so they are more likely to rent, which will further strengthen the rental market. The real losers in the situation are the speculators. Serious investors won't be affected at all.'

It was a lie of ludicrous proportions. Real sophisticated investors would not have touched Dubai with a barge pole in these market conditions. But as I sugar-wrapped my outrageous claims in some kind of misguided theory, Rav looked somewhat convinced.

'Hmm, maybe you're right.' He frowned and scribbled something on the notepad in front of him. 'I just have one more question.' Another question? I was not out of the woods just yet. 'Would you be able to survive if we, say, removed your salary and increased your commissions?'

I froze. Rav had called my bluff. If what I had just told him about my growing pipeline was true, then surely I should welcome commissions over salary, as I was the only one in the company who stood to close any deals. On the other hand, if I made it obvious that having no salary was an issue, it would show a clear lack of confidence in my bold statements. I had to think fast.

'Well, as you know, Rav, investment transactions take a little longer to close due to the more stringent due diligence procedures. I would need an income while I am working through my deal pipeline.' It was the best I could do. But whether Rav, and ultimately Tariq, would buy it was yet to be seen.

Two weeks later, and as expected, it was announced that salaries were being scrapped and commissions were being increased to 40 per cent across the board. There was outrage. Not only had senior management gone back on their word regarding salaries, the revised commissions were at least 10 percent less than most other firms were offering to their teams. Naturally, many salespeople began to arrange interviews with other brokerage houses; others threatened to leave. But they were missing the big picture. What did the level of commission matter if there were no deals to close?

I, on the other hand, had been spared. There had been no notification that my salary had been removed or cut in any way, much to my relief. Nevertheless, the message was clear. Based on what I had told Rav, the pressure was now on me to bring in the bacon and save Milestone. While I was safe for now, the countdown to oblivion had begun.

22

The Great Escape

2008 became the year of the flipper, the jumper and the runner.

The flippers were the luckiest of the three. Having seen the early signs of a correction on the horizon, they had successfully flipped their assets in time and left the market relatively unscathed. Some flippers settled for a small profit on their exits, others even a loss, but their primary aim was an urgent escape before the tsunami arrived and wiped them out completely. Unfortunately, flippers were firmly in the minority.

Jumpers were taken by surprise by the sudden turmoil. Faced with the prospect of bounced cheques, rising debts and looming unemployment, these foolhardy investors settled up and left town with whatever dignity they could salvage. They closed their accounts, paid their credit card debts and bought one-way tickets for their home country with a heavy heart and fond memories of the desert.

The runners weren't so dignified. Drowning in debt and unable to pay demanding creditors, they saw no way out except to drop everything and run for the border. They left behind their property investments, credit card debts and unpaid bills. Their only alternative to absconding was debtor's prison followed by certain deportation. Stories abounded of runners abandoning their cars at the airport with the keys in the ignition and an apology note on the windscreen reading 'Expat out of money. Sorry!'

Dubai was unforgiving of the plight of its more unfortunate guests. As soon as an expat lost their job, their visa was cancelled, giving them just thirty days to leave the country. Although many scrambled to sell their car, pay outstanding debts, shift their belongings and wish friends goodbye within the allotted timeframe, it was perhaps no wonder that many cut their losses and made a run for it. The country that they had called home for years and that they had defended so vehemently in the face of outside detractors and doubters had turned its back on them in their time of need. Many expats felt utterly betrayed, and reluctantly accepted that they had overstayed their welcome.

One British entrepreneur and 'runner' skipped town after his company, a speciality gift service, couldn't pay its bills. He responded by writing an emotional letter to the 'Dubai public' that was subsequently published in the press. In it he acknowledged that he owed money, and explained that he had fled due to the lack of structured bankruptcy laws and a banking system that had zero flexibility on loan repayments, which drove him to make a 'horrible decision'. He revealed that personal threats were being made against him and his family due to high levels of debt, which left him no choice but to take them out of the country. As Dubai lacked bankruptcy laws or US-style Chapter 11 protection, business owners were personally responsible for their debt obligations and were left with little choice.

Heads rolled and cheques bounced as redundancies and layoffs increased daily across the city. On average, one in every twenty cheques written was sent back by a bank marked 'Insufficient Funds'. Many businesses were forced to lay off a large portion of their workforce, and many more closed down. Dubai's jail cells, once reserved for drink-drivers and illegal immigrants, today were brimming with forlorn expatriates with bad debts; the sorry victims of the dark side of the good life.

Many of the old heroes of the heyday became villains overnight. Among them was Benito Valli of DCA. Once he had been the golden boy of Dubai real estate; today DCA's investors wanted his head on a stick. Construction of three of the company's projects had halted indefinitely in 2008, and two others were over a year behind schedule. Benito's investors had not received a return for months and their patience was running thin. He reacted by deflecting responsibility for DCA's woes and blamed the delays on his South Korean contractors, who filed for bankruptcy in December 2008. Nevertheless, it soon emerged in the press that Benito had sent substantial funds to South America and had paid a company in Panama seven hundred and fifty thousand euros for a new South American identity. He was arrested at Dubai airport in February 2009 trying to board a plane to Panama. Benito was never heard of again.

Throughout the unravelling of Dubai, there were no official announcements or press releases from the authorities. It was as if the government was burying its head in the proverbial sand and consciously brushing its growing problems under the carpet. This odd radio silence only exacerbated the rumour mill, causing the crisis of confidence to worsen daily. The flawless Dubai PR machine, which had meticulously managed each stage of the city's propulsion onto the global stage, was somehow broken, raising serious concerns about the government's ability to deal with the crash.

Eventually an announcement did come. In 2009, Dubai caused shockwaves throughout the world when it declared that it was bust. Dubai World, the holding company of national corporate gems such as Nakheel and Dubai Ports, told its creditors that it could not pay its massive twenty-five billion dollar debts, causing global financial markets to go into panic. The news shattered the premise that the city's institutions were government backed, and confidence among Dubai's key stakeholders disappeared overnight.

The Emirate's creditors had always acted on the underlying belief that the government had provided an iron-clad guarantee to its institutions. On this dubious premise, Dubai's companies and institutions were regarded too big to fail, as a bailout by the authorities was beyond doubt. But the Dubai World announcement proved that this was all a huge fallacy. The government had distanced itself from its business interests in challenging times, and in doing so rid itself of the liabilities. It seemed that Dubai's business model had been flawed from the beginning. 'Dubai Inc. Was far from the invincible leviathan everybody had been led to believe. In reality it was verging on bankruptcy.

The worst of Dubai World's debt problems were in its prized development company Nakheel. An army of auditors were brought in to sort out the mess, and what they found wasn't pretty. Nakheel's balance sheet was a disaster and fears were growing that the company's woes could even bring down the entire economy. Dubai desperately needed money to avoid a default and save face. The lack of meaningful oil revenues had always plagued the city, and the absence of a nest egg for a rainy day meant that it was forced to raise money by selling its most valuable assets. A buyer was waiting in the wings, licking its lips and rubbing its palms with delight – cash-rich Abu Dhabi.

The deal was likely to have been struck directly between the two sheikhs in the private Majlis, so nobody knew the exact details of what was agreed. But it was unlikely that big brother helped out its desperate neighbour for free. There were rumours that Dubai was forced to give up significant stakes in most of its most prized assets, namely the Atlantis hotel, Dubai Ports and Emirates airline. Considering Abu Dhabi's close relationship with the US, Dubai was also encouraged to scale back its historical trade relations with Iran, by freezing company accounts and ceasing operations for a number of Iranian companies in the Emirate. In the blink of an eye, Dubai lost much of what it had spent years building. Like a sandcastle on the beach, brand Dubai was swept away by the ruthless tide of politics.

In January 2009, the Burj Dubai, the world's tallest building and the jewel of the property bonanza, was finally unveiled to the world, albeit with subdued gusto. But there was a distinctive alteration in the proceedings. 'Burj Dubai' had been renamed 'Burj Khalifah' after the Sheikh of Abu Dhabi and the ruler of the UAE, Sheikh Khalifah Bin Zayed Al Nahyan. The last minute change of name was explained as an act of tribute and the ultimate mark of respect to the country's ruler. But to many it was the final stamp of humiliation by Abu Dhabi to ensure that Dubai had learnt its valuable lesson.

The titans of Western media had a field day from the moment the news of Dubai's problems began to surface. Despite the fact that their own economies were crumbling before their eyes, the tragic rise and fall of the Emirate was a more commercially viable story, as well as a useful distraction from domestic economic woes. For years while the city had boomed, outside observers had chastised Dubai for reliance on slave labour, disregard of environmental concerns and contempt for democratic values. To them this demise was poetic justice, and a flurry of damning and sensationalised articles surfaced almost daily. Dragging Dubai's name through the mud was both a commercial coup and a satisfying act of revenge.

Many Emiratis took the media onslaught personally. The publication of a cartoon of their beloved Sheikh Mohammed drowning in a sea of debt was seen by many as the final insult, prompting a bitter backlash. Emirati journalists began blaming the decline of Dubai on the immoral influence of Western expats, who had poisoned the moral fabric of its society with a culture of greed and indulgence. The expats were likened to criminals who exploited Dubai through excessive financing and loans, and fled when they couldn't afford to pay their debts. One prominent Emirati journalist responded with a damning article on the UK's own questionable historical human rights record as the debate became an embittered battle for national pride.

And so Dubai's love affair with its Western expatriates and foreign investors was over. The cultural chasm the city had been so desperate to seal was only widened, and the ambitious experiment to bridge two worlds failed with dramatic consequences.

***

Just a few weeks after the news of Dubai's debt problems went public, a most peculiar trend emerged at Milestone. One by one, team members began to disappear, never to be seen again. There was no announcement from the management and no goodbyes. They were simply there one day and gone the next. The more senior team members were the first to go. Had they quit or had they been let go? It didn't make any sense for Milestone to fire these guys. They were the heavy hitters who had pulled in the most money through the good years. They also had the biggest clients and the best knowledge of the market. If anybody was going to pull the company out of this mess, surely it would be them. Their sudden departures caused a stir among more junior team members; if these guys were being let go, what possible chance of survival could they have?

After a movie at the mall one weekend, a chance encounter helped clear up the mystery. Sitting on a bench inside near the food court, his head in his hands, was someone I had not seen in the office for over a month.

'Syed? Is that you?'

He looked up at me through weary eyes. 'It's all over, Adam, the dream is over!'

'What happened, Syed? Were you let go? Did you leave?' I asked.

'What difference does it make?'

I convinced him to join me for a coffee, where he spilled the beans.

'Edward called me into his office a week ago. He asked me if I had some cash in the bank. I didn't have any idea why he was asking, but I told him I had a little. The next thing I knew, I received a letter saying I had been let go.'

'But why you ahead of the others?'

'I don't know. I guess my crime was that I had made a little money, so they assumed I could survive in Dubai longer than others. The fact that I had been with the company since 2003 meant nothing to them. I put my blood and guts into Milestone. I worked hard every day and this is how they repay me. There's no loyalty in this business,' he said and shook his head.

'So what are you going to do now?' I asked.

'I have no clue. No rival firm will hire me because they're all cutting back like Milestone. I have no other skills. I have no choice but to head back to Pakistan. Except I'm almost out of money, so I don't know how I can possibly afford the ticket home.'

I felt sorry for Syed, but there was nothing I could do to help him. Like so many other young real estate agents across the city, the market had callously chewed him up and spat him out. Sure, some of them had made a little money, but now without a hope of finding another job in the industry, many of them were struggling to stay afloat. It was game over and a full-blown fight for survival had begun.

As much as the few surviving team members at Milestone hit the phones and pleaded with investors, there was not so much as a whisper of a potential deal in the pipeline. Over the following long and painful weeks, more and more salespeople fell away. Some looked to change careers and find jobs in other industries; others packed up and left the country. Tariq's business empire was crumbling before his eyes and the heyday of Milestone was now nothing but a distant memory.

As I watched the decline helplessly from the sidelines, I knew my days were numbered. I tried to bide my time, keep my head down and hang on to a salary as long as I could. But it was the morning that Connor, the darling of Milestone, failed to make it to his desk that I finally realised the game was up. So I did what was timely, honourable and right. I made a preemptive move that I was sure would save me from the inevitable embarrassment around the corner.

I resigned with immediate effect.

23

Apocalypse Now

'Judgment day is coming.'

'Excuse me?'

'Allah is angry with our greed. We are close to the end of the world.' There was a foreboding tone behind the taxi driver's words that made me quite uncomfortable.

'Why do you say that?' I asked earnestly.

He looked at me in his rear-view mirror. 'Sir, there is a famous old teaching of the prophet Mohammed; may God bless him. A man asked the Prophet, "What are the signs of the Day of Judgment?" The Prophet replied, "When the barefooted shepherds are competing to build tall buildings." So you see, sir, this is now coming true. Just look around us. The end of the world is close.'

Whether by 'barefooted shepherds' the prophet had meant the Emiratis was up for debate. But it was difficult to doubt that 2009 felt like the end of the world in Dubai.

As the dust finally began to settle, the ramshackle city that emerged was a tragic shadow of its former glory. All along the Sheikh Zayed Road, frozen building sites, motionless cranes and unfinished skyscrapers were a familiar sight. Skeletal shells of buildings with windows missing and steel beams exposed looked less incomplete than obliterated, like the remnants of a nuclear tragedy which had ripped through a once thriving metropolis.

The luxury hotel lobbies were empty, the apartment blocks looked deserted and the highways were quieter than ever. As I drove towards the Marina, I recalled the former promise of most of the hollow structures surrounding me. Many had been launched to great fanfare and pomp, snatching headlines across the region. Today the world's newspapers were lamenting their tragic demise. The vacant streets reminded me of the movie set of an ill-fated blockbuster whose

292

producers had pulled the plug, leaving behind an empty, soulless back lot.

Across the city's *shisha* cafés, the property market was still the hot topic of conversation. But the boasting of quick profits and short-term flips had turned into hopeless sob stories, as many lamented how much they had lost and how they should have known better. A blame game ensued as investors pointed fingers at developers for delays, developers blamed the banks for failing to honour their financing commitments and banks blamed the unforeseen global crisis. Those who had enough faith in Dubai's courts to gamble on legal proceedings were in for a long and expensive haul. Developers exploited loopholes in poorly drafted contracts that were heavily biased in their favour to shift any liability back onto investors. Other developers faced with litigation for not honouring their commitments simply closed up and fled.

After resigning from Milestone, I spent most of the next two weeks in my apartment feeling sorry for myself. I stayed in my pyjamas, I didn't shave and I lived on toast and Pot Noodles. As I sat alone on the balcony in deep contemplation, I couldn't help but wallow in self-pity. Where had it all gone wrong?

As much I tried, there was no use in trying to rationalise events. The fact remained that my grand adventure had ended in failure, and here I was jobless, hopeless and Porscheless. I was at the lowest point of my life and I wanted nothing more but the ground to open and swallow me up.

After a small bite in the kitchen, I was heading back to the sanctity of my bed when my phone rang.

'Hello?'

'Adam?' said a familiar voice.

'Yes, who's this?'

'Adam. It's your father.'

I was speechless for a moment.

'Dad... this is a big surprise.'

'Yes, well, I have some news.'

'What news?'

'I'm coming to see you in Dubai.'

I almost dropped the phone. 'Erm, Dad, right now is not really the best time.'

'Nonsense! There is no better time. Besides, I have already booked my flights. Pick me up at the airport on Wednesday. See you in a couple of days.'

As soon as he hung up, I slammed down the handset in anger. Surely some kind of warning would have been nice? I had never been very close to my father after my parents' divorce, and I had spent much of my life trying to prove to him that I didn't need him around to be successful. But instead of appreciating how well I was doing, he would now see me in the most desperate state ever. If he had only visited just three months ago, he would have viewed his son as a promising young businessman reaching for the stars, instead of the unemployed bum I had become. His timing couldn't have been worse.

**

I met him at the airport early in the morning and we took a taxi over to my apartment. My father had never been to Dubai before, but considering he was a builder by trade, I had assumed it would be like dying and going to heaven for him. As we drove down the Sheikh Zayed Road, I pointed out the landmarks and new developments, hoping to invoke a reaction. But he just listened without saying a word.

Over the next few days, I took him to see the Emirates Towers, the mighty Burj Khalifah and the Burj Al Arab. Like a tour guide, I gave him the lowdown on each iconic project by rolling off every fact I knew about the developer, the launch price, and even how much steel and concrete had been used. But as before, there was no reaction from my father. He just observed.

If he hadn't been impressed so far, I was certain the next stop on the itinerary would blow him away. As we left the coast and drove onto the Palm Jumeirah, I stared at his face, hoping for some inkling of excitement. I remembered the moment I had first driven onto the Palm and the overwhelming feeling of wonder. Yet again, he gave nothing away, which was beginning to frustrate me.

On the last day of his short visit, I took him to Bar 44 at the Grosvenor House hotel, which boasted impressive 360-degree views of the Dubai Marina. Over a cocktail, I finally broke my silence.

'So, Dad, you haven't said a word about Dubai since you got here. Aren't you impressed with what you've seen?'

'It's okay,' he replied.

'Just okay?'

'Yes. Just okay.'

I sighed heavily. 'Dad, don't you think it's amazing what they've done here? Aren't you even a little bit impressed by the feats of human ambition and engineering you've seen?'

He turned and looked into my eyes. 'Not really, son. To throw a bunch of money into building some nice-looking buildings is not really difficult. Building a real, practical, functioning city takes a lot longer. That's true success.'

'What do you mean? Are you saying Dubai is not a "real" city?'

'Son, when you look around at this place, all you see is big shiny buildings. That's all. I see beyond that. And let me tell you, I haven't been too impressed.' I had no idea what he was talking about. 'Do you want to know what I have noticed over the past few days?'

'What did you notice, Dad?' I asked, rolling my eyes sarcastically.

'I noticed that there wasn't a single phone box in Dubai.'

'What?'

'A simple phone box. I haven't seen a single one in the six days I've been here.'

'How do you know that?' I was starting to get agitated.

'I was looking out for them. Not a single one.' He shook his head adamantly.

'Okay, but what's that got to do with anything?'

'It's a perfect example of what I mean. The glitzy façade is superficial. What matters is the thought and planning. These are the things that don't come overnight.'

295

'Whatever, Dad.' I accepted that our conversation was going nowhere fast.

He suddenly started at me earnestly which made me uncomfortable. 'Son, I never objected to you coming to Dubai,' he said. 'Even though you had a good job and prospects in London, I never stopped you.'

'And why is that, then?'

'Because I could see that you had a lot of growing up to do. You were stupid and naive back then, with your ridiculous pipe dreams of quick money and overnight success. This place attracted you because everybody here thought the way you did. It was paradise for the lazy. You foolishly thought you could cut corners and avoid the difficult path. But just look at this place now. Look at you now. It's all over, just as I expected. All I hope is that you have learnt your lesson, son.'

'What lesson?'

'That there's no such thing as a quick buck. And that even if you make it, you lose two when things go against you. And they always will.'

As much as I hated to admit it, he had summed up my Dubai experience perfectly in a few simple words. I had nothing to say.

'This experience has taught you some lessons that you had to learn. But one thing I'm certain of more than anything right now is that for the first time in my life I'm not sitting with my little boy any more. I'm sitting face to face with a man.'

I stayed quiet as I allowed his profound words to soak in. It was the most honest moment I had shared with my father in my whole life. I couldn't doubt a single word he had said. He was absolutely right. Suddenly a lump formed in my throat, my bottom lip began to quiver and my eyes filled up. Within seconds, I was a complete wreck and as much as I tried, I couldn't hold back the tears. My father leaned in to comfort me, but I just grabbed his shoulder and bawled my eyes out. It had been a long, long time since I had cried like this. Back then I had been a child, on a beach holding a bucket and spade, feeling as utterly helpless as I did right now.

I dropped my dad off at the airport the next day with a new-found respect for him. Somehow he had put everything into context for me. His visit was a much-needed reality check and I was grateful. I decided there and then that feeling sorry for myself was getting me nowhere. The moment I returned to my apartment from the airport, I decided to do something I should have done weeks ago: throw caution to the winds and have some fun.

I didn't have a great deal of money left, but I had enough to stuff a bag in the back of a hired 4x4, fill up the tank and hit the road. I didn't really know where I was going, I just drove and drove. I headed north along the Emirates Road towards the northern Emirates of Ras al Khaimah and Fujairah. I had never even been outside the borders of Dubai, so I was extremely excited to see what lay ahead.

As I reached the city walls, the Dubai skyline dispersed behind me and I was engulfed by the sand dunes of the open Arabian Desert. This was the real Arabia I had wanted to see since I arrived. There was not a single building or skyscraper in sight. To my right was a herd of camels grazing aimlessly across the golden sands. They were beautiful, imposing beasts, once the lifeline of Bedouin existence; today as much a figment of history as the Bedouins themselves.

The desert landscape soon turned into mountains and valleys. A road sign informed me that I had passed into Ras al Khaimah, which boasted some of the most beautiful natural scenery I had ever seen. There were hills and springs and lakes, and not a single manmade structure or settlement for miles. Dusk was fast approaching, so I decided to set up a small camp on the beach nearby.

I had no idea how to erect a tent and as I struggled, some young Emiratis who were camping close by came over to help me. They didn't speak any English, but somehow we bonded as they asked me to join them to roast marshmallows over their roaring fire. We spent the evening singing traditional Bedouin chants and smoking from a shared *shisha* pipe. They then invited me to offer the night prayer with them, so we lined up facing the endless ocean and knelt together in complete submission to God. It was the most spiritually fulfilling moment of my life, and I hugged each of them tightly before retiring for the night.

As the fire finally went out, I lay under the star-spangled sky for an hour. It wasn't a cold night nor was it too warm, but thankfully the

297

simple blanket I had packed was enough to keep me suitably cosy. The sky above me seemed endless and I felt completely insignificant as I marvelled at its majesty. Eventually my eyes began to grow weary and the gentle rhythm of the ocean whispered me into a long, deep slumber.

I was woken by the gentle ocean breeze a few minutes before sunrise. The morning air was delightfully crisp, and the sky was beginning to turn a brilliant pink with the first rays of the new day. I washed my face in the cold waters of the ocean, and as I looked up, there before me unfolded the most glorious sunrise I had ever witnessed. I watched in utter awe as the sun rose higher over the vast waters like a majestic beacon of light. I saw its beams as rays of hope, heralding a new beginning and granting all it touched another chance to emerge from the receding darkness.

I sat alone on the beach, the sheer beauty and peace of my natural surroundings allowing me think clearly for the first time in a long while. I thought about the city and how people had seen beauty in blocks of glass and steel and concrete. How greed had brought out the worst in them, and how ugly they had become. What they were chasing was a mere mirage; it wasn't real. Before me was real beauty. It was God's masterpiece; an eternal beauty that could never be compromised.

And then it hit me. The answer was suddenly crystal clear. It all finally made sense and I knew now what I had to do. I could not have wished for a better end to my Arabian adventure than this, but I had not a shadow of doubt of what I must do. It was time to go home.

Epilogue

When I was a child, there was always one story I would repeatedly pester my father to tell me each night before bedtime. Carlo Collodi's tale of an ambitious wooden puppet called Pinocchio, who aspires to find his way in the world and become a 'real boy', fascinated me more every time I heard it. On his perilous quest, Pinocchio encounters countless challenges and obstacles. He is swallowed by a shark, caught in a weasel trap by a farmer, and conned by a cunning fox. But the episode that fascinated me most was when Pinocchio follows a boy named Romeo to the Land of Toys, where children play but never work. After having the time of his life watching puppets, bouncing on balls and riding wooden horses, Pinocchio awakes to the horror that he has grown donkey ears and a tail, a chilling symbol of ignorance and foolishness, which terrified me every time.

In late 2009, after five years in the Gulf's Land of Toys, I finally returned home to face reality. But instead of feeling defeated and demoralised, I experienced a peace within myself that I had not felt for a long time. Like so many other ambitious expats, I had foolishly bought into the promise of endless sunshine and unlimited tax-free riches, only to fall victim to an inevitable reversal in fate. I had not made the great fortune I had dreamed of, but I didn't care. I had gained something more important that no sum of money could ever buy: self-esteem.

The story of Dubai's rise and fall is both unique and familiar. Like the great empires of history, its foundations were based on the fickle ambitions of visionary men who craved recognition and praise, only to be undone by the most primal of human flaws: their own pride. Every stakeholder played an equal part in Dubai's demise. Speculators forfeited their sense of reason for quick profits. Developers built towers they couldn't afford to meet the insatiable demand. The authorities failed to implement laws and regulations while the city grew at breakneck speed. And the banks lent recklessly to capitalise on the boom. It was perhaps fitting that they were all penalised accordingly when the tide turned.

Looking back, as tempting as it was to deny it at the time, Dubai had all of the hallmarks of an archetypal investment bubble from the outset. My friend Cameron's early investment represented the smart money that went in before the masses. From my time at Imperial Bank to my first experience at Cityscape, the Dubai real estate story gained massive momentum as new investors latched on to the money-making potential of the boom; the 'awareness' phase. And the lavish parties, outrageous new buildings and global interest that underpinned my time at Milestone were characteristic of the 'mania' phase that always precedes a devastating crash.

In the midst of every bubble, there are always a few solitary voices who raise their concerns, only to be drowned out by those too greedy to care. In 2008, the Morgan Stanley report was that voice for the market at large, while I tried to warn my Milestone colleagues; we were both mocked and silenced. From the Dutch Tulip Bubble of 1637 to the dot-com crash of 2002, bubbles have remained ingrained in the human condition, and this truth is unlikely to change any time soon. As hard as the faithful try to convince us that 'this time is different', they are always proved wrong. It is never different, and Dubai was no exception. Whether Arab, Western, Asian or African, history has proven time and again that humankind remains driven by two raw emotions that will haunt our decisions for centuries to come: fear and greed.

What became of some of the characters I met on my adventure? The last I heard, Jerome remains in Dubai and is working in recruitment, although he is still seeking the deal that will make him a millionaire. Jamal left Dubai for Miami, where he is setting up a distressed real estate fund with some Cuban investors. The exact source of their money is unknown. Sharaz and his wife divorced and she went back to London with their son. He is now living with his new Russian girlfriend, Anna.

I never heard from Tariq again after I left Milestone. There were rumours circulating that he had been sued for his entire fortune by some powerful disgruntled investors, and that he had even spent some time in prison. His was one of the saddest stories of the Dubai collapse: a man who had spent his life building his legacy, only to see all of his work disappear in an instant.

At the time of writing, some Dubai property prices have fallen by as much as 65 per cent from their 2008 peak. More than half of the incomplete projects have been cancelled. Many investors have lost their entire life savings, and some are still fighting a lost battle against developers who they haven't heard from in years. Conservative estimates suggest that the amount of money still hanging in the balance in the Emirate's property market is over one and a half billion dollars; funds that investors have committed to projects that are yet to come to fruition. Until these disputes are settled, Dubai will find it difficult to shake off the crisis of confidence, and disillusioned investors, many of whom staked their life savings on the fortunes of the market, will continue to remember the city as a graveyard of dreams. It seems that the fallout of the decade-long property misadventure will continue for some time yet.

Can Dubai's property sector ever rekindle its glory days? Perhaps, but the 'build it and they will come' approach is no longer the answer. Long gone are the deep-pocketed speculators, lavish property launches and taxi-driving realtors. The true market dynamics of supply and demand have exposed a glut of inventory yet to come online and a worrying lack of end buyers. Today, property purchasers are more concerned with the alignment of the kitchen tiles and the colour of the walls than finding the next fool to flip to. Dubai has grown up and become a real city with sensible problems.

But neither will Dubai disappear into oblivion, as some predicted after the crash. The recent events of the Arab Spring have worked in its favour, as dislocated citizens from falling regimes seek a regional haven with relative stability in the increasing turmoil. As much as the new wave of expatriates spreading across the Gulf today talk up the emerging opportunity in Doha or Abu Dhabi, they would all move in a flash if they were offered a similar position in Dubai. The Emirate's world-class infrastructure and liberal lifestyle are unparalleled in the region and will continue to attract new settlers. The luxury hotels will still bustle with Eastern tourists, and weekend shoppers from South Asia and the neighbouring Arab states will continue to pack the malls. The Middle East needs Dubai, and the neighbouring kingdoms know full well that a full recovery of the city's fortunes is in the interests of the entire Gulf.

Looking back today, three years after the crash, I still think about what was and may have been. I will always remember fondly a unique period in history when I was fortunate enough to witness the birth of a new city. In those four incredible years, I saw the best and the worst of

301

humankind. And despite coming excruciatingly close to being set up for life and failing, I learnt lessons I will never forget.

Life back in London is not as fast or wild or glamorous as it was during those crazy few years in Dubai. I miss the buzz, the excitement and the spontaneity. But despite all the tall buildings, super-malls, endless beaches, Michelin-starred restaurants, trendy bars and hot night clubs, there remains one thing I miss about Dubai more than anything else: a water pipe in every bathroom to wash my backside with...

THE END

About the Author

JR Roth is an author, commentator and satirist. He has written for various publications on topics as diverse as politics, history, literature, economics and popular culture. He is celebrated for his witty and often controversial style. JR enjoys reading, art, music and the theatre.

JR is a graduate of Oxford University. He currently lives between London, New York and Dubai.

You can follow JR on Twitter *@Jrroth_author*, and on Facebook.

For updates and bonus material, sign up at
www.sheikhsliesandrealestate.com